INVASION: DELIVERANCE

THE INVASION UK SERIES

DC ALDEN

GLOSSARY

- 160th SOAR (Special Operations Aviation Regiment)
- 2IC – Second in Command
- ACOG – Advanced Combat Optical Gunsight
- AFB – Air Force Base
- AFV – Armoured Fighting Vehicle
- ANPR – Automatic Number Plate Recognition
- ARV – Armoured Reconnaissance Vehicle (LAV-25 replacement)
- ATC – Air Traffic Control
- ATV – All-Terrain Vehicle
- AV – Audio/Visual
- AWACS – Airborne Early Warning and Control
- Basha – A waterproof, plastic sheet used for shelter and/or groundsheet
- CASE-VAC – Casualty Evacuation
- CBRN – Chemical, Biological, Radiological, and Nuclear
- CDS – Chief of Defence Staff
- CID – Criminal Investigation Department

- Civpop – Civilian Population
- CO – Commanding Officer
- Common Purpose – Alleged Marxist cult posing as Leadership Charity
- CP – Close Protection (close protection officer/team)
- CQB – Close Quarter Battle
- CSM – Company Sergeant Major
- DEVGRU – Navy Special Warfare Development Group (formerly SEAL Team 6)
- DMR – Designated Marksman Rifle
- EXFIL – Exfiltration (Extraction) – to escape a hostile area
- GMLRS – Guided Multiple Launch Rocket System
- Haji – Slang term for anyone wearing the caliphate uniform
- HEAT – High Explosive Anti-Tank
- HUMINT – Human-Sourced Intelligence
- HVT – High-Value Target
- IFF – Identify Friend or Foe (aviation transponder)
- ISR Brigade – Intelligence, Surveillance, and Reconnaissance Brigade (UK)
- JAASM-XR – Joint Air Surface Stand-Off Missile (Extreme Range)
- JLTV – Joint Light Tactical Vehicle (Humvee replacement)
- KIA – Killed in Action
- LAV – Light Armoured Vehicle
- LRASM – Long Range Anti-Ship Missile
- M-ATV – Mine-Resistant-All Terrain Vehicle
- M-27 – Heckler & Koch Infantry Automatic Rifle
- MIA – Missing in Action
- MilGPS – Military navigation application
- MOD – Ministry of Defence
- MRAP (vehicle) – Mine-Resistant, Ambush-Protected

- MSS-2 – Multi-Mission Special Operations Aircraft
- MTVR – Medium Tactical Vehicle Replacement
- NCO – Non-Commissioned Officer
- NEST – Nuclear Emergency Support Team
- NMCC – National Military Command Centre – Pentagon
- NSA – National Security Agency
- OC – Officer Commanding
- OP – Observation Post
- QRF – Quick Reaction Force
- REMF – Rear Echelon Motherfucker – A soldier with no combat experience
- RSM – Regimental Sergeant Major
- RTU – Returned to Unit
- RV – Rendezvous
- SAS – Special Air Service
- SAW – Squad Automatic Weapon
- SBS – Special Boat Squadron
- SHORAD – Short Range Air Defence system.
- SITREP – A situation report on the current military situation in a particular area
- SLS – Space Launch System
- SRR – Special Reconnaissance Regiment
- TAC Tablet – A tablet-based navigation system
- UAV – Unmanned Aerial Vehicle
- UFV – Unmanned Fighting Vehicle
- UGV – Unmanned Ground Vehicle
- UISV – Unmanned Infantry Support Vehicle
- UKSTRATCOM – UK Strategic Command – Tri-Service Command Group
- USEUCOM (EUCOM) – United States European Command
- USCENTCOM (CENTCOM) – United States Central Command

- VLS (Vertical Launch System)

EPISODE FOUR

'There are few die well that die in battle.'

Shakespeare - *Henry V*

PROLOGUE

THE PILOT BANKED THE AIRCRAFT HARD OVER SO HIS SON, strapped into the co-pilot's seat beside him, could see the remains of the village below. There wasn't much to look at, the pilot observed. All the structures had collapsed, leaving behind ruined, grey stone walls choked with weeds. The single road that had once twisted its way up through the village was now fractured, its black tarmac teeth jutting through a beige carpet of wild grasses. Like many other centres of human habitation across this dark land, nature had waited until there was no one left to resist it before resuming its slow march of conquest.

'There it is! There's the church!'

The pilot smiled. His 10-year-old beamed beneath the rim of his flight helmet, his excited voice hissing through his own headset. 'Well spotted, son. We're landing. Standby.' He banked the Explorer over the gaping roof of the church and set it down on a narrow stretch of open moor just above the western edge of the village. The pilot climbed out first, looping an automatic rifle over his helmet and chambering a shock round. The aircraft's thermal imaging pods had detected nothing of any concern, but one couldn't be too careful, not here, far beyond the borderlands. He walked around the nose of the aircraft and helped his son down onto the grass. The boy still wore his helmet, and his flight suit was a little too big for him, but he would soon grow into it. Another few years and he would pilot his own Explorer. How quickly time flies, the pilot thought. The boy who was still scared of the dark, who still doted on his father's every word and looked up at him with wide, bright eyes, would soon break free of his childlike dependence and make his own way out into the world. The idea of it made him sad.

He put aside the cheerless thought and focussed on their security, sweeping the gun barrel across the village below as he squinted through the sight. The weapon registered no thermal returns, either amongst the ruins or along the overgrown road that snaked south towards the wooded valley below. He saw no movement at all, nothing other than a gentle breeze that stirred the distant pines, but the pilot knew that wouldn't last.

'Let's go.' He let the boy run a few meters ahead, conscious of the child's need to explore, to discover this abandoned world, to build his confidence, and feed his inquisitive mind. That mind, young and impressionable though it was, had already formed intelligent thought and reasoning skills. The pilot and his wife had discussed the child's future with the education board. There was talk of enrolment into the advanced preteen programs: engineering, physics, astronomy. All these subjects excited his son, and the pilot and his wife had decided that they wouldn't stand in the educators' way if they selected him for one of those curricula. That would mean the boy leaving home. That made him sad too.

He watched the boy now, clambering over the broken stone wall and wading through waist-high grasses. He saw his small hands plucking at flora and fauna, saw him filming the flight of frightened birds. As they headed deeper into the graveyard, the pilot closed the space between them, his own eyes probing a world of quiet shadows. His heart beat fast. Many years had passed since his last visit, and much had changed. The graves were barely visible now, but some memorials still rose above the grass and weeds, the angels and cherubs of an imagined heaven, their stone faces blighted by moss, the tilted Celtic crosses strangled by wild ivy, but still serving as sign-posts to the final resting place the pilot sought and the purpose of his trip across the ocean.

'This way,' the pilot said, taking the lead, and the boy followed him through the thick grass to a spot close to the wall of the church itself. The west tower had toppled over since his last visit, bringing down with it a transept wall and revealing the interior nave, its remaining pews almost lost beneath a thick carpet of vegetation and what remained of the collapsed roof. Thick weeds had taken root in the window frames, and insects flitted through bars of weak autumn sunlight.

'Where is it, father?'

'Here.'

The pilot looped the gun around his back and bent down. He yanked and trampled the tall grass and ferns until he'd revealed the faded headstone. It was a simple slab of concrete, bearing only the man's name, rank, and the dates of his physical existence on this earth. The inscription had faded, as had the man's memory, which made him a worthy subject for the boy's history presentation. The pilot watched him now, using his tablet to capture footage of the grave itself, the overgrown burial ground, the crumbling church, the ancient stillness of the site. Pleased with his efforts, the boy wandered around the abandoned settlement, capturing the weather-beaten ruins, the broken, weed-choked road, and even a derelict car that sprouted thick ferns, until a primeval cry reached the pilot's ears. His head snapped around and he raised his gun. Far below, something stirred in the wooded valley. He couldn't see any thermal returns, but the sound was unmistakable.

'What is it, father?'

'A wolf. Do you have what you need?'

The boy held up his glass tablet. 'Affirmative.'

'Then we should go.'

7

They picked their way through the lava field of cracked tarmac, skirted the rusted corrugated shell of a prehistoric barn, and headed out onto open moorland. Every few seconds, the pilot would turn and peer through his sight, checking to see if they were being stalked, but he saw no movement. That wouldn't last, he knew. Soon the sun would dip behind the mountains, and the wolves and bears and wild boar would venture forth from their hides to hunt and feed.

They headed uphill to the Explorer. The pilot helped his son inside and buckled him in. He ducked under the plexiglass nose of the aircraft and climbed aboard, securing the weapon behind his seat. He powered up the flight systems and moments later, the Explorer lifted off, hovering eight feet above the long grass that shimmered beneath the quiet hum of the power plant. The pilot checked his instrumentation and saw everything was in the green. Increasing power, he gained a little height before allowing the aircraft to drift above the uninhabited village. As he looked down, a sudden feeling struck him; he would never return to this place again. His intermittent pilgrimage had run its course, and the baton handed to his son. He banked around once more, circling the village above the sagging rooftops. He saw the church, and the exposed headstone, and said his own silent farewell. He levelled out and powered up, the aircraft humming through the darkening sky as he left the past far behind.

The landscape rose and fell beneath him, and after a flight lasting 20 minutes, the pilot set the Explorer down on one of several designated landing sites, a narrow plateau beneath a crooked granite mountain peak. There, protected from high winds and predators, they settled into the weather-beaten habitation pod and built a fire in the wood burner. The pilot prepared food, and they sat outside and ate, listening to the cries of eagles and watching the light die as darkness swallowed the eastern mountains. Later, they climbed into their sleeping bags and watched the fire, the thick curved walls of the pod warmed by its red glow. They lay side by side on their cots, and once again the pilot experienced a painful stab of emotion. The child he knew now, who was so full of curiosity, who still needed the love, support, and guidance of his parents, would soon leave. He watched him now, the glass tablet held in his small hands as he scrolled back through the footage of the graveyard. The boy sensed his father watching and rolled over towards him.

'Who was he, father?'

The pilot propped himself up on an elbow. 'Some said he was a great man, others a misguided one. Naive. Do you know what that means?'

The boy flipped the small pane of flexible glass around. Text scrolled across the screen: Naive: inexperienced, immature, raw.

'That's right, although I think history has judged him harshly.'

'Did you meet him?'

The pilot shook his head. 'No, but my great-great-grandfather did, years after the war. He was just a boy, but he remembered shaking his hand. And the men who gathered around him, he called them heroes. They were, in their own way.'

'Will you tell me what happened?'

The pilot reached over and took the tablet from the boy's hand. He didn't want this recorded. 'I can tell you about him. About the end, and what it was like for those who were there. Would you like to hear that story?'

His son nodded. The pilot turned towards the wood burner, his mind recalling the stories he'd heard, of the papers handed down through generations, first scattered, then lost. They told of shadowy rooms, where grey-haired men wearing dark coats and coloured ribbons would gather to remember the fallen. The firelight danced in the pilot's eyes.

'It was a time of war. A time of great suffering and great joy. And he was there, at the beginning, and at the very end...'

[1]
KING'S SHILLING

Seventeen-year-old Devon Barclay stood at the bottom of the stairs and shouted, 'Mum! I'm away out!'

He heard the creak of floorboards above his head as his mother hurried to the landing. She appeared at the top of the stairs, a thin silhouette against the window behind her. She said nothing as she looked down at him, at his pressed chinos, his polished shoes, the shirt and tie beneath his navy blazer. Her narrow, lined face folded. Devon braced himself.

'No, Devon. No!'

Devon smiled, his best smile, the one reserved only for his mum. 'I'm going, Mum. Please don't be mad.'

He watched her as she walked down towards him, stair treads creaking beneath her worn slippers. She stood in front of him, shorter and forty pounds lighter. She'd aged these last few years. They all had.

'I don't want you going down there. Please, Devon.'

Devon's smile faded. They were going to butt heads. Again. 'I can't stay locked in here for the rest of my life, Mum. I'm not a kid anymore.'

'You're seventeen. I won't sign the papers.'

'It's my birthday next month. After that, I won't need your permission.'

Her tired eyes filled with tears. 'I can't lose you and your father. I just can't.'

'You won't lose me. Besides, it's what I want, Mum.'

'Your dad had that same look on his face when he left. Look where it got him.'

It had got him hung outside the local mall. Devon still had nightmares of his dad dangling from scaffolding outside the shopping centre, the rope around his neck creaking as his eyes bulged and his legs kicked and thrashed. And the noises he'd made, the choking and gurgling. Inhuman sounds. He remembered his mother screaming, collapsing to her knees, and being restrained by an angry, frightened crowd. There were other bodies dangling from that same scaffold, each of them with a hand-drawn sign around their necks that declared them to be thieves. Dad's crime was trying to swipe food from a supermarket. The Barclay family had run out of money and supplies. They were starving. What was Dad supposed to do? Most days, Devon purged the memory from his mind. He needed to move on, move away. Start again. Today was the first step on that road.

But his mum wouldn't hear of it. 'I can't bear the thought of anything happening to you, Devon. You're all I've got left. There could be others out there, targeting people like you. Like your dad.'

'They didn't kill him because he was black, Mum. He was trying to feed us, remember?'

'I don't want you to go.'

He reached down for her hand. She squeezed it tight, her eyes glassy. 'We're not in danger anymore, Mum. The Atlantic Alliance is in charge now. There are tanks and soldiers all over the place. They reckon they'll recapture London soon. Then it's all over.'

'You're too young to join the army.'

'I'm joining the air force, remember? And once I'm settled, you can come and visit. Get out of this place.'

Tears ran down her face, but she smiled and held a warm hand against his cheek. 'You're my beautiful boy, always will be. I look at you and I see your dad. That same smile, same eyes. Gentle. But strong too.' She dropped her hand. 'Where are you going?'

'Dunfold community centre.'

She smiled through her tears and fixed his tie. 'Well, they'd be lucky to have you. Promise me you'll be careful.'

Devon nodded. 'I will.'

'Go, before I change my mind.'

Devon beamed and wrapped his arms around her. He could feel her bones. 'I love you, Mum.'

She slipped from his arms and trotted back upstairs. He heard the creak of the floorboards in the bedroom above, heard her quiet sobs. His resolve wavered. Maybe he should wait. The war wasn't over yet. Then again, he didn't want it to pass him by. Some of his friends had already joined up. It was his turn now.

He left the house, a modest two-up two-down on a terrace where the front doors emptied onto the pavement. There was no Internet, and the phone lines were still down, so the neighbours gathered in groups, chatting on doorsteps and street corners. He heard laughter too, which was good. No one had laughed much these last few years. He walked past a row of shops, where a long queue snaked towards the local chippy. Several people smiled and said hello because everyone knew what had happened to Devon's dad.

He left his red-bricked neighbourhood and headed downhill towards the town centre. As he got closer, he passed looted shops and burned-out cars. He avoided the broken pavements and bubbling water mains on the high street, where men and women busied themselves, hammering, sawing, and sweeping. Maybe one day the town would look like it did before the war, but Devon wouldn't stick around long enough to find out.

He heard a muted roar and looked up. Four planes were flying overhead, big fat grey ones. C-17 Globemasters, Devon knew, and he smiled. That was his dream, to be a pilot. He hadn't decided what aircraft he wanted to fly, but one of his friends told him it depended on how well he tested. Despite the disruption to his education, Devon had continued to hit the books and complete his college coursework. He was also skilled in using Microsoft Flight Simulator. Maybe he would get the chance to show someone those skills and prove he was a viable candidate for flight school. Fat transports or sleek stealth jets, Devon Barclay didn't care. He just wanted to fly.

'Devon!'

He stopped and turned around. His friend Omar was waving as he hurried up behind him.

'Hey, Omar. What's happening?'

Omar was a year older than Devon and they'd both attended the same high school. However, whereas Devon was a bright kid and excelled, Omar struggled with learning difficulties. But he was funny and popular, and Devon had liked him from the start. He was also overweight, and he leaned against a lamppost as he caught his breath. A year ago, Devon had seen a naked woman hanging from the same lamppost.

'Are you going where I think you're going?' Omar said, panting.

Devon studied his friend. He'd combed his thick black hair, and he wore a white shirt buttoned to the neck beneath his favourite winter coat, a double-breasted duffel. Trousers and shoes too, Devon noticed. 'I'm going to the community centre. To sign up.'

'Me too. What did your mum say?'

Devon shrugged. 'She's cool. But what about your dad? He's pro-caliphate.'

'Doesn't matter. He's gone.'

'Gone where?'

'Belgium,' Omar said. 'He took my sister too.'

Devon's eyebrows arched. 'He left you on your own? Who's going to take care of you?'

'I'm nineteen,' Omar said, standing a little straighter. 'And I'm signing up, too. I want to be a driver. Think they'd let me drive a tank or something?'

'They'll let you do anything if you test well.'

'And there's a $100 signing-on bounty, right?'

Devon grinned. 'Correct.'

Omar beamed. 'Then what are we waiting for? Let's go.'

They headed off, past boarded-up shops and a bustling mini-supermarket. Their appearance and direction of travel prompted shouts of *Good luck* and *God bless*, and Devon felt ten feet tall as he strode past them. The only nagging doubt he had was his fitness. Since the rumours began about the Atlantic Alliance landing in Ireland, his mum had confined him to the house. The most exercise he'd had in the last few months was walking to the shops and kicking a ball around their tiny backyard. But once he signed on the dotted line, Mum wouldn't be able to object to him going out running. He just had to convince her it was safe to do so. She had to see the regular patrols and the friendly aircraft that crisscrossed the skies. He would even point them out and tell her which ones he might be flying.

As they left the high street behind them, a steady rain began to fall. They hurried past a small park with a children's playground and a single football pitch. Next to the park, behind a fence of black railings, stood the community centre. Devon's heart beat faster. There was a JLTV parked outside on the road, painted in grey and blue, with huge black tyres and a big gun mounted on the roof. The driver saw Devon staring and waved. Devon waved back, flushed with excitement. Inside the gates, a Union Jack and the Stars & Stripes had replaced the black caliphate flag on the flagpole.

The people in the queue were mostly men and older than Devon and Omar, and he counted over 30 people standing in the rain. He saw other men and women leaving the building and heading back to the pavement, excited smiles on their faces. His stomach was alive with butterflies. If accepted, they would send him to America. Exactly where he didn't know, but Devon was unconcerned. Anywhere else but Britain would suit him just fine.

'Get your IDs ready,' said a soldier standing by the glass-panelled front doors. He wore a camouflaged peaked cap on his head and a pistol on a belt around his waist. A Union Jack patch decorated the front of his ballistic vest and the one on his arm told Devon he was a member of the 216th Pennsylvania battalion, British Volunteers.

'How cool does he look?' Devon whispered to his friend.

Omar spoke from the corner of his mouth. 'Check out the gun. Think it's loaded?'

'Of course. Not much point of having it without bullets.'

'My dad said they wouldn't be expecting trouble.'

'He shouldn't have left you.'

'He told me I had to be a man.'

'That's stupid,' Devon said.

'Next ten, inside,' the soldier said, yanking the door open.

Devon grinned and nudged Omar as they followed the others through the lobby and into the main hall. It was busy, maybe a hundred people milling around, and the air buzzed with chatter. There were three groups of tables clustered around three walls, each with colourful banners that read: *ARMY, NAVY, AIR FORCE*. Behind the tables sat men and women from each branch of each service. Devon saw smiles and handshakes, and signatures being scrawled on dotted lines. He veered across to the Air Force table and queued up behind a line of men and women. He heard Omar whisper in his ear.

'Is there still time to change my mind?'

Devon turned around. Omar's mood had changed, his earlier enthusiasm replaced by doubt. Devon didn't feel the same way. Walking into this hall was the right thing to do, of that he was certain. But he understood Omar's sudden reluctance. This was a huge commitment, and not everyone would feel like Devon.

'Look, the Air Force needs drivers too,' he said. 'Maybe they'll send us to the same base. How slick would that be?'

'Pretty slick,' Omar echoed. He cleared his throat and stood a little straighter. 'My dad said I would have doubts. Said it was natural.'

16

'He's right, even though he's a shitbag for leaving you.' Omar looked at him, his brow furrowed, then his face relaxed and he smiled.

'Next.'

Devon spun around. There was no one between him and the lady behind the desk. He stepped forward and stood straight, his arms by his side, his eyes fixed on the wall where there were more flags and banners. A big sign hung above his head: *ENLIST TODAY!* Devon intended to do just that.

The lady in the blue Air Force uniform smiled. 'To be clear, this is the air force recruitment desk. Are you interested in joining the Air Force, sir?'

The lady was dark and pretty, and he blushed. No one had ever called Devon Barclay sir. 'I want to be a pilot,' he declared, making his voice sound deeper than it was.

'How old are you?'

'Seventeen. I'll be eighteen next month.'

'Good, because we always need pilots.' She handed him a thick envelope. 'That's your information packet. Make sure you read it thoroughly. If you're still interested, fill in the form and come back to us within seven days. At that point, your application will be processed, and we'll pay you a bounty of $100. How does that sound?'

'Sounds great,' Devon said, hefting the envelope in his hand. He couldn't smile any wider.

The recruiter's fingers hovered over her keyboard. 'Can I get your name, please? First and last, and any middle names.'

'Devon Barclay. That's it,' he added.

The woman's fingers were a blur. She handed him a plastic disc with a number on it and pointed to the other side of the room. 'Take that to the desk marked administration. Thank you, Devon, and good luck.' She smiled and looked past him. 'Next.'

Devon took a few paces and waited for Omar. He wanted to be

close in case his friend needed a little support. Omar still looked a little unsure as he stood in front of the pretty air force sergeant.

'You want to join the Air Force, yes?'

Omar nodded and licked his lips. 'That's right. I'm nineteen,' he said.

She pushed an information packet across the table. Omar didn't pick it up. The recruiter looked at the envelope and then at Omar. Devon thought she'd read his mind.

'You don't have to decide today,' she told him, smiling. 'Just read and digest. Take your time. Okay?'

Omar bobbed his head. 'Okay.'

'What's your name?'

Omar cleared his throat. 'Allah.'

'Excuse me?'

Devon frowned. He wanted to hiss at his friend, tell him to stop messing about. This was no time to play the fool.

Omar giggled. 'My dad told me to say that.'

The recruiter cocked her head. 'Say what?'

'Allah Akbar.'

He showed her the small silver tube with the red button in his hand. The woman screamed something that Devon didn't understand, and suddenly he was frightened. Everyone was looking at them. Soldiers were piling into the hall, shouting. Omar looked at him and smiled.

'Close your eyes, Devon.'

Instead, Devon turned to run. His friend laughed and blew everyone to pieces.

[2]

BEANO

THE PASSENGERS' SPIRITS REMAINED HIGH AS THE LUXURY coach turned off the M3 motorway at Lightwater and headed south into the Surrey countryside. One of them had hooked up a phone to the vehicle's media system, and a playlist of old tunes had kept them all entertained for much of the journey. Alcohol was still being consumed as the coach turned onto a dark country road.

A small, dapper man in his late fifties got to his feet and swayed towards the front of the coach. He powered up a microphone, tapping it several times. Ed Sheeran's reminisces of a hilltop castle faded, and curious eyes peered over headrests. Leo Daly, ruler of the Eastern Territories and a National Assembly member, cleared his throat and spoke into the microphone.

'Ladies and gentlemen, if I could have your attention for just a moment ...'

Daly's audience responded with audible groans and some good-natured banter.

'He's not going to sing, is he?'

'Put the music back on!'

'Stand up if you're going to speak!'

That drew a laugh, and a fake smile from his wife Lucy, who stood four inches taller than the diminutive ruler of Essex and Suffolk, even without her obligatory heels. Daly took the teasing as he always did, with good humour and a mental note of who said what.

'Apologies to the Ed Sheeran fans.'

'Get on with it!'

Daly waved his hand. 'Okay, settle down, this won't take long.' He took a moment to look around the coach as he waited for silence. The lights were low and most of the 56 faces that swayed with the motion of the vehicle were lost in shadow, but Daly didn't need to see them. It was his words that were important.

'Most of you have known me for some time. Over the previous two days at Hatfield, I've had the pleasure of meeting the rest of our assembly colleagues, especially you brave ladies and gents from the northern territories. Sadly, there were absentees, some killed in terror attacks, others captured by the so-called liberators, but the rest of us have been lucky. I can only speak for myself here, but I feel privileged to be part of this assembly and honoured to have met you all.'

There was a murmur of appreciation, and a few *Hear hear's*. Daly cleared his throat and carried on.

'As you know, I've arranged transport to France. A plane waits on the tarmac at Farnborough Airport, and soon we'll all be enjoying new lives on the continent. You heard Governor Spencer's speech back at Hatfield: we are important cogs in the machine and will be treated as such once we're all settled in France. Or I should say, once *you're* settled in France.'

He saw the puzzled frowns and raised eyebrows amongst the seats.

'You're not coming?' a voice asked.

'That's right.' He puffed up his narrow chest. 'Governor Spencer has made me an offer I can't refuse. In fact, she's asked me to move to London, where Lucy and I will be moving into our new house, the governor's residence in Hampstead.'

Another voice said, 'What's going on, Leo?'

'Important business,' he told them, relishing his own self-importance. Not even Lucy knew that the old bird hadn't offered him anything concrete, but she'd given her word that he was valuable to her, and she'd look after them both. But those were details his colleagues – *former* colleagues – didn't need to know. 'I can't go into specifics, only that I will bid you all farewell at Farnborough. Lucy?'

Daly's wife got to her high heels and tottered along the aisle in a tight red dress. She handed him a flute of champagne, her smile wide and proud. Daly raised his glass and waited for Lucy to retake her seat, and for the men to refocus their attention on him.

'A toast if you will.' Along the length of the coach, glasses raised above the headrests. 'To our friendship, and to our good fortune. Long may they both continue.'

'Hear, hear!' someone shouted.

Daly sipped his champagne and then he slopped it over the floor as the coach braked hard. He dropped the microphone and braced a hand against the driver's seat. The coach stopped with a loud hiss of air brakes. Through the windscreen, Daly saw a Humvee blocking the road ahead. A man in uniform was waving a red wand.

'It's alright, everyone. It's just a checkpoint. Can't be too careful these days, eh?' Daly remained standing. They'd stopped on a quiet stretch of road, dark and wooded. He saw a figure walking towards the coach. The driver yanked a handle, and the door hissed open. The man stepped aboard, dressed in a dark coat, his head shaved. He had a hard face and hard eyes, and Daly thought he looked familiar. Then it came to him like a bolt from the blue. He snapped his fingers.

'You're Governor Spencer's man.'

The new arrival smiled. 'Good of you to remember, sir.'

'What's going on?' a voice shouted from the back. It was Bertie who answered.

'There's been an incident up the road. Nothing serious, but you'll have to wait for a few minutes. Sorry for the inconvenience.'

'Hurry up,' another voice said.

'Of course.' He turned to Daly. 'Would you step off the coach, sir?'

Before he could reply, the manservant had exited the vehicle. Daly followed him and was grateful for the fresh air. The last couple of days had been boozy affairs, with most of the assembly members getting pissed day and night. No one knew exactly what was waiting for them in France, so they were all making the most of it. Daly didn't blame them.

Bertie smiled in the darkness. 'I need your luggage, sir. I'll be taking it to the house in Hampstead.'

Daly looked around him. They were in the middle of nowhere. 'Now?'

The gopher stepped a little closer and spoke in a low voice. 'Governor Spencer is waiting at Farnborough to bid the assembly a personal farewell. A surprise, you understand. She's arranged for a limousine to take you and your good lady back to the London house. She told me to collect your luggage and have it waiting for you when you get home, sir.'

Daly felt his cheeks flush. 'That's bloody decent of her.'

The gopher pointed to the luggage compartments. 'Your bags, please.'

Daly and the driver yanked out half a dozen suitcases and a large trunk. The gopher whistled, and four black-clad militia trotted out of the darkness and wheeled the luggage towards a dark-coloured van parked by the side of the road, a Mercedes Vito if Daly wasn't mistaken. 'Be careful with those,' he snapped, watching the militia load the cases on board the van.

The gopher smiled. 'Don't you worry, sir. I'll take good care of them. And remember, the governor wants it to be a surprise.'

'Fine,' Daly said, still watching the van. His life was in those cases.

'See you back at the house, sir. I'll have a nightcap waiting.'

Daly refocused. 'What did you say your name was?'

'Bertie, sir.'

'Right.' He watched the gopher climb into the Mercedes, swing it around in a tight circle and drive off. Daly got back on the coach and slammed the door shut. He held up his hands for silence.

'Listen, everyone.' All heads turned towards him. 'Governor Spencer is waiting at Farnborough for us. She wants to surprise us, wish us bon voyage, so no more booze, okay? She might have company, the kind that frowns upon alcohol, so break out the mints and the bottled water and let's not embarrass ourselves, okay?'

He took his seat. Next to him, Lucy squirmed in her skin-tight dress. Daly told her about the luggage.

'Why didn't we go with him?'

Daly spluttered. 'In a van? Turning up in Hampstead like a couple of pikeys? I don't think so, love.'

'I'm tired and my feet hurt. I need a bath.'

'I'll get the servants to run you one as soon as we get back.' He squeezed her hand. 'This is the start of a new chapter, Luce. You'll see.'

The door opened again, and a blast of cool night air wafted around the coach. Daly heard footsteps and craned his neck. A man in a camouflaged uniform boarded the coach and stood in the aisle, his hands behind his back. He saw the microphone, picked it up and blew into it. He smiled as he heard the sound amplified around the coach. The soldier began to sing. Badly.

'Regrets, I've had a few, but then again, too few to mention ...'

He laughed at his own joke. Sinatra would be rolling in his grave, Daly thought. But there was something about this man he didn't like. It was insolence. A lack of respect.

'My name is Aziz,' the soldier said. 'Remain in your seats, and you'll be on your way shortly. Understood?'

Daly opened his mouth to speak, and Lucy elbowed him in the ribs, hard enough that Daly felt a flash of anger. He glared at her, and she shook her head, her eyes boring into his. Maybe she was right. Some of these caliphate soldiers could be twitchy at the best of times.

Aziz dropped the microphone onto the driver's seat and stepped off the coach, slamming the door behind him. The gesture troubled Daly. They were all important people, for God's sake. Didn't this Aziz bloke realise that?

The coach hummed with a low, impatient murmur. Daly thought about getting to his feet again and calling for order, but Lucy had her hand firmly entwined in his and she wasn't letting go.

'What are those militia blokes up to?'

'Looks like trouble,' someone else said.

Daly looked past Lucy and saw the militia lining up along the edge of the woods, barely visible in the darkness. 'It's a security cordon,' he told them.

'He's coming back,' someone up front said.

The door opened with a hiss. Aziz stepped aboard, but this time he didn't come all the way up the stairs. Instead, he threw something along the aisle, and Daly heard a metallic *zing*. The door slammed, and someone shouted in alarm. The object rolled along the floor, only stopping as it came to rest against Daly's patent leather shoe. He looked down and knew what it was. He sobbed, just once.

It was all the time he had left.

WATCHING FROM FURTHER UP THE ROAD, BERTIE SAW THE flash of the grenade. He knew it was coming, but the bang still startled him. He saw the windows of the coach blow out, and then he heard screaming and shouting, all mixed into one bone-chilling cacophony of noise. Then the militia guns opened up, their deafening chatter stitching hundreds of holes along the length of the coach. The storm lasted for maybe 20 seconds, then stopped, the thunder rolling away through the woods. Bertie heard more screaming, and the pleading and moaning of the wounded. He saw the distant figure of Aziz climb aboard, heard the hollow pop of his pistol ...

'I think we're done here,' said the tall, black woman with the shaved head who stood by Bertie's van. She wore a black leather coat, skin-tight black trousers, and knee-length boots. Her name was

Clarke, and if it wasn't for the crossed swords lapel pin, Bertie thought she could pass for a civil rights activist. Or a hooker.

'Give the governor my regards.'

'Yes, ma'am.'

Bertie climbed inside the van. He slipped the Mercedes into gear and drove away, keeping the lights off until he was some distance away. He felt no remorse for his part in the ambush. The traitors had sent countless people to their deaths and had got everything they deserved. What bothered Bertie was his own continued presence in England. He should've been in France by now, unpacking The Witch's belongings, setting up home for him and Cheryl, but all travel for non-caliphate citizens was now prohibited. Even The Witch couldn't pull her usual strings. So, they had to wait, and with every day that passed, the mood on the streets was becoming more apprehensive. Birmingham had been wiped off the map. Hundreds of thousands of refugees were heading south, clogging the roads, ports, and airports. Air raid sirens wailed over London. Things were going to get desperate soon, and when that happened, all bets would be off. They may never get out of the country, and that was bad news as far as Bertie was concerned. Because it was all about survival now. His, Cheryl's, and if he had anything to do with it, Judge Hardy's too.

Dead or alive, the day was coming. The day of Britain's liberation.

'Deliver us, oh Lord, from every evil,' Bertie whispered. He put his foot down, and the Mercedes sped up into the darkness.

[3]

FROZEN OUT

WHEN HARRY SQUINTED HIS EYES, IT WASN'T HARD TO IMAGINE he was standing on a desolate planet on the far side of the universe. The air was crisp and cold, the surrounding landscape rocky and inhospitable, the nearby habitation domes resembling a high-tech moon base that stretched towards a black sea dotted with towering ice floes. On a nearby granite outcrop, a cluster of futuristic radar arrays jutted into a pale blue sky. A few short hours ago, that same sky had unveiled the Milky Way in all its breathtaking wonder. Its beauty had humbled Harry, made him feel small. It was a feeling that still lingered.

But he wasn't standing on some alien world. He stood on the concrete apron of Thule Air Force Base, home to the 12th Space Warning Squadron amongst others and the remotest place that Harry had ever visited. Located on the north-eastern coast of Greenland, the US Space Force installation was 750 miles north of the Arctic Circle and just under 1000 miles shy of the North Pole. A remnant of the Cold War era, the Mitchell administration had ordered a complete renovation of the base, its missile defence systems, and its massive radar complex that could track multiple 'high interest' objects in space and around earth's upper atmosphere. He'd learned all of that from the base commander's dime tour, but the man elaborated no further. Harry had found himself piqued by his mild air of disdain, as if Harry's presence at the base was something to be tolerated and nothing more. Or was he imagining it? His chief of staff had tried to reassure him, but Harry was unconvinced.

He heard laughter and saw the base commander sharing a joke with the Russian delegation. An icy wind snatched away their merriment, and Harry was glad of it. Although they'd exchanged handshakes and smiles the previous day, Harry knew he was playing second fiddle to the Russian party as they ingratiated themselves with their star-spangled hosts. Standing next to him, Wilde's impatient boot-stamping was doing nothing to improve Harry's mood.

'How much longer?' his chief of staff whispered from behind his fur-lined hood.

'Any moment now. And stop stamping your bloody feet. It's not that cold. Thank your lucky stars we didn't come in January. Then you'd have something to complain about.'

'It's four degrees.'

'Better than minus 20.'

Wilde glanced over Harry's shoulder towards the Russians, dressed in their green parkas and black Ushanka fur hats. 'Orlov's not made much of an effort to communicate.'

'Why would he?'

'Protocol. You're Prime Minister of Great Britain after all.'

'That might've meant something a few years ago. Not anymore.'

Wilde's eyes flicked back to his boss. 'You've been in a strange mood for weeks, Harry, and I'm not the only one who's noticed it. What's wrong?'

'Now's not the time, Lee.'

A metallic voice blared across the permafrost. 'Air Force One is inbound, approaching from the west. ETA, 30 seconds. All photography is prohibited.'

Excitement rippled through the small crowd waiting on the

concrete apron. Presidents avoided these barren outposts, but this meeting with the Russians was extraordinary. Harry was out of the loop on this one, even though Mitchell had asked him to be present, and once again he felt a stab of paranoia. He had better things to do than freeze his backside off in Greenland. England was still in the grip of war, and its second-largest city had been wiped from the map. Harry needed to be back home.

'Here they come!' a voice declared.

Harry looked out towards the wide bay. Above the berg-dotted sea, a white object was inbound towards the runway, barely visible against the powder blue sky. It swept in over the shoreline and Harry failed to recognise the aircraft. It looked like a plane, but its stubby delta wings looked too small to give the craft sufficient lift, and it had military-style twin fins at its rear. It was approaching the runway low and fast.

'He's going to overshoot,' Wilde said, and Harry was about to concur when the plane decelerated with a blast of air and its landing gear deployed. Not wheels, Harry noticed, but ski-like plates on thick black legs. It settled on the ground a hundred yards away, with a grace reserved for figure skaters. There was another short blast of air and a gentle wave of tiny ice-crystals rolled over the now-silent crowd. The aircraft was larger than a private jet but smaller than a 777, and what impressed Harry – and no doubt those around him – was the lack of any significant noise. There were no visible engines, but the air beneath the tail fins rippled as if heated, although Harry could see no exhaust ports.

'Remarkable,' Wilde said, his voice a pitch higher than normal.

Harry was about to answer him, but then the fuselage appeared to shimmer, and the skin of the aircraft changed to the familiar livery of Air Force One. Despite himself, Harry joined in with the spontaneous applause.

'It's like a Las Vegas magic show,' Wilde said, gloved hands pumping together.

Harry cocked his head at the Russians. 'Not for our benefit.'

President Mitchell stepped down a ramp at the rear of the aircraft and headed towards them. He wore a thick winter parka and aviator sunglasses and was flanked by Zack Radanovich and Eliot Bird. The small reception crowd was still clapping, still beaming behind their sunglasses. Mitchell shook hands with Orlov first, then the other Russians, and finally the base commander. He saw Harry and smiled.

'Prime Minister. Thank you for coming.'

'That's quite a ride you have there,' Harry said.

'She's something, isn't she?'

He pumped a few more hands and then they were moving inside, into the warmth of the terminal building. As Harry shed his coat, he looked out of a triple glazed window and saw the strange aircraft take off again, rising vertically before banking over the building.

Enlisted staff disappeared, leaving the politicians alone. The base commander led them down a staircase to a tunnel below ground. At its end was a conference room. Harry unzipped the neck of his fleece as he took his seat around the table. Despite being constructed of poured concrete, the room was dry and warm. Harry wasn't expecting that, not in a space buried several feet beneath the permafrost.

Refreshments were wheeled inside, and Wilde did the honours, handing a coffee to Harry. Everyone settled around the table. Mitchell was at the head, flanked by Chief of Staff Radanovich and Bird, his national security advisor. Despite his creeping paranoia, Harry felt intrigued by the prospect of this meeting and had speculated with Wilde during their journey to the top of the world. Now all was about to be revealed. Mitchell cleared his throat and addressed the Russian across the table.

'Once again, Andrei, thank you for coming.'

Orlov nodded his head. 'An honour, Mr President. And may I say, an impressive entrance.'

Orlov was a big man, just like his younger brother, President of the Russian Federation Yuri Orlov, and he often went to great pains to convince foreigners that politics held no interest for him. He was fooling no one, of course. Andrei Orlov was the billionaire chairman of Gazprom, the largest company in Russia and the biggest publicly listed natural gas company in the world. When a man rose to that kind of power and influence, politics always played a part.

Harry looked at Orlov's hands. They were like shovels, his knuckles like pebbles, and Harry wondered how many people he'd killed with them, because no one in Russia rose to such power without getting their hands dirty. That observation might've intimidated Harry in the past, but not anymore. Given the right motivation, killing a man was easy. He'd proved that. He refocussed as Orlov continued.

'So, when do we get a tour of your Air Force One, Mr President? After all, that's why you wanted us to see her, yes?'

Mitchell's smile faded just a little. Bereft of his thick parka and exposed beneath the bright LED panel suspended from the concrete ceiling, he looked like the 71-year-old man he was. Instead of answering Orlov, he turned to Radanovich. 'Bring him in.'

Mitchell's chief of staff gestured to a suit standing by the sound-proofed door and it swung open. Footsteps echoed in the corridor outside. Then a man entered the room. Harry didn't recognise him until he entered the pool of light and sat in the empty chair next to Radanovich.

Orlov was the first to react. 'Mr Vice President,' he said, acknowledging the late arrival with a nod. Harry noticed Orlov was no longer smiling. No one enjoys being ambushed. Harry didn't blame him, and again, his own paranoia rose its ugly head.

Vice President Curtis J. Riley didn't shake hands with anyone but Orlov, and as the men leaned across the table, Harry guessed that in another time and place, they might've resorted to arm-wrestling. Riley was as big as Orlov, a former NFL football player and a special forces soldier when he'd served in the US military. He was also a former senator, Missouri, Harry recalled, and the rumour was, Mitchell looked upon the 48-year-old VP as the son he never had.

Rumours meant nothing, of course, but Riley's presence spoke volumes. Mitchell continued.

'I've asked Curtis to be here because the Russian administration should know that, contrary to former appointments, this vice president is my true second in command. And soon, my chosen successor. He speaks for me, period.'

Orlov raised a black, bushy eyebrow. 'You are unwell, Mr President?'

'My heart condition is common knowledge,' Mitchell said, 'and I don't intend to make it worse by occupying the Oval Office for much longer.'

Harry struggled to hide his shock. Announcements like that were reserved for domestic audiences, not for Russian oligarchs in arctic bunkers.

Orlov's eyes flicked between Mitchell and Riley. Then he smiled. 'I appreciate your candour, Mr President. No doubt Vice President Riley will honour your legacy.' He gave Riley a conspiratorial wink. 'And will be ready to do business, perhaps?'

Riley returned the smile, wide and white. His skin was tanned, and his receding grey hair shaved close to the skull. Like Orlov, he wore a polo-neck sweater and military-style trousers. He rapped the table with a knuckle. 'You are correct, Mr Orlov. The United States is always willing to listen to mutually advantageous proposals from our allies.'

'Andrei, please,' Orlov insisted.

Riley held Orlov's steady gaze as he held up his hand. An aide stepped out of the shadows and handed him a thin manila folder before retreating to the wall. Riley laid it down on the table and smoothed it out. He didn't open it.

Harry caught Wilde's sideways glance and knew what he was thinking. There was a lot of theatre unfolding here. Riley and Orlov faced off across the wide conference table while Mitchell sat back in his chair, watching. Yet there was a confidence in the president's eyes, a hint of a smile on his thin lips, like a card player who knows he has the winning hand. Bird and Radanovich were observers too, as were the other Americans and Russians in the room, and for the first time in many years, Harry felt completely impotent. He stifled his bemusement and focussed. Mitchell had asked him here for a reason. He was about to find out what that reason was.

Riley flipped open the folder and scanned the printed papers. 'These are the last publicly available figures of Gazprom's natural gas exports into Europe. According to these numbers, Russia pumped 272 billion cubic metres into the continent before Wazir's armies trampled over international borders. The year preceding the outbreak of war, Gazprom made a profit of 34 billion dollars, which was almost 10% of your country's GDP. That's pretty impressive.'

Orlov nodded. 'A tribute to the hard work and ingenuity of our workforce.'

'In fact, energy revenues across the board account for over 80% of Russian exports,' Riley continued. 'You have the largest proven gas reserves on the planet and the World Bank estimates the value of your natural resources at 75 trillion dollars.'

'God has blessed —'

'On the political front, you've handed over your southern republics to Wazir for the annexation of Poland and the Baltic states. Russian troops are also helping to prop up caliphate regimes across Scandinavia.'

'As you say, these are political matters,' Orlov said, his eyes narrowing. Harry wondered how many people had ever interrupted the man and lived to tell the tale. Riley pressed him.

'I'm guessing that if he was so inclined, Wazir could order those 28 million Russian Muslims along your southern border to stir up serious trouble inside the Motherland.'

'Our Islamic communities have enjoyed recognition in Russian politics for many decades now,' Orlov explained. 'Even a casual study of our history will reveal that Islam forms an important part of the Russian cultural code.'

'And yet you freeze out its followers from key positions in your military and economic infrastructure. They're barred from any control of your nuclear arsenal, not to mention strategic management roles in energy, finance, and transportation. It's a trust thing, am I right? They might be ethnic Russians, but their lives and loyalties are guided by religion, not by the state.'

Orlov didn't answer straight away. Instead, he leaned back in his chair and eyed the American across the table. 'What is it you want, Mr Vice President?'

'We're going to need you to shut down the Nord Stream 2 gas pipeline. End all gas exports to Europe.'

'Why would we do that?'

'Including all exports of crude oil and solid fossil fuels.'

'You're not making sense.'

'Europe relies on Russia for more than half of its energy needs. Winter is a few months away. We'd like to make things difficult there.'

Harry swallowed. Hadn't the Europeans suffered enough? He glanced at Mitchell, desperate to voice his concerns, but the president caught his eye and shook his head once. Harry looked away, troubled by the direction the conversation was going. And by his obvious impotence.

Across the table, Orlov was speaking. 'Such actions would violate our treaties with Baghdad. It would put us on a path to conflict.'

'Wazir has enough problems right now. And you can blame the shutdown on us. Hacking and whatnot. Seems only fair, as the United States has blamed you guys for everything short of the weather in the past.'

Orlov shook his head. 'This proposal of yours is bad for business —'

'Oh, and all Russian troops out of Scandinavia and the Baltic. A phased withdrawal, so there's no loss of face. We'll leave the details to you.'

Orlov said nothing. He stared across the table at Riley, then at

President Mitchell. Harry could almost hear the gears turning inside his skull.

'Your proposal is absurd ... unless there's something that could prove advantageous to Mother Russia.' He raised an eyebrow and Riley smiled.

'Okay, let's lay our cards on the table here.' He glanced over his shoulder. 'Start the slide deck, please.'

A black-and-white image appeared on the wall to Harry's left. It showed a man, his face pixilated, wearing coveralls and carrying a clipboard. He was standing in front of two large, grey industrial cabinets, much like the ones in the basement of Downing Street, though these were larger, about eight feet tall and half as wide. There appeared to be a digital display panel mounted on the front of each unit, but nothing else. Harry guessed that the cabinets themselves were the subject of the photograph, but he wasn't sure why. Orlov asked the obvious question for all of them.

'What is this?'

'Those are APGUs. Advanced Power Generation Units. In fact, the ones you're looking at now provide light and heat for this facility. In the past, power used to be delivered by a mixture of technologies: generators, thermal, and solar plants. Not anymore. Next slide, please.'

The black-and-white image changed to a night-time aerial view of one of the most famous cities in the world, an oasis of light and colour in the middle of the Nevada desert.

'Las Vegas, as if it needs any introduction. Last year the city consumed over 28 million megawatts of power, drawn from an electrical grid supplied by over 6,000 national power-generating sources including coal, natural gas, oil, the sun, moving water, biomass, whatever. But that was last year.'

The picture on the wall changed again, and Harry saw a clean, white-walled room with two long rows of identical, grey-panelled APGUs.

'Today, the local APGU system you see here in the photograph serves Las Vegas and the surrounding metropolitan areas, including McCarran Airport.'

Orlov snorted. 'Is this a joke?'

Riley continued as if he hadn't heard. 'There's no longer any requirement for vast power stations, or giant transformers, or hundreds of miles of pylons carrying high-voltage wires. They're still there because we're keeping this technology under wraps for now, but you and your brother should know, Andrei, that what you're looking at is real, and by comparison, astoundingly cheap to produce.'

Harry saw a flicker of fear in Orlov's eyes. He doubted the man feared anything, except maybe seeing Gazprom's share price fall through the floor. 'How is this possible?' the Russian asked.

'It's a by-product of the power plant we use in Air Force One. It's taken many decades to develop these technologies to a point where they have practical applications. The next slide is a case in point.'

Up on the screen, Harry saw another night shot, a magnificent timber villa perched on the edge of a lake, its glass walls throwing light across the dark waters. Behind that glass, Harry saw men and women, drinking, socialising—

The table shook as Orlov thumped it with a huge fist. His face twisted into a frightening snarl. 'You're spying on my own dacha? This is a fucking outrage!'

The tension in the room skyrocketed. Riley held up a hand. 'Relax, Andrei. We didn't invade your privacy, only the airspace above Lake Ladoga. A manned stealth aircraft took that photograph, one that employs the same technology as Air Force One. What's the Russian phrase for ground-breaking? Anyway, no one saw or heard it, including the 18 security guards who patrol your property.'

Orlov's voice dripped with menace. 'An American military aircraft entering Russian airspace without authorisation is an act of war.'

'It's an act of expediency. US troops are fighting and dying as we speak. This war serves only Wazir, and it must end.'

Orlov glowered beneath his thick black eyebrows. 'My brother will consider this a violation.'

'He needs to understand our position.'

'So, if we don't starve Europe of power, you'll market your black magic to the rest of the world, yes?'

Riley spread his hands and smiled. 'Correct. Every nation on the planet will benefit from American innovation and generosity. In less than a decade, probably sooner, the global energy market will collapse, and with it, the economies of Russia and Wazir's caliphate.'

Orlov simmered. 'This is blackmail.'

'It's progress, and the United States is giving you the opportunity to join us. Become partners in an energy revolution that will change the world.'

'In exchange for what?'

'The end of the caliphate. At least, an end to Wazir's warmongering. Shutting off Europe's power supply will be the first step in overthrowing the regime in Baghdad. Its inability to market its natural resources will do the rest.'

Orlov glanced at Mitchell. The American president smiled. 'Speak to Yuri, Andrei. Tell him we're looking for partners, not adversaries.'

Orlov took a deep breath and exhaled through flared nostrils. 'Then we should leave as soon as possible.'

'Let us help you out,' President Mitchell said. 'I'll fly you back to Moscow in Air Force One if you can arrange a safe landing for us. Somewhere private, of course. And it'll be a night flight, naturally.'

Harry saw Orlov brighten. 'I will speak to my brother.' The Russian delegation got to their feet. Harry and the others stood too, and Mitchell and Orlov left the room with their aides. Riley remained and glanced at Wilde. Harry turned to his chief of staff.

'Leave us, would you, Lee?'

'Of course.' Wilde headed for the door and closed it behind him. Riley offered his hand. Harry took it and felt the strength there.

'That was quite a show,' Harry said. 'Those power units, are they real?'

'As the nose on my face.'

'I heard a rumour some years ago about California. No more summer blackouts because of a new technology. Your Department of Energy said it was some kind of innovative transformer.'

'It was a prototype. California was a test bed. There were some problems, but we worked them out. The APGUs are the real deal.'

'How is it possible?'

'That's classified, I'm afraid.'

'Of course. And the president's health?'

'He's fine, but his heart condition is genetic, and the presidency has taken its toll. He wants to see his grandkids graduate.'

'Understandable.' There was a moment of silence between them. Harry filled it. 'What am I doing here, Mr Vice President? It's not like I had anything to offer your negotiation.'

Riley sat on the edge of the conference table and folded his arms. 'I'll be frank with you, Prime Minister ...'

'Harry, please.'

'Okay, Harry.' His cold blue eyes were unblinking. 'I don't share the president's sentimentality for Britain. You're an ally, yes, and I respect our mutual history, but whatever special relationship our countries once enjoyed no longer exists. Before the invasion, half of your country – including your own parliament – made no attempt to hide their loathing of all things American. To coin a phrase, you embraced the Dark Side, and this is where it's led you. Despite that, American men and women are – once again – giving their lives to bail out the UK, and that doesn't sit well with me.'

'I see,' was all Harry could offer as a response. Riley's bitter words shook him, and the vice president wasn't stopping there.

'The United States has committed blood and treasure to this conflict because you guys don't have the numbers or the firepower to finish the job. This is our war now, and before the president steps down, he wants to win it and bring the troops home. I intend to help him do just that.'

Harry saw the determination in Riley's eyes. There was something else there, too. Not hostility, or open resentment, but a feeling that one or the other bubbled just below the surface. 'There are local truces in place. Caliphate forces are pulling back —'

'Not fast enough. We're going to hurry them along.'

'I can understand your frustration, Mr Vice President ...'

Harry paused, but there was no reciprocal offer for him to use Riley's first name, another indicator that Harry's standing with the future administration wouldn't be as cordial as the one he thought he enjoyed. Things had certainly changed. Harry banished the thought from his mind and pressed on.

'The United States has exceeded every expectation one can have in a friend and ally, but there is much to consider here. The aftermath, for example. A dangerous period in the wake of any major conflict. My people have discussed it, but any post-war strategy has yet to be formalised. We can't do that on our own.'

'Then you're going to have to work it out. The American people are tired of war. We've played our part, shed enough blood. It's time for you guys to stand on your own two feet.' Riley got to his own. 'I suggest you speak to your Cabinet and draw up that strategy. We'll help, of course, but to quote a former president, "It's America first, now."'

'If I could speak with President Mitchell, I'm sure we —'

'I speak for him.'

'With all due respect —'

'We're done here,' Riley said, looking at his watch. 'There's a weather front moving in, so you should plan to leave ASAP. We'll talk again, Prime Minister. Have a safe trip.'

The vice president left the room and the door open. Harry saw Wilde waiting outside and beckoned him in.

'Well? How did it go?'

'I'm not sure.'

Wilde frowned. 'What does that mean?'

Harry dropped back into his chair. He swivelled left and right, rubbing his jawline. Wilde sat opposite him.

'Harry?'

He stopped swivelling, ceased his aimless thinking. He knew what Riley meant. It was as clear as that nose on the president-in-waiting's face. He turned to Wilde.

'If I understood him correctly, when all this is over, we're on our own.'

[4]

DROP SHIP

EDDIE PACKED HIS DAYSACK, SNAPPED THE CLASPS HOME, AND took a last look around his room. He wasn't coming back. His training was complete and now the room had to be vacated for the next recruit. Which Eddie thought was a shame, because the room was a good size, had a decent bed, and an en suite with a big bath and a walk-in shower. Luxury, compared to every single facility he'd ever used during his time in uniform. But there was a war on, and Strathan Manor, a sprawling period property that occupied the rising ground at the western end of Loch Arkaig, was no holiday camp. Appropriated by the Atlantic Alliance, it was now a British government facility and home to the training staff of the 4th ISR Brigade.

Eddie stood at the big bay window that overlooked the mirror-like waters of the loch. His eyes swept across the dark flanks of the surrounding hills he now knew so well, in daylight, in darkness, and in all weathers. He'd seen that same ground rush towards him at terminal velocity as he'd fallen from the sky above. He'd swum the waters of the loch too, its frigid depths and inky blackness feeding the folktales told to him and the other recruits by the directing staff before taking the plunge in their dry suits and scuba gear. Tales of strange water-borne monsters and missing fisherman. It was all bull-shit, Eddie knew that, but swimming alone, deep beneath the surface, it wasn't hard to imagine something big and hungry and prehistoric looming out of the darkness.

He'd sharpened his military skills along the way, but many of his newly-acquired proficiencies were what the DS referred to as soft skills: situational awareness; memory retention and decision-making; and observation and orientation – all designed to ensure that Eddie didn't draw attention to himself.

He pulled on his coat, slipped the daysack over his shoulder, and left the room. Downstairs in the lobby, the DS staff shook his hand, wished him luck, and closed the door behind him. The waiting Land Rover drove him to a meadow outside of Fort William. There, a helicopter ferried him south to the civilian airport at Cambeltown, on the Kintyre Peninsular. As the aircraft settled on the tarmac, Eddie ducked beneath the rotors and headed for the large cluster of portacabins sandwiched between a taxiway and the edge of the runway. Behind them, squatting at the far end of the airstrip, was a Boeing X45 Unmanned Aerial Vehicle, its light grey body almost lost in the blanket of fine rain and low cloud that had settled across the peninsular. A couple of ground support guys in wet-weather gear inspected it by torchlight. Eddie's heart rate picked up a little.

'Eddie!'

He saw Hawkins waving from a portacabin door and veered towards him. The helicopter thundered overhead and disappeared into the mist. Inside, the cabin was warm and dry. There were a couple of desks occupied by a man and woman in civilian clothes, and they gave Eddie a passing look before resuming their industrious keyboard tapping. Hawkins wore a blue Barbour jacket and jeans. He shook Eddie's hand and guided him to a table at the other end of the cabin.

'Tea, coffee?'

Eddie shook his head as he sat down. 'I'm good, thanks, boss.'

'I see the beard's coming along.'

Eddie stroked the thick, black growth. 'It's taken long enough.'

'It suits you. And you'll blend in.' He pointed to the window. 'Your transport's almost ready to go. Questions?'

'I think we covered everything back at the manor.'

Hawkins pointed to the grilled window. 'The UAV out there is a stealthy insertion vehicle retrofitted to carry a single passenger. A remote pilot will fly you south to the drop zone. You know where to stash your gear?' Eddie nodded. 'Good. Someone will collect it later. When you get to the station, wait for the first tube to leave, and board the second. You know where you're going?'

'It's all up there,' Eddie said, tapping his temple.

'Take some time to recce your surroundings, bone up on your back story. And for God's sake, don't get caught, because it won't be like Birmingham. There'll be no cavalry riding to the rescue. Once you leave that aircraft, you're on your own.'

'I understand.'

Hawkins got to his feet. 'That's it, then. Go next door and ask for Brian. He's the jumpmaster. He'll get you kitted out.' Hawkins held out his hand. 'Good luck, Eddie.'

'Thanks, boss.'

Inside the adjacent portacabin, he met Brian, a former paratrooper who limped on a prosthetic leg. Eddie followed him to a row of trestle tables. His accent was Northern Irish and strong.

'As you know, this isn't a combat jump, so you'll be travelling light.' He pointed to the items on the table. 'Goggles, helmet, jumpsuit, digital altimeter, and your chute. I packed it myself, but if you feel the need to redo it, you can go fuck yourself.' Brian grimaced, and Eddie realised it was the grizzled vet's version of a smile. 'I've done more jumps than you can count, wee man, so trust me, she'll deploy when you need her to.' He looked at his watch. 'Sunset is in 20 minutes. You'll be airborne in an hour.'

Darkness enveloped the peninsular. Blackout blinds covered the windows and red lights replaced the white ones. Eddie ate a sandwich and drank coffee. He thought about the trip ahead and ran through a mental checklist of things he had to do and places he needed to go. Brian hobbled back inside the portacabin and barked a ten-minute warning. Eddie pulled the baggy black jumpsuit over his civilian clothes and Brian helped him into his parachute container, checking his straps, buckles, and harnesses. Satisfied, he patted Eddie on the shoulder.

'You're all set,' he said, picking up Eddie's daysack. 'Let's get this show on the road.'

Outside, the sky was as black as coal and a fine mist clung low to the ground. They threaded their way between the portacabins and headed out towards the edge of the runway where the UAV waited, its turbofan engine whistling in the darkness. Eddie looked to his left but couldn't see any building lights. The engine noise increased as they got closer, and he saw the ground support team decoupling cables from the aircraft and dragging them out of the way. One of them approached – a short guy wearing dark waterproofs with yellow hi-vis bands around the sleeves. Eddie saw only his nose and jaw beneath the wide brim of his baseball cap.

'Is he good to go?' the technician said.

'Aye.' Brian nodded, then he turned to Eddie and said, 'I'll be in the command cabin with the pilot. Do as she says and trust in your equipment, okay? Good luck.' He shook Eddie's hand and limped back into the mist.

'Follow me,' the tech said.

Eddie obeyed, ducking under the wing of the aircraft, its fuselage slick with rain. Beneath its fat body was a large rectangular hatch.

'It's pretty tight inside,' the tech told him, slapping a hand against the aircraft's underbelly, 'so try not to move around. Above the seat you'll see a single button, which operates a drop-down screen. That'll give you a view from the forward-looking nose camera, plus your flight stats, height, speed, distance to drop zone, etc. No in-flight movie, I'm afraid. It also serves as a comms system with ground control, so leave it in the down position.'

'How stealthy is she?' Eddie wanted to know.

'If you're asking about the likelihood of getting blown out of the sky, I wouldn't worry. This baby has flown over 50 missions as far south as the French coast without a scratch. Her radar returns are insignificant, and Brandy is a hell of a pilot. She'll take good care of you. Okay, let's get you aboard.'

Eddie shuffled beneath the hatch and stood up. He pulled himself inside, twisted round, and sat down in the padded seat. The tech passed him his daysack and Eddie strapped it to his chest harness. 'How do I get out?'

'Brandy will open the hatch remotely before you drop.'

'Okay.'

'Safe trip, brother. Watch your feet.'

A hydraulic whine filled the cramped cabin, and Eddie lifted his legs as the hatch sealed itself below his Salomon boots. He took a deep breath to calm a sudden stab of claustrophobia as he settled inside the small, padded tube. He hit the button above his head. A flatscreen monitor folded down in front of him and the picture crackled before settling into a clear image. He saw a faded white line on the runway ahead, and a damp mist swirled in across the camera lens, but everything beyond it was dark. Still, it helped.

He felt the turbofan engine wind up, and the soundproofed cabin made it very easy to hear the silky southern voice inside his headphones.

'Hi Eddie, my name is Brandy and I'll be your pilot today. Sit back and relax, and I will get you to where y'all need to be. I can see you're buckled in.'

Eddie gave the in-built camera a thumbs up. 'Ready when you are.'

'We launch in 30 seconds. Stand by.'

Eddie settled a little deeper into the chair and grabbed the armrests. The engine noise increased, and he felt the cabin trembling around him. Then the aircraft was moving, and on the screen, Eddie saw white lines slipping beneath the nose, faster now, the acceleration pushing him back into his seat. The white lines fell away, and the undercarriage thumped up inside the fuselage. He watched the altimeter on the screen, the digital readout scrolling ever upward. He saw nothing but fog, and droplets of rain obscured the camera lens. The aircraft bumped and vibrated its way up through the low cloud before it levelled out into smoother air at 28,000 feet.

Eddie took a deep breath and exhaled, relaxing a little. Flight time was roughly 80 minutes, and there was nothing to occupy him other than the TV screen, which was broadcasting an inky blackness. That would change once they crossed the frontline which was now south of Birmingham. Much had happened these last few weeks, and despite a shaky truce, the war would continue.

Eddie had only ever seen one side of that war, the view from a combat infantryman's perspective, right up there at the sharp end. Soon, he would see another side, as a civilian living under occupation. He'd been behind enemy lines already, that was a fact, but Embleton was a village that was insulated from the worst of the war and Birmingham was practically home soil for the invaders. London would be a different story.

On paper, it was an unnerving prospect, fraught with danger, but Eddie had the training and the documentation to pass unnoticed. And he felt proud to be doing something different, something important. Back at the 2nd Mass, he was just a name and a number, but now he was a man on a mission, able to operate autonomously, and trusted to make his own decisions. Whatever they asked him to do, it might prove important enough to save lives. Or it could cost them dearly. That was also true. As a private in the King's Continental Army, he'd always been reliant on the chain of command. Orders came down that chain and there was no questioning them. That made life easy for the troops. Now it would be different. There would be no Mac to give Eddie support and guidance when he needed it. Nor would Mac be there in a fight, and Eddie felt that familiar squeeze of emotion in his throat when he thought about his friends. Now it was just him, and he was in a new fight, a different one to be sure, but no less deadly.

His mind drifted as the UAV flew unseen through the night sky. It was Brandy's voice in his headphones that interrupted an unexpected doze.

'Eddie? Are you still with us?'

He opened his eyes. On the TV screen, distant pinpricks of light punctuated the darkness. 'Yes, I'm here,' he replied.

'We're approaching the drop zone. ETA, one-zero minutes.'

'Copy.'

Eddie unbuckled his seat belt. He rechecked his parachute container harness, the straps and buckles, then his altimeter. They were below 10,000 feet now, and Eddie could feel the draw of gravity as the UAV nosed into a gentle dive. He checked his helmet and goggles were secure and then he sat upright, his elbows tucked into his sides, his fingers interlocked across his daysack. He was ready.

'Sixty seconds until outboard,' Brandy warned him. 'Standby for green light.' There was a pause, and then she said, 'Good luck.'

Eddie felt it through his boots as the pressurised hatch whined open, revealing a rectangle of inky blackness. Cold air buffeted the cabin. Eddie glanced at the TV screen and saw the aircraft had dropped below 9000 feet. He punched the overhead button and watched it fold into its recess. Darkness enveloped the cabin. His heart pounded.

A green light pulsed. Eddie tipped forward and dropped head-first through the hatch.

The night air roared around his ears. He kicked out his arms and legs, stabilising his fall, checking his altimeter, the ground, the surrounding sky, the altimeter again. He kept his eyes moving, his mind focused on the jump, but he could not control the sheer exhilaration he felt as he plummeted to earth. Below, he saw patchwork fields of shadow, grey ribbons of road bordered by the angled roofs of buildings. He passed below 1200 feet and pulled his ripcord. The chute deployed as Brian had promised, snapping him upwards as he decelerated from terminal velocity to a gentle earthbound drift. He looked below his dangling legs and saw the pale, man-made shapes to his left, his visual landing reference. Yanking his left toggle, he brought his rig around, keeping the sandy excavations in sight and aiming for the wide area of grass between them. He made a gentle right turn to the south, drifting low over a stand of trees, and then the ground opened up before him, wide and flat. He yanked both toggles to slow his descent and forward motion and stepped gently onto the 9th fairway of Chartridge Park Golf Course in Chesham. The chute deflated, and Eddie squatted in the darkness, eyes and ears sweeping the surrounding fairways, the tree lines, the nearby houses. There was no sound at all, which was perfect. He unhooked his harness, gathered up his rig, and headed for the thick copse of trees in the south-eastern corner of the course. There, he stripped off his gear and bundled everything inside the parachute canopy, stuffing it into an adjacent thicket. Then he crawled in behind it and wrapped himself inside the canopy. He would wait until the sun rose, and the trains started running from Chesham underground station, just over a mile away. His destination was far to the south, on the other side of London. With a little luck, he would be there by midday. He smiled in the darkness.

Eddie Novak was back in business.

And back in the war.

[5]
MINE CRAFT

THE SENTINEL HAD BEEN HELD PRISONER BENEATH THE SEA FOR too long. Thirty months had passed since it had settled on the seabed, guarding the entrance to Europe's largest and most important port. It had spent that time waiting for unsuspecting mariners to venture its way, so it could wrap them in its deadly embrace and drag them to their deaths on the cold and murky seabed. Yet no such seafarers had come close, and when the time came for it to be replaced by another younger sentinel, its masters overlooked its location. And so it remained, moored to the seabed, tethered in place by strong chains, to be pushed and pulled as the coastal tides of the North Sea dictated.

But chains are only as strong as their weakest links. Assaulted by the constant pressures of movement, temperature, and oxidisation, one of those links failed, and the forgotten guardian of Rotterdam drifted away with the evening tide.

Held beneath the surface by its rusted tether, the sentinel coasted southwards, floating in the dappled green world 15 feet beneath the surface of the sea, twisting and swirling in the undercurrents of the Dutch coast, until it entered the waters close to the town of West-kapelle. As it passed the westernmost tip of the Scheldt Estuary, yet another undertow caught it and drew it further out to sea. By a miracle, it drifted through the busy shipping lanes that served the Belgian port of Antwerp and continued travelling eastwards, its progress stalled by the weight of its rusted tail. It passed other sentinels guarding shallower waters, and then it moved beyond them, to a world that was colder, darker, and deeper. The sentinel was incapable of thought and feeling, so it neither knew nor cared where the sea would take it. Contact with another solid object was the sole reason for its creation. That, and the death that would follow.

And so, the Chinese Moored-4 naval mine drifted onwards, ever eastward, heading for the straights of Dover and the busiest shipping lane in the world.

[6]

HUMAN WASTE

'CHERYL! COME AND LOOK AT THIS!'

Bertie stepped back and waited for her to enter the room. She appeared a few moments later, wiping her hands on her apron.

'What is it? I'm busy.'

Bertie said nothing. Instead, he swept his hand across the long dining room table. Arranged across its highly polished surface in neat piles was more money and jewellery than either of them had ever seen. Cheryl's mouth made a perfect *Oh*.

She took a step closer, running a finger across the stacks of bonded dollar bills, across the felt bags emptied of their treasures: timepieces, necklaces, earrings, bracelets. Precious stones glinted beneath the long-drop lights. 'Oh my God.'

'There's at least a million in cash. I stopped counting.'

'Where d'you think it all came from?'

'Daly had access to all the banks in his region, plus he targeted a lot of wealthy people, had them killed or deported, took everything they had. It's not that much, considering the size of the area he governed.'

'What do you think the jewellery's worth?'

Bertie picked up a black velvet box and opened it. Nestled inside, like a pearl cosseted by its oyster, was a stainless-steel wristwatch. 'That's a Patek Philippe Rose Gold Reference 2499, manufactured in 1957 and sold at Christie's in Geneva for just under three million dollars.'

Cheryl's eyes widened. 'Are you serious?'

'Daly has the paperwork to prove it.'

'And you say he's been arrested?'

Bertie nodded. Cheryl didn't need to know the ugly truth. 'For crimes against the caliphate, or something like that. Anyway, he was going to use this little treasure trove to buy this house, but now he no longer needs it. Her ladyship says we should pack it all up and bring it to France. Which is good because we might need some of this cash to grease the wheels.'

'What do you mean?'

Bertie jerked a thumb towards the window. 'It's getting busy out there. A lot of troops, and a lot of refugees coming down from the Midlands. I've heard the M25 is like a car park, day and night, likewise a lot of roads leading through London. Everyone's getting out.'

Cheryl bit her lip. 'Then maybe we should stay. Maybe it won't be as bad as we think.'

Bertie shook his head. 'We can't afford to take that chance. Once the government folds, there'll be a power vacuum. It'll be mob rule on the streets until our boys get here and restore order. That could take weeks, and anyone who worked for the administration will be fair game, including you and me. The mobs won't care that we needed the work, that we had to support ourselves. That won't mean shit to them. All they'll want is blood, and if we don't go, it could be ours they spill.'

Cheryl's face paled. 'You're frightening me, Bertie.'

He drew her towards him and held her close. 'Don't be frightened, love. I won't let anything bad happen to you.'

She looked up at him and stroked his stubbled cheek with a soft hand. 'France it is, then.'

'Just until things settle down. They'll probably sign some sort of peace deal, eventually. Give it a couple of years and we should be able to come back.'

'I trust you, Bertie,' she said, kissing his cheek.

'What are you doing right now?'

'Cleaning the entrance hall. Why?'

Bertie pointed to the treasure, the open suitcases, and the clothes scattered across the wooden floor. 'I'm going to pick up the van from Stoke Newington. Any chance you could clear this lot up and make an inventory of all the cash and jewels? Your handwriting is much better than mine, and what with the traffic, I might not get back before Lady Edith gets here.'

'What time is she due?'

'Sixish. She's having dinner and staying the night.'

'Okay. Leave it to me,' Cheryl said.

Bertie kissed her and left the room. He slapped a flat cap on his close-cropped head and cut across the back garden, leaving the grounds by the back gate. He kept to the shadows of the tree-lined pavement, his eyes and ears open for trouble. The streets of Highgate were quiet, like always, but Bertie knew that once things fell apart, nowhere would be safe. They needed to be gone before that happened. That was the bonus of being The Witch's hired help: she would know when to get out, and she'd make sure she had enough time to do it.

He hurried through the leafy, affluent lanes towards the High Street. With any luck, he would be back before The Witch was home. He didn't know where she was or what she was doing, but she'd told him she had important business to take care of.

'LADIES AND GENTLEMEN, THE BARGES HAVE NOW MOORED, AND the disembarkation process will begin shortly.'

Edith led her judicial team towards the third-floor windows of the administration building. As expected, the view was unimpressive.

Below her, a wide concrete apron stretched towards a sluggish slate loop of the River Thames. Across the dark waters lay the urban sprawl of east London, an ugly landscape of industrial roofs, high-rise housing, and monstrous electricity pylons. She'd never visited a waste management plant in her life, and she wondered why anyone would choose to work in such a place. The administration building was surrounded by rusted industrial buildings festooned with pipes, and towering smokestacks belched plumes of black filth into the leaden sky. A swirling mass of seagulls whirled and screeched as they circled over mountains of rotting rubbish. If Edith had ever witnessed a more dismal scene, she couldn't think of one.

There were rumours that the Atlantic Alliance was heading unopposed towards the city. She'd heard talk of *tightening nooses*, and the phrase made Edith's heart beat like a rabbit's. The urge to escape to France was growing stronger every day. There were preparations to be made, and the official visit to this decrepit installation was wasting her precious time.

She felt an elbow brush against hers and caught the waft of his familiar cologne. He whispered in her ear.

'What on earth are we doing here, Edith?'

She turned her head towards him and responded from the corner of her mouth. 'It's been in the diary for weeks. We must keep up appearances, Victor. Show unity and strength.'

'Here comes the militia,' she heard one of her judicial team say. Then she saw them, emerging from the darkness of the incinerator building, two lines of black uniforms and helmets greasy with rain. Some held rifles, while others carried long sticks, and they formed a narrow channel that led from the dock to the incinerator. Rain swept across the river, across the four dark, ugly barges tied up alongside. Dock workers in hooded yellow rain slickers used ropes to draw back the damp tarpaulins, revealing the cargo inside.

People. Hundreds of them.

Edith saw their pale faces tilted toward the complex of rusted buildings, but she couldn't read those distant faces. A voice echoed across the room behind her, and Edith recognised the throaty, working-class rasp of the facility's senior manager, a creature named Jarvis who wore a cheap suit and reeked of rubbish.

'We're processing about a thousand a day,' he boomed, pride dripping from his poorly enunciated words. 'They're shipped upriver overnight, so the public don't see 'em. That lot down there arrived a couple of hours before dawn, from Wandsworth Prison.'

Edith watched the yellow slickers secure ramps against the barges, and the prisoners were bullied ashore, many wearing blue boiler suits with yellow stripes down their arms and legs. Others wore civilian garb, and all of them looked wet and miserable. Still, their discomfort would soon be at an end. As if they'd read her thoughts, stick-wielding militiamen began thrashing the condemned through a channel of black uniforms towards the incinerator building.

'How do you handle the termination process?'

Edith glanced along the row of faces and saw Judge Advocate General Andrea Clarke, asking Jarvis the question. The facility manager pointed through the glass.

'It's quite simple, really. Inside that incinerator building, there's a big corridor with walls of sheet steel. The prisoners go in there, and a bulldozer shoves 'em straight into the feeder chute, which empties into the burn chamber. The chamber burns at over a thousand degrees, so it's quick and clean. And it all feeds into the local grid, providing energy to the homes and businesses you can see across the river.'

'Can you scale up if need be?' Clarke asked.

Jarvis nodded. 'Absolutely, your worship...' Edith rolled her eyes at the man's bungled address. 'We can process as many as you need, but our only concern is visibility. As you can see, dockside operations are shielded from prying eyes, but if we have to stack the barges during daylight hours, some busybody might see what's happening.'

'We'll keep you posted,' Clarke told him.

'Dear God,' Edith heard Victor whisper. She gave him a look that told him to keep his mouth closed and his emotions in check.

She turned back to the window, watching hundreds of criminals, Resistance fighters, political opponents and various other ne'er-do-wells being herded towards the dark entrance of the incinerator building. Edith knew that some of her people were uncomfortable attending executions. Names and numbers on a spreadsheet were easily deleted, but to hear the howls of fear, to see the blood and bodies, could affect one's ability to function. As it had Victor. But things had changed, and her team had to realise what was at stake. The war was lost, and the enemies of the state had to disappear before the avenging armies entered the city. Edith felt a shiver of fear.

She turned towards a familiar clicking sound and saw a hijab'd woman taking photographs. Caught by the lens, Edith smiled. The photographer kept moving, switching between the faces at the glass and the condemned herd below. Edith considered ordering her to stop but the woman was brown-skinned and wore a rain jacket with the cross swords of the caliphate emblazoned on the left breast. The rest of Edith's team smiled and nodded at her, as did Jarvis, gurning like a simpleton for the camera. Everyone except Victor, who kept his head turned away.

'It won't save you, you know.'

'I don't want my picture taken, Edith. Not here. I don't want to be a party to the slaughter.'

'A little late for that, don't you think?'

'How much longer must we endure this horror show?'

'Stop talking.' She watched the photographer scroll through her photographs, pack the camera away and leave the room. Edith turned back to the window. The barges were almost empty now, and she saw the last of the pathetic, rain-soaked figures being whipped and beaten out onto the dockside. The lines of militia folded inwards and drove the herd towards the dark entrance of the incinerator building. Inside, the walls glowed red. *Like a gateway to hell,* Edith thought. Jarvis' voice filled the room.

'That's the last of this shipment. If anyone wants to see the termination process, please follow me.'

The party followed Jarvis out of the room. Andrea Clarke paused on her way out.

'Governor? Chief Justice? Are you not joining us?'

Edith shook her head at the tall, black woman with close-cropped hair. Clarke wore a long, black leather coat with a cross swords lapel pin. 'Victor and I have urgent business to attend to back in Whitehall.'

'When are we leaving the country? Have you heard anything yet?'

'I'm hoping for news any day now. Stay close to your phone, Andrea.'

'I will. Thank you, Governor.'

Clarke spun on a booted heel and followed the others from the room. Victor snorted in her wake.

'From human rights champion to the Angel of Death in three short years. Terrifying.'

'She's your protégé.'

'She was forced upon me. A diversity appointment. She would never have made the grade otherwise.'

'Bring my car around,' Edith barked at one of Jarvis' flunkies. The young man scuttled away, and Edith turned to Victor. 'We must leave,' she told him. 'I need a long, hot bath.'

Victor tore his eyes away from the windows. 'What have we become, Edith?'

'Enough of the self-pity. You can wallow to your heart's content when we're settled in Provence. Come.'

They headed for the elevator. Outside the building, Edith's black Mercedes idled in the rain, bracketed by two escort vehicles. Security guards used umbrellas to shield them from the rain as they ducked inside the car. Moments later, they were clear of the facility and headed towards Greenwich.

'Whitehall,' she told the driver, then powered up the sound-proofed glass panel. Satisfied he could not hear them, Edith turned to Victor. 'You're right, things are going to get worse, but we must both hold our nerve. Al-Taha has assured me we'll be gone before the machine breaks down.'

Victor bit his lip. 'I'm not convinced, Edith. What do they owe us? Really? They've played us for fools.'

'The caliphate has always rewarded loyalty.'

'Did you see any caliphate people there? Apart from the photographer? No, you didn't. And you know why she was taking pictures, don't you? It was evidence to be used against us. They'll hunt us for the rest of our lives.'

'Which we'll spend in great comfort, and in far sunnier climes. We'll be safe, Victor.'

'Maybe. Maybe not —'

'Enough!' She glanced at the driver, but the man was oblivious. 'Neither of us will live forever, but what time we do have left will be spent in sun-kissed luxury. Focus on that.'

Victor bowed his head. 'You're right, Edith. I'm sorry.'

She turned away and watched the streets of south-east London pass outside her smoked-glass windows. They were grey and dismal, like the people she saw. No one paid any attention to her discreet convoy, not until they neared the queue of traffic at the entrance to the Rotherhithe tunnel. Their lights and sirens carved a path through the congestion, and Edith glimpsed their faces, sullen, scowling, and she wondered what would happen if their convoy stalled. Would they swamp the vehicles, attack the occupants? Probably not. The caliphate remained a force to be feared. No, the people of this city would bide their time, wait until the invaders had fled before daring to challenge the authority of their betters and seek their own violent justice.

And when they did, Edith was in no doubt that the streets of London would run with blood.

[7]

BATTERSEA BOY

EDDIE WOKE TO THE SOUND OF A TRAIN CLATTERING ON THE tracks outside his fourth-floor window. He sat up on the single bed and yawned, shrugging off his sleeping bag. He parted the thin curtain and saw a multitude of train tracks that crisscrossed this area of south-west London. To his right, multiple lines headed into Clapham Junction station just over a mile away, and to his left, the busy spur that fed the nearby Battersea Park station. The sky above was a pale grey, and Eddie watched as a police surveillance blimp drifted low overhead, its unmanned platform bristling with cameras.

He let the curtain drop and slumped back onto the bed. He felt tired, not only from a lack of sleep since his journey south; now he was a military intelligence operative behind enemy lines, and that came with its own energy-sapping stresses. That stress had begun 24 hours ago, when he'd crawled out from a golf course thicket and slipped onto the streets of Chesham in Buckinghamshire, 25 miles from central London.

He'd made his way to Chesham tube station, keeping his pace steady, his head up, his stride confident, as if he belonged there. He wore jeans and Nike trainers, a white t-shirt, and a navy-blue hoodie.

Tinted glasses completed the look. With his cropped hair and thick beard, he might also be mistaken for a brother of the faith.

As he navigated his way through the quiet suburban streets, he saw the scars of a country that had been at war for several years. Boarded up and burned down houses. Abandoned cars and rubbish-strewn streets. Stray dogs and feral cats. As he neared Chesham High Street, he saw other people trudging along the pavement, shoulders slumped and heads bowed. Eddie slowed and cast his eyes down. This wasn't like Birmingham, where the city had embraced the occupation. What he saw now was the weight of oppression.

The tube station itself was a quaint little building from a bygone age. Eddie closed the gap between himself and the couple in front, a man and woman in their thirties, carrying laptop bags. Eddie wondered if they worked for the caliphate, or the quisling British administration. There was no way of knowing, but they didn't flinch when they saw the four militiamen standing outside the station entrance. They were a scruffy bunch, armed with pistols and clubs, and Eddie passed them with silent headphones plugged into his ears. He only caught a couple of words. *Birmingham* was one, and Eddie remembered his close call with death; he still woke up in a cold sweat sometimes.

He'd swiped through the barrier and followed the other commuters onto the platform. The journey into central London was uneventful, but at Victoria he saw thousands of people queuing to get into the station. Eddie had walked south instead, catching a bus across Chelsea Bridge into Battersea.

His destination was the sprawling Francis Chichester housing estate, where brutal towers of grey concrete loomed over Battersea Park Road. The estate had seen better days, Eddie guessed. Everywhere he looked he saw dozens of abandoned and burned-out vehicles and boarded-up windows in the surrounding tower blocks.

Eddie's safe house was in one of the smaller blocks, a red-bricked 1950s era maisonette. The fourth-floor, two-bedroomed flat in Newtown Court was a short distance from Battersea Park and

Chelsea Bridge Road. The property was a former MI5 safe house, decrepit from the outside, the front door and kitchen window protected with steel grilles. Eddie had used a security key to unlock them, then used the same key to open the front door and slipped inside, locking everything behind him. He'd leaned against the door and exhaled a long sigh of relief.

The flat was basic, the walls papered with cheap patterned rolls, and the blackout curtains covered the windows of two small bedrooms and sparse living room. The water was on, as was the electricity, and Eddie had enjoyed a long shower in the cramped but clean bathroom. There were a couple of tins of soup in the kitchen, but they were out of date by over six months, so Eddie cooked a pack of noodles from his daysack. He'd spent most of the night listening to the sounds of the block, the traffic on the nearby roads, and the trains that rumbled past his window. There would be a pattern to life here, and he had to listen to its rhythm, absorb it, learn its beats, lulls, and crescendos. He'd spent most of the day waiting, reading one of the well-thumbed paperbacks on a shelf in the living room, stretching, exercising, then catching up on some more sleep. When the sun dipped behind the grey towers outside his balcony, Eddie went to work.

He swung his legs off the bed and drew every curtain and blind in the flat. In the hallway, he opened the airing cupboard door. Inside was a hot water cylinder wrapped in insulation, but Eddie knew it was redundant. He disconnected the plastic water pipe at the bottom of the tank, grabbed it with both hands, and lifted it up. The tank swung out towards him on a hinged bracket and Eddie crawled beneath it, getting to his feet in the narrow space behind it. Then he placed his hands against the back wall, held his breath, and pushed it hard. He heard a click, then the entire wall moved backwards six inches. Eddie slid the panel to his left, exposing the equipment store behind, divided into several shelves. Eddie checked the inventory. There was a laptop in a toughened case, a satellite phone, spare batteries for both, a small spotter scope, an RF signal decoder, several boxes of MRE rations, a covert tactical vest, and in the grey steel gun locker, a Springfield Armoury sub-compact 9mm pistol and a Heckler & Koch MP5K, a close-quarters weapon that was easily concealed, plus 800 rounds of ammunition for both weapons. There was also a brick of cash – $5000 sealed in a plastic container. That would come in useful, Eddie thought, peeling off 500 in twenties and recording the withdrawal on the inventory sheet.

He took the weapons into the living room and checked them, then loaded all the magazines. He returned the HK to the locker, but he kept the pistol close. He typed up a brief report on the laptop, connected the satellite phone, and sent the tiny, encrypted file back to Scotland. Transmission time took hundreds of a second, so the chances of his signal being tracked were almost zero. Almost.

Eddie was swinging the cylinder back into place when he heard the knock at the door. He peered through the spy-hole and saw a man standing outside. He had a thin face and greasy, scraped-back hair tied in a bun at the back of his head. Eddie recalled the brief back in Scotland:

William Griffin, 42 years old, self-employed florist, married, wife Zoe, 39, two children, Alfie, 6, and Freddie, 8. As a teenager, he served 14 months in the Royal Regiment of Fusiliers before being dishonourably discharged.

Eddie flipped the two deadlocks and cracked open the door. The man on the balcony smiled and nodded.

'I'm from next door,' he said, jerking a thumb at the adjacent flat. 'Thought I'd say hello, introduce myself.'

Eddie opened the door wider. 'I'm Eddie. Eddie Shaw.' He'd repeated the name a thousand times since they'd issued him his IDs, but it still wasn't rolling off the tongue.

'Billy Griffin,' the man said, shaking Eddie's hand. 'Call me Griff. Everyone else does.' His neighbour grimaced, pointing to the coloured swirls of graffiti that decorated the front door and the kitchen window. 'I didn't see 'em do it. Little shits, eh? I guess they were pissed off that they couldn't get in, what with the steel grills.'

And the reinforced front door with the steel frame that wouldn't shift without using explosives. 'You're probably right,' Eddie agreed. The man had been standing on his doorstep for too long now. Others might be watching from one of the countless windows overlooking Newtown Court. 'D'you want to come in? I can make us a brew. Powdered milk only, I'm afraid.'

Griff brightened. 'How about a beer? The missus is putting the kids to bed. What you might call a window of opportunity. I've got a six-pack of cold ones in the fridge.'

The thought of a beer sounded too good to resist. 'Sure, why not?'

'Sweet. Back in two.'

He was quicker than that, and Eddie bolted the door behind him. They sat in the living room, flopping onto the dated three-piece suite. There was a cheap wooden coffee table between them but little else, no pictures on the walls, no TV, nothing. Griff cracked open a couple of Spanish imports and handed one to Eddie. 'There you go.'

Griff was right, the beer tasted good. His neighbour waved a hand around the room. 'Where's the rest of your furniture?'

'Storage,' Eddie lied. He eyed his guest. Griff was a small guy, thin too, with sunken cheeks and crooked teeth. His stonewashed jeans and vintage *Vanns* t-shirt hung off his slight frame. 'So, what's your story, Griff?'

'Since the invasion?' He took a swig of beer as he dug into his memories. 'Jesus, what a night that was.' He shook his head and refocused. 'I've got a flower stall on the Waterloo Road, right outside the station. I was packing things up when the bombs went off. *Boom! Boom! Boom!* Three of 'em, one after the other, right at the height of rush hour. Then came the stampede, people pouring down the stairs and out into the street, screaming and crying, some of them covered in blood, others with their clothes blown off. Suicide bombers, someone said. Blew themselves up on the main concourse. It was chaos. I saw people trampled at the bottom of the escalator – kids, old people ... a baby and its mum. It was awful.'

He took another swig of beer and belched into his hand.

'So, I locked up, jumped on my pushbike and headed home. Down on the embankment, there were crowds of people, all watching the smoke and fires across the river. Some said they saw planes go down, and we heard more bombs going off across the city. Gunfire, too. So, I kept going, made it home about 20 minutes later. Zoe was in bits, absolutely terrified.' Griff chuckled. 'Mind you, so was I. Anyway, the TV and radio were off the air and neither of us had a phone signal, so we just battened down the hatches. We stayed like that all night, sitting in the dark, door bolted, curtains drawn, just trying to keep the kids quiet. There was trouble on the estate, and a few cars got torched, but no one came down this end. A couple of days later, we saw long lines of trucks full of IS troops, and by then we had a good idea of what had happened. When the power came back, we put the TV on. BBC and Sky were talking about the Prime Minister, blaming him and his government for stirring trouble ...'

Eddie remembered the days and months after the invasion, when the British media and political classes had scrambled to praise Wazir, blaming society for a plague of discrimination and xenophobia. The displaced Brits watching from America had been outraged.

Griff cracked open another beer and kept talking. 'D'you remember that prison riot a month before the invasion? When all those Muslim prisoners were killed? And the refugee dinghies, rammed by British fisherman out in the Channel?'

Eddie nodded. He remembered the jerky phone footage of blood-splashed cells and the bodies of women and children washed up on the beaches of Kent.

'All bullshit,' Griff said. 'Those people died, but I think they were sacrificed, you know, to justify what came next. The invasion. Anyway, things got back to normal, eventually. They cleared the streets, got the traffic moving again, the trains and tubes too. They told everyone to go back to work, and we all did. What else could we do, right? The shops reopened, but a lot of the West End was closed off while they knocked buildings down. No one knows what happened to the bodies. Put 'em in mass graves, I expect. Tens of thousands of people had gone missing. The cops just shrugged their shoulders, and after a while they started enforcing new laws, getting heavy-handed. I've seen entire families evicted from the estate. No one knows where they've gone, though some people say they got shipped abroad. Me and Zoe keep our heads down, stay out of trouble. We take the kids to the park, go shopping in Clapham Junction, and that's about it.'

'What about this so-called resistance?' Eddie asked him. 'I've heard they've caused a few problems.'

Griff snorted. 'And look what happens to 'em. They crucified the last lot. Crucified 'em, for fuck's sake.' He shook his head. 'I didn't go to watch it, but I know people who did. Christ knows why. Planted them all around Marble Arch. Took days for some of 'em to die.' Griff finished his beer and cracked open two more, handing one to Eddie. 'So, what about you?'

Eddie stroked his beard. 'I was down on the coast when it all kicked off. Me and my mate ended up on his uncle's farm outside of Eastbourne. Stayed there, kept our heads down.'

'Very wise,' Griff said, looking around the room. 'This is your place, then?'

'Yes.'

'I've seen a few different people come and go over the years.'

'I rent it out,' Eddie said, adding another layer to the lie. 'Management company was taking care of it for me.'

'Right.' Griff necked his beer. 'Is that why you've come back? Because they're leaving?'

'Who?'

'The caliphate. Everyone's talking about it. Quietly, of course, but we all know they got booted out of Ireland.'

'What else have you heard?'

'That our boys and the Yanks are kicking their arses. That's why they nuked Birmingham. To stop us. It didn't work, apparently.'

For a moment, Eddie was back on the roof of that building. He could still smell the cordite, the burning jet fuel, the metallic tang of blood. 'I wouldn't get too complacent.'

Griff's jaw dropped open. 'You don't think they'd nuke London, do you?'

'That would be a big mistake on their part.'

'I wouldn't put it past 'em. But they're going, that's for sure.'

'You've seen it?'

Griff nodded. 'I work at Waterloo, remember? They're packing onto trains and heading for the coast. Hundreds of 'em, families mostly, all queuing up with their suitcases. A dozen trains a day, I've heard. And that's just Waterloo. Same thing's happening at St Pancras, London Bridge, Charing Cross, you name it.'

'I saw a big crowd outside Victoria.'

'There you go, then. And it's not just the immigrants. There's a lot of Brits going too, the ones who worked for the government. Good riddance, I say.'

'What about the soldiers? The militia, the cops? What are they up to?'

Griff frowned. 'There're still plenty of soldiers about, but not as many as we're used to seeing.' He smiled, crooked crockery on display. 'As for the militia and the cops, they're shitting themselves. You can see it on their faces.'

Eddie sipped his beer. 'What about checkpoints?'

'Worse than usual. Like they're clamping down. Stupid, really. They must know what's going to happen to them when our boys get here.'

'Maybe there won't be any trouble,' Eddie suggested. 'Maybe we'll wake up one morning and they'll all be gone.'

'Maybe,' Griff said, shrugging. 'I've seen some odd things, though.'

'Like what?'

'They're piling onto every train going south, right? But I've seen a lot of trucks and equipment heading north across Waterloo Bridge.

Civilian trucks mostly. Big rigs, trailers with tarps thrown over them. It's odd.'

'Why?'

'I've been on that patch since they got here, remember? I'm out there every day, watching the world go by. Sometimes those trucks are nose to tail all the way back across the bridge. Never seen it before.'

Eddie finished his beer and stood up. 'I'm calling it a night, Griff. Appreciate the brew.'

'My pleasure.' The older man got to his feet. 'Anything you need, just knock. If I'm not in, ask Zoe. I work until six, Monday to Saturday. If you're ever passing the station, come say hello.'

'I will.'

Eddie closed the door behind him and dropped the deadbolts. He fished out the laptop, sent an update to Scotland, then packed it away again. As he brushed his teeth, he guessed Scotland would learn nothing new. Someone, somewhere, would've reported those unusual truck movements. The allied war machine wouldn't grind to a halt, waiting for Eddie Novak to fill in the blanks. He turned off all the lights, padded to the bedroom and lay back on his bed.

Big rigs, with tarps thrown over them. All heading into the city. Not out.

Maybe the Hajis were gearing up for something? Or maybe the rigs were there to transport stolen goods. Eddie had seen the intelligence reports: banks; data centres; engineering and farming equipment; millions of tons of cabling; designer stores; jeweller's shops; car dealers. It was all being nicked and shipped overseas. The ultimate shopping spree.

He lay in the dark of his bedroom and decided he would find out what was going on. Eddie didn't know what the future had in store for him, but if Hawkins was right and the fighting was entering its ultimate phase, he hoped he would still have the chance to make a difference.

[8]

WAR PIGS

THE REAR ELEMENT OF THE ISLAMIC STATE'S 3RD (ABU BAKR Assiddeeq) Combat Division cleared the outskirts of the Welsh city of Newport just after 1 am, massing along the eastbound lanes of the M4 motorway as they travelled towards the Prince of Wales Bridge. Beyond it, across the River Severn, lay the relative safety of England.

Behind them, pre-recorded military radio traffic filled the airwaves above the cities of Cardiff and Newport, designed to convince the trailing American forces that IS units remained present in both cities. The IS commanders knew it was a pointless exercise; enemy UAVs would track their eastbound progress and relay that information back to the Yankee ships in the Irish Sea. That explained the long-range missiles that were chipping away at their trailing formations, forcing the commanders to employ desperate tactics and buy themselves time to escape across the river into England. So, they called upon the martyrs to engage the enemy where they could. These men and women would die on Welsh soil, but none of them feared death. Like all martyrs, what they dreaded most was failing in their task – stalling the Yankee advance and killing as many infidels as possible.

On the A48 motorway heading east out of Cardiff, Afghan engineers blew the road bridge over the motorway, bringing down a large section of concrete onto the highway in a cloud of grey dust. When it cleared, the Afghans realised the rubble wouldn't halt the progress of the infidel armoured column heading at speed towards their positions. Their well-armed comrades, hiding amongst the embankment shrubbery, opened fire on the speeding American convoy with a mixture of TOW, Javelin, M47 Dragon, and French APILAS anti-tank guided missiles. The swarm of weapons streaked through the night air in a blaze of smoke and solid-fuel flame, ripping into the American front-runners in a series of deafening explosions, disabling four M1A3 Abrams tanks, and destroying a single, ageing LAV-25 APC. Trailing American armour fired off chaff and smoke, twisting left and right as they sought to evade the incoming weapons. The American crews had the bit between their teeth and were in no mood for a protracted firefight.

As a disabled Abrams opened fire on its attackers with its 120mm gun, another 60-ton monster flattened the barrier at the side of the road and drove up the embankment, running along it at an ungoverned 50 miles per hour and at a dangerous tilt, chewing up trees and bushes with its clattering tracks and blind firing its secondary guns as it bore down on its attackers. Such was the speed and ferocity of the advance that many of the Afghans were left screaming beneath a thundering monster of US heavy metal. Leaving the chewed-up meat of its attackers behind it, the marauding Abrams breached the top of the embankment and slammed down on the other side with a seismic boom, rocking to a halt in the middle of the road. Its big gun swung to the right and fired a snapshot round at a car heading away in the opposite direction. The high explosive shell scored a direct hit, blowing the vehicle and its unknown occupants to pieces. In a cloud of blue exhaust fumes, the tank lurched forward, raced down the opposite embankment, and rattled back onto the A48 motorway.

Joined by two more M1s and a fast-moving Stryker mobile gun platform, the newly formed convoy skirted the rubble of the bridge and opened up on the embankments on either side, shredding the undergrowth with thousands of high-calibre rounds, shattering signs, fences, and advertising hoardings. No one was thinking about collateral damage. Everyone wanted to make it home. If civilians were stupid enough to wander around a war zone this late at night, then on their heads be it. There had been enough warnings – leaflet drops, broadcasts over local FM and AM frequencies, illumination shells fired above every major population centre along the southern Welsh coast, lighting up the sky and letting everyone know that the Atlantic Alliance was coming. If people hadn't got that message by now, fuck 'em. Stupidity was punishable by death.

Behind the front runners, a Caterpillar D9 armoured bulldozer made quick work of the fallen bridge section and the armoured column formed up once again, this time over-watched by a Predator drone armed with Hellfire missiles. At the Coryton roundabout, a mixed troop of armoured vehicles swerved off onto Northern Avenue and headed south towards Cardiff city centre. Above and ahead of them, the Predator's onboard integrated sensor platform was already searching for targets.

In his cramped control booth aboard the *U.S.S. John Kennedy*, the Predator pilot saw wild tracer rounds lancing up into the air around his aircraft and banked towards the source of gunfire. His thermal imaging revealed a large group of enemy fighters on the rooftop of the St David's shopping centre on Bridge Street. With the freedom to operate autonomously, the pilot locked and launched a Hellfire missile and watched it streak across the city sky and strike its target, blowing the roof to pieces and killing everyone on top of it. As he banked the aircraft around the target in a wide, prudent circle, the pilot saw flames leaping up from the bowels of the mall beneath the newly-ventilated roof. Black smoke and burning red embers boiled into the night sky, and on his third pass, the pilot noticed that some of those embers were smoking in the gutters of the adjacent Metropolitan Cathedral. Within minutes, a fire caught hold and engulfed the entire roof in a terrible inferno. The last thing he saw before banking away was a stream of people stumbling out of the cathedral.

The pilot increased power, accelerating to the west. He located the friendly armour and reported his contact to the troop commander. Then he raced ahead of them, banking to the east, searching for enemy formations, for stragglers and rogue elements like the rooftop jokers whose charred remains were now scattered across Cardiff's shopping district.

For the good folk of Cardiff, there would be no military liberation of their city, no triumphant parades of British and American troops through the streets, no cheering crowds or blizzards of ticker tape. The immediate mission of the Atlantic Alliance was to drive the enemy east, out of Wales and into England, and then snap at their heels, all the way to London and the coast, where, according to the latest intelligence, boats and planes were criss-crossing the English Channel at an exponential rate.

In the Bristol Channel, four landing craft powered their way through the fast-moving tidal waters and made landfall on Severn Beach, less than eight miles from Bristol city centre. As ramps slapped down onto a narrow strip of sand and pebbles, 16 Ripsaw UFVs powered up the empty beach. When all 16 remotely-operated tracked vehicles had formed a column along Station Road, their operators, squeezed into cramped cubicles on the America-class amphibious assault ship U.S.S. *Bougainville*, powered their charges into the darkness, steering them through empty streets in a matte-black convoy of autonomous armour.

As their HD gun cameras swivelled left and right, the operators glimpsed frightened faces at the windows of the quiet residential neighbourhood. At the end of Church Road, the lead Ripsaw bullied its five-ton body through the wooden fence and rolled out onto the empty M49 motorway. One by one, they turned northwards, accelerating to their maximum speed of 60 miles per hour towards the road junction 3 miles ahead. When they got there, the fast-moving column veered left and up onto the Prince of Wales Bridge, the six-lane vehicle span that linked England and Wales above the muddy brown waters of the River Severn. As they crested the on-ramp, the operators saw that the bridge lights were out. However, their low-light optics picked up the eastbound lanes that were packed full of military vehicles, moving at low speed towards the darkened county of Gloucestershire. Intelligence officers had promised the operators a target-rich environment. They didn't disappoint.

The formation split up. The leading eight Ripsaws sped up towards the middle of the bridge while the trailing eight slowed, rolling line abreast as they opened fire with their 30 mm autocannons. All eight guns tracked along the convoy, their armour-piercing shells chopping up the troop carriers and logistics vehicles prioritised in their target packages. As the enemy returned fire, the Ripsaw operators used the vehicles' excellent manoeuvrability to avoid the incoming rounds, accelerating, braking, reversing, then surging forward again, firing off smoke and punching shells into the stalled convoy. In less than a minute, 20 enemy vehicles were ablaze, the belching black smoke adding to the confusion.

The other Ripsaws were running at full speed towards the middle of the bridge, their M61, Vulcan 20 mm rotary cannons locked into position at 90 degrees to the road. Receiving the remote command, all eight Ripsaws opened up, tracking their explosive rounds along the length of the convoy. Sixty rounds raked the length of a fuel truck and it exploded, the giant fireball swallowing every vehicle around it in a shockwave of fire and death. As incoming rounds pinged off their black armoured hides, the Ripsaws fired off smoke and spun around on their tracks, heading back towards their comrades, their guns cutting men and machinery to pieces. Oily black smoke trailed back across the bridge and burning fuel spilt to the river 120 feet below. In their cubicles back on the *Bougainville*, the American operators were pushing their Ripsaws to their limits, spending their ammunition as fast as possible. They knew that the fight wouldn't last long. And so it proved.

IS AFVs broke free of the stalled convoy and crashed through the central reservation, all guns blasting, taking out three of the Ripsaws in a matter of seconds. To the east, more armour headed back over the bridge to join the fight and soon the autonomous mini-tanks were battling against a deadly crossfire. A duel ensued. The bridge lit up with incoming and outgoing 30 mm and 20 mm rounds, the pall of smoke enveloping the bridge and pulsing like a lightning storm. IS troops joined the battle, launching RPGs from cover and opening up with their heavy machine guns. The American operators worked with impressive dexterity, but the suicide mission was over. As the last of the working Ripsaws emptied its magazines, another incoming shell blew it to pieces.

The battle was over. The bridge was a mess of debris, of scorched tarmac littered with thousands of empty brass cases and pools of burning fuel. At least 100 IS vehicles burned, the flames rippling into the night sky. Hundreds of troops lay dead and wounded, and desperate divisional commanders ordered the vehicle drivers to break protocol and use every lane on the bridge to reach safety on the other side. They knew, as did everyone else on that bridge, that the fires would be seen for miles.

At that precise moment, six Boeing F/A-18/F Advanced Super Hornets rumbled across the deserted nature reserve of Lundy Island, their weapons bays and wing mounts heavy with ordinance. At 5 nautical miles past the island – and 66 to their target – the lead F18s launched their AGM-158 anti-ship missiles before banking left and right respectively and allowing the trailing pairs to do the same. Each plane launched two cruise missiles, and they streaked towards their targets, the two concrete towers that supported the bridge's central section. The missiles screamed out of the darkness and hit both pylons with their 1000-pound penetrator warheads. Of the 12 missiles launched, only 1 missed its targets and self-detonated in the sky above Chepstow, the resulting thunder shaking windows and dislodging roof tiles across the city.

Back on the bridge, the central road span shuddered as the towers were hit repeatedly, the exploding warheads punching giant holes in the reinforced structures and raining concrete across the road below. The 240 steel cable stays sang as they vibrated like giant guitar strings, and then in rapid succession they snapped, whipping across the bridge, and scything through flesh, concrete, and metal. Its base reduced to a crumbling ruin, the westernmost pylon collapsed in a thunderous roar, pulling its dying sister onto a road deck below that was already straining beneath the weight of hundreds of immobile vehicles and armour. As the easternmost tower crashed down onto the bridge, the central section gave way and collapsed into the black waters below.

And still, the carnage continued.

The F/18s circled back and headed fast and low towards the Monmouthshire countryside, rising and falling with the contours of the land until the ground fell away and the eastern approaches of the bridge were laid bare. On the ground, panic ensued, but the desperate attempts to organise any kind of air defence were too little and far too late. Working in pairs, the F/18s unloaded their ordnance into the confusion of men and vehicles caught on the Welsh bank. Rockeye cluster munitions rained down, the explosions rippling across the surrounding hills and echoing out into the Bristol Channel. The F/18s banked away to the west, leaving death and destruction in their wake, and severing a major artery between England and Wales.

ONE HUNDRED AND TWENTY-EIGHT MILES TO THE WEST, another convoy moved through the darkness, except this one had no fear of an aerial attack. In the preceding daylight hours, the convoy organisers had seen the mighty ships sailing offshore and had witnessed the countless planes and helicopters criss-crossing the skies, and they knew.

Liberation was nigh.

For three long years, the residents of Newquay had suffered beneath the yoke of tyranny. They'd watched from behind barbed wire fences as caliphate bigwigs had enjoyed their sandy beaches. They'd been forced to listen to music and laughter carried on summer winds, as English lapdogs had partied in the Headland and Fistral Beach hotels. The people had suffered the torment of lock-downs, food shortages, and curfews, while their oppressors had taken full advantage of everything the popular Cornish city offered.

That oppression extended itself to anyone who dared question the legitimacy of the Newquay Security Council, staffed by local politicians who'd scrambled to align themselves with their new masters. Like countless bureaucrats across the country, the council-lors of Newquay could not face being deprived of the power and privilege they'd become accustomed to.

One such man was the council's leader, Lewis Monk. He too had seen the grey ships out at sea, had cringed in fear as the jets had screamed overhead, had peered through his office blinds as allied helicopters had skirted the town. His days were numbered, and the people he'd ruled over for so long glared at him as he'd passed them in his official car, their vengeful intentions suppressed by Monk's still-loyal militia. So, he'd stayed at home – a luxurious house overlooking Fistral Bay, the one he'd seized from a local entrepreneur – and waited for the promised phone call. When it came, Monk would drive the short distance to Pentire Headland and board the waiting helicopter that would whisk him and his wife to safety. He was still waiting for that call.

He saw the first sign of trouble through an upstairs window: the militia detail guarding his house had disappeared. The second sign was the long line of headlights speeding up Esplanade Road towards his property. As he ran to the bedroom and screamed at his wife to hide, he knew he was already too late. Downstairs, the front door splintered and crashed open. Angry voices filled the house and pounding feet stampeded up the stairs. Monk yanked open his bedside drawer, fumbling for the pistol inside. He would do his wife first, then put a bullet through his own head. His fingers brushed metal, but the feet and voices were already in the room. Something struck him on the side of the head and supernovas exploded behind his eyes. Strong hands grabbed him and dragged him downstairs. His wife's screams filled the house, and then suddenly choked off. A jeering mob waited outside in the driveway, and someone spat in his face as they bundled him into the back of a waiting van. He lay face down on the filthy metal floor, his broken nose running with blood, his body pinned by booted feet that kicked at his ribs and genitals.

The journey was quick, and when they dragged him out feet-first, a gusting wind whipped his thinning hair and thin shirt. They stood him up, and he felt grass beneath his feet. Headlights lit up the headland and threw the angry faces around him into shadow. Headlights flared and bounced as more vehicles arrived. Monk shivered, more from fear than the chilly wind, and then he saw other faces stumbling towards him, familiar, bloodied, and beaten. His council colleagues, men and women who'd taken their 30 pieces of silver, the same people who Monk was preparing to abandon. There was going to be a reckoning, and the prospect terrified the former dictator.

'I have money,' he gasped at the nearest man, a hulking shadow with long hair and earrings who stood in front of Monk and his cowering councillors. Monk couldn't help but imagine pirates had captured him, and now he was about to walk the plank.

'Your money won't save you now,' the man drawled in a thick West Country accent. He grabbed Monk by the arm and shoved him forwards. More hands accosted him, squeezing his neck, his arms, grabbing his sparse hair. He heard a woman scream behind him, and he wondered what had happened to his wife. Killed, he imagined. He stumbled forward, penned in by the surrounding louts. He heard the crashing of waves ahead, and that's when he realised where he was.

Those same hands dragged him to a halt and ripped the shirt

from his back, as well as his jeans and underwear. They shoved the other councillors forward, all of them stripped naked and shivering, their hands covering their private parts. A stiff wind gusted. The pirate chief spoke.

'Your job was to take care of this community, yet you sided with the enemy. We've all lost people – friends, family, workmates. Some you gave up to the firing squads, others you had hung for nothing. You're the worst sort of people, traitors and scumbags. Now you're all going to die. How does that feel?'

Monk blubbed. 'No! Please, I'm begging you!'

'You can't do this!' another councillor wailed.

The pirate chief pointed at Monk and barked his order. 'Save him 'til last.'

The mob closed in, manhandling his colleagues towards the lip of the hole. The Witch's Cauldron was a cavern carved out of the rock beneath the headland by a million years of tidal erosion. It was a frigid and dark cathedral, where the sea surged in, swirling and pounding itself to spray on a sharp, glistening bed of rocky outcrops 40 feet below.

Monk moaned as ruffians ran the pleading town clerk towards the hole and shoved her hard. She tumbled out of sight, her scream shrill and echoing until the rocks cut it short below. Waves boomed and crashed as the rest of the council followed her into the cauldron.

Then it was Monk's turn. He tried to back away, knowing he had only moments to live. In those moments, he regretted the decisions he'd made over the last three years, the lives he'd destroyed, the power that had destroyed him. Strong hands grabbed him, lips cursing and spitting hatred as they ran him towards the edge—

Then pulled him short of the gaping chasm. They locked his arms behind his back, his feet scraping the rocky lip. Monk looked down, saw white foam, and the pale, twisted bodies of his team dotted on the wet rocks. Some were still moving ...

'Oh God, please —'

'This is for the people of Newquay.'

A shove, and then he was flying, his arms windmilling through the air, the damp chill of the cavern already eating into his bones as he plummeted towards the rocks below. The bodies rushed up towards him, like skinless seals broken and bleeding on the jagged stones.

He closed his eyes and prayed he would die on impact.

[9]

ROZZER

THE TRAFFIC JAM WAS HUGE AND STRETCHED NOSE-TO-TAIL down Haverstock Hill towards Camden Town. As Bertie drove past on the other side of the road, he saw vehicles of every description – cars, SUVs, pickups, vans, and small trucks, all crawling north, many of them crammed with people and luggage. He saw an estate car parked by the side of the road, the roof rack piled high with cases, the hood propped open. Steam belched from the engine block. A family stood on the pavement, parents, grandparents, kids, all looking lost and frantic. As well they might, Bertie thought, because there was no AA anymore, no RAC to come to the rescue. No mobile phone network either, not for the likes of ordinary folk. He saw the man pleading with passing drivers, but no one would stop, not now that the *Great Liberation* had become the *Great Escape*. Bertie had no sympathy for the stricken driver. He looked normal enough, a pasty bloke wearing a t-shirt and shorts, but there was no guessing what he'd done, what he'd been a party to. *If they run, they're guilty.* That was Bertie's motto. He was running too, but for good reason. Sticking around might get him killed. Cheryl too. How was that fair? Maybe that stranded man was like Bertie, labelled as a traitor, with no choice but to run. Maybe.

'I've never seen the traffic so bad. How will we get home, Bertie?'

He glanced in the rear-view mirror. The Witch sat behind him, handbag clutched in her lap, staring at the congestion through the tinted privacy windows. *You look old,* he wanted to tell her, *old and weak and frightened.* But he didn't.

'They're diverting them down Belsize Lane to Swiss Cottage,' he said. 'From there, they'll pick up the North Circular and use that to get around to the south. We'll go another way back. I'll flash my credentials if need be.'

'Be careful, Bertie.'

'Of course. Your safety is my priority, Lady Edith.'

'Bless you.'

His words, his physical presence behind the wheel, were a comfort to her. She'd let her official car go, not because she had any sympathy for the stranger who drove her Mercedes, but because terrorists had attacked an official car the day before. The man was some local bigwig over in south-east London. They'd rammed the car and stabbed the occupants to death. The news shook The Witch, and now Bertie had to drive her everywhere in the Toyota. It was a prudent move, but it put Bertie in the firing line, too. That's why he carried his gun, the one that Judge Hardy had given him. It was a Glock 26, a small, 9mm automatic concealed in a plastic holster clipped to his waistband. He had a permit too, tucked into his impressive wallet, the one with the gold badge of crossed swords. It could open all sorts of doors. It could also get him killed if he turned the wrong corner. Bertie was in no doubt - the sooner he and Cheryl got lost in the French countryside, the better.

He pulled into an empty lane at the King's Cross checkpoint. The security presence was heavier than usual, which didn't surprise Bertie, given the size of the crowd waiting to enter the city. Many of them waved papers, passports, and ID cards, desperate to get inside London's security envelope that stretched all the way out to City

Airport. That's where The Witch would travel from, while Bertie and Cheryl drove the van down to the coast. Today was all about getting those travel permits. Without them, everyone was screwed.

As the car idled behind the security barrier, Bertie watched the soldiers from behind his Oakley's. They looked jumpy, especially the guy sitting behind the big gun mounted on the roof of his jeep. His head swivelled left and right, his eyes hidden behind wraparounds. Bertie noticed everyone had guns now, even the spotty militia kid manning the barrier. He carried an AK slung across his chest that looked far too big for him. The cop in the booth handed Bertie his ID, and the barrier hummed upwards. Bertie cursed them all under his breath as they drove through.

'Thank God we're out of that mess,' The Witch muttered behind him.

'It's going to get a lot worse,' Bertie said, stoking her fear. It wouldn't hurt to keep her on her toes.

'Let's just get there, shall we?'

'Yes, ma'am.'

Beyond the security cordon, traffic lights were out of commission. Bertie saw several military vehicles blocking roads, and a big green truck rumbled past in the other direction, packed with sullen-faced troops. Bertie smiled. The military evacuation was underway, and he hoped those troops were shitting themselves at the prospect of facing off against the Atlantic Alliance. But his smile soon faded. What would happen after those soldiers left was anyone's guess, and Bertie had a feeling that Londoners wouldn't be in the mood for street parties and conga lines. More like blood-letting and unbridled revenge.

The IS troops wouldn't be going back empty-handed, though. As he drove into Bloomsbury, Bertie saw broken shop windows, empty shelves, and pavements littered with glass and abandoned plunder. He saw hotels, restaurants, supermarkets, and coffee shops, all ransacked. He dreaded to think of the mess on Oxford Street.

'This is awful,' he heard The Witch whisper. As they drove

around Russell Square and into Montague Place, Bertie pointed through the windshield. 'Looks like they're cleaning out the British Museum too.'

At the rear of the world-famous institution, scores of soldiers were loading crates into a long line of removal lorries parked nose-to-tail along the street.

'One might argue that we stole those artefacts from their rightful owners,' The Witch said.

'You were right to take those paintings, Lady Edith. Imagine that lot getting hold of them.' He pointed to four soldiers puffing and bellowing at each other as they manhandled a large marble antiquity up a vehicle ramp.

'Perish the thought,' she said, watching them as they drove by.

Bertie turned onto Malet Street. The iconic art deco Senate House loomed ahead, and hundreds of people eager to get inside had formed an orderly queue that stretched back to the British Museum.

'We're here,' he announced, pulling into the kerb outside the main entrance. Behind the coils of razor wire, armed guards watched the Toyota. 'Not sure I should wait, Lady Edith. These guys look pretty nervous.'

'Find somewhere to park. I'll call you when I'm on my way out.'

Bertie checked his phone signal. The secure network was still up, but that might not last once the dominoes toppled.

'Yes, ma'am.'

He got out, flashing his gold badge to the nearest guards, and opened the Toyota's rear door. The Witch climbed out and passed through the security gate. Bertie got back in the car and pulled away. He drove around the block and parked on Keppel Street, opposite the School of Tropical Medicine. Stopping in a space behind another car, he made sure he had a good view of the main gate and could scoop up the Old Bag as soon as she appeared.

He settled into his seat, his eyes watching the mirrors, the badge on his lap ready to ward off evil. He turned on the radio, but it was just a lot of looped music stations and warning messages to obey the night time curfew. The traitors weren't taking much notice of that. He'd seen some of The Witch's neighbours in Hampstead, their cars creeping out of their driveways before heading off into the night, getting out before the coming storm.

Because it was coming. A big one. And by the time it broke over the city, Bertie hoped and prayed he'd be long gone.

EDITH ENTERED THE BUILDING, PASSING THROUGH ITS impressive marble and limestone entrance hall to an elevator that whisked her up to the 18th floor of the 19-storey building. There, Edith crossed the carpeted lobby and pushed her way through a set of double doors into a large open plan office.

She hesitated on the threshold. Admin staff hurried back-and-forth, clutching arms full of documents and folders. Shredders buzzed like angry wasps. Frantic hands emptied drawers and filing cabinets, and papers littered the carpet beneath her feet.

She waited, unwilling to plunge into the hectic bustle. If the mounting disorder on the streets was a clue, the sense of panic that swirled around the room was confirmation that the end was nigh. And approaching much faster than she had imagined.

'Governor Spencer!'

She saw the Secretary General of the British Territories, Nassir Al-Taha, standing with a group of suits and robes, looking out of place in jeans and a tailored shirt. He detached himself and beckoned her to follow him. She hurried through rows of desks and lifeless computers into the calm of a wood-panelled office. Beyond its large windows, Edith saw a distant column of black smoke towering into the sky. Her stomach churned, and she wanted to leave.

Al-Taha walked around his desk and flopped into a leather chair. 'How are you, Edith?'

'I'm well, thank you Secretary-General.'

He gestured towards the door. 'Have you come to help?'

She raised an eyebrow. 'Excuse me?'

Al-Taha smiled. 'Relax, I'm teasing. Among many other things, they're destroying movement records. The criminals you had shipped overseas.'

'I see,' Edith said.

'I didn't realise how efficient you'd been, Edith. Over a million deportations. That's impressive.'

'Just doing my duty,' she said.

Al-Taha nodded, then he opened a desk drawer and retrieved a small, padded envelope. 'These are for you,' he said, tossing the envelope across the desk. Edith ignored the impolite gesture and scooped up the envelope. She peered inside.

'What's this?'

'Your authority to travel. Rubber wristbands, to be exact. There's no time to issue a whole new batch of travel documents, so we came up with this. The wearer will be given priority access to any mode of transport heading for the continent. Behind caliphate citizens, of course.'

Edith fished into the envelope and plucked out a band. It resembled the gaudy loops that some people wore around their wrists for good causes and charities. Thankfully, these were a subtle dark green and inscribed with white lettering that read, *Priority Passenger – Office of the Secretary General*. Edith hoped that the thin loop of rubber would stay on her bony wrist.

'You're sure this is all we need?'

'Absolutely. We've notified the travel hubs. Don't trouble yourself, Edith.'

She dropped the band back into the envelope and nestled it deep into her Louis Vuitton, snapping the clasp shut. 'When can we leave?'

'The military has priority right now. There are still several divisions waiting to be shipped out of the country. Once they're clear, it will be your turn. You have your secure phone, yes?' Edith nodded. 'Keep it on at all times. You'll receive a text message when the time comes. When it does, make haste to your nearest point of departure. Are you still at the Corinthia?'

'Yes.'

'Good. London City Airport would be your best choice. It's central and well-protected.'

Al-Taha pushed his chair back and stood. He walked around the desk and sat on the edge, his arms folded, and she caught a waft of his cologne, something strong and musky.

'Once most military personnel have departed these shores, the only people left to protect the city will be the militia and the police. I wouldn't give much for their chances once the infidels get here, and I imagine those people in uniform will think the same. You won't have long to act, Edith.'

Behind Al-Taha, the distant smoke was an ominous black smudge against the clear blue sky. 'I'm Governor of the British Territories. Can I not leave sooner?'

Al-Taha winced. 'Sorry. You'll have to wait.'

'How long? Realistically?'

'A week. Maybe two.'

'What about you, Nassir?'

'I leave for Paris tonight.'

'Tonight?' She felt the blood drain from her face. It was happening too fast.

'Don't concern yourself, Edith. The UN is about to intervene on our behalf, to stall any pre-emptive attack on London. You'll have plenty of time.'

Edith swallowed. 'Attack London? Surely not.'

'I wouldn't rule it out. Your fellow countrymen appear to have the bit between their teeth.' He stood up and held out his hand. 'You should go back to your hotel. And be ready to leave at a moment's notice.'

She took it, shook it. 'Goodbye, Nassir.'

Outside, she gripped her bag as she dodged the fast-moving bodies. The lift took her down to the busy entrance hall, and she paused behind one of its marble columns. She took out her phone and was about to dial Bertie's number when a voice in her ear said, 'Governor Spencer. What a surprise.'

Edith turned. Her skin pimpled with fear. Colonel Al-Huda, the senior CID investigator, was standing less than three feet away, a smile on his bearded face. Edith thought – hoped – she'd seen the last of the man who'd invaded her office, who'd probed and badgered her while he investigated Timothy's death, a man with whom she'd conspired to replace former Governor Davies. Now he was here, standing in front of her, so close that she could smell the garlic on his breath. He wore a dark suit, a tieless white shirt buttoned to the neck and a small, crossed swords lapel pin. Her heart picked up the pace.

'Colonel Al-Huda. How are you?'

'Very well, although disappointed to be leaving these shores. There was much work to be done here.'

'I'm sure the Caliph has his reasons.' She smiled. 'Peace be upon him,' she added, cringing at her blunder. She glanced at her watch. 'Forgive me, I must go. I wish you well, Colonel.'

She'd taken five paces before Al-Huda's next words stopped her in her tracks.

'Where is Albert Payne?'

She froze, then willed herself to thaw. She spun on her heel. 'Excuse me?'

'I attended the crucifixion at Marble Arch, only to discover that he'd been released from Lewes prison. On your order.'

Edith met his gaze, her jaw set, her legs like water. 'A forgery. The work of a mole, we believe. I have started an investigation.'

'Really?'

'Yes.'

'I checked with your office. There's no warrant for Payne's arrest.'

'An oversight, I imagine. Unsurprising, given the circumstances.'

'What circumstances?'

Are you an idiot? 'The withdrawal, of course. I shall remedy the situation as soon as possible.'

'Albert Payne is a dangerous criminal, not the simpleton you said he was.'

He made a fool of you, Edith realised. *Good for you, Bertie.'*

The colonel stepped closer, and once again Edith was in range of his rancid breath. 'To be clear, you've had no contact with Payne since his escape from prison?'

Al-Huda's voice had taken on a harder edge. Edith swallowed, and she felt her face flush. She imagined a sign dangling around her neck that screamed *Guilty!* Al-Huda's eyes bored into her. He was reading her mind. She was sure of it. She forced herself to focus and injected a little steel into her own voice.

'After what he did, I would have him shot on sight.'

Al-Huda stepped back and looked her up and down. 'Trouble seems to follow you, Governor Spencer. First there was the business with your friend Gates, a practising homosexual, and his relationship to the traitor Al-Kaabi. Now this. Some might say your conduct is unbecoming of a caliphate public servant.'

Edith's blood thawed and boiled. *Public servant indeed. The audacity of the man.* 'I serve at the pleasure of Chief Judge of the Supreme Judicial Assembly of Europe, Abdul bin Abdelaziz,' she said. 'Perhaps you should take the matter up with him?'

Al-Huda smiled and nodded. 'Abdul is a friend, so perhaps I will. You're still at the Corinthia Hotel, yes?'

Edith's resentment fizzled and died, and once again her blood chilled. She gripped the straps of her Louis Vuitton to stop her hands from shaking.

'That's correct. Now, if you'll excuse me, there are matters of state to attend to. Good day.'

She turned and hurried out of the building, her shoes clacking past the long queues, her passage observed by dozens of soldiers. Any moment now, Al-Huda's voice would bellow her name, and a thousand pairs of eyes would turn in her direction. Soldiers would close in around her, trapping her and sealing her fate ...

But the shout never came, and she passed through the security gate unmolested. She looked up and down the street and noticed car headlights pulsing from a side road. She saw the Toyota pull out of a parking spot and brake. Bertie got out and opened the back door for her. She almost screamed at him.

'Get back in, Bertie. Now!' Bertie complied. She jumped in and slammed the door. 'Go,' she said. 'Back to Hampstead.'

Bertie stared at her in the rear-view mirror. 'Is everything all right, Lady Edith?'

There was no point telling him now, not until they were all together. Then they would thrash out a new plan, a new timetable that would see them to safety. Because Al-Huda was the tenacious type, who would follow every lead wherever it took him. And if he didn't have any leads, well, he would do what they always did in the caliphate. What she herself had done countless times – have everyone arrested and thrown into the deepest, darkest cell from which there would be no escape.

On the back seat of the Toyota, Edith shivered.

[10]

NEW MODEL ARMY

THE STEEL DOOR SWEPT OPEN, AND WAZIR MARCHED INTO THE underground command bunker, his black-clad Pretorian guard fanning out in the shadows behind him. They carried guns, a practice forbidden inside Baghdad's defence ministry, but Wazir's guards were an exception to that rule. He took his seat at the head of the conference table and waved a hand at the officers who stood rigid around it. They sat as one, clearing throats and shuffling papers. Wazir could read people by their mannerisms, body language, and facial expressions. People communicated far more by their gestures than the words they spoke, and what he saw now was depressing. He saw folded arms and knitted brows, and digital maps infected with troubling red rashes. He saw concern and frustration. And he saw fear.

'What news from China?' Wazir opened without preamble, pouring himself a glass of chilled water.

Air Chief Marshal Al-Issa, Chief of Staff of the Military High Command and one of this small group of commanders unafraid to speak their mind in the Caliph's presence, answered the question.

'I have spoken with General Mousa earlier today. The stalemate continues, Holy One.'

'Casualties?'

'Significant. Confirmed deaths 120,000, and twice that number wounded. Combat formations have been decimated.'

'Can we reinforce?'

'We're throttling food supplies in Bangladesh, Sub-Sahara Africa, and Indonesia. The shortages will encourage military enlistment in those territories, but General Mousa is still predicting over a million casualties by the end of the winter.'

Squeezed on two fronts. For the first time since his meteoric rise, the future troubled Wazir. The next words out of Al-Issa's mouth were inevitable.

'We should discuss the nuclear option, if only to remove it from the table.'

Wazir studied the surrounding faces. They'd already reached the same conclusion. 'To employ such weapons would invite our own destruction. The Chinese have an excuse to launch against us, as do the British. We have built an empire without their use and without the threat of their use. Our possession of such weapons was enough to give our enemies pause. Those tables have now turned. Nukes are not an option.'

'Note the Caliph's decision for the record,' Al-Issa barked to a uniform hovering in the shadows.

'Instead, we must focus on saving our forces in Britain,' Wazir continued. He scrutinised the wall display, registering the thick concentration of blue and green icons that represented retreating caliphate forces. And the red symbols too, the enemy pushing west from Lands' End, pressing down from the Midlands, leap-frogging the devastated city of Birmingham. It didn't look hopeful.

'The enemy struck our 3rd Division as it was withdrawing from Wales,' Al-Issa informed him. 'Enemy aircraft destroyed the Prince of Wales Bridge, cutting off half the force. Fighter-bombers attacked the stranded formation. There's nothing left, Holy One.'

'Was there not a local truce in place?'

'The Alliance gave us a 12-hour window to withdraw into England. That deadline was still three hours away when the attack began.'

Wazir felt his blood boil. 'They're breaking their word.'

'Their tone has changed. Since the nuke in Birmingham. Their strategy is becoming increasingly aggressive.'

'Which is a mistake,' Wazir said. 'The destruction of the bridge is evidence of that. Severing a major artery was a foolish move.'

'I agree, but the Americans would know this, so it begs the question: why?'

'Expediency,' Wazir said. 'They want this over with.'

Al-Issa continued. 'Infidel minesweepers are clearing sea lanes towards the port of Plymouth. Once our forces are clear of Bristol, they will use the airport to fly in men and equipment. If we cannot withdraw fast enough, we could lose the rest of the 3rd Division and almost certainly other formations.'

Wazir's commander of special operations, General Baban, spoke from the other side of the table. 'So, we blow the runways, make the airport unusable. If we move fast, we can destroy the other major bridge across the Severn River.'

Al-Issa didn't look convinced. 'It's risky. And could invite further attacks.'

'We must do something.'

'I agree, but at the risk of annihilation?'

Baban smiled beneath his thick black moustache. 'The Yankees attack anyway. You said it yourself. They grow bolder, more aggressive by the day. We must give them pause.'

'How?' Al-Issa said, shrugging his shoulders. 'They own the skies, the seas to the west. Their technology surpasses anything we have inherited, and our supplies of Chinese missiles and other ordinance are all but spent.'

'We still have the NATO arsenals,' Baban countered.

'Depleted, thanks to the Chinese conflict. Since the infidel armies landed in Ireland, we've lost every major engagement, and our anti-aircraft capability is woefully deficient. Frankly, I'm surprised they haven't pressed their advantage.'

Baban thumped his fist on the table. 'So, we drop our trousers and bend over, is that it?'

Wazir watched the two men debating across the table. This is what he encouraged from his senior officers, the freedom to exchange views, however controversial, in the language of fighting men. He bowed his head and winced, pinching his nose to quell the sudden pain behind his eyes. The headaches were a symptom of stress, but that didn't make them any easier to deal with, and he wondered where the architect of their recent misfortunes was right now. Wazir prayed his nephew was still alive and his existence proving to be a miserable one. He sipped his water and cleared his throat.

'Marshal Al-Issa is correct,' Wazir said, directing his words at Baban. 'We must avoid military engagements and preserve our forces at all costs.' He interlinked his fingers and refocused. 'So, let's discuss the evacuation.'

The logistics officer at the far end of the table took his cue. He glanced at the sheaf of papers spread out across the table in front of him.

'We have already moved 12 full divisions back to Europe,' said the grey-haired General Talib. 'Every port and airport in the south-east of England is being used to evacuate remaining military personnel and equipment. In 48 hours, we will abandon the eastern port of Harwich after the last ship leaves. In the west, Weymouth will follow suit. All evacuation operations will then be concentrated on the south coast, and the airports at Heathrow, Gatwick, Southampton, and London City will ferry VIPs and their families out of the country in order of seniority.'

'Is there a protocol in place?' Wazir asked.

Talib nodded. 'Secretary-General Al-Taha is keen to ensure our people reach safety, including those who have given loyal service to the caliphate.' Talib cleared his throat. 'The problem is the civilians.

The emigres, who travelled to Britain to start a new life, and those who aim to continue their lives in the caliphate. These are ordinary people, and they know we are withdrawing. Millions are on the move, heading for the coast. Some roads are already unmanageable.'

'We can't allow them to impede the military evacuation,' Al-Issa said.

'Then we must prioritise,' Wazir said. 'Military and political personnel must be given primacy. After that, God will decide.'

There was a murmur of approval around the table.

'We must reach out to our friends at the United Nations, apply some pressure there.' He heard a faint murmur of discord and silenced it with a raised finger. 'Given the growing refugee problem, and its potential to impede the military withdrawal, we will declare a humanitarian crisis in the south-east of England. The UN will agree, and the Americans will have little choice but to comply. This will buy us valuable time and give General Baban more time to organise his people.'

All eyes turned to the smiling general. Wazir smiled too. 'General Baban, please share your news with us.'

'Thank you, Holy One.' Baban looked around the table. 'We may have lost Britain, my brothers, but we're not leaving without a serious fight. My people in London have recruited an army, volunteers from our regular forces and supplemented by local militia. Right now, we have several thousand fighters moving into position across the city. When the time is right, they will strike.'

Al-Issa frowned. 'Isn't this playing into the infidel's hands?'

Wazir spoke before anyone could answer. 'Many of our people died to liberate Britain. Now we must leave with our tail between our legs...'

Scuttling across the Channel like cowardly dogs! His nephew's words had struck a chord. Wazir knew he'd mellowed in his old age, but it was his thirst for war that had driven his rise to power. Why deny that urge again?

'General Baban's army is unsanctioned by this administration.

We will brand them as deserters, rebels, undisciplined, and uncontrollable. Unofficially, they will be heroes of the caliphate, and their names will be carved in stone along the Avenue of the Martyrs. When the last ships and planes have left those ignorant shores for good, they will fight the battle we could not. They will take the war to the infidels, make them shed blood for their precious capital city. General Baban, please stand.'

The general obeyed, his chair rolling backwards as he stood ramrod straight.

'The general will leave us tonight. His destination is London, where he will lead that army.'

'It is my honour, Holy One.'

Al-Issa was the first to move, circling the table to embrace his friend. Wazir watched the others do the same, kissing Baban's cheeks and embracing him. In a time of chaos and defeat, it was an uplifting moment.

Wazir got to his feet. 'Evacuate our forces with all speed,' he told his commanders. 'Get everybody out. Take everything of value and destroy the rest. Lay waste to the jewel in their unholy crown.'

'It will be done,' Al-Issa said, bowing. The others bowed too, and Wazir left the room, his security team falling in around him. Though the fight would be ultimately futile, the thought of Baban and his army meeting the infidels head-on filled Wazir's heart with joy.

As the elevator whisked him to the surface, he noticed that the pounding in his head had disappeared.

[11]

HARRY'S GAME

HARRY STOOD BY THE WINDOW, A SATELLITE PHONE CLAMPED TO his ear, listening to the voice on the other end as he looked out over the grounds of Higham Hall. Beyond the landscaped gardens, dramatic peaks rose around Bassenthwaite Lake, yet Harry saw none of it. All he saw was the depressing mental picture the commander of USCENTCOM was painting for him. When General McKenzie had finished talking, Harry thanked him, ended the call, then replaced the phone back in its cradle.

'Harry? Is everything alright?'

He stood at the window for a few more seconds, then turned to face his chief of staff. 'Let's join the others, shall we, Lee?'

He could see Wilde was keen to probe, but instead he led the way down to the ground floor. In the entrance hall, workers busied themselves fixing lights and running cables. Domestic staff brushed and polished and smiled as Harry passed. The Victorian manor house had fared well during the occupation, and its function as an adult educational arts facility meant that there was little for the invaders to plunder. There were some broken windows and furniture, but overall, the damage was limited. Now it was being refurbished, and soldiers and anti-aircraft units encircled the new home of the UK government.

Wilde led the way, turning into the shadowy west wing corridor and entering the last room on the left. The 20 men and women sitting around the substantial conference table got to their feet and Harry waved them back down. As Wilde peeled away to a chair against the wall, Harry took his seat at the head of the table. Ballistic shields and sound-reduction blackout drapes covered the walls and windows, and a suspended rectangle of light hung above the conference table. It wasn't Downing Street, but it was a start. He looked at the faces gathered around him and forced a smile.

'I'd like to welcome everyone to the inaugural session of the government of the United Kingdom. This is a historic moment, bittersweet of course, but we're back on British soil and it's important that the people of this country know that a working government is here and functioning.'

There were several murmurs of *Hear, hear,* accompanied by a tattoo of knuckles on the table. Somewhere in the shadows, Harry heard the photographer's camera clicking. He saw a young woman in combat uniform hovering near the end of the table, a camera pressed to her eye. 'That'll be all, thank you.' He waited until the door had closed behind her before getting straight down to business.

'I've just spoken to General McKenzie. The Prince of Wales Bridge has been destroyed.'

'Destroyed?' the Welsh Secretary echoed. His name was Ceri Maddox, and he'd served as a Senedd commissioner before the invasion. 'How bad is it?'

Harry didn't sugar-coat it. 'The entire central road deck, supporting towers, and a significant number of enemy vehicles are all lying at the bottom of the River Severn. At low tide, it's completely blocked. It's going to be a hell of a job to clean up.'

'Jesus Christ,' Maddox muttered. 'Why? Why destroy it?'

'They were targeting an enemy convoy.'

'Heading *into* Wales?'

The voice belonged to Foreign Secretary Shelley Walker, one of several new appointments. The others were the Home Secretary, Defence, Health, Transport, and the Scottish and Welsh Secretaries. Remaining ministers served without portfolios, but they would form a vital voting block intended to keep Harry's government account-able, transparent, and democratic. It was how he intended to govern from this point on.

'No, they were withdrawing into England,' he told Walker.

Maddox's face flushed with anger. 'So why attack them?'

'It was a snap decision. Surveillance imagery had ...' Harry's words tailed off. Maddox and the others watched him, waiting. 'Truth be told, I think McKenzie was fobbing me off. He left me with the impression that the Americans saw a big juicy target and hit it.'

'Have you spoken to President Mitchell?' asked Simon Chisholm, Harry's Defence Secretary.

'Not yet.'

'What about these local truces we keep hearing about?'

Harry shrugged his shoulders. 'They're negotiated arbitrarily with regional commanders, but USCENTCOM controls the entire process. There's no transparency. We're out of the loop in that regard.'

'But this is *our* country. We must have some influence in these decisions.'

'You would think so.' Harry turned to Maddox. 'Cardiff city centre was hit, too. A shopping centre was severely damaged. And a cathedral. Casualties are significant.'

'Sounds like our American friends are a little trigger-happy.'

All eyes turned towards the gravel voice at the other end of the table. Faye Junger was Harry's Home Secretary and the youngest Cabinet minister he'd appointed. At 42 years old, Junger was a grad-uate of the London School of Economics, with degrees in political science and economics. A north London native, she'd worked in PR for a decade before being parachuted into Essex and winning an important by-election. She was smart and confident, and she took no nonsense from anyone, which is how she'd come to Harry's attention. In Boston, she'd volunteered to join Harry, Nina, and the rest of his small team at McIntyre Castle, but Harry had denied her request. He wanted as few people as possible in harm's way. *And look where that got you.*

Unlike Nina, Faye Junger was a plain woman, unremarkable in the looks department, her copper-red hair cut short and neatly parted, her thin frame habitually clothed in tailored trouser suits. There were rumours, but Harry was unconcerned about her sexuality or marital status. Junger had proved herself and had a track record in consensus-building. That skill had drawn the light of scrutiny upon her. Even Nina had thought her a rising star, and that was good enough for Harry.

'The White House is keen to see an end to this conflict,' he told her.

'Caliphate forces are withdrawing,' Chisholm said. 'Attacking them unnecessarily could prolong the conflict, not shorten it.'

'Baghdad is in no position to dig its heels in,' Walker responded. 'China remains their biggest concern, and that conflict won't end anytime soon.'

'Shelley's right,' Harry said. 'There's something else. Mitchell has struck a deal. Russia is going to cut off all energy supplies to Europe.'

There was a stunned silence around the table, but it didn't last long.

'What's the nature of this deal?' Walker asked.

The lie rolled off Harry's tongue. 'I'm not privy to the details.'

Walker pressed. 'Why would Orlov help the Americans? He's aligned with Baghdad.'

'I don't know, but whatever happens, Europe faces a harsh winter.'

'What does that mean for us?' Junger asked.

All eyes turned to Harry. He recalled Vice President Riley's words back in Greenland, his cold admission that he was not the United Kingdom's friend. When the VP ascended to the Oval Office, Britain faced a potentially harsh and uncertain future.

'This war will soon end,' Harry told the room. 'What follows will be the biggest battle this administration will ever face. Somehow, we must get this country back on its feet. That task is going to take many years and an infinite amount of money. But it will also give us the opportunity to rebuild.'

Harry tapped a finger on the table.

'I'm not talking about the physical reconstruction, though that will present its own opportunities. I'm talking about society, the way we do things. The old system is no longer fit for purpose. It was a monolithic monstrosity. It controlled us, and we were powerless to act against it. That system is no more, and now we can change things. I'm talking about a fairer and more just political system. True representation of the people, and a smaller, more efficient government.'

He clasped his hands together, his mind imagining the brave new world of his recent reflections.

'I have so many thoughts about this, so many ideas, but I believe we can achieve something truly extraordinary here. A reconstruction of our society, formed on the bedrock of freedoms fought for in blood. We must codify a new constitution, a single document with no unwritten ambiguities ...' He stopped talking. He studied the faces around the table and said, 'I'm getting ahead of myself, aren't I?'

Junger came to his aid. 'No, Prime Minister. You're right, this is an opportunity. One we have a duty to explore.'

'We can't have a catch-all constitution,' Maddox said. 'The people of Wales can't be expected to swallow something cooked up in London.'

'Ditto for Scotland,' said Shona Nicol, the Scottish Secretary. 'Our self-determination rights didn't end after the evacuation. Once those Scots come home, they'll expect to be governed from Holyrood, not Westminster.'

'Of course,' Harry said, waving his hand. 'I'm expressing some ideas, that's all. Constitutional discussions are still a long way off.'

'If we agree to them taking place at all,' Maddox grumbled.

Harry's heart sank. Their first meeting as a Cabinet, and already there was division. The exchange depressed him, and he missed the country of his youth, its singularity; its quirky, nostalgic character; its place in a world it had explored and studied for hundreds of years, leaving its indelible mark. Even as a boy, Harry knew Britain had its problems, but as his father often said, when good folk came together, those troubles are often fixable. By the time Harry entered politics, that had all changed.

The country was at war with itself, its people divided on countless issues. National identity, a sense of belonging, shared values, unity, tradition, it was all crumbling to dust by the time he'd waved for the cameras outside Downing Street. He'd known the enormity of the task ahead. He knew his primary role would be negotiator, one shackled by the chains of office and held accountable by two ancient houses riddled with corruption.

And he knew that beyond the bubble of Westminster, a quiet war was being waged across the country. The population flourished unchecked. Communities became hostile – with each other, with the authorities – demanding their slice of a pie that was shrinking year on year. Infrastructure was crumbling. Interest rates soared. Unemployment skyrocketed. The future looked bleak, but Harry hadn't cared. Lying in bed that first night, with a belly full of champagne and Ellen by his side, Harry Beecham was going to fix all of it.

But he didn't. Couldn't.

And then came the bomb.

'Prime Minister?' Harry looked up. Junger was smiling at the other end of the table. 'The post-war reconstruction; I assume the Americans will help us finance that recovery?'

Harry lied again. *So much for transparency.* 'We haven't

discussed specifics yet. However, now is the time to plan a framework strategy. We'll need to get into it fairly quickly.'

'We should discuss the refugee problem,' a minister-without-portfolio said. 'The event in Birmingham has triggered an exodus from the Midlands and elsewhere.'

Harry turned to Chisholm. 'Do we have an update on local conditions?'

The Defence Secretary nodded. 'Ground zero is still a hot zone, but a joint US/UK CBRN team is monitoring the area. Thankfully, the bomb was a low-yield weapon. Outside the hot zone, radiation levels are approaching normal.'

Harry nodded. 'That's good news.'

'About those refugees,' Junger said, steering the conversation back to the subject. Harry listened, but he already knew the scale of the problem. As the allied forces advanced, people were leaving towns and cities that stood in their path. Lancashire and Yorkshire had seen vast movements of people. Many were British citizens whose allegiance had always been to the caliphate. Then there were the collaborators, local politicians, civil servants, police officers, all fleeing south, skirting the devastation of Birmingham. And the émigrés, of course, from the Gulf States, from Pakistan and other areas of Europe. Countless people had settled in an occupied Britain to start new lives. Now they were heading back.

'Why are so many leaving?' Maddox asked. 'I'm struggling to understand.'

'Many people have adapted to life under Wazir's rule,' Junger answered. 'For them, regime change brought stability, law and order, opportunities for employment. The caliphate values family, tradition, mutual respect. These are powerful messages.'

'You're forgetting the public executions and mass deportations,' Chisholm reminded her, but Junger continued as if she hadn't heard.

'Now they're promising a fresh start for anyone resettling on the continent,' she said. 'Who wouldn't want to spend the winter on the Costa Del Sol? Many people know that life in Britain is going to be a bleak experience for years to come. Many low-income families will take their chances abroad. Better the devil you know.'

'Faye has a point,' Walker said. 'I've heard similar stories.'

'Good riddance,' Maddox said. 'They won't be welcomed back, not in Wales.'

'Is there any update on the ceasefire?' Harry asked Walker, keen to move the meeting on.

She shook her head. 'The US has yet to respond.'

'Baghdad has a point,' Chisholm said. 'All those people trapped between two opposing armies. It doesn't bear thinking about if the war escalated.'

'I'll speak to President Mitchell,' Harry said. He turned in his seat and located Wilde in the gloom behind him. 'Lee, set up a call, would you?'

Wilde left the room. Harry and his team spent a few minutes discussing other business, which included the relocation of remaining UK government personnel from Boston to Cumbria. He ended the meeting and left the room.

He caught up with his chief of staff in the corridor outside. 'What time did you schedule the call for?'

Wilde grimaced. 'Tomorrow. 11 pm, UK time.'

'Tomorrow? What the bloody hell is Mitchell playing at?' Harry faked a smile as his ministers passed by. He waited until the last one was out of earshot before speaking. 'What about Riley?'

'He's unavailable.'

'Jesus Christ. What do I tell the Cabinet tomorrow morning? I rang the White House but no one's at home?'

'You lie. Again,' Wilde added.

Harry shrugged his shoulders. 'What choice did I have? Tell them that Riley's uninterested in a post-war Britain?'

'We're going to have to plan for it, Harry.'

'And pay for it how? Go cap in hand to Beijing? The Russians?' Harry shook his head. 'I never expected this from Mitchell. He *has* to help us.'

Wilde looked over his shoulder before he spoke. 'And what if he doesn't? What happens when he steps down and hands the reins to Riley?'

Harry thought about that. It took him less than five seconds to reach his conclusion.

'In that case, this country might be finished.'

[12]

HEAD HUNTERS

THE SCREAM CUT THROUGH THE MIST, STOPPING THE PATROL commander in his tracks. He held up a gloved fist and sought cover behind a tree. He peered around its trunk, his eyes searching the grey mist that clung to the ground ahead. The scream cut short, tailing off as it echoed through the trees. An animal caught in a trap. Or being eaten alive.

The 24-year-old sergeant from Utah glanced over his shoulder. The 12 men under his command had spread out behind cover, their weapons ready. His dawn patrol was a fighting one, light on gear but heavy on weapons and ammunition. Not that the sergeant was expecting trouble. The pre-dawn intelligence brief showed that the closest enemy units were some miles to the south, but the sergeant took that information with a big pinch of salt. Intelligence was like the weather; it wasn't wise to get caught out if it changed.

He brought his M-27 up and squinted through the optics. The mist between the trees swirled and shifted and remained impenetrable. His 2IC, squatting behind another tree, shook his head. The wood wasn't dense, but the top cover trapped the light. The ground in front of them sloped downhill into the mist and the open field beyond. Where the fog was heavier. And where the scream had come from.

The sergeant didn't need to check his map. Their route should've taken them down to the tree line, then around the field before sweeping through another wood on the other side of the valley. But things had changed, as things often did in war. He couldn't use one of their mini drones, nor could he call up a bigger bird, not in this weather. No, the sergeant would need to get eyes on.

He stayed in position for another 60 seconds, his senses on high alert, the same senses that had kept him alive this far. He didn't think that—

Another scream shattered the silence. A bird exploded from the tree above him, clattering its way unseen through the wood, its frightened shriek piercing the gloom. The sergeant's heart beat fast. Goddam thing had spooked him. Then he heard his 2IC's voice in his ear.

'What the fuck, sarge?'

The sergeant keyed his microphone. 'It's coming from the field ahead. I'm taking the Alpha element down to the tree line. You follow on with Bravo, but keep a 20-metre spread between us, copy?'

'Copy.'

'And watch our flanks. If we get engaged, fall back to RV Two.'

'Roger that.'

The sergeant gave the order, his voice just above a whisper, and five of his team got to their feet and followed him. They moved in a loose arrowhead formation, watching their step, watching the mist, until the trees thinned out and the light brightened. Another raised fist brought his guys to a halt at the edge of a field. It's where the scream had come from, of that he was certain. He closed his eyes and listened, but the silence was almost oppressive, the air cold, damp, and dead.

He opened his eyes. There was something out there in the mist, he was sure of it, but what? He wondered if he was being lured into a trap. Less than a week ago, another patrol had been engaged in a neighbouring sector. Americans had been killed and prisoners taken. The sergeant wouldn't let that happen to his men. He ordered them to hold position and stepped out of cover and into the field.

The ground was flat, the grass knee-high. He moved in slow motion, his M-27 jammed tight into his shoulder, his finger curled around the trigger, barrel sweeping left and right. The wall of fog moved with him, not yet ready to reveal whatever it was hiding. The sergeant took one careful step at a time, his head moving from side to side beneath his helmet. He glanced behind him and could barely see the wood he'd just left. He took another few steps and turned again. Now it was gone. He felt a faint flutter of unease. Disorientation could get him killed, so he checked his bearing on his wristwatch. If anything happened, he would pull a 180 and head back to the trees.

He pushed further into the field, feeling alone and exposed. He took another slow ten paces, stopped and listened. Nothing. He took another ten, counting them off in his head. The silence was deafening. He stopped and squinted. He saw shapes ahead, tall and straight. *A stand of trees?* He didn't recall that feature on his map. He moved closer. Not trees. Wooden stakes planted in the ground. *A fence?*

He swallowed, knowing that if he heard that scream again, close by, he might just shit his pants. He crept forward, his gun held ready, his heart pounding. The mist yielded, swirling around the posts. The closest stake was six feet away, almost close enough to touch. It towered above him, and the sergeant looked up ...

A bald, severed head looked down at him, its eyes and mouth frozen open in death, the stake painted crimson with blood.

Fresh blood.

The other stakes, the nearest ones, all sported heads, faces twisted in pain and fear. He started backing away, his finger tight on the trigger, his eyes sweeping left and right. The stakes faded, consumed by the opaque mist.

The sergeant took two more steps backwards, then he turned and bolted towards the unseen tree line.

· · ·

GENERAL BABAN STOOD ON THE PLATFORM, WATCHING THE passenger train rumble across the river into London Blackfriars. Like his officers around him, Baban wore civilian clothes. In his case, green cargo pants, a navy-blue summer shirt, and Nike trainers. He also wore an automatic pistol on his belt, which was hidden by the shirt's loose folds. The commuter train squealed to a halt beneath the roof. Blackfriars Station was unique because all four platforms spanned the River Thames, the only bridge in London to provide such a convenience. The north and south bank entrances were now barricaded, and two stationary trains occupied tracks 1 and 4, restricting views of the bridge and allowing passengers to disembark unseen onto platforms 2 and 3.

Baban watched the new arrivals crowding along the platform. The men streamed past, five hundred on each train, all dressed in civilian clothes. They headed for the ticket hall, where curious eyes could not penetrate the shuttered walls. Baban's 2IC, Lieutenant-Colonel Naji, filled his boss in on the specifics.

'The trains come in from the south-east and the tube station beneath our feet transports them to where they need to be. No one on the surface is any the wiser.'

Baban watched the last group of fighters pass by, mostly young girls in boots and combat trousers, corralled by several hijab'd mother hens clucking around them.

'And the weapons and ammunition?'

'Also shipped into the city via tube train.' Naji smiled. 'Impressive engineering, I must say. Enables us to move men and equipment all over town without being spotted.'

'Stockpiles?'

'Growing fast. We shut down the entire network to the public last night.'

'What about the surface trains?'

'Still running evacuees to the south, but that won't last for much longer. Once the last plane leaves Heathrow, the infidels will have a straight shot into the city.'

'Let them come,' Baban said. 'What's the status with the engineers?'

'They've been working around the clock,' Naji said. 'They should finish in the next 36 hours.'

'And our anti-aircraft coverage?'

'We have 18 mobile systems on the ground plus 50 Stingers from Turkish inventories. They're old units, so they might not be as reliable as we hope.'

'It doesn't matter,' Baban said. 'Their presence will be enough to give the infidels pause.'

'I've positioned them on several high-rise buildings across the city. Right now, they're passive.'

'Keep them that way until I give the order.'

'Yes, general.'

Baban had seen and heard enough. 'Okay, let's get back to Leicester Square, work the details.'

The small group of officers headed back to the ticket hall. Naji paused, and Baban waited for the others to move out of earshot.

'Speak your mind, my friend.'

'I've placed a helicopter on standby. It can take us to France, should you so choose.' Naji paused, then said, 'Rather than die in the rubble of this city.'

Baban smiled and slapped a hand on his subordinate's shoulder. 'Once again, you've thought of everything, my friend. Let's see what happens, shall we?'

[13]

CONVOY

IF THE CROWDS AT WATERLOO STATION WERE ANYTHING TO GO by, Eddie estimated that the evacuees leaving London numbered in the hundreds of thousands. Maybe more. The station concourse, warmed by sunlight streaming through the glass roof, was jammed with tens of thousands of people. Yet it wasn't like the old days, the pre-war London rush hour, with endless rivers of commuters streaming through the station in all directions like colliding atoms. No, this was different.

Digital ad boards played endless video loops of Wazir. Beneath them, steel fences set in concrete blocks separated the main concourse from the public, and caliphate soldiers in full battle dress patrolled its length, watching for trouble. Beyond the fences, thousands of people snaked through a maze of crowd control barriers towards the platforms. Eddie studied the evacuees and saw they were well-heeled in clean robes and colourful saris. There was no sense of urgency, no concerned faces. Instead, laughing children ran back and forth, excited, as if they were about to embark on a holiday. New arrivals streamed into the station via the taxi drop-off, trailing expensive luggage and family members as they passed through a checkpoint.

'Step back.'

Eddie turned. A soldier gestured an Asian couple away from the fence with the barrel of his AK. They were young, Eddie saw, and the gowned woman was pushing a toddler in a stroller. The man had a wheelie suitcase in his hand, and he was saying something about losing his papers, but the uniform wasn't buying it. 'Step back. Now,' he repeated, a dangerous edge to his voice. The Asian woman dragged her pleading husband away.

So, not everyone is getting preferential treatment. Eddie waited until the soldier had strolled away before resuming his observations. With his full beard, T-shirt, jeans, and trainers, he blended in well with the others queuing behind him at the food kiosk.

'Yes, brother,' said the man behind the raised counter. Eddie ordered two lamb shish kebabs in wraps and a couple of drinks. As he waited, he watched the crowds as they filtered through the barriers and onto the platforms, where trains waited to transport them south. Some would go to the airport at Gatwick, some to the coast, to the ferries. It was a bustling scene, devoid of any panic, and Eddie wondered how long that would last.

He paid for the food and took the escalator back down to the street. Griff's flower stall was close to the main entrance, and the man himself was perched on his stool.

'Nice one, bruv,' he said, as Eddie handed him his foil-wrapped lunch. Griff took a huge bite of his kebab. Lamb and onions spilt onto the pavement.

'Lovely,' he mumbled.

'It's busy up there. A lot of people on the move.'

'It's been like that for weeks. The fences went up a few days ago, just after they cancelled normal services.' He glanced over Eddie's shoulder. 'Don't make it obvious, but here comes one of those convoys I was telling you about.'

Eddie took a bite of his own food and turned around. At the traffic lights by The Old Vic theatre, cops were waving through one articulated lorry after another. Eddie watched them as they rumbled past the station. He counted six, all towing bulky cargo on sheeted, flat-bed trailers. Each truck had a driver and a passenger, but they didn't resemble your average British lorry driver. They were young, brown-skinned, and the passengers scanned the pavements. Eddie knew that look – they were threat-assessing, and he figured they had weapons in easy reach. He watched the last truck grumble past, followed by a dark-coloured van, and Eddie noticed it was full of fighting-age men in civvies. Escort team. Something odd was happening. He wrapped up his kebab.

'I'm going for a wander,' he told Griff. 'Back soon.'

Griff winked an acknowledgement, still focused on his meat-filled wrap. Eddie headed north up Waterloo Road and turned onto Stamford Street. By the time he got there, the last truck was disappearing over the bridge. Behind it, jeeps and police vehicles swerved across the road and blocked it off. He had to find out what was going on.

He walked towards the riverbank, hoping he would get a better view of the bridge, but as he approached the Festival Hall complex, he saw cops and militia standing behind steel barriers, blocking access to the River Thames. Behind his wraparounds, Eddie's eyes darted left and right. The streets were quiet. He thought about changing direction, but two cops had noticed his approach and were watching him. Turning away now might look suspect, so Eddie headed straight for the barrier. He gave them a friendly nod.

'Afternoon,' he said. 'Can I get to the river down here?'

One cop, overweight and sweating behind his own dark glasses, shook his bald head. 'Restricted area, I'm afraid.'

'Since when?' Eddie said. He held up the foil-wrapped food in his hand. 'I normally have my lunch down there. Watch the world go by.'

'Are you deaf?'

Eddie saw a militiaman marching towards him, a small guy, his sleeves bunched at the elbow, his baggy trousers tucked into his boots. He looked like a boy playing grownups, but there was nothing juvenile about his gnarly face and the gun on his hip.

'Excuse me?' Eddie answered him.

The man stood behind the barrier and gripped the top rung. 'Comedian, are ya?'

Small-man syndrome. Eddie knew not to push people like that. Uniforms and bullies gravitated towards each other, and a tyrant like this one could be a danger in Eddie's profession. He shook his head.

'Sorry, I just wanted to have a quiet lunch, that's all. I enjoy watching the river, see? Helps with my anxiety.'

Mini-militia waved his arm. 'It's restricted.'

'They've closed Waterloo Bridge,' Eddie said. 'Any idea why?'

'They're all closed. Jog on.'

'Sure. Thanks.'

Eddie moved off, knowing he'd pushed the man as far as he dared. But what did he mean, *all closed*? That couldn't be right. He headed west along the embankment, towards Hungerford Bridge, the railway span that connected Waterloo East station to Charing Cross on the opposite riverbank. He wondered if the public bridge that ran alongside it was open, but after a casual five-minute stroll, he saw that someone had blocked the stairway leading up to the bridge with barbed wire. So maybe they *were* all closed. He had to confirm it.

He headed back to the flower stall where Griff was wrapping an arrangement of lilies for a sad-faced old lady. She laid them on top of her shopping trolley and wheeled it away.

'That's a lot of my business right there,' Griff said, pointing at the departing pensioner. 'People want flowers for graves. Or they lay 'em at places where people died. Everywhere you look, there are dead flowers.'

'What time are you packing up?' Eddie asked him.

'I'm not exactly rushed off my feet.' Griff looked at his watch and shrugged. 'Might as well call it a day.'

He closed the shutters and padlocked his stall. He'd parked his battered Renault van in a side street, and they drove off towards Lambeth. Passing St Thomas' Hospital, Eddie saw police cars and steel barriers blocking the road on Westminster Bridge. Lambeth Bridge was the same, and Vauxhall too.

'What the hell's going on?' Griff said. 'They've cut the city in half.'

Eddie frowned. 'Must be something to do with the evacuation.'

'They shut the tube last night. The entire network.'

Eddie looked at him. 'Why?'

'It was on the news. They said it was a public safety issue. Didn't you see the crowds at the bus stops?'

Eddie had but didn't give it much thought. This was London, after all. So, no trains or tubes, and now they were closing bridges. Eddie felt it in his bones. Something big was happening. 'Can we look at Chelsea Bridge? Just to confirm?'

Griff nodded. 'I'll cut down Nine Elms Lane towards the dog's home. We can take a run up to the river from there.'

'Nice one.'

Nine Elms Lane was busy with traffic. With the bridges closed, that would only get worse.

'They killed them all, you know.'

Eddie turned to look at Griff. 'What?'

'Battersea Dogs Home. They don't like dogs, so about a month after the invasion, they killed them all. The cats too. They use it as a jail, now.'

Eddie didn't respond. He'd seen a lot of cruelty, but there was something especially brutal about killing defenceless animals.

Griff turned right at the roundabout and drove past Battersea Park towards the distant Chelsea Bridge. Even from a distance, Eddie saw cars and vans turning around and driving back towards them.

'So, looks like this bridge is closed too.'

'Spin her around, Griff. I've seen enough.'

It took less than ten minutes to drive back to Newtown Court.

Griff parked his van under a railway arch, and they walked back to the apartment block. Griff paused outside his front door. 'Fancy joining us for dinner tonight? Zoe's cooking pasta. She always does too much.'

Eddie shrugged. 'Sure. That'd be great.'

'See you in an hour. I'll chill the beers.'

THE LAYOUT OF GRIFF'S PLACE WAS THE SAME AS EDDIE'S, BUT that was the only resemblance. The Griffin household was a place of life and colour, the kitchen walls a shrine of family photographs. Kiddie art covered the fridge door, and Griff's children, Leo and Freddie, were a couple of blond-haired live wires. Excused from the table, they were now terrorising each other in the living room. Eddie, Griff, and Zoe remained seated around the kitchen table. Eddie was on his second glass of red. On top of the three beers he'd had before dinner, he was feeling a little pissed. *Lightweight,* he told himself. *But no more.*

It had been a while since Eddie had enjoyed a family meal, and Griff had been right about Zoe cooking too much pasta. He watched her as she cleared plates and loaded the dishwasher. He saw a mum with dyed blonde hair and dark circles under her brown eyes. She was thin and tired and frayed around the edges. Given the life she'd led these last few years, who wouldn't be? She sat back down and poured herself a glass of wine.

'Thanks again for dinner,' Eddie said, raising his glass to her.

'You're welcome.' She took a sip and set her glass down. 'What is it you do, Eddie?'

'Property,' he lied. 'Before the invasion —'

'Liberation,' Griff corrected, smirking.

'Yes, well, before that I had a couple of properties, rented them out. The one next door and one down in Sussex.' *Keep it vague, Eddie. Just give them the broad strokes.*

'Not bad going for a young bloke,' she said.

113

'I got lucky. My nan died, left me her house. That's how I got started.'

'Wish I had a nan like yours,' Griff said, filling his glass with the Aussie Merlot. A loud bang from the other room interrupted the conversation. The kids started yelling at each other.

'I'll go,' Zoe said. 'It's time for their bed, anyway.'

She stood up and left the kitchen. Eddie waited a few more seconds before speaking.

'I need to get across the river. ASAP.'

Griff shrugged. 'Don't see how if they're blocking the bridges. Why the urgency?'

Eddie lied again. 'It's personal. Family stuff.'

'Can't it wait? This'll all be over in a few weeks.'

'Or maybe it'll get worse. I can't take that chance. Lives might be at stake.'

'Whose lives?'

Zoe had slipped back into the kitchen. She sat down, sipped her wine, waiting for an answer.

'Eddie needs to get over the water,' Griff told her.

She stared at Eddie. 'Why?'

'I've got a disabled niece over there. I haven't heard from her.'

'So, take a tube.'

Griff shook his head. 'He can't. They shut down the network, babe. Remember?'

'D'you think this'll be over soon?' Zoe asked Eddie. 'Everyone says they're leaving, but I can't see them just walking away, can you?'

'They'll go. The Yanks are too strong for them.'

'What about the nuke?' Griff said. 'Everyone thinks that was the Yanks.'

Eddie shook his head. 'It was the caliphate. A rogue element, I heard.'

Griff swallowed a mouthful of wine. 'Birmingham's like Baghdad. Why nuke their own people?'

'It was a false flag op.'

114

'A what?'

Watch your language, Eddie chided himself. 'They tried to make out we did it.'

'You think there'll be more bombs?' Zoe asked him.

'I doubt it. Wazir isn't that stupid. He'd get annihilated.'

'So, how will this end?'

Eddie stroked his beard. He could see Zoe was scared. 'Hard to say, but it'll probably be a huge anti-climax. You'll wake up one day soon and it'll all be over.'

'You think so? God, that would be great.' There was a thump from out in the hallway. Zoe pushed her chair back. 'Those kids drive me mad sometimes.'

She left the room. Eddie kept his voice low. 'I still need to get across that river. Any ideas?'

Griff said, 'Sure. You could walk across.'

Eddie felt a spark of optimism. He'd sent an update about the convoy, and the reply was swift. *Get eyes on and report back.* So now he had a mission. 'What d'you mean, walk?'

Griff pushed his chair back and stood. 'Come with me.' Eddie followed him out onto the balcony. Griff pointed to the multitude of train tracks running beside Newtown Court. 'That line there runs into Vauxhall, then Waterloo.' He pointed to a sooty viaduct that ran past the block. 'That bridge is the Victoria spur. Goes straight across the river.'

'Inside, both of you!'

Eddie turned. Zoe was standing on the doorstep, arms folded, her narrow face dark with anger. He followed Griff inside, and she closed the door behind them. She had her husband squarely in her sights.

'What d'you think you're doing?'

'What's up, love?'

She pointed a chipped nail at Eddie. 'You're telling him how to sneak across the river.'

'So?'

'So, there's a reason they're blocking the bridges off. They don't

115

want you going over there. Stop talking as if you're some sort of resistance fighter. You're not. You're a husband and father. You sell flowers, for God's sake.'

'It's alright,' Eddie said, seeing Griff's face darken. 'Forget I mentioned it. You're right, probably best if I wait until our boys get here.'

Zoe looked at him with cold eyes. The friendly host had vanished. Now Eddie felt like an intruder. He'd seen a lot of things since coming ashore in Ireland, things that had aged him, but these people had far more life experience than him, and for the first time, Eddie's confidence in his abilities as an intelligence operative waned. Maybe Zoe had seen through him, through his cover story. Maybe he hadn't applied the lessons taught to him back in Scotland.

'Fuck it, I'm having another drink,' Griff said, a rebellious scowl on his face.

Zoe glared at him. 'I'm going to bed, so keep the noise down. If you wake those kids, there'll be hell to pay.'

'Thanks for the food,' Eddie said, flashing her his best smile. It didn't work. She rounded on him.

'If you want to do something stupid, fine, but don't drag my husband into it. We've survived this far by keeping our heads down. You want to get yourself killed, fine. But leave him out of it.'

She made a sharp about-turn and left the room. Eddie heard the bedroom door close behind her. Griff nudged him.

'Come on, let's go to yours for a nightcap.'

Back in Eddie's living room, they poured the rest of the Merlot. Eddie sat on the sofa, and Griff slumped into an easy chair.

'Sorry about Zoe,' he said. 'She doesn't like it when I talk about doing stuff like that.'

'Stuff like what?'

'Dodgy stuff.' He took a sip of wine and kicked his legs out. 'I did a bit of bird just after Freddie was born. We were broke, and kids cost money, so I handled some stolen goods. I got six months for receiving, served three. Zoe read me the riot act, and I promised I'd never do anything like that again. I kept my word too.' He swirled the claret liquid around his glass. 'I've been a father to the boys, put the graft in at the flower stand, made a living despite what's gone on ...' His voice trailed off.

'But?'

Griff put his glass down and sat forward. 'I feel like a coward. When all this started, I saw blokes pack up their families and get out. There were rumours of ships and planes up north. I wanted to go, but Zoe wouldn't risk it, not with the kids. So, we stayed.'

He shook his head, his eyes watching some past horror.

'Since then, we've seen a lot of nasty shit. People killed for lipping off – shot, and beaten. Entire families have gone missing from the estate. Some said they'd been carted off abroad. I wanted to do something, maybe join the Resistance, fight back, but Zoe wouldn't even talk about it. When we heard the Alliance had liberated Ireland, we were over the moon. When they took Newcastle, well, some people around here got cocky. The police and militia came down hard on 'em. If I had a gun...' He bit his lip, took another swig of vino.

'You're not a coward,' Eddie said. 'Family comes first, right?' He thought of Steve and the battle to reunite him with Maddy. It had cost him his life, but on reflection, what life would Steve have had, knowing they'd raped his wife and traded his daughter in a slave market somewhere? How could any man live with that? *Family comes first.* Empty words.

'When all this is over, what will I tell my boys?' Griff said. 'That I was a good husband and father? That I could've got them out but didn't? Because of me, they've seen people hanging from lampposts, others shot and killed. Those kids have suffered. They're still suffering, bless 'em. What do I tell them when they get older? When they ask me, "What did you do in the war, Dad?"'

'You did what you had to do.'

Griff shook his head. 'No, I did what Zoe wanted me to do. Kept my nose clean. Stayed out of trouble. What happens when Beecham is back in Downing Street and the pubs reopen? When the taps are flowing, and everyone is swapping war stories, what am I going to say? That I sold a hijab some carnations that were on the turn?'

'Not everyone's in the Resistance, Griff. You're no different from most.'

Griff swallowed a mouthful of wine and stared into his glass. 'I was in the army once, back when I was a kid. Did 14 months in the Fusiliers until I got caught selling weed. Sometimes I wonder how my life would've turned out if I hadn't been so stupid. I could be on that frontline right now, getting ready to march on London. Imagine that, eh?'

'In that life, you might not have Zoe and the boys.'

Griff waved a frustrated hand. 'You know what I mean. In three years, I never stepped up, never fought back. Not once. That makes me a coward. And that's what they'll call me when all this is over.'

Eddie understood how he felt. When he found out Kyle was dead, Eddie had wanted to fight, and the Department of Defence had given him that chance. They'd trained him, given him a gun, and sent him across the Atlantic. He'd been through so much since then, lost so much, and now the end was in sight. When it was over, Eddie could walk into any bar, civilian or military, and hold his head high. Griff couldn't. If Eddie was in his shoes, it would eat him alive.

'Look, I have to get over that river,' he told Griff. 'Maybe you could draw me a map? Give me some intel about the live rails, what to look out for, that sort of thing. That would be a big help.'

'I used to go tagging when I was a kid,' Griff said. 'Me and my mates did all the bridges around here. I know those tracks like the back of my hand.' He tipped his wine back. When he looked at Eddie, his eyes never blinked. 'I'll take you into Victoria.'

'Look, I don't want to get you into trouble —'

'Leave Zoe to me.' He stood up, hitched his jeans, and walked out. At the door, he paused. 'I've heard a lot of bullshit in my time, Eddie. So, here's what I think. There's no disabled niece, which is fine because I don't care. But I have a favour to ask.'

Eddie's cheeks burned, just like his cover. 'Go on.'

'Whatever it is you're doing, I want in, okay?'

Eddie got to his feet. 'We'll talk tomorrow.'

'Sure.'

Griff left the apartment, and Eddie locked the door behind him. He knocked off the living room light and sat in the darkness. His cover was blown, so now he had to decide. Stay and bluff it out? Or let command know and disappear to another safe house. Hawkins would see the move as a failure. Eddie's new journey had only just begun. Griff was a bump in that road, and his gut told him that the man wasn't a threat.

So, he would stay. Because something strange was happening across the river, a mystery the American spy satellites could neither see nor solve.

Eddie had to find out what it was.

[14]

WOLF HALL

EDITH STOOD BEHIND HER DESK, SIFTING THROUGH HER personal possessions. There was much to discard and very little worth keeping, which felt liberating to her. She was making a fresh start, embarking on another phase of her life. She'd emptied her desk drawers, the contents now spread across her desk in a disorderly jumble. Much of it was worthless, she decided. Bank statements for non-existent accounts, photographs, private correspondence, and other knickknacks she'd accumulated over the years. She placed some personal letters and photographs in a cardboard box on her desk. The rest went into a rubbish bag, destined for the shredder.

Her desk clear, she sat down and smoothed out the inventory typed up by Mrs Parker. She perched her glasses on the end of her nose and ran her eye down the long list of treasures donated by the Daly creature. And she had to admit, it was quite a haul – jewellery; object d'art; gold and platinum ingots; and a significant amount of cash. She knew people like Daly taxed their citizens in this way, but the man had taken full advantage of his position. She did a rough calculation in her head and determined that the treasure trove, including the paintings liberated from her office, would provide her with enough money to live in luxury for several lifetimes.

She sat back in her chair and looked around her private study, now bathed in early evening sunlight. She would miss this quiet haven, its comforting smells of wood polish and fresh flowers, the warming winter fires that burned in its hearth. A place where she could be alone with her thoughts and deliberations. She thought of building a similar sanctuary in the Provence house and she smiled. But then her immediate predicament invaded her thoughts, and the smile faded.

There was a knock on the door, and Mrs Parker appeared, advancing only as far as the threshold.

'Chief Justice Hardy is here to see you, Lady Edith.'

Victor entered, accompanied by his wife Margaret. She was a rotund lady with grey hair piled high beneath a chiffon veil, and her heavy frame draped in a patterned summer dress. Victor beamed, and Margaret grinned, exposing a mouthful of horse-like teeth.

'Lady Edith,' Victor said, addressing her formally for the benefit of his wife. 'You remember Margaret, I take it?'

Edith stood and walked around her desk. She pumped Margaret's chubby hand. 'Of course. How are you, Margaret?'

'Very well, Lady Edith, given the circumstances.'

Victor squeezed his wife's hand. 'She's bearing up, aren't you, poppet?'

'A suite at the Corinthia will calm the nerves,' she said, smiling.

Margaret was a social climber, Edith knew. Like most of her kind, she basked in the reflected power and status of her spouse, believing herself to be just a few rungs short of royalty. Edith took some pleasure in delivering the unexpected news.

'A change of plan, I'm afraid. Victor, can we speak privately?'

Victor frowned, but he knew how the game was played. He ushered his disappointed wife from the study, instructing her to wait downstairs. He closed the door behind her and crossed the room.

Edith met him halfway. She folded her arms and glanced down at her Roger Vivier buckled shoes. Victor stood, waiting. She looked up into his ruddy face.

'I warned you, did I not?'

Victor frowned. 'What are you talking about?'

'Releasing Bertie was a mistake.'

'You've lost me.'

'I picked up our travel permits today. While I was there, a certain colonel from the Criminal Investigation Department accosted me.'

Victor paled. 'Al-Huda?'

'The same. He knows Bertie was freed from prison on my order. He's onto us, Victor.'

'How can you be sure?'

'Because he's not an idiot!' She bit her lip, regretting the outburst. Allowing her emotions to get the better of her would do them no good. 'We have to give Bertie up. Can we find someone else to take care of things?'

'Like whom?'

'What about your man Theo?'

'He was yours originally, remember? Besides, I've let him go.'

'There must be someone, Victor. Think!'

Edith turned away and walked to the window. The city looked serene from Hampstead's elevated rise, and there was no sign of the smoke she'd seen from the building in Bloomsbury. She closed her eyes and imagined waking up in her bed, the world outside returned to what it was, a world where she was Lord Chief Justice once more, and the *Great Liberation* was nothing more than a tormented dream of a failed Iraqi rabble-rouser ...

'Edith, listen to me.'

She opened her eyes. A distant flight of military helicopters clattered across the city like a flock of deadly birds. She turned away from the window. Victor was shaking his head.

'We can't do that to Bertie. Not after everything he's done for us.'

'He threatened to kill me.'

'He was angry. He felt betrayed. What do you expect?'

'Then we'll send him on his way.'

'No, Edith. We need him.'

'Don't you understand, Victor? If Al-Huda discovers the truth, he'll arrest us. And we both know what will happen then. Is that what you want? To be transported down the Thames in a filthy barge? Bulldozed into an incinerator?'

Her head spun. She couldn't breathe. A stab of pain shot across her chest. She was having a heart attack. Victor eased her onto the Chesterfield, then crossed the room. She heard a faint note of crystal, then he thrust a cut-glass tumbler into her hand.

'Drink.'

She obeyed, tossing the cognac back in three deep gulps. She felt her heart rate settle as the alcohol went to work. Victor sat on the couch beside her. He took the glass from her hand and squeezed her flesh. She couldn't remember the last time someone had attempted such an intimate gesture, and she found herself comforted by Victor's smooth skin.

'You need to get a grip on yourself, Edith. Al-Huda will think twice before denouncing you.'

'I name-dropped Chief Judge Aziz, hoping the very mention of the man might persuade Al-Huda to desist with his inquiry.' She turned and looked at Victor with frightened eyes. 'He didn't believe me. How many people have lied to us from the dock, Victor? Too many to count, yes? It's easy to tell a lie when one has the power to punish such transgressions.'

'Call the Secretary-General. Make a complaint.'

'Nassir is leaving the country. After he's gone, there'll be no one to shut Al-Huda down. We're on our own.'

Victor got to his feet, and she felt his hand slip from her own. 'Al-Taha's leaving already?'

'Yes.'

'That doesn't bode well.' Victor rubbed his jaw. 'But perhaps that means Al-Huda will leave too?'

Edith got to her feet. She felt stronger now. The fog of fear was lifting. 'No. He has the bit between his teeth. He thinks someone has played him for a fool. It's about honour now.' She stepped closer to Victor. 'And he knows I'm at the Corinthia, which means none of us can go there. You and Margaret will stay here until we get the signal to leave.'

'When is that likely to be?'

'A week. Maybe two.'

Victor raised a troubled eyebrow. 'That long?'

'Focus, Victor. Bertie is our immediate problem.'

'You're right. He has to disappear.'

'We need to discuss the details. Bertie will claim he's been staying here. The Parker woman will corroborate. She has to go too.' She wagged a finger. 'That's it! We can accuse her of harbouring Bertie beneath our very noses! We blame everything on her —'

'No,' Victor said, in a tone that Edith hadn't heard for a very long time. 'We're not throwing Bertie or Mrs P to the wolves. I won't allow it, Edith. But there is another way.'

Edith folded her arms. 'Then you'd better explain it to me.'

THE VAN WAS A PREVIOUSLY OWNED MERCEDES SPRINTER, complete with passenger seating and a cargo bay large enough to accommodate the trunks and luggage now stacked in the house's utility room. The paintwork was midnight blue, and in the house's post-sunset shadow, it looked black. Bertie had paid extra to have the passenger windows coated with privacy film and steel bumpers fitted front and back. He'd also paid for a full service, upgraded shocks, new tyres, two spares, three 20-litre diesel containers full of fuel, a couple of litres of oil, and a decent toolkit. The precautions were overkill, he knew that, but he wouldn't make the same mistake as the guy on Haverstock Hill. Especially with the cargo that Bertie would be carrying.

He'd lashed the extra fuel and tyres to the roof rack and covered them with black weatherproof sheeting. The works of art were also aboard, packed inside their transportation crates and braced against the back of the passenger seats with padded lengths of timber. Bertie spent the next hour moving back and forth between the utility room and the van, packing and stacking Daly's treasure chests and The Witch's personals. There was so much to think about but thank God he had Cheryl. She was a master organiser and had transformed his life in ways he'd never expected. He wouldn't admit it to anyone, not yet, but Bertie Payne had found love again.

The first time didn't really count. They were both too young, the marriage a spontaneous union, and neither Bertie nor his ex-wife ever declared their undying love long past the honeymoon. They thought it was the real thing. It wasn't. What he felt now was so much different. And Cheryl felt the same, too. Somewhere down the line, when things settled, he would ask her to marry him. He already had the ring. A gem lifted from Daly's trunk before Cheryl had the chance to list it. It wasn't flashy, but the rock was impressive, and the dealer's stamp read 1909. An antique, Bertie reckoned, and Cheryl liked antiques. He'd stashed it in the van, in a void beneath the steering wheel. When he thought about giving it to her, his heart raced. But that was the future. First, they had to survive the present.

'Bertie?'

He turned around and saw Judge Hardy standing in the doorway. He gestured for Bertie to follow him outside to the garage. Bertie closed the door behind him. The judge leaned against the Toyota, his arms folded, his face grave. Bertie's heart thumped faster.

'Everything alright, Judge?'

'We have a problem. Colonel Al-Huda. He's the man who —'

'I know who he is.' Bertie swallowed, and he rubbed his left hand. He'd never forget that hammer. His left hand still ached and would do for the rest of his life, Bertie reckoned. 'What about him?'

'He knows you're free.'

Bertie's stomach lurched. 'What? How?'

'He wanted to see you hung on that cross. When he discovered you were free, he followed the paper trail. Lady Edith told him it was an inside job, a mole on her staff, but she doesn't think he believed her.'

The judge's voice faded in Bertie's ears. All he heard now was the metallic ring of foot-long, rusted nails driving through his wrists and his own terrible screams.

'What are we going to do?'

'You must leave, head for France. If you're not here, Al-Huda can't join the dots.'

'When?'

'Now. Tonight.'

'There's still so much stuff to pack.'

'Then I suggest you get on with it. The colonel might decide to make a house call. You must speak to Mrs Parker too, make sure she's onboard.'

Bertie's mind raced. He forced himself to take a breath, think. 'Wait,' he said. 'What's stopping him following us to France?'

'What d'you mean?'

'If he knows I'm alive, he won't stop. Even when we get to France, he'll come looking.'

The judge shook his head. 'Unlikely. For now, you must pack up the van and head for Dover. Your priority travel authorisation will get you aboard a ship.' He headed for the door, then paused. 'When you go, don't drive through London. There's a chance that Al-Huda has flagged your name at the checkpoints.'

'I'll head west, then south,' Bertie said.

'Good. I'll let you get on.'

Judge Hardy left the garage and Bertie stood for a moment, his mind whirling. The only shot he and Cheryl had at a future was by The Witch's side, hidden away in the south of France. Bertie had to get out of Dodge before Al-Huda came knocking, but he needed

Cheryl with him. He couldn't take the risk of leaving her behind, just in case things went to hell faster than any of them expected. If that happened, The Witch and Judge Hardy would abandon Cheryl to her fate. Bertie couldn't allow that. He'd rather die on that cross.

He hurried from the garage, slamming the door behind him.

[15]

LUTON AIRPORT

THE DEFIANT HELICOPTER FLEW FAST AND LOW ACROSS THE city of Luton. Harry had his nose pressed against the cargo door window and watched the Apache escort choppers spitting out dozens of anti-missile flares in a blaze of burning magnesium. Alliance forces had driven the enemy out of the city 24 hours ago, but the possibility remained that someone, somewhere, might launch a surprise attack with a shoulder-mounted weapon. Harry's escort was taking no chances.

Surprise attacks were the reason the city had suffered such a heavy bombardment. Mounting losses of men and materiel was a source of serious concern at the Pentagon. Suicide attacks and booby traps made it difficult to discern friend from foe. Luton was a cautionary tale.

Harry watched the city pass beneath the helicopter, dismayed by the damage. He saw a blazing tower block burning like a Roman candle spewing thick black smoke into the grey sky. He saw another block missing half of its outer walls, exposing shattered, blackened interiors. Missile strikes, Harry guessed. As they thundered past, a shower of dust and concrete tumbled to the ground below.

And then the towers were behind them. Now they were flying over a broad tract of terraced housing, peppered by a ragged pattern of bomb craters filled with water, masonry, and blackened timbers. Harry saw hundreds of burned-out cars, toppled church spires, and the fractured domes of Luton's countless mosques. And he saw fires everywhere, some small and isolated, some engulfing whole buildings.

He caught Lee Wilde's grim expression from the opposite seat. Before he could comment, he heard the voice of his escort commander, an infantry colonel from the 2nd Battalion, New York Volunteers (British), in his headphones.

'As well as regular troops, half the city turned out to defend it. We called for ground support, but USCENTCOM launched an aerial assault instead. Probably saved a lot of casualties, but on the other hand ... well, you can see.'

Harry saw. He also saw long convoys of armour and support vehicles snaking through the shattered city. He'd been told that Luton would be a tough nut to crack. The Americans had not just cracked it. They'd smashed it to pieces.

'Two minutes out,' the pilot announced over the net. Harry's stomach lurched as the chopper nosed into a rapid descent, thundering over thousands of abandoned cars surrounding Luton Airport. Terminal buildings flashed beneath them. The aircraft flared, then set down on the concrete apron. Harry ducked beneath the twin rotors, following his security team towards a large maintenance hangar. They wound their way down two flights of stairs to a bleak concrete basement, now serving as temporary HQ for the Brigade Combat Team, King's Continental Army Division.

The ops room was a wide space with low ceilings filled with battlefield systems operators hunched over their computers. Harry saw a thick knot of British and American officers gathered before a sizeable display screen and headed towards them. They turned as he approached. Their fatigue was noticeable from across the room.

Lieutenant-General Nick Wheeler, Deputy CDS, broke away

from the group. He wore full battle dress and a distinctive blue cravat around his neck. He shook Harry's hand, then Wilde's.

'Appreciate the ride in,' Harry said.

Wheeler was stony-faced. 'Against my better judgement, you understand.'

'Point taken. Is there somewhere we can talk?'

'Of course.'

Wheeler led them into a scruffy office with cheap wooden furniture and naked, pale-yellow walls. The soldier arranged the chairs, and they sat in a loose circle. The Deputy CDS opened the conversation.

'You shouldn't be here, Harry. It's too close to the frontline.'

'We've tried parking me somewhere safe, remember? Look how that worked out.'

'McIntyre was a terrible business,' Wheeler admitted. 'But you should reconsider these visits. Imagine if we lost Churchill during the Second World War. That would've been a significant blow to this country.'

Harry laughed for the first time in a while. 'I'm flattered, but I think we can both agree that I'm no Churchill. Besides, you're close to the front yourself. I'm surprised Sir David has sanctioned such a move.'

'He needs reliable eyes and ears on the ground.'

There was a moment of silence between them. Harry broke it. 'Are you saying he's lost trust with our allies?'

'He's being prudent, that's all.'

'Very diplomatic. Where is he now?'

'With USCENTCOM. At an undisclosed location.'

It was Wilde who spoke next. 'Our recent discussions with Washington have been somewhat tense. Have you or Sir David experienced anything similar?'

Wheeler's eyes narrowed. 'Is there something I should know about?'

'You know about the Prince of Wales Bridge?' Harry asked him.

'Of course.'

'Excessive, wouldn't you say?'

'If I'm being honest, yes.'

'That bridge was a vital economic asset. The clean-up alone will take years and cost tens of millions. Now Luton has been pulverised. This wilful destruction is getting out of hand. The caliphate is withdrawing. Their army is boarding ships as we speak.'

'Luton was a pro-Wazir city, and not the only one. They made a decision to hit the enemy hard.'

'The Americans, you mean.'

'Yes,' Wheeler said.

Harry pointed to the concrete ceiling. 'Have you seen the devastation up there? I dread to think how many civilians were killed.'

'We gave ample warning. And time to evacuate. Anyone who stayed behind knew the risks.'

'What about the elderly and infirm? The sick? Children?'

'We employed precision strikes where possible.'

Harry grimaced. 'What I saw was quite the opposite.'

Wheeler shrugged. 'We're not in charge, Harry.'

'We should be. Especially when the likelihood of significant collateral and infrastructure damage is high.'

Wilde piled in too. 'We agreed to the prosecution of this war long before the first ships set sail for Ireland. They promised us tactical and targeting oversight.'

'Show me that in writing.'

Wilde didn't respond. Harry refused to concede the point that easily.

'Come on, Nick. We both know that protecting lives and property was a strategic objective. When this war is over, the country will have to be rebuilt from the ground up. A task made so much harder if they've reduced our cities to rubble.'

Wheeler's nostrils flared. When he spoke, it was with one eye on the room beyond the office window. 'What started out as a partnership has transformed into something else. Something subordinate.'

'The nuke,' Harry said.

'Precisely,' Wheeler said, tipping his head. 'That event triggered a sea change in attitude. Since then, tactical consultations between the King's Division and USCENTCOM have been virtually non-existent. Officially, we're still partners. In reality, they've relegated us to the role of observers.'

Harry bit his lip. 'Then it's worse than I suspected. Sir David should've said something. He's my CDS after all.'

'He's doing his best under difficult circumstances.'

'That's not good enough. He must insist on his voice being heard.'

'He's trying to bring General McKenzie back around to our position. That takes time, diplomacy. Influence. He's also conflicted.'

Harry raised an eyebrow. 'Meaning?'

Wheeler leaned forward. 'When we left Scotland, the British armed forces ceased to exist as an operational organisation. After the restructure and formation of the King's Continental Army, our land forces numbered 27,000. Twelve hundred were killed in Ireland and eighteen hundred seriously wounded. For various reasons, most of the wounded will never wear the uniform again.'

Wheeler ticked off the fingers of his left hand.

'In Scotland, we sent 20,000 combat troops through Tom and Jerry. Subsequent operations have accounted for another 4000 killed and wounded. Additional casualties – non-combat injuries, illness, desertions, etcetera – number around a thousand and that number is rising each day. That's 8000 British casualties so far, which is over 30% of our entire land army. Those numbers are unsustainable, and if Luton is anything to go by, there might still be a lot of hard fighting ahead of us.'

Harry chewed his lip. He knew the figures were sobering, but to hear them reeled off like that was jarring. Losing a road bridge paled into insignificance by comparison.

'It's the reason Sir David is reluctant to press our allies,' Wheeler continued. 'He's sensitive to mounting casualties and feels that some collateral and infrastructure damage is a price worth paying. Given the certainty of further casualties, I'm inclined to agree with him.'

'He has a point,' Harry conceded. 'But this is our country. We're going to have to live with the aftermath long after US troops have departed these shores.'

'And if it wasn't for the Americans, we wouldn't be having this conversation.'

Which was true as well. The US had come to Britain's rescue and saved millions of her citizens. She'd given them shelter and a chance to take back their country. Harry couldn't have it both ways.

'What about British reserves?' Wilde asked the general.

'We held back 4000 to support the assaults through *Tom* and *Jerry*. We've used them all to plug the gaps.'

'Can we recruit more people into the ranks?'

'We can,' Wheeler said. 'But recruitment amongst the British diaspora has dwindled. News footage of hangars filled with flag-draped caskets isn't helping.'

'What about locally?' Harry asked. 'The liberated Brits? I thought we had a program to recruit volunteers.'

'Yes, that,' Wheeler said, a bitter note in his voice. 'The take-up was impressive, but a lot of recruitment centres have been attacked by suicide bombers and suchlike. We've suspended the program for now.'

'Jesus,' Harry muttered. He stretched his legs out and folded his arms, processing what he'd seen and heard. 'Look, I'm not a military strategist,' he told Wheeler. 'But we're pushing the enemy hard, snapping at their heels. We're forcing them to turn and fight, and then we engage them with extreme prejudice. Why can't we take our foot off the gas? Give them a chance to run.'

'Harry's right,' Wilde said. 'Just let them go, for God's sake.'

Wheeler shrugged. 'In theory, I agree. Is there any news on the UN ceasefire?'

'Still no word from the White House,' Harry said.

'Then everything hinges on President Mitchell. If they agree to honour Wazir's ceasefire, that might buy Sir David time to work on McKenzie, tap the brakes a little.'

Harry shook his head. 'It's not McKenzie that's driving this. I need to speak to Mitchell directly. If Lee can arrange a meeting, can you provide conference facilities?'

'We have a secure comms room down the corridor,' Wheeler said.

'Good.' Harry got to his feet and held out his hand. 'I appreciate the candour, Nick. I'm going to stick around if you don't mind.'

Wheeler managed a smile as he shook Harry's hand. 'Do I have a choice?'

Harry returned the smile. 'No.'

Wilde waited until the general had left the room. 'You think Mitchell will agree to a slowdown?'

'I hope so.'

'And if he doesn't?'

Harry stared through the window at the officers gathered around the display. 'In that case, I dread to think what might be ahead of us.'

[16]

CRY ME A RIVER

THREE MILES TO THE SOUTH-WEST OF LUTON AIRPORT, FOUR squadrons of armoured cavalry charged southbound along the M1 motorway. The convoy consisted of a range of US mechanised fire-power, from M1A3 Abrams tanks to the venerable Bradley, but most of the vehicles were eight-wheeled Strykers in all their variants – ground support, anti-aircraft, medical, and command. They raced along the empty motorway, pushing their ungoverned power plants to the max. Their objective was the major road junction with the M25, the orbital highway that circled the outskirts of London. From that intersection, it was less than 20 miles to St Paul's Cathedral, and the convoy had one job – to clear the road and open up a major artery into the heart of the city.

Half-a-mile ahead of the main element, six JLTVs were racing toward the intersection, fat black tyres humming on the asphalt. They carried an assortment of weapons, from M134 mini-guns to SHORAD air defence systems that scanned the unfolding terrain ahead. Flying unseen on their flanks, hugging that same flat land-scape, two flights of AH-1Z Viper attack helicopters were ready to engage any potential threat.

The driver of the lead JLTV pumped his brakes as they closed in on the tailback ahead. Standing above him, behind his protective armour, the top gunner swivelled his M134 mini-gun and started tracking it across the mass of civilian traffic blocking every lane of the M1s southbound carriageway. With the M25 junction still over a mile away, the troop commander signalled his convoy, and the JLTVs slowed to a crawl. He reached for his radio and called up the Abrams tanks, tooling towards his position. A couple of minutes later, two 60-ton monsters made quick work of the central reservation, crushing the metal barrier into the ground and creating an enormous gap that would allow the trailing squadrons to pass through onto the north-bound carriageway.

Obstacle duly negotiated, the JLTVs surged through the gap and raced towards the distant junction, rumbling past the thousands of crawling vehicles desperate to escape the advancing mechanised storm. Arriving at the off-ramp, the commander watched dozens of panicked drivers peel their vehicles away from the edges of the jam and speed south along the M1. He ordered his gunner to open up with his mini-gun. The ripping sound was unmistakable, and hundreds of tracer rounds lanced a glowing path beneath the low cloud cover. No more vehicles attempted to head south.

The two Abrams tanks caught up, crushing more sections of central reservation and blocking the southbound carriageway. One of them nosed its way into the traffic, bullying a path through the massed ranks of vehicles before crashing through the roadside under-growth and opening up a route through to a lane on the other side. The tank roared backwards in a cloud of exhaust fumes and re-joined the monstrous armoured barrier across the southbound carriageway, its massive 120mm gun barrel tracking across the traffic jam. The closest civilian vehicles got the message and drove through the crushed undergrowth and out onto the lane. In minutes, hundreds of cars were emptying off the motorway. Where they went was none of the troop commander's concern. All that mattered was clearing the junction.

A dozen US troops dismounted from the JLTVs and started directing the civilians off the motorway. The troop commander exited his vehicle and joined them as they scattered flares across the road. Most of the faces that watched him and his soldiers looked scared. Some stared with open hostility. Many were caliphate citizens who'd emigrated to England and Wales, but there were others too, Brits, with their families, cars loaded with luggage. That was a phenomenon the commander just didn't understand.

He heard a low rumble of thunder behind him. He turned and saw several flights of transport helicopters heading southeast. Their mission was to secure the other major junctions at the A1, the A10, the A405, and the M11. By nightfall, the northern section of the M25 motorway would be closed to civilian traffic. He climbed back into his JLTV and listened to the command net. To the west, another Atlantic Alliance battle group was forming outside of Windsor, waiting for the last pockets of resistance to be eliminated in a town called Slough. Waves of A-10 Warthogs were ripping up an enemy that was dug in deep, dropping munitions and hosing the streets with their 30mm auto-cannons. He asked his driver to skim through the civilian radio frequencies and heard the same message being broadcast:

Remain in your homes until further notice!

Failure to comply could lead to serious injury and death!

Stay tuned for further messages from the allied authorities!

It won't be long now, the commander told himself. The road trembled as the trailing squadrons of armour leapfrogged his position and continued south, rumbling down the motorway towards the outskirts of London.

DESPITE THE SOUND-ABSORPTION PANELS, EDDIE COULD STILL hear muted shouting through the walls and suspected that Griff had broken the news to Zoe. He hoped they would sort it out quickly because if Eddie could hear it, so could others. He didn't think the cops would show up, though, because he hadn't seen one all day. What he had seen were plenty of trains clattering past his window, all of them filled with evacuees.

He refocused on his mission prep. Behind drawn curtains, he'd laid his inventory out on the bed. Three days of rations, bottled water, satellite phone, spare batteries, spotter scope, the RF signal decoder, tactical vest, the pistol, and the MP5 with its suppressor attached. He was taking 120 rounds for the MP5, 50 rounds for the pistol, and $1000 in cash. He was going loaded for bear, as his American friends would say. If they stopped and searched him, it would be over. In fact, any interaction with the enemy would be fraught with danger. Eddie could get killed for looking at someone the wrong way. So, he would go across that river armed and dangerous.

He packed his daysack and slipped a navy rain jacket over the MP5 and tactical vest that carried his spare magazines and satellite phone. He wore jeans, a green T-shirt, and Nike trainers. Slipping the daysack over his shoulders, he cinched the straps tight and bounced up and down. Nothing rattled, scraped, or sloshed around. He was good to go.

The latest update from Scotland told him that allied forces were massing to the north and west of London, and IS troops were using every means of transport to escape to the continent from the south and east. The war had its own momentum now, but the last days of any conflict were unpredictable and dangerous. Again, he pondered the mystery of the convoys. Satellite reconnaissance had revealed nothing, but Eddie thought it would be easy to hide articulated lorries in a city. He was keen to get over the water and find out why.

Outside, the sun had set. There was still lots of cloud cover, which was good. Rain would be better, but he couldn't have everything. Eddie scanned the darkness of the viaduct, and he felt a sudden knot of apprehension in his stomach. Local knowledge was hard to beat and navigating his own way across that bridge was a daunting thought. One trip, one foot on the wrong rail, and it would be over. He hoped they'd worked it out next door. He could use Griff's eyes and experience.

Out in the hallway, he caught it again, a muffled voice, female, raised and angry. It was still kicking off next door. Now Eddie had a decision to make – Griff or no Griff. If he made it across in one piece, he needed to find a base from which to operate out of. That shouldn't be too hard. There were thousands of empty properties and looted stores—

Eddie froze as a shadow passed by the kitchen window. He heard a sharp rap on the door and squinted through the spyhole. It was Griff. He opened the door.

'I'm ready,' Griff announced. He was wearing dark track bottoms, trainers, and a black hoodie. On his back, he carried a small rucksack. Eddie ushered him inside and closed the door.

'I heard shouting,' he said.

Griff waved a dismissive hand. 'It's nothing. She doesn't want me to go, obviously.'

'Maybe she has a point. It'll be dangerous.'

Griff frowned. 'I meant what I said. I wanna do my bit.'

'Fair enough, but once we're out there, we work as a team. I talk, you listen, and vice versa. Deal?'

'Deal.' Griff held out his fist and Eddie bumped it.

Outside, Eddie locked the door and grille. As they walked past Griff's place, the front door opened. Zoe stood immobile, her arms folded, her eyes raw and smudged with mascara. Griff stopped and squeezed her arm.

'Don't worry, babe. I'll see you soon, I promise. Kiss the boys for me, yeah?'

But Zoe wasn't listening. She shrugged off her husband's hand and glared at Eddie. 'You'd better bring him back in one piece, you hear me?'

'I will,' Eddie said. At that moment, he promised himself he would cut Griff loose the moment he got across that river. Zoe scowled and slammed the door closed.

Behind Newtown Court, there were two types of vehicles in the car park: burned out or barely serviceable. They skirted the vehicular graveyard and headed for the shadows that bordered the estate. Griff pushed his way through the overgrown shrubbery and Eddie followed, one arm up to protect his face from the branches and brambles. He smelled shit, too. A torchlight flared, and he grabbed Griff's arm.

'No lights, mate.'

Griff pocketed the torch. A few steps ahead, a fence of rusted steel railings separated them from the tracks beyond. Griff ran his hand along the spikes, then stopped. Using both hands, he twisted one of them and lifted it upwards. Eddie helped him lift a couple more until they'd created a gap at the bottom of the fence. They crawled through, then lowered the spikes back down.

Eddie stood less than six feet from the closest train track. Beyond it, more lines stretched away into the darkness.

Pointing, Griff whispered, 'All those tracks lead in and out of Waterloo Station. We're going up.' Eddie saw the viaduct above their heads, and he followed Griff to a steel ladder bolted to the wall. The older man went first, and Eddie followed, scaling all 30 feet until they were up on the elevated bridge. They crouched in the darkness, watching and listening. They didn't see any trains headed their way, and Eddie was grateful for it. There were only four tracks on the viaduct itself, all heading into Battersea Park train station a short distance away, and the gap between the rails and the viaduct wall was tight. If a train came their way at speed, it could prove lethal. Griff read his mind.

'Don't worry,' he said, whispering in the darkness. 'There's more room than you think. Stay a few feet behind me and make sure you follow my footsteps. I'll let you know if there's anything to be worried about. If a train comes, don't panic. Just watch me, okay?'

Eddie nodded, feeling like a raw recruit being given basic instructions on night movement. But Griff's movement and noise discipline impressed him, and it was obvious he'd done this before. Eddie followed him along a path of narrow paving slabs running beside the track. Eddie looked over the parapet and saw a large roundabout, but traffic was minimal. A car passed below, then a couple of pushbikes, and a single electric scooter whizzed into the black expanse of Battersea Park. Traffic cones blocked access to Chelsea Bridge Road, and he saw cops armed with rifles pacing up and down behind them.

They kept moving, leaving the bright and empty platforms of Battersea Park station behind them. Apartment blocks rose on either side of the tracks, and to Eddie's right, the giant, redundant smoke-stacks of Battersea Power Station towered into the night sky. There were lots of lights in lots of windows. Eddie glimpsed figures and the flickering light of TVs. It all seemed so surreal, so normal. Maybe the war will pass London by, he thought. Maybe it will all be over sooner than any of us have hoped.

Maybe.

Ahead, he saw more tracks converging, forming a wide stretch of rails and sleepers that ran across the river to the opposite bank. Griff held up a hand, and they both took a knee in the darkness. Eddie felt very exposed.

Beneath his hood, Griff whispered, 'There's a footpath on the other side of the tracks. It's used by maintenance crews to cross the bridge. That's our way in. Follow me, and walk where I walk, okay?'

Eddie nodded. 'Roger that.'

Griff cut across the tracks towards the eastern boundary of the railway lines. Halfway across, Eddie felt the vibration through his Nikes. The rails sang, and then Griff was waving him towards a maintenance shed squatting between two sets of rails. They took shelter behind it and the vibration grew into a rumble. A train thun-dered past, and Eddie caught glimpses of the passengers inside, packed in tight like some pre-invasion commuter train. More refugees, heading south towards the coast. The exodus seemed endless.

The trailing wind battered them as the last carriage rumbled past. Running lights faded into the distance, and then they were on the move again, lifting their knees like flamingos as they stepped across the rails. They made it to the other side without further incident, and Eddie was glad to feel the concrete path beneath his feet. They moved faster now, the empty bridge stretching out ahead of them. Halfway across, Griff froze, crouching down, and Eddie did the same. He heard voices close by, echoing somewhere below him. His right hand slipped inside the Velcro panel below his armpit. Ripping it open would allow him to extract the MP5 slung beneath it. Griff leaned towards him.

'There's someone below us. Working on the bridge.'

Eddie listened. He could still hear the voices, but it was difficult to work out what was being said. 'What are they doing?'

'Engineering works, I suppose. They're always doing something.'

They kept moving. Embankment lights rippled across the surface of the river, and further to the east, bright skyscrapers towered above the city. At moments like this, it was hard for Eddie to believe the country was at war, but then he saw a distant line of red tracer rounds burning into the night sky. The Hajis had probably detected a drone or something. Seconds later, the *thump, thump, thump* of booming guns rolled across the river.

After another few minutes of careful progress, they left the River Thames behind. The darkness of the station approach swallowed them. Dozens more railway spurs merged, forming a wide mass of steel rails that converged beneath the bright flare of platform lights at Victoria station. Eddie guessed they were still 300 yards short of those platforms, but even from this distance, he could hear the echo of the public-address system blaring across the station. He sensed an urgency in that voice and imagined thousands of people massed beneath the departures board waiting to board the next train. He imagined a stampede towards the trains, the crowds desperate to escape. Eddie hoped that was the case. The more panic there was, the better.

He heard a faint hum, and he pushed Griff towards the bridge ahead of them. From its inky shadows, they watched an unmanned security blimp drift above them, collision lights blinking, the word *POLICE* stencilled in white letters on its black belly. Its battery-powered engines hummed as it headed towards the river. They waited for it to disappear, and for two empty trains to clatter past and vanish into the distant station. Griff pointed to the sooty brick arch above their heads.

'That's Ebury Bridge Road. There's a staircase on the other side that leads up to the street. Come on.'

Emerging from the shadows of the bridge, Eddie followed Griff up a rusted steel staircase to a thick wooden gate topped with barbed wire. 'What's the plan now?' he asked Eddie.

'You're going back.'

Beneath his hoodie, Griff shook his head. 'You don't know the city like I do. Tell me where you're going, and I'll get you there.'

'I'm heading for the West End. Charing Cross, Kingsway, that area.' He didn't tell Griff that satellite imagery had revealed a large truck parked on a side street near Waterloo Bridge. 'You should go. If either of us gets caught, they'll shoot us, no question.' As Eddie twisted the lock, Griff grabbed his arm.

'I can help you, Eddie. Please.'

Eddie hesitated. Griff could be useful, but when he thought about the man's kids, he felt a stab of guilt. But the mission came first. 'Stay out of sight and don't move around,' he told Griff. 'When you hear a car stop outside this gate, it'll be me. If I'm not back in 15 minutes, leave. If you smell trouble, leave. Got it?'

Eddie opened the gate and pulled it closed behind him. He stood on an empty pavement. To his left was a collection of multi-storey council blocks. To his right, the empty junction at Buckingham Palace Road. He didn't see a single car or pedestrian anywhere, but the glare of white neon streetlights gave him nowhere to hide. He had to work fast.

He headed for Buckingham Palace Road, conscious of the CCTV. He couldn't avoid it, so he had to move fast. From the corner building, he saw several Metropolitan Police vehicles parked outside

Belgravia police station. Perfect. Eddie headed for a BMW estate close by. He crouched by the passenger door and plucked the RF signal decoder from his tactical vest. He aimed it at the dashboard and punched the button. The alphanumeric display scrolled through thousands of combinations per second until a small green light glowed. Eddie pushed the button beneath it and heard the quiet *thunk* of the car unlocking. He crawled into the driver's seat and pushed the ignition button. The hybrid engine purred into life as the dashboard displays glowed. He waited for the needles to settle: half a tank of diesel and a power cell at 65%. He checked over his shoulder – Buckingham Palace Road was devoid of traffic. He pulled away, keeping the lights off, and turned the corner onto Ebury Bridge Road.

A few moments later, Griff was climbing into the passenger seat. He closed the door, a broad grin on his face.

'First time I've sat in the front of one of these.'

Eddie hit the boot release button and found what he was looking for. He tugged a high-visibility yellow police vest over his jacket and climbed back behind the wheel. He handed another vest to Griff and a baseball cap with a chequered band. 'Lose the hood and cover up that hair.'

Griff did as he was told, and Eddie pulled away from the curb. A few seconds later, they were driving through the back streets of Pimlico. The car radio was on, but the police chatter was minimal. No one was saying anything about a stolen car. *Maybe they've all run for the hills*, Eddie thought.

'I didn't think we'd be joyriding a cop car,' Griff said, chuckling.

'You can still go back. Maybe you should.'

'Forget it.' Griff looked at him. 'So, what's the plan?'

Eddie shifted in his seat. Beneath his lightweight jacket, the MP5 lay across his lap, and the pistol dug into his right side. 'We head to the embankment and drive into the West End from there.'

Griff winced. 'Could be dodgy,' he said. 'I've seen checkpoints along Millbank.'

'I don't want to get caught in a backstreet,' Eddie said. 'We might need to get out of trouble fast. Besides, we're cops, right?'

Griff pulled his cap down a little lower. 'I suppose we are.'

Eddie turned onto Grosvenor Road, which would take them along the Thames embankment towards Vauxhall Bridge, a huge intersection where 16 lanes of traffic converged. As the BMW cruised towards the junction, Griff saw it first.

'They've shut off the embankment,' he said.

Eddie saw it too. Steel barriers blocked the road on either side, reinforced by coils of razor wire. Eddie counted 20-plus militia mooching around, rifles slung, chatting, and smoking. But no police.

'We're going to bluff our way through,' he told Griff. 'Are you ready for this?'

Griff sat a little straighter in his seat. 'Bit late to back out now, eh?'

He was scared. So was Eddie, but he'd learned to control it. He glanced at the control pad on the dashboard and punched a button. The BMWs roof lights flickered blue as he slowed for the roadblock. Heads turned their way.

'Jesus,' Griff whispered.

'Relax. Say nothing and follow my lead.' Eddie powered down his window and rested his arm on the sill. A cover story about an escaped prisoner waited behind his lips. The plan was to stop short of the razor wire so he could make good his escape if he needed to. He dangled his arm out of the window, the other resting on the steering wheel. *Nothing to see here. Just two cops patrolling.* He cleared his throat, ready to engage, but then the razor wire rolled out of the way and a militiaman waved them through. Beyond, an empty Millbank beckoned. Eddie waved a hand in thanks.

'Fuck me,' Griff said, exhaling as he watched his rear-view mirror. 'Mate, that was cool as fuck. Balls of steel, that's what you've got.'

'We're not out of the woods yet,' Eddie said.

Millbank Tower rose above the road, then fell behind them. At the next roundabout, Eddie saw that Blackfriars Bridge was closed to traffic. He kept driving, nice and steady, towards Parliament Square. The road narrowed, squeezed on either side by tall wooden hoardings. Eddie knew what lay behind them – nothing but desolate spaces of bulldozed rubble.

'Makes me want to weep,' Griff said. 'They started knocking everything down as soon as they got here. Houses of Parliament, Westminster Abbey, Big Ben, Whitehall. It's all gone.'

Eddie recalled watching the TV news reports back in Boston. Everyone had been horrified when the wrecking balls had destroyed some of the most iconic landmarks in the world. He'd once visited London on a school trip, and he remembered seeing Westminster Abbey and the Tomb of the Unknown Soldier, a memorial that had lit its own flame inside him. He remembered the scruffy protest mob in Parliament Square and Big Ben's emphatic ring. And he remembered the Palace of Westminster, the mother of all Parliaments, where Oliver Cromwell had stood guard outside with his sword raised aloft. Now it was all gone.

Griff spoke, his voice gloomy. 'They said it was bomb damage, that the buildings were unsafe and had to come down. Nobody bought it. It was all about wiping away our history. Year Zero, or some bullshit like that. Look.'

Griff pointed through the windscreen. Beyond a bulldozed Parliament Square, Eddie saw Whitehall was nothing but a vast, empty space behind steel fencing. A distant row of buildings was all that remained, naked beneath tall arc lights and propped up by a network of scaffold poles. Blue weatherproof sheeting rippled in the night breeze.

'That's Downing Street.'

Eddie turned in his seat. 'What?'

'It's where it all began, apparently.'

'Someone must've said something about this,' Eddie said.

Griff shook his head. 'Our own politicians banned any protests. Too busy taking the knee for Wazir and praising his *timely intervention*. They stood and clapped when they brought Big Ben down.

Fucking traitors.' He brightened. 'They'll stand trial, with any luck. I'm looking forward to that day.'

'Most of them will be on those trains, I reckon.'

Eddie followed the road back onto the embankment, unsettled by the empty skyline around him. He saw Westminster Bridge, barricaded and deserted. He drove past Scotland Yard, keeping his speed down, gliding past the vast empty tract of land where the Ministry of Defence building once stood.

'We need somewhere quiet to park,' Eddie said. 'Any ideas?'

Griff directed him. After they'd driven beneath the twin bridges of Waterloo and Hungerford, Eddie turned left into Savoy Place and parked in the shadows of the London Memorial Garden. He switched off the engine. Griff looked at him.

'Is this quiet enough?'

'Yep.'

'Now what?'

'We need somewhere to lie low,' Eddie said. 'Should be easy enough. Somewhere that's been looted already.'

Griff shrugged off his Hi-Viz. 'You mean somewhere low-profile, with more than one point of entry so we've got an escape route. Maybe somewhere with a decent vantage point too.'

Eddie smiled. 'You've done this before.'

'I told you, I was a bad lad back in the day.' Griff winked and got out of the car. Eddie followed him, shrugging off his own Hi-Viz and locking the car with his gizmo.

'I must get one of those,' Griff said, flipping his hood up.

Eddie grinned. 'Now that would be a bad idea.'

'You're probably right.' Griff headed up the street and away from the embankment. 'Follow me. I know just the place.'

[17]

RAIDERS OF THE LOST CAUSE

BERTIE HURRIED INTO THE BATHROOM, CLUTCHING A PLASTIC carrier bag. He dumped the contents of the small pedal bin into it, then he plucked his toothbrush from the glass next to the cold tap. Walking out of the room, he spun around and checked the cupboards once more. He had to be certain he'd left no traces of his recent stay in The Witch's house. It was paranoia, he knew that. He also knew he was short on time.

Back in Cheryl's room – *their* room – he threw the carrier bag into a larger bin liner. Cheryl had emptied the wardrobe of Bertie's clothes and laid them out on the bed. She handed him a couple of shirts.

'Hang those up in your old room,' she said without turning around.

'We should get rid of everything.'

'You used to live here, didn't you? When they took you away, did they give you time to pack?'

Bertie shook his head. 'Of course not.'

'Exactly. It would look odd if there were no traces of you at all.'

Bertie watched her pack a neat pile of folded T-shirts into his travel bag. She'd packed everything for his trip to France, even his French phrase books. She was the best. Better than the best. And he'd made up his mind. 'I'm not leaving without you, Cheryl.'

She turned and stared at him. 'But you must, Bertie. If that man comes for you, it'll be over. I've just found you. I won't lose you again.'

'And I can't leave you here.' He pointed to the ceiling and lowered his voice. 'I don't trust that lot up there. I'll talk to Lady Edith, explain that I need you in France. To prepare the house ready for her arrival.'

Cheryl frowned. 'It could be a couple of weeks before they leave. They'll have no one to take care of them or look after the house.'

'They're not crippled, love. It won't hurt them for a week or two.' He took her hands in his. 'You're coming with me, that's final. I'll talk to her, don't worry.'

Out in the corridor, a buzzer rasped long and loud. Bertie's heart pounded. He felt the splinters piercing his back as they laid him down on the wooden cross —

Cheryl hurried past him. He followed her to the end of the base-ment corridor and stopped in front of the security panel. On the CCTV monitor, beneath the glare of the security light, Bertie saw The Witch's neighbour, Mr Clemens, waiting on the pavement. Bertie deflated, relieved.

'What does he want at this time of night?'

Cheryl held down the intercom button. 'How may I help you, Mr Clemens?'

Clemens' voice crackled. 'I need to see Lady Edith. Now.'

He didn't look at the camera, Bertie observed. Clemens was some sort of textile millionaire whose business had barely skipped a beat since the invasion. He was a snob too and didn't like explaining himself to the hired help.

'Please come in. I'll let Lady Edith know you're here.' She stabbed the entry button. On the screen, Clemens pushed open the pedestrian gate. 'I need to announce him,' she told Bertie. 'Finish your packing.'

'Okay, love.'

Cheryl hurried upstairs. The CCTV screen flickered.

Bertie turned to walk away—

Then stopped.

'WHAT'S FOR DINNER, DARLING?'

Victor stared at his wife. She was sitting on the sofa, her legs curled up beneath her and an upturned novel on her lap. An inquisitive eyebrow was raised in his direction. Victor put down his own book, a cricketing autobiography, one that aroused fond memories of long and boozy days spent at Lord's cricket ground. He doubted those days would ever return.

'Dinner?' Margaret repeated.

'I've no idea, darling. Perhaps you'd like me to fetch a menu?'

His wife's eyebrow dropped like a guillotine. 'Don't be facetious, Victor. It's unbecoming.'

'This isn't a hotel, dear. And if things get much worse, we might have to fend for ourselves. You must prepare yourself for the ordeal.'

Margaret's scowl morphed into a smile as Edith entered the library room. She swung her chunky calves to the floor as Victor puffed to his feet. Edith smiled, and Victor noticed it required some effort on her part. Margaret gushed.

'Lady Edith, why don't you join us? It's so peaceful in here.'

Victor watched her cross the Persian rug, her eyes wandering over the book-lined walls. 'I shall miss this room. Perhaps I should ask Bertie to fill a few boxes, take them to Provence.'

'Not a good idea, Edith. We don't want to overload the van, do we? The last thing Bertie needs is a breakdown.'

She didn't react to Victor's abandonment of her title. Instead, she perched herself on the edge of a chair, squeezing her hands together. 'I'm troubled, Victor.'

'How so?'

'Bertie's travelling with so much of my personal wealth. If anything happens ...' Her voice tailed off.

'Nothing will happen,' Victor said, positioning his backside over the chair. Before he could sit, there was a tap at the door and Mrs P entered the room.

'You have visitors, Lady Edith. Shall I show them into the reception room?'

Victor straightened up. 'What visitors?'

The library door swung open, and Colonel Al-Huda entered the room. Trailing behind him was the rangy figure of Andrea Clarke, dressed in her customary long black leather coat and matching boots. Victor's heart raced. They were all in serious trouble.

Edith scrambled to her feet. Margaret stared open-mouthed, then looked at Victor. He shook his head, and she stayed in her seat. Another man entered the room, small, grey-haired, and dapper in tan slacks and a canary-yellow sweater. Edith looked confused and frightened.

'Colonel Al-Huda? Andrea? What are you both doing here?' Her eyes flicked to her neighbour. 'Jeremy? What's going on?'

'Just doing my duty,' the man said. He folded his arms, his chin cocked as if daring Edith to challenge him.

'What are you talking about?'

Al-Huda smiled and took a few steps towards her. 'You know exactly what I'm talking about, Spencer.'

Victor watched Edith's face darken. 'You forget your place, Colonel. You will refer to me as Governor Spencer.'

Al-Huda slapped her, a backhanded swipe that knocked Edith off her feet and onto the sofa next to Margaret.

'Stop that!' Victor said, rushing to Edith's side. She slumped over the sofa arm, her glasses broken, her lower lip bleeding. She touched it with trembling fingers. Shock, Victor guessed. He felt it too, his heart racing at a reckless speed. He handed her his linen handkerchief, but she waved it away. Victor stepped back as she got to her feet, keeping one hand on the sofa for balance. She stared at a smiling Al-Huda.

'You've just ended your career,' Edith told him in a calm, cold voice. Victor knew it wasn't courage that was driving Edith. It was sheer outrage. But Al-Huda didn't appear intimidated at all. Standing behind the colonel, Clarke observed with an amused expression on her ebony face.

'You lied to me,' Al-Huda replied. 'You're harbouring an escaped criminal.'

Edith dabbed her lip with a tissue. 'I don't know what you're talking about.'

Al-Huda raised his hand and Victor stepped between them. 'Please, Colonel, there's no need for —'

The open hand connected with Victor's chubby jowl. His head snapped sideways, and he staggered a step or two.

'You're under arrest, Hardy.' Al-Huda pointed a finger at Margaret. 'Her too. Everyone in this house!'

'Where is he?' Clarke said, no longer smiling. Whatever cold streak of cruelty Edith possessed, Clarke trumped it in spades. 'You had me execute the National Assembly, remember? And you sent your man Payne to pick up Daly's luggage.'

Victor glanced at Al-Huda. 'You're mistaken, Andrea —'

She whipped around to face him, leather coat tails flapping. 'I've seen his mug shot! What did you think? That I'm some dumb house nigger, doing the white man's bidding?'

Victor grimaced. 'What are you talking about?'

She turned back to Edith. 'Admit it, you dirty old bitch! Speak now, or you and your friends will find yourselves on a slow barge to an east London incinerator.'

'Enough!' Victor snapped. He turned to face Al-Huda, his voice softening. 'The Atlantic Alliance is bearing down on this city and your only concern is finding a petty criminal? We're all on the same side, for God's sake.' His chest rose and fell, and he was finding it difficult to take a deep breath. 'Please, let's talk this through like civilised people.'

Al-Huda nodded. 'You're right. Cooler heads must prevail.' He reached inside his jacket and produced a small pistol. He held it by his leg and turned to Edith. 'Now, tell me, Spencer. Where is the criminal Payne? And please, think carefully before you answer.'

Victor saw Edith was terrified. Margaret's face was ashen. And standing by the door, poor Mrs P, an unwitting victim, was—

The housekeeper had disappeared.

AT THE TOP OF THE BASEMENT STAIRS, BERTIE STEPPED ASIDE AS Cheryl hurried past him, carrying a silver coffee tray filled with pots and crockery. He followed her towards the half-open library door. His hand shook. Yes, he'd done this before, and that night still haunted him, but tonight was different. This was about survival, nothing more, nothing less.

Cheryl swerved around the door and disappeared inside. Bertie heard her voice.

'I brought coffee for you and your guests, Lady Edith.'

Bertie stepped closer to the library door. Inside, he saw Clemens standing against the wall, arms folded across his horrible yellow jumper. Everyone else was out of sight. Bertie would have to move fast. Surprise was vital.

Cheryl cried out, and he heard the tray crash to the carpet. He took a deep breath and stepped into the room. Al-Huda and the black woman had their backs to him. Cheryl knelt on the carpet, fussing over broken crockery. Victor turned in his direction. The Witch saw him, and her mouth opened. He took two more steps and raised the gun, aiming it at the back of Al-Huda's greasy head. He pulled the trigger. The bang was deafening. Bertie switched aim. The black woman spun around, and he shot her in the chest. She stumbled backwards, hands reaching for something to grab, and then she collapsed on the carpet. Bertie twisted around.

'Get on the fucking floor!' he yelled at Clemens, pointing the gun. The little man obeyed, whimpering as he lay face down. Bertie knew he'd be no trouble. He turned to the others. 'Is everyone okay?'

The Witch approached him, her face painted with Al-Huda's blood. She raised a trembling claw and held it against his cheek. Her skin was cold. 'God bless you, Bertie. God bless you.'

Victor slapped him on the shoulder. 'Using Mrs P as a diversion. Good thinking, Bertie.'

'What about Clemens?' Bertie motioned to the man trembling on the floor.

'Please don't kill me,' he pleaded. Bertie kicked him over. Not too hard, though. Just enough to know he meant business.

'Get up.'

Clemens obeyed, and Bertie slammed him against the shelves. Books tumbled to the floor. He jammed the Glock into Clemens' neck. The textiles magnate trembled like a leaf in a breeze. 'I'm going to let you go,' Bertie said. 'Then I'm going to make a phone call. If you speak about this – ever – some friends of mine will pay you and your good lady a visit. And their faces will be the last you'll ever see. Do you understand me, Mr Clemens?'

The little man's head bobbed up and down several times. 'Perfectly,' he stammered.

Bertie took a step closer and leaned into Clemens' face. 'Good. Now fuck off.'

Clemens bolted from the room. A moment later, the front door slammed behind him.

'Do you think he'll talk?' Judge Hardy asked him.

Bertie shook his head. 'Doubtful.' He slipped the gun into his trouser waistband and hugged Cheryl tight. 'Good job, love. Now go, pack our bags, and put them in the van.' As Cheryl hurried from the room, Bertie turned to the others. 'Same for all of you. We can't stay here, not now. Grab your things and load them in the van. Essential items only. And be quick about it. Al-Huda might've arranged for backup.'

Judge Hardy helped his ashen-faced wife off the sofa and ushered both ladies out of the room. Bertie went through Al-Huda's pockets and found a car key. Outside, the street was silent. He pressed the key fob and saw orange lights blink in the darkness further down the street. He climbed inside the car, an electric BMW, and drove it into The Witch's driveway. After closing the gates, he parked it inside the double garage next to the Toyota. He popped the hood and disconnected the battery, then he took a claw hammer to the control panel. No battery, no electrics, no GPS signal. He ducked back into the basement and killed the external building lights. With a lot of effort, he dragged the bodies of Al-Huda and the black woman through the house to the French doors. Cheryl passed him, her hands laden with luggage. She returned a minute later, mopping the bloody trail, the mop head fizzing left and right like a broom handler in a curling competition. After he'd relieved both bodies of their phones, Bertie stuffed the corpses inside the BMW with Cheryl's help. Their dead heads lolled together like lovers.

Bertie secured the garage, then the house, leaving the alarm off. Everyone had gathered at the back of the Mercedes van. As he caught his breath, Bertie studied his travel companions. They'd dressed down as he'd advised, losing any obvious jewellery or expensive clothes. Ordinary, that's how they had to look from this point on. Their IDs would do the talking.

'Okay, let's get aboard.'

'Wait.'

Everyone turned to look at The Witch, but her eyes were elsewhere, travelling the length and breadth of the building, her pale face drawn and sombre. She'd dressed in a dark double-breasted overcoat, knee-length skirt, and low-heeled boots, and she'd pulled a knitted green beanie over her grey hair. She looked small and frail, and to Bertie's surprise, she was crying. He felt a twinge of pity, but it lasted for less than a second. He took her elbow and steered her back towards the van.

'Come on, Lady Edith. Let's not upset ourselves. A new life

awaits, yes?' He looked at the others for support. Judge Hardy came to his rescue and ushered the ladies into the crew seat. Cheryl climbed into the front, next to Bertie. She wore a hoodie and jeans, and Bertie wore the same, his close-cropped head covered with a Tottenham Hotspur baseball cap. He lifted his left hand to reveal the green band around his wrist.

'Okay, let's see 'em. You've all got them on, right?' Hands raised behind him like obedient schoolchildren. 'Excellent stuff. Okay, let's go.'

He started the engine but kept the lights off. The gates opened, and he rolled the Mercedes through them, checking that they'd closed behind him. He heard The Witch sob once, a final expression of regret. Two in one day, Bertie thought. He doubted he would ever see that again.

'What's the plan, Bertie? You still haven't told us.'

Bertie turned in his seat, the black leather creaking beneath his backside. 'Remember you told me to find another route out, just in case things went bad?' The judge nodded. 'Well, that's what we're doing. Plan B.'

'And where does Plan B take us?'

Bertie dropped the van into gear. 'Farnborough Airport. And we need to get there in a hurry.'

He drove away at low speed until he'd made a couple of turns. Then he flipped the van's lights on and put his foot down, heading west.

[18]

SECOND FIDDLE

THE KNOCK AT THE DOOR DRAGGED HARRY FROM A FITFUL sleep. He shifted on the lumpy couch and saw a young woman in combat uniform peering around the door.

'Sorry to disturb you, Prime Minister, but you're needed in the conference room.'

'I'll be there shortly,' he mumbled, flushed with a mild embarrassment. He'd fallen asleep in his clothes, his walking boots kicked off to one side, his head buried beneath his coat. His thick grey hair was a wild mop, and he hadn't shaved for two days. *You're letting yourself go, Harry.* He couldn't tell if that inner voice belonged to Ellen or Nina, but whoever it was, they were right. He was losing *something*. Confidence, authority, control – it was all slipping away. He swallowed a flutter of panic and stood up, kicking an empty half-bottle of whiskey across the floor. He remembered cracking it open, a nip to help him sleep, but not finishing it. That wasn't good. He shoved the bottle down the side of the sofa and trudged to the bathroom.

There was no time for a shower, but a cold-water wash made him feel better. The feeling didn't last. His shirt needed changing, as did his underwear. Someone had mislaid his travel bag in transit to

Luton, and it didn't seem appropriate to demand its return given the circumstances. Yet appearances were important, and it was unacceptable to perform his duties looking frayed at the edges. That simply wouldn't do for a prime minister, especially a wartime one.

Lee Wilde was waiting for him inside the conference room, a medium-sized box of rough concrete walls lit by a single fluorescent light. At one end of the room was a large monitor on a mobile stand and a rectangular table surrounded by cheap wooden chairs. Two soldiers fussed over cables and AV equipment then left the room. Harry turned to his chief of staff.

'What's going on, Lee?'

'The Oval Office has scheduled an update.'

Harry glanced at his watch. 'It's the middle of the night over there. Something must've happened.'

The TV flickered, and the White House logo appeared. Harry sat down and Wilde sat down out of camera shot. On the screen, a digital clock counted down from thirty seconds. Harry cleared his throat, laying his palms on the table's worn wooden surface. He opened his mouth and stretched his face, allowing his muscles to relax. *We're just two colleagues working through a problem, that's all.*

On the screen, Vice President Riley's square-jawed countenance replaced the White House logo. Harry's heart sank. He forced a smile. 'Good morning, Mr Vice President. Is President Mitchell joining us?'

Riley shook his head. 'Not today.'

No explanation, no apology. Harry lost the battle to keep the smile on his face. 'I was hoping to speak to him.'

Riley remained stoic. 'I wanted to let you know that the United States has rejected Baghdad's ceasefire proposal. Instead, the president has issued an ultimatum – all IS military forces must leave the British Isles by 6 am tomorrow morning. GMT,' he added. 'Any troops or formations failing to meet that deadline – and unwilling to surrender – will be engaged.'

Harry leaned back in his chair, struggling to control his rising temper. 'So, once again, you've excluded me from the decision-making process. Can I remind you, Mr Vice President, that I'm the Prime Minister of Great Britain? My voice needs to be heard.' In his peripheral vision, he saw Wilde gesturing with hands. *Calm down, Harry.*

But Riley wasn't holding back. 'With respect, you're prime minister of nothing. I'm sorry, but that's the truth. The United States is rectifying that situation.'

Harry inhaled a deep breath through his nostrils. He had to remain calm. Back in the day, before the world was turned upside down, Harry used to be good at conciliation.

'The nation is indebted to you, as I've publicly stated on many occasions. But what I'm asking for – and I don't think I'm being unreasonable – is a little transparency.' He kept his tone agreeable, upbeat. It made him feel sick.

On the screen, Riley nodded once. 'I'll take that under consideration.'

That's big of you. 'Can we talk about infrastructure damage? Because it's been considerable. The Prince of Wales Bridge, for example. Given the looming deadline, it's clear that some of Wazir's forces won't get out in time. If they're engaged with the same level of ...' Harry fumbled for an appropriate term. '... determination, then I fear that further destruction is unavoidable, not to mention the potential for significant loss of life.'

Riley leaned towards the camera. 'What are you asking for, Harry? That we take our foot off the gas?' The VP shook his head in slow motion. 'The American people are tired of foreign wars. President Mitchell came to your aid because Great Britain needed our help. Again. We stepped up, and in doing so we earned the right to dictate policy and prosecute this war as we see fit.'

'No one is doubting your commitment,' Harry responded. 'But reducing this country to rubble when we have our boot on the enemy's throat makes no sense. All I'm asking is that you consult us before you launch any major attack. When this war is over, I'll have

159

to explain to the British people why many of their cities have been reduced to rubble.'

'At least they'll be free,' Reilly said. 'And besides, *reduced to rubble* is a little melodramatic, wouldn't you say?'

Harry pointed to the ceiling. 'Have you seen the damage in Luton? It's not just American firepower that's causing it either. IS troops are ransacking every high street they're retreating through. They've set ablaze entire towns. They've looted banks, destroyed communication hubs, blown up power lines, burned crops —'

'So, the quicker they leave, the better, yes?' Riley's eyes were like cold pebbles, his jaw working on a stubborn stick of gum. 'Look at this.' He held up a photograph, and Harry leaned forward to get a better view. For a moment, he didn't understand what Riley was showing him. Then the penny dropped.

Heads on poles. Scores of them.

'Jesus Christ.'

Riley tapped the photograph. 'US servicemen and women, beheaded, then arranged across an English field like some goddamn horror movie.' Harry was grateful when Riley put down the photograph. 'They were prisoners, and whether or not Baghdad sanctioned this atrocity, the United States government will not let this pass. When the deadline expires, any enemy troops still on British soil and holding a gun will be engaged with maximum prejudice.' He tapped the photograph on his desk. 'And this never happened. Are we clear?'

'You're sweeping a war crime under the carpet?'

Riley nodded. 'They were travelling home when their plane crashed into the Atlantic. There'll be a ceremony, and we'll honour them as heroes. Their families don't need to know how they died. It doesn't help anyone.'

It was cold, but Harry found himself in agreement. Going public would stoke the flames of an endless cycle of revenge and cause the bereaved to live in torment. Sometimes, ignorance was bliss. He marshalled his thoughts.

'Look, all I'm asking is that you keep me in the loop. If you don't, my Cabinet will lose confidence in my leadership, and that's the last thing we need right now. So, respectfully, include me, even if it's only informative. Keeping me in the dark serves no one.'

'I can't promise anything.' On the screen, Riley checked his watch. 'Okay, time's up. We'll speak again.'

The White House logo replaced the live feed, and after a moment, that too disappeared. Harry stared at his own reflection.

'What just happened?'

Wilde got up from his seat. 'He cut you off. Bloody rude.'

Harry ran a hand through his thick grey hair. 'What will I tell the Cabinet? That the White House isn't interested?'

'I don't see you have much choice.'

'They'll think I'm finished. That I'm burned out.' He laughed, low and bitter. 'Wheeler likened me to Churchill, remember? The only thing we'll have in common is post-war rejection.'

'We can spin it. Tell the Cabinet the meeting was confidential.'

'Sounds desperate.'

Wilde smiled. 'These are desperate times.'

'I didn't choose them for their gullibility, Lee.' He bit his lip. 'I never imagined the liberation of Britain would depress me so thoroughly.'

'There's still a long road ahead, Harry. We need to keep you front and centre. A photo-op with frontline troops, and a stirring speech. Like the one you gave in Otterburn, before the assault on Newcastle.'

Harry was good at it, too. 'That's an idea.'

'The Cabinet won't like it, but they also think being this far south is risky. Your continued presence here, close to the frontline, will boost your credibility.'

'Leaving them to conspire against me.'

Wilde frowned. 'Don't get paranoid, Harry. Look, if you think we should go back to Cumbria, then so be it. The Cabinet will know you've been frozen out, and the cards will lie where they fall. Or you could stay here, keep them in the dark a little longer, see how this plays out. The end could be less than a month away, and things might not be as bad as we imagine. Once they get the TV and radio networks back up and running, the British public will see and hear you. The others can't compete with you on that stage. So, whether you stay or go, it's a choice only you can make.'

Harry processed that for several long, silent moments. Despite Wilde's wise counsel, the panic that plucked at him spiked. Riley was right about one thing – the sooner it was over, the better. Harry wanted to see an end to hostilities, too, but not from the side-lines. Not now that the end was just over the horizon.

'To hell with Cumbria. We stay here, make ourselves busy, see this thing through. Wherever it leads us.'

[19]

HEATHROW EXPRESS

Nabil Zain gathered his family together in the hallway of his Hounslow home, making sure everyone was ready to go. He'd told them to pack a single bag and to wear comfortable clothes they could move fast in, especially footwear. That meant no heels for his wife Salma. His twin eight-year-old girls, Sunita and Suresh, wore matching yellow Disney sweaters and red leggings (Nabil wanted them to stand out in any crowd). They looked up at their father with wide brown eyes. They were carrying pink backpacks, both of which were filled with bricks of $100 bills. Salma wore a dark designer tracksuit and a Chanel sports bag slung over her shoulder, also stuffed with cash. She'd hidden her jewellery collection in her wash bag. She stared at her husband with eyes wider than their two beloved daughters.

'We're going to be okay, aren't we?'

Nabil pulled her in tight, then wrapped his other arm around his twin girls. 'We're going to be fine, trust me.'

'We should have left weeks ago.'

Nabil shot his wife a warning smile. 'Let's not go over that again, eh?' He checked the twins' backpacks, making sure he'd sealed them tight, and then he scooped up his car fob from the hallway dresser. 'Ready?' All three girls nodded. He opened the front door.

A cool night breeze swirled around the hallway, scattering pizza flyers across the carpet. He stepped outside, looking up and down the residential street. Nothing moved beneath the white glare of the streetlights. This was a decent neighbourhood with neighbours much like him – entrepreneurs, local politicians, plus a few caliphate bigwigs. Most of them had left. And most of them had warned Nabil to take his family and run. And he would've done so sooner had it not been for the containers of food, clothing, and electrical goods waiting to be offloaded at Tilbury Docks. Commercial shipping had to wait at anchor until the military was clear (*fucking pussies*, Nabil had raged to the shipping agent), so the wait for dock space to free up was a gamble. Salma had begged him to leave, but he'd refused. He had $140,000 tied up in that shipment.

The shipping agent was a Brit and a pragmatist like Nabil. Wars come and go, the Essex native had said, but business never stops. They'd met in a car park in south-east London and the agent had paid Nabil, minus his 10% fee. Now his girls were carrying the rest.

Nabil threw open the rear door of his Range Rover Sport. 'Get in, quickly.' The twins climbed aboard and buckled up. Salma sat up front. Nabil fired up the engine, pulled out of the driveway, and turned south towards Heathrow Airport.

They cruised through the empty streets of Hayes, but when Nabil drove over Harlington Bridge, he looked right and saw the largest traffic jam he'd ever seen, jamming both sides of the M4 motorway for as far as he could see. A tide of humanity flowed through the congestion like water as people abandoned their rides and headed for the airport on foot. It was over three kilometres away. Nabil doubted they'd make it.

'What are we going to do?' Salma said. 'The airport will be overrun.'

He reached for Salma's hand and squeezed it, conscious of her fear infecting the twins. 'It's all good. Just hang on, okay?' He glanced in the mirror at the girls, secured safely in their seat belts. 'This is fun, right girls?'

The wide-eyed eight-year-olds nodded in unison, but Nabil knew their nocturnal adventure might soon deteriorate into a nightmare. His stomach churned. Perhaps he *had* left it too late. But then he shook the thought from his mind. He had an instinct for timing. It's what had made him a successful businessman, knowing when to push and when to sit back and wait. They would make it. *Insha'Allah*, he added. Just in case.

He put his foot down, the Range Rover powering across the bridge and over the traffic jam. On the other side they found themselves driving through a quiet suburb of private homes. Nabil didn't see a single light. He had no idea if they were abandoned or the families inside were just lying low, but neither did he care. All that mattered now was getting out.

He slammed on the brakes at the junction of Bath Road. Dead ahead was the airport perimeter fence, and he watched an airliner lifting off into the night sky. That spurred him on. He swung the wheel to the right and sped up towards the airport tunnel. Salma gasped and grabbed the handhold above her head. Nabil saw it too. IS tanks blocked both sides of the road, their guns pointed at the approaching traffic. Nabil watched a couple of cars turning around and racing back past him at high speed. He hit his hazard lights and slowed the Range Rover, powering down the window. Soldiers crowded the gaps between the tanks, their guns ready. Nabil turned off his lights so he wouldn't blind them. Or piss them off. Hands waved for him to stop. The Range Rover idled as an officer approached the window. Nabil already had their passports ready. He offered them to the soldier – a captain – who took them without a word and flipped through the pages. Nabil watched him. The man wore full battle gear but instead of a helmet he wore a beret with a crossed swords badge above his left eye.

'From Beirut, huh?'

'That's right. Hamra.'

'No shit. I'm from Jnah.'

Nabil smiled. 'Loved that place as a kid. Sun, sea, and girls, right?' *Please don't speak, Salma.*

The captain handed back the passports. 'You're cutting it fine. Another ten minutes and we abandon our posts.'

'We've had some problems,' Nabil told him. 'The girls, they —'

'Go. Right now. Terminal Two is where you need to be. Good luck.'

He slapped the roof and pointed Nabil towards the tunnel that led to Heathrow's terminals. When he got there, Nabil saw another row of armoured vehicles blocking the motorway approach road. Behind the armour was every car in west London, choking all four lanes and stretching far into the distance. He swung the wheel to the left and floored the accelerator. There were other cars ahead of him, racing through the tunnel towards the airport. The engine roared, echoing off the tunnel walls. Roof lights flicked above them, faster and faster.

'We're too late!' Salma was on the verge of hysteria. Nabil squeezed her hand again, but harder this time.

'We'll be fine.' His eyes flicked to the digital display clock. Eight minutes until those soldiers abandon their posts. When that happened, all hell would break loose.

The tunnel emptied into the neon glare of the airport complex. Salma pointed through the windscreen.

'Terminal Two!'

Nabil saw the glowing sign high above the distant terminal building. He rounded a bend and brake lights blazed in front of him. He stamped on the brakes. The car skidded, then righted itself, screeching to a stop less than a metre from the tail end of another traffic jam. One they wouldn't get out of in time. Nabil saw people abandoning their cars and running for the terminal building.

'Let's go!' He flung open his door and unbuckled the twins. 'Do exactly as Daddy says. Don't be frightened, nothing is going to happen, but we're going to have to run, okay?'

'Yes, Daddy,' they said in unison, their voices high-pitched and anxious.

Salma slung her bag over her back and grabbed Sunita's hand. Nabil took Suresh's and led the way. He weaved through the cars, yanking his daughter's arm, then his foot caught a discarded suitcase and he stumbled, letting go. A man in a suit barged the little girl to the ground and Suresh screamed as more people staggered over her. Nabil hurled himself into the panicked herd and snatched her up.

'Daddy's here, baby.' He yelled over his shoulder at Salma, 'Carry her!'

They started moving again, his sobbing daughter bouncing in his arms. He could barely hear himself think above the shouts and screams, the car horns and pounding feet. This wasn't the marginally flustered exodus he imagined. The system was breaking down and Nabil was frightened. *Instinctive timing, my arse! You screwed up!*

Above a sea of bobbing heads, he saw soldiers' helmets. They were funnelling everyone through the terminal entrance, checking passports and papers. The crowd bulged as it slowed. Nabil pushed Salma ahead, bodies squeezing in around them as they siphoned between nervous-looking uniforms. Nabil reached for the passports in his back pocket, fanning them out like a hand of cards, making sure the crossed-swords covers were visible. The building loomed above him and he could see inside the terminal. People were running towards the departure gate. He waved his passports at the nearest soldier, but the man wasn't looking. He was shouting into his radio.

That's when Nabil heard it, a low rumble, like thunder, but it wasn't a plane. He turned and looked over the heads of the crowd, saw a stampede of humanity charging towards the terminal. The surrounding crowd panicked and pushed. The cordon crumbled, and Nabil and his girls swept through the doors into the building.

'Run!' he yelled above the noise.

They scrambled through the empty check-in desks, through the security zone, and into the departure lounge. They staggered past looted and lifeless shops and along the vast passenger concourse that fed the aircraft gates. Nabil saw a soldier and shouted, 'Where's the plane?'

The soldier, barely a kid, pointed. 'Last gate! You'd better move! They're closing the doors.'

Nabil cursed his luck as he charged onwards. The concourse stretched away into the distance and people were overtaking them all the time. His daughter was an anchor wrapped around his neck. Next to him, Salma slowed as she gasped for breath.

Nabil's heart sank as he dodged an obstacle course of abandoned luggage. Suresh was sobbing in his ear. His arms, legs, and lungs screamed for oxygen. He heard a rising thunder and looked behind him. What he saw was a tsunami, a wall-to-wall wave of human panic stampeding towards them. Nabil and his girls were about to get hit, then go under. Salma knew it too.

'There!' she gasped and veered towards a door. She barged through it and Nabil followed, just as the tsunami thundered past them.

'Go!' he shouted. 'Quickly!'

Salma led them down a couple of flights of metal stairs to the ground floor. A door covered in airside warning signs barred their entry. Nabil slammed the bar and pushed his way through. Outside, the wind whipped across a vast concrete apron. Distant lights shimmered, but none of them were aircraft. He looked to his right, towards the last gate, the last jetway.

It was empty. There was no plane.

Hope faded. He'd left it too late.

'What are we going to do now?' Salma wailed above the wind.

'We go back home, wait it out.'

'They'll throw us in jail! They'll take the girls from us!'

Nabil turned on her. 'What choice do we have?'

Lights flared, and Nabil saw a military Humvee approaching. He watched it roll past at speed, and then it screeched to a stop in a blue cloud of smoking rubber. Nabil saw a waving arm. He didn't hesitate.

'Go! Go!'

The Humvee reversed as they ran towards it. The rear door flew open, and a helmeted soldier clambered out and helped them inside. Nabil and Salma bundled the girls in and sat them on their laps. The soldier squeezed in next to them as the driver crunched gears and screeched away. The front seat passenger turned around. A man with a crossed-swords beret. The captain from Jnah.

'You must enjoy living dangerously, my friend,' he said, grinning.

'There was no plane,' Nabil said.

'The pilot had to taxi away before the plane got swamped. It's waiting at the end of the runway. Last plane out.'

The Humvee hurtled along the apron. Through the windscreen, Nabil saw a big commercial passenger jet ahead, its collision lights blinking. They raced towards it. Behind them, hundreds of desperate people spilt from the terminal and ran for the plane.

Thirty seconds later, the Humvee screeched to a halt at the bottom of a mobile passenger stairway.

'Move!' the captain said, kicking open his door. Nabil ushered his family up the steps, the wind whipping his hair, the massive engines whistling as they idled. He stepped inside the aircraft. To his left, he saw the darkened cockpit, the pilots tapping touch screens.

'Let's get those doors closed!' one of them shouted over his shoulder. Hijab'd cabin crew directed Nabil, the girls, and the soldiers into first-class seats. The rest of the plane was full, the lights dimmed and filled with silent, anxious faces. He heard the cabin door thump shut behind him and the plane started moving.

Nabil felt the pressure as the plane sped up. He took Suresh's hand in his and squeezed it, smiling. His daughter smiled back. *Praise God!* He looked beyond her to the window and saw tiny figures flashing by on the runway apron, chasing a plane they would never catch. Engines roared and then his stomach dropped beneath him as the plane nosed up into the air. He felt the thump of the raised undercarriage and saw sheer relief on the faces of the seated cabin crew. The plane climbed higher into the night sky. Silent minutes ticked by. Wispy clouds flashed past the windows, and then the plane levelled out. The seatbelt sign stayed on. Nabil leaned out into the aisle and caught the eye of a stewardess.

'Where are we going?' he asked her.

'Paris. From there, you can transit to your onward destination. All services are normal across the caliphate.'

'Good to know,' Nabil said, and for the first time that evening, he relaxed a little.

'Let's get their bags off,' Salma said, and Nabil helped his twins out of their pink backpacks. He unzipped one of them, took his daughter's things out, and dumped them on Salma's lap. 'Back in a sec.'

He unbuckled his seat belt and walked three rows back, the garish backpack dangling from a loop on his finger. The captain from Jnah looked up at him and smiled.

'That was close, eh? An exciting story to tell those kids when they get older.'

'Have you got kids?'

The captain nodded. 'Three boys. Haven't seen them for two years.'

'When you do, buy them something nice.' Nabil dropped the bag at the captain's feet and walked back to his seat. He sunk into the leather and exhaled, tired but elated. His instincts were right, after all. He'd made it.

Countless others wouldn't be so lucky.

BACK ON THE GROUND, HEAVILY ARMED MEN FORCED Heathrow's air traffic controllers out of their 280-foot tower and went to work on the equipment with sledgehammers and crowbars. Elsewhere, other teams destroyed the communications apparatus, radar dishes, and radio transmitter masts. An aviation fuel truck was driven through the glass wall of Terminal Five and set alight, and trucks, buses, cars, and coaches burned along the tarmac of Heathrow's main runways.

By the time the flight carrying Nabil and his family touched down in Paris, fires had spread across the UK's premier airport and giant plumes of oily black smoke belched into the night sky. RAF Northolt suffered a similar fate, as did Stansted Airport. At Gatwick, four airliners laden with fuel taxied onto both runways and came to a stop, nose to tail, roughly in the middle of each landing strip. Once the pilots had made good their escape, 30mm tracer rounds ignited all four aircraft, blowing them to pieces and scattering burning debris across the airfield. Like Heathrow, insurgents destroyed every usable flight system. The wilful destruction was widespread, and on a scale large enough to deny the use of all four airports to the approaching infidel army.

THE LAST COLUMN OF ISLAMIC STATE MILITARY VEHICLES began moving towards Dover port's number nine ramp and the gaping hold of the P&O vehicle ferry waiting to receive them. Aboard *The Spirit of Britain,* space was at a premium, every nook and cranny crammed with troops, support staff, and equipment. Vehicle decks bulged with armoured vehicles, trucks, and jeeps, and the air was thick with diesel fumes as troops and the ship's crew battled to secure the decks for crossing. As the last tracked vehicle clanked aboard, the propellors engaged. Alarms blared as bow doors whined shut. Deck-hands and dockworkers untethered the ship from its berth. Unlike the air terminals, the seaports would remain open, ferrying civilian passengers across the channel to the safety of the caliphate. Now that the final military-requisitioned vessel was leaving English shores, the ferries would operate on a first come, first served basis. It was going to be a chaotic situation.

For the last three years, the dock workers had witnessed a lot of comings and goings. In the early days, they'd worked the cargo ships and ferries filled with IS troops and vehicles, landing day after day, week after week. They'd seen prison ships going the other way, holds packed with captured British military personnel, police officers, and other civil servants. As the months passed, civilians followed, tens of thousands of them, never to return. There was nothing anyone could do to object. There were too many snitches around the port, and too many Dover residents had disappeared because of them. But for those who'd endured, who'd kept their heads down and their mouths shut, who'd mourned the loss of their land and liberty in silence, they would soon have their day.

As *The Spirit of Britain* churned the waters to white foam and slipped away from its berth, a small group of dockworkers stood and watched it sail into the darkness. On the pier behind them, hundreds of vehicles lay abandoned, keys thrown into the sea as a final, petulant gesture. Beyond the car park, beyond the towers of rusted shipping containers and the port buildings, thousands of people had gathered at the barbed wire fences to seek passage abroad. Further out, miles of traffic blocked every approach road to Dover.

A ship's horn droned across the port, and the dock workers saw an inbound ship moving at low knots around the harbour wall. A radio message told them to head for number seven ramp, where the empty vessel would be readied to accept the first wave of evacuees desperate to escape this green and pleasant land for the rigid embrace of Wazir's caliphate.

And the good men and women of Dover would work around the clock to see them on their way.

[20]

BRIDGE OF SORROWS

EDDIE TEXTED HIS LATEST SITREP AND SENT IT BACK TO Scotland (or wherever the 4th ISR Brigade HQ was now based) via his sat phone. The report itself was thin, confirming he was across the river and on the hunt for the mystery trucks. A few seconds later, he received an acknowledgement, but there was no update on the wider progress of the war. He was in the dark as much as the rest of London's civilian population.

He powered off the phone to preserve the battery. From the cutting floor window, he looked down onto Maiden Lane, but there wasn't much to see. The only things moving on the narrow street were stiff-legged pigeons and litter – lots of litter – being bullied around by an early morning breeze. Eddie had to give kudos to Griff. It was a good spot.

After abandoning the police car, he'd followed Griff across an empty Strand to the narrow backstreets of Covent Garden. Their destination was a fashion design shop on Maiden Lane, a business Griff had delivered flowers to on many occasions. Behind a security grill, the window display comprised a single, androgynous mannequin swathed in a silky Islamic robe. Griff had used his shoulder to make quick work of the lock, and once inside, Eddie had discovered a labyrinth of private dressing, storage, and cutting rooms, and a large kitchen diner, spread over four floors. There was a back door that led to a narrow courtyard and beyond, an alleyway with access out onto the Strand.

After Eddie had bolted the front door, they sat in the dark, listening to the sounds of the city. Big guns fired every so often, but they were distant. Eddie took the first watch and Griff slept on a couch in the client room beneath a length of purple cloth that served as a blanket. Eddie never woke him. Instead, after a couple of hours of watching and listening, he got his own head down, confident that their insertion into the West End had gone unnoticed. He stirred in a big easy chair when daylight crept across the cutting room floor.

Eddie's hand gripped the pistol on his hip when he heard a creak on the stairs. Griff appeared, yawning. 'Morning,' he said, smiling through his fatigue. He jerked a thumb over his shoulder. 'I found some brew kit in the kitchen. I hope you like your coffee black.'

'Perfect,' Eddie said.

They sat at the table in the kitchen diner, nursing steaming mugs of instant coffee. Griff winked at Eddie across the table.

'So, what are you, then? Army? Recce Reg? I know you're something like that.'

'It's that obvious, eh?'

'I'm not stupid. That lump on your right hip – it's a pistol, right?'

Eddie nodded. 'And I've got an MP5 with the rest of my kit upstairs. I'm military intelligence but that's all I can tell you.'

'I knew it,' Griff said, slapping the table. 'I always thought there was something suspect about next door. Different people coming and going over the years, all of them friendly enough, but you couldn't get two words out of 'em, you know? You're the youngest I've seen, though. They should have given you a better cover story.'

'Yeah, maybe.' Eddie felt mildly irritated. Griff had seen through him from the start. Or at least suspected something wasn't right. 'Until a few months ago, I was a regular in the 2nd Massachusetts

Battalion, 14th Infantry Brigade Combat Team, King's Continental Army Division —'

'Fuck me ...'

'My brother Kyle was killed on the Scottish border three years ago. I joined up in America, and I was in the first wave that hit the beaches in Ireland. I've been fighting ever since.'

Griff looked at him with wide-eyed awe. 'You lucky bastard,' he said.

'A lot of my friends weren't so lucky.'

'I didn't mean it like that. I'm sorry for your loss, I really am. I just wish I could've joined you, that's all. Instead of being stuck here, selling flowers.'

Eddie winked. 'You might be a little old for frontline infantry work.'

'Maybe, but I still would've joined, done my bit.'

Eddie thought about that as he finished his coffee. He pushed the mug to one side. 'While you were sleeping, I took a good look around this place. Did you know they had a basement?'

Griff nodded. 'There's nothing down there but boxes of material and big rolls of cloth.'

'Which is perfect. Follow me. I've got an idea.'

It took Eddie and Griff over 30 minutes to get everything into place. When they'd finished, boxes of material and large bolts of cloth plugged the far end of the long and narrow basement from floor to ceiling. As a final touch, Eddie brought a mannequin down from upstairs and stood it against the barricade. He brought his MP5 down too. Griff saw it slung beneath his arm and whistled.

'That's a sweet piece of kit.'

'I'm going to put a couple of rounds through it, make sure it's fully functional. You can do the same with the pistol.' He unclipped it from his belt and offered it. As Griff's hand reached out, Eddie snatched it back. 'You remember your weapon drills, right?'

Griff nodded. 'Pretty much.'

'This is a Springfield subcompact 9mm. It's got an ambidextrous thumb safety and a ten-round mag. It's light, accurate, and packs a punch.' He handed it to Griff. 'Clear it.'

Griff took it and turned the barrel downrange. 'Safety is on,' he said, checking. He released the magazine and pulled back the slide, checking the breech. 'Gun clear,' he said, locking the slide into the open position.

Eddie smiled. 'Nothing wrong with that.'

'It's small,' Griff said, weighing the gun in his hand.

Eddie dangled a strip of silk in front of Griff. 'Tear that up and stuff it in your ears.'

Taking cover behind a brick pier, Eddie and Griff took turns to fire three rounds each from both the MP5 and the Springfield. Unsurprisingly, the pistol's sharp report was louder than Eddie's suppressed weapon, but despite a slight ringing in both men's ears, it was the splintered and perforated mannequin that had fared the worst. Back in the canteen, they found a couple of tins of soup and Eddie shared a packet of noodles between them. The weapons lay at the far end of the table.

'So, what now?' Griff asked, sucking noodles through his lips.

'One of those articulated lorries is parked a few streets over, near Kingsway. I need to check it out.'

Griff nodded at the guns lying at the end of the table. 'Are we going strapped?'

Eddie got to his feet and placed his empty bowl in the sink. He turned and faced Griff. 'You should go home, mate. If anything goes wrong, you could get killed. You've got a wife and kids.'

Noodles dangled from Griff's fork as he pointed it at Eddie. 'That's true, but it's my choice.'

'I know you want to do your bit. I get it, but we're approaching the endgame now. There's no telling what might happen, and everyone will be on edge. Even walking the streets might get you killed. You should be with your family, Griff.'

The older man stared at his food, then he raised his head. 'Yeah. Maybe.'

'You've done enough. And you'll have a story to tell,' Eddie said. 'How will you get back?'

'I could cross Hungerford Bridge after dark. Might take me a couple of hours to get home, but it'll be safe enough.'

Eddie picked up the weapons from the table. 'I'll give it an hour then recce the local area, make a plan.'

'Let me know if you need help,' Griff said. 'I might as well make myself useful while I'm still here.'

THE SEPTEMBER SUN HAD DIPPED IN THE PALE BLUE SKY BY THE time Eddie and Griff left the relative safety of their hideout. Earlier, Eddie had scouted The Strand, but there were few people around. Those he noticed hurried along the pavement, bent against a fresh wind. In Trafalgar Square, where Lord Nelson had once looked out over the city with a watchful eye, a twin-barrelled anti-aircraft gun loitered beneath a sagging camouflage net. Eddie saw a family on Charing Cross Road, standing by the roadside, surrounded by luggage. The man hailed a cab – one of several, Eddie noticed – and when the minivan pulled into the kerb, the man bundled his wife, kids, and bags inside. That scene gave Eddie an idea.

He found a minicab parked on a side street to the south of Covent Garden square, a silver Toyota Prius. The thin film of dust on the windscreen and the litter gathered beneath its tyres suggested no one had used the car for a few days at least. Stealing it was a risk, but he doubted car theft was high on any cop's list of priorities right now. He used the scrambler to unlock the vehicle and drove off on battery power. He made a couple of turns and stopped on another side road close to The Strand. Griff was waiting in the shadows of an empty shop doorway. Eddie climbed out and left the door open.

'You drive. I'm your passenger, okay? If anyone stops us, I'll do the talking.'

Griff nodded. 'No problem.'

Inside the car, Griff tapped the map screen. 'Portugal Street is where that truck is, right? That's less than a mile, but we have to loop around because of the one-way system on Kingsway.'

'Good. The longer we're off the main roads, the better.'

Griff dropped the car into drive and cruised through the rat runs of Covent Garden towards Holborn. 'What d'you think will happen now?' he asked.

'Short term? Hard to say,' Eddie replied, watching the streets. 'With luck, any opposition will disappear, and our boys will roll into the city uncontested.'

'And if they make a stand?'

'Then it'll take more time, but either way, we win.'

Griff glanced in his rear-view mirror. 'I'm having trouble remembering what life was like before the invasion. That sounds mad, right? It's only been three years, but so much has changed.'

'Things will never be the same,' Eddie said, staring out of the window. 'Even England doesn't feel the same anymore.'

'You got that right.'

The Prius twisted and turned through the narrow streets. Looters had emptied all the big shops, and Griff had to swerve around piles of debris. He turned onto the wide avenue of Kingsway and headed south.

'Portugal Street coming up on the left,' he said.

'Make the turn,' Eddie said. 'Nice and easy.'

Griff slowed the Prius and spun the wheel. The street was narrow and squeezed by the surrounding buildings. Eddie saw the Peacock Theatre on his left, the windows still intact and filled with images of men and women in robes and saris. He doubted there'd be another performance anytime soon.

'Shit!'

Griff stamped on the brakes as a large group of black-clad militia fanned out across the road, arms waving at them to stop.

'Say nothing,' Eddie said through ventriloquist's lips. He stopped counting at 20. They were mostly militia, but there were some cops amongst them, too. And they were all heavily armed. They swarmed around the vehicle like bees on a honeypot. A clenched fist thumped off Griff's window.

'Turn that fucking engine off! Now!'

Eddie opened his door and climbed out. 'It's okay, guys. I've got business here.'

The uniforms closed in. Hands grabbed him and spun him around, slamming him against the Toyota. On the other side of the car, Griff was also getting searched. Eddie wasn't too worried; the guns were back at the safe house, and this was just a recce. But Eddie had to do the talking and do it fast.

'He's a cab driver,' Eddie explained to the cops searching Griff. 'I asked him to take me here.'

'Quiet,' said a man about Eddie's age, an AK-308 gripped in his hands. More hands spun him around and slammed him back against the car. Eddie winced. 'Take it easy, guys. We're on the same side.'

He looked at the faces crowding around him. Older men, fifties and sixties, unshaven and hard-eyed, and teenage boys, playing soldiers, lost in their baggy black coveralls. They carried older weapons, AKs and a couple of SA80s with iron sights. Eddie noticed everyone was wearing body armour and webbing, which was a recent development. Like their comrades at Vauxhall Bridge, they'd rigged themselves out for combat. Why? What chance would they have against seasoned troops?

'Make a hole!'

A woman pushed her way through the surrounding uniforms. She stood in front of Eddie, forties, tall and thin, her face lined, her dirty blonde hair scraped back off a lined forehead. Her coveralls were dark blue, and she wore an assault rig across her narrow chest. The sergeant's tabs on her epaulettes shouted, *leader,* because no one else was wearing any. She carried an AK-12 and magazines filled her pouches. Her lined brow furrowed. 'State your business.'

Eddie folded his arms and leaned against the Prius, calm and casual. 'My boss is a commercial landlord. He's got me riding around town, making sure his buildings are secure.'

The woman's eyes narrowed. 'Now?'

'I found this, sarge.' A shaven-headed kid with a pimply chin emerged from the Prius with the prop taken from the safe house, a large metal loop filled with keys of all descriptions. He jangled it in his hand. 'They must be his. To get into buildings.'

'Ya think so, Sherlock?' The sergeant spat on the ground and refocused on Eddie. 'Which one is yours?' she said, her breath stinking of cigarettes.

'That one.' Eddie pointed to the ransacked hairdressers on the corner behind her. Glass from the windows carpeted the pavement.

The woman grinned with yellowed teeth. 'Hope your boss is insured.' Her laugh sounded more like an animal bark, and it didn't last long. The shutters came down again, and she held out her hand. 'Show me your ID.'

Eddie gave her the photo card issued back up in Scotland. The woman studied it for a moment and handed it back. 'Do yourself a favour. Get out of the area and don't come back.'

'What about you?' Eddie asked her.

The woman spat again. 'What about me?'

'All of you, I mean.' Eddie looked at their faces. 'You've done your best, but maybe you should think about saving yourselves. Before the Alliance gets here.'

'We'll take our chances.'

Eddie tried his best to sound like he gave a shit. 'But you could get killed.'

'Not before we kill some of them.' She half-turned towards the narrow lane behind the theatre. Eddie could only see a corner of the truck – still parked in the same spot he'd seen on the satellite images – but there was something on the flatbed, something big, something covered with a tarpaulin. And above the truck, a camouflage net rippled in the breeze. Eddie heard the spotty youth talking.

'It's not just our group, you know. There're loads of us all over the city.'

The woman wheeled on him like a Rottweiler. 'Shut your fucking piehole!'

The kid wilted, and Eddie almost felt sorry for him. His eyes flicked back to the flatbed, and he glimpsed two bearded men chatting. They both wore civilian clothes and tactical vests, and they carried themselves and their weapons with a confidence that marked them out as seasoned soldiers. Eddie winked at Sergeant Hagface. 'Don't worry, I didn't hear a thing.'

She didn't look convinced. 'Best be on your way, then. And if you're running for the coast, be advised – Charing Cross is closed and the last train leaves London Bridge at sundown.' She stepped closer, another sneer twisting her mouth. 'You might as well stay and fight. You and your driver. If you've got the guts.'

Eddie didn't blink. 'I'm no coward, but I'm not stupid either. The odds of surviving are shit.'

'Fuck the odds!' she snarled. 'This city ain't gonna fall that easy, mark my words!'

'We don't have guns or anything.'

Eddie cringed when he heard Griff's voice. The hag shot him a look. 'We can spare a couple of uniforms, and guns are no problem. You want in? Say the word. But make sure you get back here before the curfew. Some of these nippers get jumpy in the dark.' She jerked her head towards the spotty youth. His cheeks reddened.

'We know where to find you,' Eddie said.

She gave Eddie one last scornful look and turned away. 'Back to your posts! Move!'

The cops and militia broke away and disappeared down a side street. Eddie slapped the roof of the car. 'Let's go.'

Griff climbed inside, dropped the car into gear, and reversed out of the street. He didn't speak until Kingsway was in his rear-view mirror and the car was sweeping around the curve of Aldwych.

'I think I might've soiled my pants.'

'You did good,' Eddie said.

'Mate, you're an iceman.'

'Only on the outside.'

'So, what now?'

'I'll wait until it's dark, go back. I need to know what's on that rig.'
Eddie watched the cars ahead of them as the Prius slowed for the
junction. The traffic lights were out, and as they neared them, the van
in front peeled off to the left.

'Where's he going?' Griff said. 'All the bridges are closed.' The
mystery was solved a moment later.

'Waterloo's reopened,' Eddie said. He saw a civilian car travelling
across the river towards them and a couple of pedestrians heading
south. 'Quick, turn left and pull over.'

Griff obeyed, turning towards the bridge, then pulling into the
pavement. Eddie leaned forward and slapped a hand on Griff's shoulder. 'Go. Get across the river before they close it again.'

'What about you?'

'I'll walk. It's not far.'

'I didn't mean that.'

Eddie nodded. 'I know. I'll be fine. Just go, okay?'

Griff twisted around in his seat and stuck out his hand. 'Good
luck, mate.'

'I'll see you back at the flat,' Eddie said. 'Put some beers in the
fridge, eh?'

'Sure.'

Eddie saw that Griff was struggling. He was torn, but it was for
the best, and they both knew it. He climbed out and watched Griff
drive off towards the bridge.

Then Eddie turned and walked away, eager to get back to the safe
house. The bang was tremendous, the shock wave knocking him to
the ground. He lay still, his hands over his head, as a storm of debris
rained down around him. A moment later, the thunder rolled away.
Eddie pushed himself up, then he flinched as another explosion
rippled across the afternoon sky.

Then another.

And another.

The detonations marched away into the distance. Eddie stayed low, waiting for the storm to abate. Rivers of glass fell like waterfalls from the surrounding buildings. Broken blinds rattled in the breeze. The ground trembled, then became still. Eddie looked towards Waterloo Bridge and saw the Prius slewed across the road, its windows smashed, its bodywork peppered with debris. He ran towards it.

As he got closer, the driver's door swung open, and Griff fell out onto the tarmac, coughing and spluttering on his hands and knees. Eddie helped him to his feet. Griff's face was running with blood.

'What the fuck happened?' he stuttered, wiping claret from his eyes with the cuff of his hoodie.

Eddie looked south. The entire centre section of Waterloo Bridge had disappeared into the river below. A few more seconds and Griff would've disappeared, too.

'They blew the bridge,' Eddie said. 'It's gone.' His head swivelled left and right, and he saw enormous clouds of smoke and dust rising above the River Thames into the darkening sky. 'Jesus Christ, it's not just Waterloo. They're all gone.'

A MILE AND A HALF TO THE EAST, THE ENGINEERS EMERGED from the basement service ramp of *Twenty-two*, a 945-foot-tall commercial building on Bishopsgate and piled into two idling Ford Transit vans. After a headcount, the vans took off at speed, driving a short distance to the road junction of Aldgate High Street and Middlesex Street. There, a Chinook helicopter waited on the ground, its massive rotors battering the air, the sound of its twin Honeywell engines thundering off the surrounding buildings. The transit vans stopped short of the junction and the engineers climbed aboard the waiting aircraft. Moments later it lifted off, dipping its nose and heading south towards the airfield at Biggin Hill, where a fixed-wing aircraft waited to ferry the engineers back across the channel.

They'd worked hard these last few weeks, cutting supporting

columns and placing thermite charges in strategic locations across several basement floors of the towering structure. Articulated lorries had delivered tons of TNT and RDX, and the engineers had spent several days positioning those explosives around specific supporting columns. They'd drilled boreholes and connected hundreds of blasting caps to smaller, primer charges. They'd run a twisting rope of electrical detonation wires up from the bowels of *Twenty-two* and onto Bishopsgate itself, laying hundreds of metres of cables before terminating them at a switch-box mounted inside a cargo van and connected to a remote RF signal repeater.

The stage had been set. Now the show could begin.

ACROSS THE SQUARE MILE OF THE CITY OF LONDON, A SIREN wailed, long and loud. Oblivious civilians, already scared witless by the proximity of war, craned their necks to the sky and wondered what was coming. Those who knew were already at a safe distance. That included General Baban, watching from the roof of an investment bank on Cheapside. He was far enough away to be safe, yet close enough to dispense with any visual aids. He wanted to see this with his own eyes.

'We're ready, General Baban.'

He turned and saw the chief architect and structural engineer hovering behind him. The engineer had a phone clamped to his ear. Surrounding them were several of Baban's leadership team, including his 2IC, Lieutenant-Colonel Naji. No one wanted to miss this.

'Do it,' Baban said, turning back to watch.

He heard the structural engineer mutter a command into his phone. Baban held his breath. A moment later, a low detonation rumbled across the city, and birds wheeled into the sky over Bishopsgate. Baban smiled. It would be the first of many.

. . .

Across the basement floors of Twenty-two, thermite charges ignited, cutting through dozens of massive steel columns like hot knives through butter. A moment later, the primary charges blew, sending a massive shockwave through the foundations of the building. The TNT and RDX detonated a millisecond later, obliterating the already weakened steel columns. With nothing left to support it below ground, the 400,000-ton building stepped off its foundations and leaned over ...

Above ground, the subterranean explosions stripped the glass skin from several floors of Twenty-two and blasted it across the street. The air was thick with dust and shrilling alarms. Broken glass showered onto the street below as an immense shockwave rippled up the tower's façade. The ground shook, and then the massive structure tilted as its subterranean support structure crumbled to dust. Tortured steel screamed in agony as the once-magnificent tower fell sideways at free-fall speed and smashed into the ancient streets below, pulverising everything beneath it and crushing the southeastern corner of the ransacked Bank of England to dust. The shock rippled outwards, and a huge pyroclastic cloud barrelled through the city, engulfing everything in its yellow, choking path. The sound travelled much further, an audible earthquake of falling steel, shattered glass, and broken stone rolling like thunder across the city. Those who heard it trembled.

As did the ground, as other buildings across the city fell too.

[21]

FLIGHT TO NOWHERE

IT TOOK BERTIE OVER SIX HOURS TO DRIVE THE FORTY-SEVEN miles from Hampstead to Farnborough Airport. The journey had started well enough, and most of the back roads around north-west London had been clear, but towards Hammersmith they ran into a traffic jam of immense proportions. Bertie had swung the van around and headed in the opposite direction, but it took over an hour to get clear of the congestion.

Sitting next to him, Cheryl had served as his guide when the sat nav had failed. She studied a road map by torchlight, plotting alternate routes and giving Bertie options, and he wondered why Cheryl had chosen a life of domestic servitude rather than making her own way in the world. Yes, she'd married and had a child, but she was smart. Despite Bertie's former career as a black cab driver, Cheryl was often two or three routes ahead of him. He told her he was rusty. That made them both smile.

But the others sitting behind them weren't laughing. Judge Hardy's wife was an emotional wreck, and her constant nervous chirping in Bertie's ear was getting on his nerves. She would bounce between long silences and short periods of panic, especially when

186

they got caught in a traffic jam. The Witch was quiet mostly, unless she was snapping at Mrs H or berating Bertie for driving them into another chaotic tailback. As for the judge, well, he was doing his best to calm his wife and deflect The Witch's anxiety. Bertie didn't envy him. *Talk about a rock and a hard place*, he thought.

In west London, Bertie swerved the chaos and cut through Acton and Ealing. There, something hit the side of the van with a heart-stopping bang. In Southall, Cheryl had spotted the makeshift road-block ahead of them and yelled a warning. Thanks to her quick thinking, she'd got them out of trouble and guided them south. Passing through a road tunnel beneath the M4, they'd all seen the gridlock above them and realised the whole of west London was at a complete standstill. So, Bertie kept to the less-used routes all the way out to Farnborough.

Passing through Chertsey, he saw a huge fire to the west and figured that something terrible had happened at Heathrow Airport. Mrs H had blubbed in his ear. The Witch said nothing, her nose pressed against the window, and Judge Hardy had popped a pill from a box in his pocket. Cheryl ignored it and urged Bertie to do the same as she studied the map. Bertie did as he was told.

Now they were travelling on a wooded road, where the lights of Farnborough Airport glowed above the trees. Dawn was fast approaching, and Bertie's hopes of a clean getaway rose. With a little more luck, they'd be in France by midday, Provence by midnight. It was quiet in the van, just the drum of the road and the hum of the heater. The Witch was asleep, her head lolling from side to side, her mouth open. Next to her, the judge's eyes were closed, and his chin rested on his chest. But Mrs H was wide awake, her face a pale mask of dread, but at least she'd stopped her ceaseless twittering. Next to him, Cheryl sat in silence, lost in her thoughts. Bertie hoped they were about him.

He saw a parking sign ahead and pulled into a cutaway. the judge and The Witch jerked awake. Bertie shut off the engine and opened his door. 'I need to stretch my legs,' he told the others. Cheryl joined him, and Bertie was grateful for the predawn silence of the woods and the cool breeze on his face. He was more tired than he realised. His eyes stung and his back ached. He stretched and yawned.

'Are you okay?' Cheryl asked him. She slipped her fingers between his and squeezed.

'I'm fine. Tired. But we're here now, thanks to you.'

'So, what's the plan?'

'We should talk to the others.' Bertie let go of her hand and yanked open the side door. His passengers represented the cream of British society under the caliphate's rule, and two of them were – *had been* – amongst the most powerful people in Britain. Now they looked like three anxious pensioners on a day out from the nursing home.

'We should go over the plan,' he told them.

Judge Hardy nodded. 'That's a good idea, Bertie. I'm sure the ladies would appreciate an update.'

Bertie put one foot on the van's step and leaned inside. He saw Cheryl drift a few paces away, watching the road. Bertie hadn't even thought to ask her. She'd done it instinctively. He refocused.

'I've spoken to a contact at Farnborough. For a price, he'll put us on the first available plane to France.' He lifted the sleeve of his sweatshirt. 'We use our travel bands to get access to the airport, then I'll find him and do the deal.'

'Bribery.' The Witch wrinkled her nose as if she'd detected a pungent fart. 'Such a grubby business.'

'I'll have to use some cash, Lady Edith.'

She scowled and tutted. 'How much?'

'For all five of us, plus the contents of the van, I'm guessing somewhere between $20-50,000.'

'Outrageous!'

'Edith, please,' Judge Hardy said. 'What's a few thousand dollars compared to the safe transportation of your precious artworks? They're worth hundreds of millions, for God's sake. If we have to pay the piper, so be it.'

The Witch growled and shifted in her seat. 'I hope you're recording these expenses, Bertie.'

'Of course,' he lied. 'Now, I suggest we get going. Have your wristbands and your ID cards ready, but don't make a big song and dance about who you are. There might be people there who won't take kindly to us jumping the queue, so let's be subtle, eh?'

'Discretion is our watchword.' the judge smiled, tapping his nose with a finger.

Bertie rounded up Cheryl, and a few moments later, they were pulling back out onto the country road. It wasn't long before the trees gave way to the chain-link perimeter fence of Farnborough Airport, and Cheryl guided Bertie towards the main entrance. Even from a distance, he could see jeeps and armoured vehicles parked outside the gates, so he slowed the Mercedes. He didn't want to spook any of the soldiers who stood beneath the white glare of security lights. Bertie swallowed a sudden bout of panic. Did they know about Al-Huda? Had they flagged his name? Cheryl didn't think so. She doubted any of the computer systems were still operating, which was a good point. Even so, the CID officer's mobile phone felt like a burning hot coal in his coat pocket.

He stopped the van at the security gate and flashed his ID card at the nearest soldier. Gold swords glinted beneath the halogen lights. More soldiers surrounded them, their eyes trying to penetrate the privacy glass. An officer stepped out of the booth with a clipboard. Bertie showed him his ID and the green loop around his exposed wrist.

'Do you all have them?' the officer said, staring past Bertie. The others raised their hands, and the officer smiled. 'You're lucky. I've turned away many people in the last 24 hours. D'you know where you're going?'

Bertie shook his head. 'I've been told to ask for Raymond Salla.'

The officer nodded. 'He's with flight operations. Over that way.' He pointed towards a collection of distant buildings. 'Turn right and follow the road to the first building you come to. He's in there. Or was. It's all a bit chaotic right now.'

'Thanks very much,' Bertie said and waited for the barrier to shiver upwards before driving beneath it. The relief in the van was almost palpable.

'Thank God,' Margaret muttered.

'Well done, Bertie,' Judge Hardy said.

'Yes, good job,' The Witch echoed.

Bertie glanced at Cheryl, and she gave him a smile. It said, *You're a rockstar, Bertie*, but they both knew they weren't out of the woods just yet.

He followed an access road that looped around the perimeter fence. A sudden roar filled the vehicle and Bertie saw a plane lifting off into the brightening sky. It was a small jet, Bertie noticed. They would need something bigger.

'A question, Bertie. How do you know this person?'

Bertie glanced at the judge in his mirror. 'Daly had arranged a charter flight for his National Assembly cronies. All the details were in his private papers. He'd given this guy Salla an upfront payment of twenty grand. I called Salla up, told him we might need to move fast. He said if I bring cash, we're golden.'

'He sounds like a ne'er-do-well,' The Witch said. 'I hope you know what you're doing, Bertie.'

'Don't you worry, Lady Edith. We'll be on a plane to France by the time the sun comes up.' *Ungrateful cow*, Bertie added, silently of course. But The Witch had a point. Could they trust anyone right now?

The terminal building loomed ahead, a modern, single-storey glass and steel cube. Bertie thought it would be brightly lit, but all he saw was darkness behind a wall of dark glass. He stopped outside and switched off the engine.

'It looks deserted,' Cheryl said.

'Pass me the envelope, love.' She reached into the glove box and handed him a thick brown packet. Inside was $25,000 in $100 bills.

There was another envelope in the glove box with the same amount. Bertie had more money stashed in strategic envelopes around the van just in case more palms needed to be greased, but he thought 25 might do the trick, especially as things were getting desperate. 'Wait here. I'll be back shortly.'

'Be careful.'

Another aircraft lifted off into the dawn sky as he yanked open the glass door and stepped inside the building. From a back office, a weak shaft of light fell across the reception desk and onto the polished black floor of the foyer. Bertie approached the desk, his trainers squeaking on the tiles and echoing around the silent building.

'Hello?'

A single light burned in the office behind reception, and Bertie saw papers and brochures scattered across the floor. A minute passed. The low rumble of jet engines filled the foyer. Bertie stepped around the reception desk and checked the office. He saw a desk, a full ashtray, and a half-empty mug of coffee. He touched it – still warm. The wheeled chair was at an angle as if somebody had recently vacated it.

Bertie stepped back out to reception. Laughter drifted along a dark corridor leading away from the foyer. Bertie followed it, his senses on full alert. Now he heard voices, foreign ones. The last door on the left was open, but only a little. Bertie peered through the gap. Another office, and beyond it, a glass wall that overlooked a staff car park surrounded by landscaped grounds. Bertie saw several soldiers and civilians smoking and chatting as they rummaged through the boot of an estate car, one of several that were parked behind the building. There were clothes and suitcases scattered everywhere, even on the grass—

Bertie's skin crawled. Not clothes or luggage. He was looking at dead bodies.

He backed away, then hurried to the foyer. He was halfway to the main door when he heard a raised voice behind him.

'Excuse me!'

Bertie stopped and turned around. He smiled at the short, bald man in a white shirt and tie who stood staring at Bertie as he buckled his trouser belt. A clerical type. 'I thought this place was empty.'

'What d'you want?'

'I'm looking for Raymond Salla.'

'Who are you?'

'I spoke to him on the phone. He said he'd arrange transport for me and four others.' Bertie thrust out his arm and pulled the cuffs of his coat and sweatshirt back. 'We've all got special passes. From Secretary General Al-Tahir himself.'

The clerk strolled towards him, his hands thrust into his pockets. He studied the wristband, then he looked up at Bertie and smiled. 'You must be VIPs. How much luggage have you got?'

'Not much,' Bertie lied.

The clerk cocked his head. 'Drive it around the back.'

'Might be easier if we go straight to the plane. That way we can load everything directly on board.'

'Round the back is fine.' He looked past Bertie towards the Mercedes parked right outside the main doors. 'That's you I take it?' Bertie nodded. The man moved past him. 'I'll drive it round.'

Bertie grabbed his arm, and the clerk spun around.

'Hey, don't touch.'

'Sorry,' Bertie said, holding up his hands. 'My passengers, they're old and frightened, that's all. A stranger might upset them. I take it there's an administration fee for all of this?' He reached inside his jacket and extracted the envelope stuffed with cash. The clerk's eyes widened, the tip of his tongue darting out and licking his top lip. He gestured behind him.

'Why don't we step into my office?'

'Sure.'

Bertie followed him behind the reception desk and into the office. The clerk flopped into the chair and wheeled it into the desk. He held out his hand for the envelope.

'How much to get us on a plane?' Bertie said. There would be no plane, he knew that now. Only death awaited them here at Farnborough.

The clerk stared at the envelope in Bertie's hand. 'How much have you got?'

'25,000.'

'How many of you did you say?'

'Five.'

'The price is 20 grand each.'

'Ray said 25,' Bertie countered.

'Ray's not here.'

'I'll ring him.' He reached inside his jacket. Al-Huda's phone slipped from his hand and bounced off the clerk's desk, disappearing beneath it. 'Sorry.'

The clerk tutted and pushed his chair backwards. He ducked under the desk and popped up a moment later, the phone in his hand. Bertie brought the ashtray down on the back of his skull with all his strength. The clerk groaned and dropped to his knees. Bertie hit him again, once, twice, and then the ashtray shattered in his hand. The clerk lay face down on the carpet and Bertie heard him groan. He lifted him into the chair and snaked his arm around the man's thin neck, squeezing as hard as he could. The man's fingers plucked at Bertie's jacket, and warm blood ran across Bertie's hands. The clerk's legs thrashed as oxygen deprivation kicked in, so Bertie squeezed harder. *Die, you fucker!*

Finally, the man went limp, and Bertie let him go. He heard that faint laughter again, so he wheeled the dead clerk out into the foyer. He found a storage cupboard filled with mops, buckets, and other cleaning materials. Wheeling the body inside, Bertie shut the door and hurried back across the foyer.

Cheryl leaned over and opened his door. Bertie climbed inside and started the engine. He dropped the van into gear and drove back towards the main gate.

'Bertie?' Cheryl said.

'Change of plan,' Bertie told her.

The Witch piped up behind him. 'What's happening, Bertie? Tell me!'

'Be quiet! Don't say a word until I tell you!'

Soldiers turned towards him as he approached the security gate. He felt Cheryl's hand on his arm, and he snatched it away. 'Not now, love.'

'You've got blood on your hands,' Cheryl said, her voice calm and measured. Bertie cleaned them as best he could, then shoved the bloody tissue in his pocket as he stopped in front of the barrier. He lowered his window and forced a sheepish smile. The same officer frowned as he stepped out of the booth.

'You again. Problem?'

Bertie cocked a thumb at Cheryl. 'My wife forgot her ID. They wouldn't let us board —'

'Sir, you're wanted on the radio!'

'Stay there,' said the officer, turning on his heel and stepping back into the booth.

Bertie wondered if he could ram the barrier at low speed. Even if he could, they wouldn't outrun the bullets that would surely follow. Maybe the officer would take an envelope and let them go. Maybe.

Bertie watched him inside the booth, speaking into a walkie-talkie. He stared at Bertie, his face grim, and he nodded several times. Bertie took the envelope out of his pocket and left it in his lap.

The officer put the radio down and stepped outside.

And drew his gun.

'We've got trouble at another gate. If you leave this airfield now, you're on your own, do you understand?'

Bertie nodded several times. 'Yes.'

'Heathrow and Gatwick are both gone. My advice would be to head for the coast, try your luck there.'

'Thanks,' Bertie said.

The security barrier shuddered upwards. The officer slapped the side of the Mercedes and Bertie put his foot down, leaving the airfield in his rear-view mirror. He headed south, driving in silence for several minutes before he found a quiet lay-by on the other side of Aldershot. Cheryl handed him a bottle of water and he took a long swig. Behind him, the judge spoke.

'Are you okay, Bertie?'

Bertie nodded without turning around. 'Farnborough was a dead end. They were killing and robbing people like us.' He turned in his seat. 'I'm sorry. I thought this plan would work.'

'What do we do?' Mrs H said, whimpering like a frightened puppy.

In the shadows behind him, Bertie saw The Witch scowl. 'You had one job, Bertie. To find a way out. You've failed us!'

The judge snapped at her. 'Be quiet, Edith. You're not helping.' He turned to Bertie. 'So, what do we do now?'

'We do what that officer said. We head to the coast and jump on a ship.'

'But that could take hours, days,' The Witch wailed. 'We could be trapped here!'

Bertie stared at her in the mirror. 'Better than lying dead in a field.'

Next to him, Cheryl was already studying the map. 'Stay on this road, Bertie. I'll tell you when to turn.'

'Right you are, love.'

He dropped the van into gear and drove off, his hopes of reaching safety fading with each mile.

[22]
WAR DRUMS

THE SKY WAS BLACK, AND THERE WERE NO STARS. HARRY STOOD
on the empty beach, watching luminous waves crashing on the shore
in front of him. He wore black trousers, boots, and a combat jacket,
but he didn't feel cold because there was no wind. The beach
stretched away on either side of him, endless. Behind him, sand
dunes towered into the inky blackness. Waves pounded the shore.
Harry watched them in silence. The man standing next to him broke
that stillness.

'I like it here. It's peaceful.'

Harry didn't answer, didn't turn his head.

'I didn't expect to be here,' the man continued. 'I thought they
would send me somewhere else.'

Harry knew what the man meant. 'You don't deserve to be here.'

'Neither do you.'

'No one's perfect.' Harry looked up into the sky. Where were all
the stars? The waves boomed, then hissed as they retreated. 'I've
always tried to do the right thing.'

Next to him, the man laughed. 'Sure. Keep telling yourself that.'

Harry turned to look at him. Black blood poured down the man's face, and Harry could see the beach through the gaping hole in his forehead.

'You murdered me in cold blood,' Vidich said. 'Was that the right thing?'

He screamed and lunged at Harry—

HARRY JERKED AWAKE, HEART THUMPING IN HIS CHEST. HE threw back the covers, swung his feet to the carpet and rubbed his face. The nightmare was now a recurring one, but he wasn't sure why. A counsellor would probably say it was guilt, but Harry felt no remorse. Vidich had deserved to die. So, maybe it was stress, the invisible tormentor, the go-to pretext for a vast multitude of ailments. Harry used to thrive on stress. Now he was drinking to take the edge off. So, he had to be careful, keep his concerns to himself. When people heard stress, they made the instinctive leap to nervous breakdown. For a prime minister, especially one who'd suffered a previous episode, that would not do at all. He reached for his satellite phone and speed-dialled Lee Wilde. His chief of staff answered after a single ring.

'Lee, find me a doctor, would you? No, it's nothing serious, just the usual aches and pains. Within the hour, please.'

IT WAS A SHORT RIDE BY JLTV TO LUTON UNIVERSITY Hospital. There were civilian ambulances and military vehicles parked everywhere, so Harry's three-vehicle convoy didn't look out of place. It snaked around the facility and stopped outside a catering service entrance. In a discreet examination room, a junior captain had diagnosed Harry with nothing specific and suggested that, given his slightly raised blood pressure, he was probably suffering from stress and mild exhaustion. He needed rest. Harry told the doctor he needed to win a war first, so he prescribed something to help him sleep. Neither mentioned anything about alcohol.

Luton Airport had grown into a huge military camp. Planes and helicopters flew in and out continuously, and the noise wasn't helping Harry's nerves. Thankfully, they'd found him new quarters, the director's suite of a private jet company, which also boasted a decent conference room. When Harry returned to it, his chief of staff was chatting with Faye Junger. They got to their feet as Harry closed the door.

'Faye? What are you doing here?' He looked around the room as if the rest of the Cabinet might be hiding, waiting to surprise him. A ridiculous thought. 'Where are the others?'

'Back in Cumbria,' Junger said. 'I thought I would travel down, talk to you in person.'

'The Cabinet has concerns,' Wilde said. 'I told Faye there was nothing to worry about.'

Harry slipped his coat off and sat down, inviting the others to sit. 'What concerns?' He stared at Junger, who'd dressed appropriately for her visit, wearing a black polo neck, olive-green trousers, and sturdy boots.

'They think – *we* think – you're being a little irresponsible.'

Harry folded his arms. 'Really? In what way?'

'Your proximity to the frontline. It puts you in danger.'

Harry's nostrils flared. 'I'm sick of hearing this argument. I need to see what's going on. Talk to people. I can't do that in Cumbria.'

'As deputy PM, I should remind you that your focus should be on governmental matters.'

'A government at war,' he reminded her. 'I will not make the same mistakes as past prime ministers. If I'm sending our young men and women into danger, they need to know I'm prepared to take the same risks.'

'You've proved yourself already, Harry.'

'To the military, perhaps, but the public should see my face, hear my voice.'

'Little early to be campaigning, don't you think?'

Harry scowled. 'Don't be facetious, Faye. This war has devastated many of our towns and cities. I've seen some terrible things.'

She raised a pencilled eyebrow. 'Is that why you're seeing a doctor?'

Harry flashed Wilde an angry look. 'That was in confidence.'

Wilde stood his ground. 'Faye's your deputy. I thought she had a right to know given the circumstances.'

'My health is nobody else's business.'

Faye leaned forward in her chair. 'You're wrong, Harry. Your health is the business of this nation. If you were killed or seriously wounded, that would be a huge psychological blow to the British public.' She paused, then said, 'Or if you were ill.'

'I'm not ill.'

'Either way, I should know if there's something to be concerned about.'

Harry rapped the table with his knuckle. 'To be clear, I am fit and healthy, as confirmed by the doctor this morning. End of discussion.' He smiled, hoping she wouldn't see through the façade.

'Good to know,' Junger said. 'So, back to the question in hand – when are you returning to Cumbria? Ally wants to get the press in, establish the face of the new British government, lots of stills around the table. She has a plan.'

Harry grimaced. 'Tell her to park it. I want to wait until the end of major combat operations —'

Wilde jumped to his feet. He was staring at his phone. 'Baghdad is making an announcement in the next few minutes.'

Harry stood too. 'We should get to the comms room.'

'... AT MIDNIGHT TONIGHT, THE LAST MILITARY FORMATIONS WILL *have left the British mainland. By dawn tomorrow morning, all Islamic State forces will have officially withdrawn from Britain. Any troops, militia, and law enforcement personnel still on British soil must lay down their arms and surrender to representatives of the*

Atlantic Alliance. Failure to do so will directly violate the orders of the Islamic State military high command. In the meantime, safe passage must be given to British citizens and other displaced persons wishing to return to the caliphate's European territories. This announcement has been authorised by His Holiness the Grand Mufti Mohammed Wazir, chief cleric of the Islamic State and supreme ruler of the caliphate. Peace be upon him, and upon all his citizens ...'

THE TV BLINKED OFF. HARRY STOOD AT THE HEAD OF THE table, his arms folded, his emotions swirling. He didn't know quite how he felt. Elated, yes. Relieved, certainly, but as all eyes in the cramped, stuffy comms room turned to him for comment, another emotion bubbled its way to the surface. Apprehension. He looked at the surrounding faces - Wilde and Junger; Nick Wheeler and his senior staff; and a couple of American uniforms, all waiting for him to speak. He broke the silence.

'Well, that makes it official, then.'

'It's not over yet,' Wheeler said, his tone cautionary. Which is exactly how Harry felt. 'Wazir is covering his arse,' the deputy CDS continued. 'He's telling us that if another nuke goes off, it's nothing to do with him.'

'He's not that stupid,' Harry replied. 'Give us the room, please general.'

The cramped comms room emptied quickly. Harry waited until the door was closed and sat down.

Wilde beamed. 'You did it, Harry. We've won.'

Harry motioned him into a chair. 'Maybe. The fact is, there will be some very angry people in Baghdad, and we certainly can't ignore the cultural ramifications. This withdrawal will hurt Wazir, and not just politically.' He took a breath and exhaled, long and loud. 'That said, it's another milestone passed. All being well, the road to London will be clear as of tomorrow morning.'

'Those combat operations might end sooner than we think,' Junger said.

'Let's hope so. But some will refuse to accept defeat. We've seen that already, suicide attacks and suchlike. There'll be more, but the sooner we take control, the sooner the country will stabilise.'

Junger winked. 'Peace in our time, right Harry?'

'God forbid I won't say anything as rash.' He turned to Wilde. 'Lee, talk to Ally, start drafting something. Nothing presumptuous, and nothing that acknowledges Wazir's announcement, understood?'

Wilde was scribbling in his notepad. 'I'm already on it, Harry.'

'Run it by me when you're done. And I'm going into London with the first wave. We'll get some footage of me in Trafalgar Square, or Whitehall. Somewhere significant. A morale booster. Talk to Nick, set it up.'

'I'll join you,' Junger said.

Harry shook his head. 'That's not an option, Faye. Besides, we shouldn't travel together, especially to London. Line of succession and all that.'

'Then we'll travel separately.'

'No.'

Junger sat back, her eyes narrowing. 'Is it the optics? You want the world to see the Prime Minister riding on a tank into the liberated city of London, while his Cabinet cowers under the table in Cumbria.'

'Don't be ridiculous.'

'Then why risk it? As Lee says, we've won. Let the military do their job and then we'll all travel to London together. A show of unity.'

Harry got to his feet and stared at a wall map of Britain. Over three years had passed since that fateful, terrible June day. The invasion was an event that had changed the course of human history, much like the Kennedy assassination and 9/11. He held himself partly to blame for what had happened. He was prime minister after all, leader of a deeply divided country. Meanwhile, Wazir's face and message were everywhere, on trains, tubes, and buses, on the evening news, reaching out to so many of Britain's communities. Hundreds of thousands marched in his name through the streets of London. He was a poster boy for foreign interference, yet politicians and the media remained silent. On reflection, Harry realised the Caliph, had he waited, could've taken Britain and Europe without firing a shot, but that wasn't the way they did things in the caliphate. Land had to be seized and blood spilt. Harry and his government had ignored the warnings, had sought to appease Baghdad instead of confronting the sabre-rattling. He recalled a televised address that Wazir had made to a global audience. Ninety thousand had packed inside Wembley Stadium while another three hundred thousand watched from outside. And that was just in London. Harry had to go to the annual party conference to find more than a dozen admirers in the same room. Was it any wonder that things had fallen apart so quickly?

'Harry?'

He turned around. Wilde and Junger were waiting for him. 'Sorry,' he said, returning to the table. He didn't sit down. Instead, he focussed on Junger.

'This London thing, it's something I have to do, Faye. The boldness of Wazir's invasion trapped so many people there, while I had access to secret tunnels and stealth helicopters. The SAS made sure I escaped with barely a scratch. Almost everyone I met that day is now dead, and some of them gave their lives so I could live. Going back to where it all started is personal. Something I have to do alone.'

Junger held Harry's gaze and nodded. 'I understand.'

Harry gripped the back of his chair. 'When we get the official all-clear, I want you and the Cabinet in London as soon as possible. Then we'll make a big show of it, lots of press. And policy announcements too, a couple of quick wins that'll give fresh hope to the people of this country. And you'll be right by my side, Faye. How does that sound?'

The deputy PM got to her feet. 'It sounds like a plan, Harry.'

Heads turned as General Wheeler knocked and entered. Harry saw his face and braced himself.

'What is it, Nick? What's happened?'

'It's London,' Wheeler said. 'They've destroyed every major bridge across the River Thames.'

'What?'

'It doesn't end there. They've brought down several buildings too. Skyscrapers, national landmarks. The damage is extensive.'

Earlier, Harry had felt apprehensive, as if something bad was waiting in the wings. That feeling had been proved correct, and now it was replaced by another emotion. Anger, raw and burning.

'I'm going to London, Nick. I need to see this for myself.'

[23]

MARCHING SAINTS

ONE HUNDRED AND FOUR MILES OFF THE RUGGED COAST OF Cornwall, the Astute-class submarine *HMS Agincourt* nosed up through the cold, dark waters of the Atlantic Ocean before levelling its planes and slowing to a near-drift. Sixty feet above the sail, a heavy squall lashed the grey waters, but the surface conditions were not a concern for the crew inside the command-and-control centre. Once the sub's movement had stabilised, the commander snatched up his comms phone and spoke directly to the weapons officer (Weo) hunched over his console in the attack centre.

'Weo, this is command. Tube's three and four are released for launch.'

He heard the weapons officer respond, his voice calm and collected. This wasn't the *Agincourt's* first dance.

'Final target prediction is valid. All launch pre-requisites are met.'

Standing next to the commander, the XO was next to speak. 'XO concurs. Pre-requisites are met.'

The commander keyed his phone. 'Weo, command, you have permission to fire.'

'Permission to fire has been granted. T minus one minute and counting.'

No one spoke above the low, steady hum of the boat's many complex systems. It was the commander himself who broke what passed for silence aboard the sophisticated hunter-killer submarine. 'Ten seconds.'

Then ...

A muted roar as missile tubes three and four were flooded with cold seawater, followed by two solid thumps of compressed air that rippled through the submarine's bulkhead.

'Missiles away.'

'Missiles away,' repeated the commander. 'Secure for dive. Make your depth three-five-zero feet.'

As the *Agincourt* dived for the deep, the twin LRASM missiles breached the ocean's surface in a storm of white water, followed by twin blasts of white-hot flame as the weapons' booster engines fired and the missiles ripped up into a leaden sky before banking east towards the English Channel. The missiles flew in formation, 50 feet apart and 190 feet above the surface of the ocean towards their target, 254 miles to the east.

'For God's sake, how much further?'

Bertie felt tired and irritable. *We all are*, he reminded himself. He gripped the wheel and kept his tone upbeat. 'Just a few more miles, Lady Edith. Shouldn't take long if the traffic stays like this.'

'But how will we get on a ship?' Mrs H said. Her voice trembled, and she was tugging furiously on Bertie's last few nerves. Even the judge was losing patience.

'Be quiet, ladies. This constant jabbering isn't helping.'

The Witch snapped at him. 'Don't be rude, Victor.'

Bertie refocussed on the road as Cheryl pointed through the windscreen. 'Make the next turn. That'll take us through Woolston towards Ocean Village. The docks are right there.'

'Good work, love.'

Cheryl had been his rock, guiding Bertie across the Hampshire countryside from Farnborough Airport to the outskirts of Southampton, while avoiding the uncertainty of the main roads. They'd stopped once, on a quiet country lane with rolling fields on either side, so people could relieve themselves and stretch their legs. The Witch had been mortified by the prospect of taking a leak *al fresco*, and Bertie had smirked when he saw her little grey head poking up from behind a bush, twisting left and right like a frightened bird as she emptied her bladder. *Oh, how the mighty fall.* Cheryl had caught him relishing in the old bag's discomfort and given him a warning nudge. Bertie had promised to behave himself.

Back on the road, the radio was devoid of working stations, and the regime's messages had stopped broadcasting, along with the looped music. They'd almost given up trying to find anything when a stern American voice had filled the van, doing nothing to soothe fragile nerves.

Bertie made the turn towards Woolston, and Cheryl announced it was less than three miles to Southampton docks.

'Not far now,' Bertie said.

'If the Americans want us to stay off the roads, maybe we should heed their warning,' Mrs H whined like a frightened pup. The Witch duly chewed her out.

'And how do you propose we get on a ship if we do as they say?' she said. 'You must get a grip on yourself, Margaret.'

So, The Witch has found a little Dutch courage, Bertie realised. He knew why. His own spirits were rising with each passing mile. The Portsmouth Road was busy with traffic, all of it heading towards the coast, but it was moving, and that was good enough for Bertie. Outside, tree-lined roads gave way to suburban housing estates and rows of shops before the trees closed in again. If they kept up the pace, they could be dockside in less than 20 minutes. Behind him, Judge Hardy posed a question.

'Have you thought about the boarding process, Bertie? There are plenty of ships at Southampton, but I can't recall seeing roll-on, roll-off ferries.'

The Witch tutted before Bertie could answer. 'How could you possibly know, Victor? Are you an expert on the workings of this port?'

'Margaret and I have sailed from here many times, back when we used to cruise. Cunard operates out of Southampton, you know.'

'Fascinating,' she said scowling, then she leaned between the front seats. 'Bertie, do you foresee any problems getting this vehicle aboard a vessel?'

Bertie was about to answer when his skin prickled with a sudden rush of dread. He hadn't considered the possibility of not finding a ship. This was Southampton, after all. But maybe Judge Hardy was right. Maybe no vehicle ferries were sailing from Southampton. What then?

Once again, Cheryl came to his rescue. 'The Red Funnel ferry ships cars and lorries, Lady Edith. They go to the Isle of Wight and back. But they could just as easily go to France, couldn't they?'

'Another expert.' The Witch leaned back in her seat and tutted again. 'This is quite unacceptable, Bertie. This vehicle is literally worth hundreds of millions of pounds, and we don't have a definitive plan to get us to safety.'

Bertie bit his tongue. 'We did, Lady Edith, but things have fallen apart quicker than we thought.'

'Your run-in with Al-Huda was a blessing in disguise,' Judge Hardy told her. 'Otherwise, we'd still be in London. Imagine that.'

Bertie glanced at the mirror. 'I've got money, Lady Edith. That talks. We'll be able to buy our way aboard any ship.'

'You're developing a knack for frittering money, Bertie. Remember, it isn't yours. Once we're in France, I'll expect you to provide an account of your expenditure.'

'I'll get right on it,' Bertie said through gritted teeth.

Cheryl lifted her nose out of the map. 'There's a mini-roundabout coming up. You should see a toll bridge there, the Itchen Bridge. The docks are on the other side.'

'Good girl,' Bertie said. He shifted in his seat and gripped the wheel a little tighter. The road ahead snaked around a gentle bend of trees and then the mini roundabout came into view. Beyond it, Bertie saw a line of toll booths. Even from a distance, he could see all the barriers were open and cars were passing through unimpeded. Bertie drove over the roundabout and passed an empty toll booth. Abandoned cars littered the side of the road. Bertie pumped the brakes as he entered the bottleneck of vehicles, his big steel bumpers warding off other drivers as they funnelled onto the narrow bridge.

'There, look!' Judge Hardy said.

Bertie saw them too, the smoking stacks of a giant ship towering over several distant blocks of waterfront apartments. And it wasn't the only one. As the bridge rose above the estuary, Bertie looked down at the water and saw it filled with boats of all types: cruisers, tugs, RIBs, dinghies, sailing boats, even a couple of old navy landing craft packed with people, all heading out towards the open sea. Bertie had never seen anything like it.

'Jesus, it's like Dunkirk in reverse.'

Cheryl screamed, 'Watch out!'

'Shit!' Bertie slammed on the brakes. The traffic ahead had slowed, forming a long line of burning brake lights snaking into the marina at Ocean Village. The Mercedes screeched to a halt just inches from the tail of the Volvo 4x4 ahead of him.

'Jesus,' Bertie said. He leaned on the wheel, cursing himself. What if he'd hit it? What if he'd cracked the radiator or busted the steering? *Wake up, Bertie!*

He rubbed his eyes and opened his window. Cool, salty air filled the van, and he took a few deep breaths. People streamed by along the pavements, hundreds of them, entire families wheeling wheelchairs, luggage, and kids' buggies, their lives crammed into holdalls and shopping bags, their faces frantic. According to the Yank, civilians would be allowed safe passage, but no one was buying it. All

Bertie had seen for the last 16 hours was panic. He felt for the rubber band beneath the cuff of his hoodie and rolled it between his fingers. He doubted any of the mob outside would have such a golden ticket wrapped around their wrists.

'Are we stuck?' The Witch asked, her voice like sandpaper.

Bertie shook his head. 'No. It's moving. Look.' And it was, albeit slowly. Bertie didn't know much about docks, but he knew cruise lines always had giant car parks for their passengers. 'I'm heading for those big ships,' he told them. 'They'll get us on board.'

The judge smiled, his first since the sun had risen. 'You're the boss, Bertie.'

And he was, but not for long. When they got to France, things would go back to normal, with Bertie at The Witch's beck and call. But he didn't mind one bit. This time, he'd have Cheryl by his side. And being in France wouldn't be too much of an ordeal, given the luxury waiting for them. The weather would soften the blow too, a mix of mild, short winters and long, glorious summers. If they were patient, they could be back in the UK in a couple of years. That would be the hard part, convincing The Witch to let them go, but there was plenty of time to come up with a plan.

He leaned over the wheel and looked up into the sky. The cloud cover was low and grey, and to the west, an ominous black wall threatened something worse. A storm was coming, but with luck, they'd all be across the channel before it hit.

Bertie smiled. Things were finally going to plan.

THE MISSILES BEGAN LOSING HEIGHT, SKIMMING OVER THE SEA before making shore and rising over the town of Weymouth, where an armada of small and medium-sized vessels sailed in and out of the harbour. In a moment they were gone, leaving the town behind, and thundering out over Weymouth Bay before making land once more and rumbling across the Dorset countryside.

The weapons flew at high subsonic speeds, and the ominous

black shapes that streaked low across the squally sky frightened those who saw them. They flashed above the northern suburbs of Bournemouth and through the smoke and fires of burning planes littering the runways at Bournemouth International airport. They skimmed over the New Forest, scattering wild horses in their wake. As they flew, the missiles received updated targeting data and a real-time battlefield snapshot from an orbiting US military satellite. That target was just over six miles away, which meant they had less than forty seconds to live.

The missiles lost height, the navigation software making tiny course adjustments to ensure an optimal path of attack. They boomed over the traffic chaos on Marchwood bypass and broke the windows of the Oaklands rest home. The land fell away, and Southampton's vast network of docks lay ahead. A French frigate was the first and only enemy vessel to see the incoming threat and opened up with its 20mm cannon. The rounds fell behind the fast-moving missiles, decapitating the smokestacks of the Marchwood power plant. The noses of the Long-Range Anti-Ship Missiles dipped in a perfect choreography of death as they made their terminal dives.

Their target was the *MV Star Khalij*, a fully loaded container ship now churning up the mud of Southampton Water just a few feet beneath its keel. Inside its cavernous hold and stacked in vast towers on its deck were containers filled with every conceivable type of ammunition and explosive ordnance used by the Islamic State forces: bombs, rockets, short-range missiles, artillery shells, ammunition of all calibres, and hundreds of tons of military-grade explosives. Ordinance stores around the country had been emptied and the stockpiles shipped to the ports of Southampton and Portsmouth. The *Star Khalij* and its precious cargo were setting sail for Karachi, Pakistan. There, the ordinance would be unloaded and transported to the Chinese front.

The missiles screamed across Southampton Water and hit their target, slamming the ship sideways. The 1000-pound fragmentation warheads sliced through the double hulls at the bow and stern, sending a crushing shock wave and a white-hot fireball through the belly of the *Star Khalij*, igniting the stored ordinance in a blast of such power that it lifted the ship out of the water and vaporised it in an instant.

BERTIE'S EYES BARELY REGISTERED THE DETONATION, OR THE shock wave that thundered towards them at a mile a second, slamming into the van. But he heard the explosion, a terrifying crack of thunder that shook heaven and earth, jolting the bridge beneath them and sucking the air from Bertie's lungs. The windscreen cracked, and Bertie saw a small car roll across the road and hit the safety rail, before flipping over the edge and plunging to the estuary below. An enormous black and white mushroom cloud engulfed Southampton Water and the docks, boiling up into the sky where the cloud base had been ripped away by the force of the blast. Through the smoke, there was nothing left of the Ocean Village marina complex or the waterfront apartment blocks.

Cheryl —

She was okay, coughing and crying at the same time. He turned around. The judge had his arms over the heads of both women, and through the painful ringing in Bertie's ears, he could hear their terrified howls. Cheryl grabbed his arm, her mouth working, her voice muffled. Bertie shook his head to clear it.

'What?'

'Get us out of here!' she screamed.

The engine was still running, the Mercedes idling in neutral. He dropped it into drive, and then he heard a whistling sound that grew to a screaming pitch. He flinched, and a moment later a giant piece of metal the size of a small house crashed onto the bridge, crushing cars and people, and impaling itself in the road. It was black and red and rusty, and Bertie knew it was part of a ship's hull. He heard another whistle, another scream – Cheryl this time – and another colossal piece of debris roared past the bridge with inches to spare before hitting the water below and sending up a huge geyser that swamped the road in sea water.

Bertie slammed his foot on the accelerator and threw the wheel around. The backend fishtailed, but he got it under control and headed back the way he came, towards the tollbooths and the Portsmouth Road. Debris rained around them, a storm of man-made meteorites small and large, and Bertie did his best to ignore it, to keep his eyes on the road and the urge to drive like a lunatic under control. The approaches to the bridge were clogged with traffic, but the road heading away from the docks was almost clear. Cheryl scrambled for the roadmap and Bertie watched for danger ahead, knowing that Southampton, like Farnborough, was a no-go. Those doors had been slammed shut. How many more would they need to try before they reached safety?

'Is everyone okay?' Bertie said, glancing over his shoulder. Judge Hardy had his arms around his wife while The Witch cowered against him like a frightened child. They were all pale and shaking, but they were unharmed. Thank God for the traffic jam.

The judge waved a hand. 'We're fine, Bertie. Just watch the road.'

Good advice, Bertie thought, as he swerved around a car that suddenly pulled to the side of the road. The further away from the docks he drove, the less traffic was in his way. He kept his headlights on full beam and his hazards on, hoping that would deter anyone from getting in his way.

'Keep going,' Cheryl told him, tracing a finger on the roadmap. 'Portsmouth is our next best bet. It's close, and we're bound to find a ship there.'

Bertie shook his head. 'No. After what just happened, everyone will head in that direction. It'll be chaos, and who knows if that port will be attacked too.'

Cheryl's eyes widened. 'You think that was our boys who attacked?'

'Who else could it be?'

'It might have been an accident,' Judge Hardy said. 'An oil tanker, perhaps.'

'I don't want to take the chance. Time for a new plan.'

'What plan?' Cheryl said.

He'd never seen her face so pale, and he was suddenly frightened for her. 'Find me a way around Portsmouth, then plot a route to Dover. It's far enough away from the frontline and the Alliance advance. I say we go there.'

'I say you're right,' Cheryl said. She looked at the map, then at Bertie. 'There's a road on your left, about a quarter of a mile ahead. Take that and head north.'

'Right you are, love.' He looked in the mirror. 'Make sure you're belted up back there. This ride could get bumpy.'

He reached out, gripped Cheryl's hand for a moment, then grabbed the steering wheel. He stared ahead through the cracked windscreen. The road was empty.

Bertie put his foot down.

[24]
ROCKET MAN

THE BLOOD ON GRIFF'S FACE AND HANDS CAME FROM superficial cuts caused by his windscreen shattering and falling out of the car. Eddie cleaned them using the first-aid kit in the kitchen/diner, but there wasn't much he could do about dressing the nicks on his face. He joked about Griff looking like a spotty teenager, but Griff wasn't in the laughing mood. Afterwards, Eddie cooked soup and noodles. They sat and ate, but they talked little. Griff was suffering from shock. Eddie knew from experience that it was best to talk.

'It wasn't just Waterloo Bridge they blew up,' he said, kicking off the conversation. 'It's all of them. The ones I could see, anyway. Remember all that shouting we heard as we crossed the river? That must've been the demolition teams working under the bridge.'

Griff nodded without looking up. 'What about all that dust, though? Where did that come from?'

Eddie remembered struggling back to the safe house with Griff leaning and bleeding all over him while distant detonations rumbled, and the earth shook beneath their feet. Weaving across The Strand like a pair of drunks, a wall of yellow dust had rolled towards them from the direction of Trafalgar Square. They'd dodged it easily enough, ducking into a side street, but the fog had been dense and silent, and it had given them both the creeps. Back in the safe house, Eddie had watched from the window as the air of Maiden Lane became opaque, and yellow dust settled on abandoned cars. Eddie knew it was fallout, but from what? He retrieved his sat phone and sent an update, and again ISR comms acknowledged the message, but that was it. Eddie wondered why he couldn't make a call. If the radio was to be believed, all IS troops should've left the country by now and the Alliance forces were closing in on London. He doubted there was anyone left to triangulate his phone signals, but his orders were explicit – no voice calls. And yet ... the Hajis at that truck were regular troops, which meant not everyone had gone. Why? Maybe Hawkins already knew. Maybe he'd received intel from other sources. The mystery of those trucks needed solving, and fast.

Eddie rinsed his bowl in the sink. Outside, the shadows were long, and dust devils swirled and died as streetlights blinked into life along the empty street. Griff washed his dishes and made coffee. Eddie took his black and sat down.

'I'm going back to Kingsway,' he said. 'I need to know what's on that truck. And if I can find out anything about the bridges and the other explosions, so much the better.'

Griff sat down across the table and sipped his coffee. 'I'll come with you.'

Eddie shook his head. 'Not this time, mate. I'm going armed, and I expect trouble. You've had a rough day. Just hold the fort until I get back.'

'I'm okay, really,' Griff said. 'The bridge thing shook me up. Another few seconds and I'd have been killed.'

'You're still in shock,' Eddie said. 'It's better if you stay here.'

'Is that what they said to you lot, over in Ireland? *You've had it rough today, lads. Take tomorrow off, have a lie-in.*'

Eddie put his mug down. 'That's different. They trained us for war. We were prepared.'

'I'm okay,' Griff repeated. 'I can watch your back.'

Griff stared at him, unblinking. Eddie saw a firmness there, and the man had proved he could move quickly and quietly. Eddie still had a mission to complete, and four eyes were better than two.

'You're on —'

'Sweet.'

'But remember, we're going armed. We've been lucky so far, but that could change. Probably will. So, you do as I say, and without hesitation or question, am I clear?'

'I won't let you down, Eddie. I promise.'

'Make sure you don't.'

THEY WAITED UNTIL IT WAS FULLY DARK AND THEN DROVE TO Kingsway where they left the car in a side street, its doors unlocked and the key inside. Eddie's MP5 was slung beneath his open coat, ready to go, and Griff wore the pistol on his belt. They crouched in the shadows of an office building across the road from Portugal Street. They couldn't see the truck, or any cops or militia. In fact, Eddie saw no movement at all – no vehicles, no people, nothing. After the earlier explosions, he doubted anyone would venture out on the streets until the Union Jacks were flying and the brass bands were marching along Whitehall.

Eddie watched through his spotter scope for another ten minutes. Still nothing. Earlier, he had counted 20 militia and cops. Now there was no one. Maybe the truck had gone too.

'We're moving in,' he told Griff. 'Stay close and quiet.'

Griff nodded in the darkness, and they broke cover. Lights blazed along Kingsway, and Eddie walked with purpose, neither hurrying nor strolling. He kept his head moving, watching the road, the pavements, the windows that overlooked one of London's busiest routes. If anyone was watching them, they had no way of knowing. If anyone was targeting them, they would know soon enough.

They reached the other side of the four-lane boulevard and

stayed in the shadows of the buildings. Portugal Street lay ahead, less than 50 paces to the south. Eddie's hands gripped the MP5, and he flipped the safety off with his thumb. Someone coughed close by. He froze. Griff was a statue behind him. Eddie watched the pavement ahead for shadows, guessing that someone was standing around the corner, a lone sentry maybe. But then he heard another cough, closer this time, wet and hacking. Then the sound of someone spitting. That's when Eddie saw the narrow alleyway just ahead. He signalled to Griff and crept towards it, peering around the edge.

A figure. Vulnerable too.

He ducked into the alley, the MP5 up in his shoulder. He powered up his barrel torch and blinded the woman squatting in the dark, her trousers gathered around her boots. She dropped her cigarette and reached for the AK-12 propped against the brickwork.

'Don't fucking move,' Eddie hissed, the thin cone of light forcing the woman to squint. It was her, the hag-faced cop sergeant from his earlier encounter. 'Put your hands on your head. Do it.' He jerked the gun barrel in her face. The hag did as she was told, but she did it slowly, her eyes never leaving Eddie's. Griff appeared by his side. 'Take her gun and watch the street,' Eddie said. A terrible stench assaulted his nostrils. 'All these empty buildings and you couldn't find a toilet?'

She stared up at him, her hands locked behind her head. 'What d'you want?'

'I want you to stand up, turn around, and put your hands against the wall.'

The sergeant did as she was told, her trousers still bunched around her boots. Eddie saw her thigh holster there. He crouched down and snatched the pistol out of it. The hag looked over her shoulder.

'Is this the part where you and your mate rape me?' She smiled with crooked yellow teeth. 'Promise I won't scream.'

Eddie snapped off his barrel torch and waited for his eyes to readjust. 'Where are the others?'

'Chilling.'

He jammed his suppressor against her back. 'Where?'

'The theatre café.' She half turned and caught his eye in the darkness. 'You're the bloke from earlier, right? The one who drove into the street. I had a feeling about you. What are ya? Army? Security services? You ain't no cop, that's for sure.'

'Is the truck still there?' A nod. 'What's on it?' She stared at the wall. 'Speak. Or I'll leave you for dead.'

She smiled at him, wide and triumphant. 'Surface-to-air missiles.'

'Crew?'

'Five of 'em, IS regulars.'

'Why are they here?'

She shrugged. 'They don't talk to us. Our job is to protect them.'

'The explosions earlier. What was all that about?'

'They blew all the bridges across the Thames. Other buildings too. Big ones, up in the city.' She grinned. 'They even brought down Admiralty Arch.'

That explains the dust cloud that rolled up The Strand, Eddie realised. 'Why all the destruction?'

'Like I told you, we're not going down without a fight.'

'What are 20 untrained losers like you lot going to do against the might of the Atlantic Alliance?'

She turned and snarled. 'It's not just us, ya cocky little shit. There're loads of us —'

She bit her tongue and stared at the brickwork. Eddie touched the back of her knee with his gun. 'Keep talking, or I'll blow them both out.'

She turned and spat on the ground. 'They're hiding in the tube stations. Don't ask me which ones because I don't know.'

'Who's hiding?'

The hag shrugged. 'IS regulars, Jihadis, some British volunteers, like my lot.' She turned, and the sneer returned. 'The army might've left, but there are thousands of us still prepared to fight. We'll make you pay for every street corner, mark my words.'

Eddie glanced at Griff, who stood at the end of the alley, watching Kingsway. The clock was ticking, and someone would soon come looking for the hag. But he had one more question.

'Why do you fight for them? After everything they've done, the invasion, the death and destruction, the deportations, the public executions. What can they offer you that the old world couldn't?'

The hag turned around, her boots moving around in short, shuffling steps, revealing her naked lower half in all its untamed glory. She lowered her hands. Eddie didn't object. There was no point.

'That old world you speak of? I was a cleaner back then, mopping floors for minimum wage. I was nothing, a nobody. After the invasion, I got a job at Holloway Prison, as a guard. Later, they asked me to join the police. I worked hard, made sergeant. The caliphate gave me the sort of opportunities I could never have dreamed of in the old world. Back then I was scum, the lowest of the low. Now look at me.'

'You could've got out with the others. Gone to Europe.'

She laughed, her cackle echoing off the walls. 'No speakee-the-lingo, bruv. Besides, this is home, and I can promise you one thing – I'm not going back to my old life. I'd rather die on these streets.'

Her chest rose and fell, and her bunched fists trembled by her bare legs. If her trousers weren't trapping her, she would try to tear his eyes out. He pulled the trigger, and the round blew out the back of her head, smacking off the brickwork in a puff of dust. Her legs folded, and she dropped to the ground, rolling into her own excrement. Eddie turned and whistled. Griff came running. He stopped short of the body.

'Jesus. What happened?'

'If there was another way, I would have taken it.' He nodded at the AK-12 in Griff's hands. 'You know how to operate that thing?'

'Piece of piss. And better than the pistol.' He knelt beside the hag's corpse and dragged a magazine from her chest rig. The rest of her was smeared in foul-smelling shit. Griff inspected the mag, then jammed it into his pocket. 'That's two full ones,' he reported.

'Don't use it unless you have to. According to our friend here, IS fighters are hiding out in tube stations. I don't want to give them an excuse to come outside.' He pointed to the other end of the alleyway. 'Let's go this way, nice and quiet.'

Eddie led the way along the narrow channel and stopped short of the end. As suspected, it emptied into the small piazza behind the theatre. He saw the truck parked on the other side of it, and Eddie clocked the tarpaulin thrown over a very large box container. Those would be the missile canisters. Cables ran from the truck to the rooftops, where the tracking radar would be located. *It's a good spot*, Eddie thought, and he wondered how many more stood ready across the city. One such truck could cause major problems. Griff had seen dozens of them. He had to get back to the safe house and report in.

'Is that you, Sarge?'

Eddie froze. A shadow stretched across the ground in front of the alleyway. A moment later, a large silhouette wearing a militia uniform blocked the light at the end of the alleyway. The man held an SA80 in the crook of his elbow, the barrel pointed at the night sky.

'Sarge? You alright?'

Silence. Eddie brought the barrel of his gun up and spoke. 'It's me. Sarge is taking a shit.'

'Who's *me*?'

The MP5 kicked in his shoulder, and the man grunted, staggering backwards, and falling to the ground. As he died, his trigger finger spasmed —

The SA80 fired twice, two loud, rapid reports that boomed off the buildings around the piazza. Eddie's reaction was instinctive. He turned to Griff. 'We're going for the missile truck. I'll go left, you go right. You see a threat, put it down! Move!'

Eddie charged across the open piazza towards the truck. As he funnelled along the left side, a bearded man jumped down from the cab. Eddie shot him twice, and the Haji dropped to his knees, his weapon clattering on the cobbles. Eddie heard the roar of the AK-12 and figured Griff had done the same to the driver. On his left, Eddie saw a light in a ground-floor window, and cables snaked up through the cammo net towards the roof. He charged towards it, opening fire, and shattering the glass. He sprayed a dozen rounds at the figures scrambling inside, then shouldered the adjacent door open. Inside the room, a camping light had been knocked over, and Eddie counted three bodies, two of them still breathing. He put safety rounds into them as Griff stumbled in behind him, breathing hard. He gestured to the radio equipment and sophisticated laptop displays scattered around the room.

'Let's disable everything and get the fuck out of here.'

They went to work, smashing the laptops to pieces. Eddie used his combat knife to sever every cable he could find. Moments later, voices echoed outside.

'Time to go.' He pushed past Griff, and the older man grabbed his arm.

'Wait!' He pointed towards the shadowy depths of the building. 'Why don't we go that way? Out through the other side.'

Eddie shook his head. 'We don't know the layout. Trust me, we don't want to be trapped in a building.'

'But that militia mob is out there.'

'And they're badly trained. A couple of rounds over their heads and they'll bolt like frightened deer. Let's go.'

Eddie stood in the doorway. The truck was right in front of him. He risked a quick look towards the piazza and saw the cops and militia gathered around the body of the man he'd shot.

'Chill time's over,' Eddie whispered in Griff's ear. 'Go around the other side of the truck. Give it ten seconds, then put a couple of rounds over their heads. When they scatter, we bolt for the alleyway and get back onto Kingsway. Don't stop, just keep going until you reach the car.'

Griff nodded. 'Understood.'

His face was pale in the shadows of the building. Eddie slapped him on the shoulder. 'Start counting.'

Eddie crept out of the building and towards the piazza, keeping tight to the truck until he reached the rear wheels. Kneeling, he could see the militia spreading out, their heads swivelling left and right. On the other side of the truck, Griff opened up, and Eddie watched the uniforms duck and hit the ground. That was unexpected. So was the volley of fire that pinged off the truck's body and eviscerated the big double tyres. Eddie crouched behind them and returned fire, the sound of his gun drowned by the roar of the militia's weapons.

'Check your fire! You're gonna hit those missiles!'

The order echoed across the piazza, and Eddie was grateful. One stray round could send up the whole truck and take out half of Kingsway. He used the lull to return fire, picking his targets, switching from one prone figure to the other until he'd dropped at least five bodies. He shot two others as they made a mad dash towards the truck and a third, who changed his mind halfway. The shooting stopped. He heard puffing and scraping and saw Griff crawling beneath the truck towards him. Eddie scanned the piazza through his gunsight, running the red dot across windows and corners. Bodies were scattered beneath the streetlamps. One of them was still moving. Eddie turned to Griff.

'We need to go before they regroup. Ready?' Griff nodded. 'Let's move.'

They rolled out from beneath the truck and stopped short of the piazza, checking left and right. Eddie saw shadows crouched behind a parked car a hundred feet away and put two suppressed rounds through the windows. The figures bolted, sprinting further down the street.

'Go!' As they crossed the piazza, Eddie heard a voice.

'Help me, please.'

He ignored it and made the alleyway seconds later. He turned around to cover Griff and saw him kneeling next to the wounded man. Eddie hissed at him.

'Griff! For fuck's sake, move! Now!'

He didn't move, didn't look up. Eddie sprinted back and took a knee next to him, the MP5 jammed in his shoulder, his head twisting left and right. 'Move now, or I'll leave you here.'

Eddie felt a hand tugging on his trouser leg, and he looked down. It was the spotty kid from earlier. His face was plaster-white, and tears ran from the corners of his eyes. His other hand was clutching his belly, where his shredded uniform revealed a rope of bloody pink intestine slipping between the kid's fingers.

'Help me, please. I don't want to die. Please.'

'We have to do something,' Griff said, his own eyes pleading with Eddie. 'He's just a kid.'

Eddie stood and fired a round through the boy's chest. He grabbed Griff's shoulder and yanked him upright, pushing him towards the alleyway. 'Move!'

A bullet cracked by them and smacked off the wall. Eddie turned to fire and felt a savage punch to his chest. He fell to the ground, fighting for breath and unable to feel his legs. Griff grabbed his arm and pulled him along the ground to the alleyway. His chest hurt, but his heart and lungs were functioning, and blood flowed through his legs once more. *Just keep moving!*

He got to his feet and pushed Griff ahead of him. They ran down the alley, leaping over the hag's body and turning hard right onto Kingsway. Griff's trainers pounded the tarmac, the AK rattling in his hands. Across the street, he stopped and took a knee. Eddie leapfrogged him and kept going, plunging into the side streets of Covent Garden. He saw a deep shop doorway and lost himself in its black embrace. From the shadows, he had a good view of Kingsway and Portugal Street in the distance. Griff barrelled in a second later and they stood together, their breathing coming in ragged gasps.

'Watch for movement,' Eddie told him.

'Are you hit?'

'Not sure.' His upper chest throbbed. He slipped his hand beneath his tactical vest and his fingers came back dry. He tugged the shattered satellite phone out of his vest pocket.

'Mystery solved,' he said, relieved. The pain he felt was bruising, impact damage, nothing more. He was lucky. Luck like that didn't last.

'Close one,' Griff whispered. He pulled up his hood and stared across Kingsway. 'Looks like we got away clean.'

'Let's keep moving.'

It took them less than 15 minutes to get back to Maiden Lane. No one had tripped Eddie's visual alarms, and they secured the premises from inside.

Up in the kitchen/diner, Eddie stripped off his gear and inspected his body by torchlight. His diagnosis was correct, the skin on his left pectoral was bruised but unbroken. He was pulling his T-shirt back on when Griff entered the room. He unloaded the AK like a pro and left it on the table.

'You're all good, then?'

'You could've got us both killed,' Eddie said, frowning.

Griff dropped his chin. 'I couldn't help it. I saw that kid's face, and he reminded me of my own boys.' He looked up. 'I'm sorry, Eddie.'

'Forget it.' He could've chewed Griff out, but what would be the point? Besides, he had bigger problems now.

Like contacting Scotland. He had to let them know about the missiles, but how? No cell or landline networks were operating, and he'd yet to see any Alliance troops. They would know about the bridges and the other explosions, so they'd be cautious. But he had to get the intel to Hawkins, and that meant finding a working satellite phone.

'I need to get home, Eddie.'

He turned around. A tea light burned on the table, throwing the rest of the kitchen into deep shadow. Griff blew out the match and slumped into a chair.

'Zoe was right. I should never have left her and the kids.'

Eddie sat opposite, wincing as he leaned on the table. Griff chewed a nail, his eyes somewhere else. Eddie had seen that look before on the faces of those unused to killing and violent deaths.

'You'll be alright, Griff. We'll get you home, don't worry. We just have to work out how.'

'I shot that bloke by the truck. He died at my feet. I saw him take his last breath.'

'You've seen death before, Griff.'

He chewed another nail. 'Yeah, but I've never taken a man's life. Not like that. And that poor kid. Stupid kid. He didn't have to be there. Probably got talked into it.' He looked up at Eddie, his narrow face lost in shadow. 'You killed him. Why did you do that? His mates might've saved him.'

'He was dying, Griff. And he would've got us killed too.'

'He was just a kid. Not much older than my boys.'

'He knew what he was doing.'

'I don't believe that.' He dropped his chin and pulled his hood over his head. 'I need to go home.'

'The bridges are gone, Griff. Remember?'

'The tubes are still there,' he said without looking up. 'We can walk through 'em, straight under the river.'

'But the stations are —'

Eddie bit his tongue. The hag said there were troops and Jihadis in those stations. That kind of operation required planning and coordination, and that meant communication. Landlines, maybe. Sat phones, almost certainly.

Eddie reached across the table and laid a hand on Griff's arm.

'I'll get you home, mate, but you're going to have to dig a little deeper to get there. Can you do that? Can you help us both get the fuck out of here?'

Griff looked up. His bloodshot eyes blinked once, and then he nodded.

'Show me the way, brother.'

[25]

PEEP SHOW

BY THE TIME THEY'D REACHED THE KENT VILLAGE OF BODIAM, Bertie had been driving for over eight hours, and exhaustion was playing tricks with his eyes. As the darkness crept in, he imagined the road ahead was crowding in around him and narrowing to nothing. Animals real and imagined darted through the headlights of the Mercedes, forcing him to skid and swerve. He needed a break, to stretch his legs and drink a coffee, but more urgently, to repair the damage to the Mercedes' windscreen.

After driving east out of Southampton, the subsequent hard stops and hurried starts, the potholes and pavement mounting, had all caused the cracks to lengthen and widen, until Bertie realised that another good jolt or unseen rut could shatter the whole windscreen. To add to the problem, the rain had swept in, forcing Bertie north, away from the busy main roads and deeper into the countryside. No one was happy about the decision, least of all Bertie, but if the windscreen blew, it could scupper their escape.

Bertie had driven through the village of Bodiam on sidelights, past a school and down a long, twisting hill bordered by trees. He passed a row of houses, and the boarded-up Castle Inn pub (what he wouldn't give to have a night out in a packed pub), and then the village surrendered to wide open fields shrouded in darkness.

Bertie found a suitable spot further down the road, an unlit, isolated property to the south of the village. He drove through the open gate and followed a rough track that wound its way around a thick stand of trees, shielding the sprawling period property and its many outbuildings from the road. Bertie stopped the van outside and switched off the engine. Rain drummed on the roof. As he reached for the door handle, Cheryl said, 'Be careful, Bertie.'

'I'm going to ask them for help, offer them a bit of cash, that's all. If they say no, we move on.' He leaned forward and looked up at the building. 'Can't see any lights, though.'

'Doesn't mean no one's home.'

He smiled. 'I'll be careful, love.'

The Witch grumbled from the crew seat. 'Make a record of any transaction, Bertie.'

'Of course.'

He climbed out and stretched, offering his face up to the rain. It felt cool and fresh and momentarily fended off his fatigue. The house was a big place, with lots of windows and tall chimneys silhouetted against the darkening sky. To the right of the main house was a huge double garage, and beside that a glass greenhouse, but even in the failing light Bertie could see most of its panes were broken or missing. The front door was scuffed, the paint cracked and peeling, and dead leaves crunched underfoot as he pushed the faded brass bell. He heard it echo deep inside the house, but no one came.

'I'll take a look around the back,' he told the others, and then he circumnavigated the building, sweeping his torch across a wet, weed-choked patio and sprawling, untended gardens. There were no lights anywhere, inside the house or beyond its boundaries. Bertie tried the handle of a patio door, and it didn't surprise him when it opened. Inside, there was an air of abandonment. Books and newspapers littered the floor of the library, and in the hallway, clothes spilt out of an open suitcase and across a scuffed parquet floor. Upstairs, antiseptic tainted the air, and the empty rooms were furnished with empty hospital beds and empty IVs. A nursing home, or more likely one of those end-of-life places, Bertie guessed. His torch picked out TVs, plastic bedpans, and framed family photographs. It made Bertie feel sad.

Outside in the rain, he yanked open the side door of the Mercedes and held a big black umbrella aloft while Judge Hardy escorted the ladies inside the house. They made camp in the kitchen, arguably the biggest room in the house, its red-tiled floor dominated by a gigantic oak dining table surrounded by chairs. There was an Aga cooker, an almost empty fridge-freezer, and a big range oven. And they had gas too. Bertie didn't want to advertise their presence there, so he retrieved a camping light from the van – and the cool box filled with sandwiches – and let Cheryl get on with settling everyone in. Bertie had more pressing issues to attend to before he could take a break.

He started in the kitchen, turning out the drawers and cupboards, then he moved outside, to the double garage, his torch probing every nook and cranny of a chaotic but well-appointed workshop, until he found what he was looking for in a workbench drawer filled with car bulbs, loose screws, and assorted tools. The two tubes of superglue were unopened, and Bertie spent the next hour tending to the windscreen, using his debit card to work the glue into the big, spidery cracks across the glass. By the time he'd finished, the tubes were empty and almost all the fractures filled. He spent another 30 minutes gaffer-taping the windscreen's rubber seal and some of the smaller cracks, just to be sure. He couldn't risk anything going wrong.

They were still over 45 miles from Dover and almost a day behind schedule. The caliphate broadcasts had stopped, but the cold American voice on the radio continued to issue dire warnings. Dover would be a beacon for those trying to get to Europe, and Bertie imagined the port would be teeming with collaborators, bureaucrats, cops, and militia, all desperate to escape. With nothing to stop them, those seeking revenge for three years of tyranny would be looking for targets to vent their rage. Dover would be full of such potential victims.

As Bertie circled the van checking the tyres, he thought of George and wondered where his former resistance contact might be. He'd been a friend, up to the point where he'd tried to have Bertie killed. He wondered if George was still alive, and despite their beef, he hoped he was. Maybe one day they would meet again, and Bertie could tell George the entire story. As he tightened the dust caps on the tyres, he thought about Gordon Tyndall, the Lovejoy brothers, and the other resistance rock stars who'd accepted their fates with their heads held high, only to suffer squalid deaths, nailed to wooden crosses in Marble Arch. He remembered the TV news, and it still gave him the creeps. Now he was heading back into that same lion's den, where public execution was still the norm, but there Bertie would live deep in the countryside and in the good graces of The Witch. And when the time was right, he and Cheryl would leave France and return to England. All wars end, he told himself. But if it didn't, and if one day they came for him in Provence, well, he would still have his gun.

Satisfied the Mercedes was fit for the road, he parked it around the side of the house and covered the windscreen with a roll of hessian cloth he'd found in the garage. The rain fell steadily, and a rumble of thunder followed him into the house. He passed through a darkened utility room and into the kitchen, where the camping light glowed, throwing the walls into deep shadow. Everyone was sitting around the table. The Witch spotted him first and barked in his direction.

'Bertie. Have you taken care of things?'

'I have, Lady Edith. We need to wait a while though, allow the glue to set before we hit the road, otherwise we could be back to square one.'

'How long?' Judge Hardy this time, sitting next to The Witch.

Bertie shrugged. 'An hour. The traffic might be lighter by then.'

'Or it could be worse,' The Witch said, chewing a sandwich like a mouse with a hunk of cheese in its claws. 'Did you not hear the thunder?'

'I did.' Cheryl handed Bertie a cup of coffee and he leaned against the worktop. The brew was strong and sweet, and he helped himself to a corned beef and tomato sandwich from the cool box. 'We'll give it half an hour. If the glue has hardened, we'll head off.'

'Only if you're sure,' The Witch mumbled.

'He's got us this far,' Judge Hardy said to her. He offered Bertie a tired smile. 'Given the circumstances, I think we should congratulate Bertie and Mrs P, don't you think, Edith?'

The Witch wouldn't concede that easily. 'Let's not get ahead of ourselves. We're not out of the woods yet.'

Bertie was too tired to argue. Cheryl put a hand on his arm and squeezed. 'I wish I could drive, give you a break.'

'I wish you could too.' He pecked her cheek. 'It's not that far now. Christ knows what Dover will be like, especially if this storm keeps up, but we should be okay, what with the wristbands and cash.'

'I hope you're right. Things seem to be falling apart.'

Bertie knew what she meant. Earlier that day, travelling east of Portsmouth, they'd passed a petrol station engulfed in flame, where blackened cars burned, and charred remains lay sprawled across the forecourt. They'd witnessed a mass brawl on the outskirts of Arundel, forcing Bertie to mount the pavement and run down two men brandishing knives and stabbing people indiscriminately. Twenty miles to the east of that encounter, a vehicle pileup blocked the A27, and once again, Cheryl had guided them out of trouble. The incidents, however, had cost them time and diesel, and Bertie had to fill the tank from the jerrycans lashed to the roof. And that's what worried him. If Dover turned out to be another dead end, and they had to head further east, they might run out of fuel. And that meant running out of options. But they had cash and lots of it. Somebody somewhere would have a boat for hire.

Mrs H got to her feet and steadied herself on the table. She'd been a bag of raw nerves since the explosion at Southampton. Her puffy face was blotchy. Her coiffure had deflated like a soggy soufflé and was now tied behind her head in a wiry grey bun.

'Where are you going?' the judge asked her.

'I must make myself useful, Victor,' she announced in a shaky voice. She pointed across the room. 'I spy oranges in that fruit bowl. I shall cut them up for the journey. It's important we get our vitamins, yes?'

The judge took one of her pudgy hands and kissed it. 'Good thinking, poppet.'

Bertie looked at Cheryl, and she raised an eyebrow. Maybe Mrs H was getting her act together. He hoped so. They would all need their wits about them when they got to Dover. He watched her slip a blade from a knife block and begin slicing fruit, her hand shaking, her hair falling in front of her face in unkempt strands. Bertie felt sorry for her. Her comfort zone was in another universe.

Cheryl headed for the table and cleared the plates, stacking them in the big Belfast sink. Bertie sipped his tea and watched her run water and squeeze in some washing-up liquid. She didn't have to, of course, but that was Cheryl. The girl had class, respect for others' property, no matter whose house she was in. Bertie loved her more each day.

He finished his sandwich and checked his watch. He'd give it another 15 minutes and check on the windscreen. After that, he'd ask Cheryl to make a flask of coffee. He'd certainly need something for the road.

He raised his mug —

And froze.

The man standing in the shadows across the room was staring at him. Bertie's heart rate skyrocketed. He put his mug down, and then he felt something cold and sharp touching the back of his neck.

'Don't fucking move, pal.'

Everyone heard the voice. Cheryl turned around, and the plate in

231

her hand slipped and smashed on the tiles. Mrs H sobbed once, and the two judges sat with wide eyes and open mouths. A strong hand pushed him in the back. He stumbled forward against the table, and the man in the shadows stepped into the pool of light. His wet hair hung down to the shoulders of his combat jacket, and he carried a sawn-off shotgun in his hands. He jerked it at Cheryl and Mrs H.

'You two. Sit.'

They obeyed, and Cheryl caught Bertie's eye. He winked at her, hoping she wasn't feeling as frightened as him. He turned around and faced off against two men. One was a big, bald lump in his forties, six-four at least, heavy around the waist but heavier across the neck and shoulders. The other one was younger, late teens or early twenties, with a tribal tattoo on his neck and a teardrop beneath his right eye. The big lump carried a knife by his right leg, the knuckles of his fist white, and the kid rested a baseball bat on his shoulder. He grinned like a boy who'd just trapped an animal in a snare. Their dark coats dripped water onto the tiles.

'Search him,' the voice with the sawn-off said.

The boy stepped forward, the grin sliding from his face. 'Try anything stupid, and he'll spill your guts all over this floor.'

'We won't give you any trouble,' Bertie said.

'Fucking right.' He put his bat down and ran his hands over Bertie's hoodie. He found the gun clipped to his belt and yanked it off.

'Look at this! He's tooled up.'

Sawn-off walked around the table, his eyes never leaving Bertie's. He had cold eyes too, Bertie saw, dark and distinctly unfriendly. They were locals, he reckoned, maybe gypsies, and that worried him. Sawn-off took the gun from the boy's hand and weighed it in his own. His fingernails were black.

'Nice,' he said, turning the weapon over. 'Custom holster too.' He looked up at Bertie. 'What are you, a cop? Militia?'

'Neither one,' Bertie said.

Thunder growled, and rain tapped against the kitchen windows.

'He carries that for security,' The Witch said. 'He has a permit. Show them, Bertie.'

'*Bertie*,' the boy echoed, sniggering.

Sawn-off pocketed the pistol. He raised the shotgun and aimed it at Bertie's midriff. 'Everything on the table. Now.'

'All of ya!' the boy shouted, marching around the room. He slapped Judge Hardy around the head and shook The Witch's arm like a rag doll. 'Come on, you old bitch. Let's see the goods.'

'How dare you!' she said, her voice shaking with indignation.

'Shut it, grandma!' The boy rested the bat on her narrow shoulder and The Witch finally got the message. She bit her lip and emptied her purse on the table, catching Bertie's subtle head shake.

He turned back to Sawn-off, who was studying the crossed swords ID.

'It's a fake,' Bertie told him. 'I'm with the resistance. Gordon Tyndall? The Lovejoys? You ever heard of 'em?'

'Looks real enough to me,' Sawn-off said. He scooped up the keys to the Mercedes and lobbed them to the boy. 'Check it out.'

'We're just leaving,' Bertie said.

Sawn-off shook his head. 'You ain't going nowhere.'

Bertie softened his tone. 'Come on, pal. The war's almost over. We've all had a rough time of it, especially these older folks. How about you let us go on our way, eh?'

Bertie watched him finger the rest of his belongings spread over the table. There wasn't much, just some coins, a packet of mints, and a mobile phone with no service.

'What are you doing here?' Sawn-off asked him.

'I came to pick up my mother,' Bertie lied. 'When we got here, the place was empty. We're waiting to see if anyone —'

The utility door slammed, and the boy ran into the room, his wet boots squeaking on the tiles. He waved one of Bertie's envelopes.

'Mickey! Look!' He showed Sawn-off – *Mickey* – the thick wad of cash.

'Jesus,' Mickey said, snatching the envelope and thumbing the notes.

The boy panted. 'The van's full of bags and stuff. There's probably more.'

'Fucking jackpot,' Mickey said, whistling.

'Tell you what,' Bertie said. 'You keep that and let us go. Everyone's a winner.'

Mickey shook his head, grinning with brown teeth. 'I don't think so.'

Bertie's heart sank. There would be no deal done here. Instead, they would take what they wanted and leave. The question was, would they leave them alive?

'That money belongs to me,' The Witch said, thumping a bony hand on the table. 'Likewise, the contents of that vehicle. You're not to touch any of it, do you hear me?'

Thunder rolled above the fields outside. Mickey stared at The Witch and burst out laughing.

'Fuck me, you've got some nuts, love, I'll say that for ya.'

'Must you speak that way? It really is rather vulgar.'

'I bet *she's* vulgar.'

Mickey's laughter faded. It was the first time the Lump had spoken. And he was looking at Cheryl.

Bertie took a step closer. 'Come on, lads. Leave us be, eh?' He knew he was wasting his breath. There were men in this world who couldn't be reasoned with. Bertie had known a few in his time and had always avoided them. There was only one way this would go.

'I think Big Willie's sweet on someone,' the boy said.

Mickey grinned. 'Who said romance was dead?'

Cheryl folded her arms and stared at the floor. The Lump pushed past Bertie and lurched around the table.

'Hey! That's far enough,' Bertie said.

Mickey was staring at Bertie. 'That's your woman, right?'

'Call your mate off,' Bertie said.

'Too late for that. He's got the flavour.' He pointed the shotgun at Bertie. 'You make a move, I'll cut you in half.'

Cheryl screamed as the Lump grabbed her by the arm and dragged her out of her chair. The judge scrambled to his feet and tugged at Cheryl's attacker's raincoat.

'Let go of her! Immediately!'

The big man swung his arm without looking, catching the judge on the temple, and sending him crashing to the floor. Bertie moved and Mickey screamed.

'On your fucking knees! Now!' He levelled the shotgun at Bertie's chest. 'Get those hands on your head!'

Bertie hesitated, then dropped to his knees. He looked up at the man with the gun. 'You can stop this. You've got the power.'

Mickey shook his head. 'It's out of my control. When the big fella gets the urge, watch out. Man, woman, or beast, he'll do 'em all.' He laughed, a cruel hack with not a trace of humour.

Bertie watched Willie push Cheryl back against the table.

'Please,' she whispered, shaking.

'You mean, *yes, please,*' Willie said, tugging off his jacket and throwing it on the table. 'Take your jeans off and climb up there.'

Cheryl shook her head. 'I won't.'

Willie held up his knife. 'Do it, or I'll carve your face off.'

'No.'

Willie roared. 'Get 'em off, you fucking slag!' He grabbed her by the jaw and held the knife against her cheek. 'Last chance. Either way, you're getting fucked.'

'Cheryl, do as he says, love.' The words tasted revolting, and Bertie spat them out like poisoned pellets. 'Just don't think about it.'

The boy laughed. 'After she's had a taste of Big Willie, that's *all* she'll think about.'

Willie grabbed the belt of Cheryl's jeans. She struggled, and Bertie winced as he slapped her face. The fury boiled inside him like a venting volcano.

'Fucking bitch!' Willie raged, yanking at her belt.

'Stop it!'

All heads turned towards the voice. Mrs H pushed her chair back and stood up. She unbuttoned the front of her dress as she spoke to the Lump.

'She's pregnant, can't you see?'

Bertie frowned. *What is she doing?*

Victor struggled to his feet. 'Margaret, sit down, please.'

Mrs H turned on him. 'Do you think you're the only man I've had relations with? I was quite the catch, in case you'd forgotten.' She eased Cheryl out of the way and stood in front of a bemused Willie. She took one of his huge paws and placed it on one of her equally large breasts, barely contained by a navy silk bra. 'There, that's what you want, isn't it? *Au naturale,* of course.' Her other hand reached for his crotch and squeezed it.

'My, my. Big Willie. Literally.' She chuckled like a mischievous schoolgirl.

'Margaret!'

She glanced over her shoulder. 'Be quiet, Victor.' She smiled at the slack-jawed Willie. Cheryl was nothing but a distant memory. 'Help me up, would you, big boy?'

She climbed up on the table, and Willie grabbed her ample backside and pushed. 'What a gent,' she puffed, rolling onto her back. She hitched up her dress and exposed her hefty, milky white thighs.

Bertie couldn't believe what was happening. A transfixed Mickey was too far away for Bertie to get to his feet *and* close the gap. The boy was on the other side of Mickey, watching proceedings, and all Willie was interested in was the triangle of navy-blue silk between Mrs H's legs.

The Lump climbed up onto the table and undid his jeans. Mrs H's eyes lit up. 'Oh yes, I can see this is going to be fun, but it won't work like this, my dear. I'll need to be on top.'

'Okay,' Willie mumbled, now putty in her hands.

The judge was close to tears. 'Margaret, for God's sake ...'

'Look away, my love.' She reached out for Willie's member and stroked it. He lay back on the table that creaked beneath their combined weight. Mrs H straddled him, then slipped him inside her.

'Ooh, I say,' she gasped.

Bertie could barely look. Nor could he comprehend what was going on. She must've had a mental breakdown or something. He glanced at the judge, who stared at the floor, his hands over his ears. *Poor bloke.*

'That's it, that's good,' Mrs H said, grinding the Lump as he mashed her breasts together. She started bouncing faster.

A transfixed Mickey whooped like a cowboy. 'Go on, my son!'

Bertie shuffled his knees closer.

'Fuck it, I'll go next,' the boy said, licking his lower lip. 'I've done old birds before.'

'Like your mum?' Mickey cackled.

'Fuck you!' the boy said, laughing, still spellbound by the live show.

Mrs H was bouncing up and down, her eyes closed. 'Here we go,' she moaned. 'I can feel it ... can you hear me, Bertie?'

Bertie jolted as if he'd been shocked. *Did she just say my name?*

'Are you ready, Bertie?'

Across the creaking table, Cheryl glanced at him and frowned.

Mrs H was bucking and puffing. 'Bertie ...?'

'Do her!' Mickey yelled, the shotgun dangling from his hand.

Bertie inched closer. Something was about to happen, and not just Willie getting his rocks off.

Mrs H threw her head back and yelled. 'Now, Bertie! Now!'

And then the knife was in her hand, held high, and she plunged it into Willie's neck. Blood sprayed across the table. Mickey roared and lifted the sawn-off. He fired, the blast taking Mrs H in the face and neck and knocking her off the table. Then Bertie was on him, grabbing the gun and trapping Mickey's hand with his own. Bertie was taller and stronger, and he yanked the gun around just as Mickey squeezed the other trigger. The cone of lead hit the boy in his midriff and sent him crashing against the Aga. Bertie grabbed the barrel and twisted it. Mickey screamed as his finger broke. Bertie ran him onto the table and snatched it away. He brought it down on Mickey's head, once, twice. On the third strike, he felt the skull give way, then blood flowed through his wet hair and across the pale oak. He slipped off the table and collapsed onto the tiles.

'Cheryl!'

Bertie tossed the sawn-off, and she caught it with both hands. He reached into Mickey's pocket and retrieved his own gun, cocking it and swivelling towards the boy, but one look and Bertie knew the kid was done. He lay on his right side, his legs splayed, his jacket shredded from armpit to groin. Blood spread in a wide puddle across the floor. Bertie took the envelope from Mickey's jacket. He found some shotgun shells and pocketed them too.

His heart pounded, and his legs were like water. Willie was still alive, still breathing, but he was choking now, and the blood no longer pumped. The hilt of the knife sunk into Willie's thick neck just below his left ear.

'Bertie! Help me!'

He ran around the table. The Witch was lying on the floor, spark out.

'She fainted,' Cheryl said, fanning The Witch's face with a table placemat.

'Check her head for damage.'

Bertie stepped over her and crouched by the judge's side. Mrs H was dead, the skin and muscle stripped from her face, exposing pale white jaw and cheekbones. Her nose and her left eye were gone too, as well as most of the hair on the right side of her head. Bertie could barely look. He put a gentle hand on the judge's back.

'There's nothing you can do, Judge.'

But the judge wasn't listening. He cooed over her body, kissing her lifeless hand.

'We have to go,' Bertie said. 'In case others come.'

'I can't leave her,' he sobbed. 'Not like this.' The judge looked up at Bertie. His white hair was dishevelled and tainted with blood, and his face creased with pain. Tears ran from his bloodshot eyes as he pointed at the now-dead body sprawled across the blood-soaked table. 'I'm not leaving her here with *them*.'

Given the circumstances, Bertie didn't blame him. But they had to move fast. 'Why don't we take her out into the garden?'

'Yes,' the judge said, nodding. 'She'd like that.'

Bertie found a wheelchair in a lounge area, but it still took 20 minutes to move her body. Outside, rain swept across the patio, and they puffed and heaved until they'd laid her to rest beside a muddy flower bed. The judge arranged her body, and Cheryl found some dried flowers in the house. The judge placed them in his wife's dead hands and Bertie left her ID card on her midriff and covered her with a discarded tartan blanket. Cheryl held the judge's hand as he muttered a painful goodbye, and then Bertie helped him back to the Mercedes. The Witch waited inside, still shaky after her fainting spell.

'Finally,' she said, as Bertie threw open the side door. 'Put the heater on, would you, Bertie? It's bitter in here.'

The judge climbed in and leaned his head against the window. Bertie got behind the wheel and started the engine. Their damp clothes steamed up the windows, and then the warm air kicked in, clearing the windscreen. The wipers went to work, and Bertie saw that, despite some small nicks in the glass, overall, visibility was good.

'Time to go,' he said over his shoulder. 'Are you strapped in back there?'

'What about the money? The envelope stolen by those ruffians?'

'I've got it, Lady Edith. They got nothing from us.'

'They took everything,' the judge said, his voice cracking.

Bertie winced. 'Yes, Judge. They did. I'm so sorry.'

'Justice has been served,' The Witch said, patting her colleague's hand. 'We must put this business behind us.'

Bertie shared a look with Cheryl, and she half-smiled.

'Get us out of here, Bertie,' she said.

He nodded, dropped the Mercedes into gear, and drove off the property. Back on the main road, he headed south as Cheryl spread the map across her legs and traced an alternative route by torchlight. Bertie put his foot down, accelerating into the night.

Dover beckoned. And he had no intention of stopping for anything until he got there.

[26]

PHOTO BOMB

THE MSS-2 SPECIAL OPERATIONS AIRCRAFT — CALL SIGN Vampire One – drifted through the night sky, its approach unnoticed by the anti-aircraft vehicles parked below. It flew above high stone walls and dense woods patrolled by US Rangers, before settling in the grounds of a sprawling private estate five miles to the southwest of Windsor Castle. Once on the ground, it rolled across manicured lawns and parked beneath a temporary shelter constructed of infrared and thermal camouflage screens. Safely hidden from prying electronic eyes, the crew took its power plant off-line and lowered the ramp.

President Bob Mitchell stepped down onto English soil for the first time in several years. He took a deep breath, savouring the fresh country air, which was distinctly milder and drier than the frigid wind and freezing rain that buffeted the West Coast of Scotland, where he'd landed in Air Force One less than three hours ago. The MSS-2 had then flown the presidential party south to this discreet estate. As they escorted him towards the shadowy, cubist building, the Marine general by his side explained that the house was owned by some British Lord, now living in the United States. And like every other exclusive home in the country during the last three years, the occupying force had first commandeered, then ransacked it.

The property hadn't fared too badly, Mitchell noted as they walked through the sprawling, interconnected cubes of glass, steel, and concrete, though it was difficult to tell given that the building was lit only by red LED lights. The general led them down into a huge basement of polished concrete floors and glass walls. Mitchell passed a cinema room, and behind another huge transparent wall, there was a vast, empty honeycomb that was once an impressive wine cellar. The owner was also a classic car collector, Mitchell learned, which explained the huge underground parking lot built alongside the basement. Naturally, the cars were gone, and USCENTCOM had filled the concrete void. It was McKenzie himself who greeted the president and his team as they passed through a steel door and into the lot that was now bathed in the electronic light of computer screens and huge, translucent battlefield displays.

'Mr President,' McKenzie said, shaking Mitchell's hand with his customary iron grip.

Mitchell noticed several curious glances directed his way. They had made his imminent arrival known only moments before, but these were professionals, and his presence caused barely a stir. McKenzie's core team waited to greet him, and he crossed the smooth concrete floor and shook hands with all of them. He studied the digital maps and saw the dense clusters of blue and green icons to the north and west of London. Red icons were barely visible, and even as he watched the real-time display, he saw two of them blink out.

'Enemy operations have officially ceased,' McKenzie told him. 'However, small groups of civilians and other quasi-military factions continue to resist. Their primary goal appears to be destruction. Heathrow Airport is currently out of commission, likewise Gatwick and Stansted, plus several smaller airports. We can't fly our transports in right now, but we've got specialist air force clean-up crews inbound from Ireland. They'll get those Heathrow runways serviceable within the next 48 hours.'

'We need to get our fighters running combat air patrols over the south-east ASAP,' explained an Air Force officer. 'The coast will need defending too with Patriot batteries and sea defences.'

'What about the Channel and the North Sea?'

'As for the latter, we're coordinating with the Russians and conducting minesweeping patrols, clearing shipping lanes between Norway and Scotland. We haven't pushed into the Channel yet, not in numbers. We'll wait until the mass exodus has run its course, then we'll begin naval operations as per the security plan.'

'How soon can all this be achieved?' Mitchell asked.

'To achieve land, air, and sea security? A month,' McKenzie said. 'The south-east is still chaotic. Some estimates suggest there are a million people still on the move. Most are headed to the ports at Dover and Folkestone, and we have no intention of stopping them. If they want to leave, so be it, but chasing them with armour and scaring the shit out of them with flybys won't make it happen any faster. We're going to let it happen at its own pace.' He paused for a moment, then said, 'We should discuss your immediate intentions. Let me start the conversation by saying your proposal is a bad idea.'

Mitchell looked around at the faces of McKenzie's command team. He didn't see any dissenters. 'Are you telling me that London isn't safe?'

'Until we get there and establish a security cordon, I'm saying your safety cannot be guaranteed.'

'How so?'

McKenzie folded his arms. 'It's their capital city, and it's already suffered significant and wilful damage. Every bridge from Kew to the Tower of London has been destroyed. The London Hilton is now a mountain of rubble blocking Park Lane, the BT Tower is gone, and a thousand-foot building in the City of London was dropped on top of the Bank of England. That took some major planning and a hell of a lot of explosives. If the enemy were prepared to go to those lengths, what else might they have up their sleeves?'

'Baghdad has denounced the destruction,' Mitchell said. 'They're accusing rogue elements and deserters. Wazir has given us a green light to take out these rebels.'

'That's true, Mr President, but a photo op at a London landmark? That's a seriously risky venture. You shouldn't go, period.'

Mitchell looked at the map and failed to see a single red dot in the centre of town. 'I'm not talking about a walking tour of the London tourist spots, if there are any left. I'm talking about a fast meet-and-greet with the troops. We wouldn't be on the ground for more than 30 minutes. Are you telling me that the combined might and technological power of the US armed forces cannot guarantee my safety for half an hour?' Mitchell waited, his eyebrows raised. McKenzie took the bait.

'That's not what I'm saying at all. Vampire One could have you in and out of there without anyone knowing. That would be the smart move.'

'At night, I take it?'

McKenzie nodded.

'Then what's the point? The American people need to know that the war has been won. If they see me in London, with the troops, that will have a great deal of psychological impact.'

'I'm not convinced.'

'Then humour me, Pat. How would you do it?'

McKenzie sighed and folded his arms. 'Okay. Well, if you choose what's left of Downing Street as your LZ, that would be good, given that they've flattened everything between Trafalgar Square and Lambeth Bridge.'

Mitchell shook his head. 'Not Downing Street. That would be rubbing Harry Beecham's nose in it. It's too raw for the man and his people. I was thinking of somewhere else, close by. Somewhere iconic.'

'Buckingham Palace,' McKenzie said without hesitation. 'The perimeter walls are still intact, as are most of the gates. Drone coverage has picked up a few looters, but it's been pretty much left alone. We lay the ground first, using special forces teams to recce the area and secure the LZ. Later, we send you in by air, fast and low, with multiple decoys and heavy jamming. You drop in, shake hands, smile for the cameras, and be out again in no time. If it's domestic media impact you want – in an environment that we can secure – then I would choose the King's former home. *If* I had to choose,' he added. 'My recommendation stands. You should wait until all hostilities have ceased, and the city is secured.'

ZACK RADANOVICH WAITED UNTIL THE MILITARY ORDERLY HAD delivered the refreshments and exited the room before he addressed the president. 'Well, what did McKenzie say?'

Mitchell helped himself to an English tea and folded himself into a comfortable easy chair. The private office was almost as large as Mitchell's oval one. Sitting on the opposite couch, Sandy Tagg, Mitchell's press secretary, and Elliott Bird, his national security adviser, waited in silence. All of them had flown with the president from the pad at Camp David to Faslane in Scotland, where they'd transferred to the MS-22. The entire trip had taken less than three hours, and they would be back in Maryland before Washington discovered they'd left the country.

They had swept the office they now occupied for bugs. It was also soundproof, but Mitchell kept his voice low anyway.

'McKenzie said what I thought he'd say. No.'

'Not a word presidents like to hear,' Zack said.

Mitchell sipped his tea. 'He has a point. There's been a lot of devastation.'

'Blowing those buildings and bridges is the biggest display of petulance I've ever seen,' Bird said.

Sandy Tagg was next to speak. The constitutional law professor from South Carolina was one of the sharpest minds on Mitchell's team, and the White House press corps had yet to best her. It was a reputation she was determined to keep.

'Okay, so McKenzie said no. What do you say, Bob?'

'The general hasn't put a foot wrong since we stormed the beaches in Ireland. I can't fault his instincts. If he says don't go, maybe we should listen to the man.'

Tagg crossed her legs and plucked an unseen speck of lint from her trousers. 'I agree, the prosecution of this campaign has been text-book, but he's not the only one with instincts. Mine are telling me that this opportunity is too good to miss. And I know Zack agrees with me.'

Tagg glanced at Zack. A rueful smile played on Mitchell's lips. 'What's this? Collusion?'

Zack shrugged. 'I agree with Sandy. It would be good for the folks at home to see the commander-in-chief on the frontline, mixing it up with the troops, especially on the grounds of a genuine royal palace. Say a few words, shake a few hands. It'll look good.'

'I would advise against recording sound,' Tagg said. 'I say we dress you up for the part, camouflage jacket, military cap, and get you in amongst those combat troops. Then we capture the footage from a distance, hand-held stuff, so it doesn't look staged. A secret visit to the frontline leaked to the media. That would reflect well with the elec-torate and be great for your numbers.'

'I'm not campaigning, Sandy. Those days are over, thank God.'

'Either way, it'll reflect well on you.'

Mitchell turned to his national security adviser. 'Let's hear it, Elliott. I can feel the disapproval radiating off you.'

Sitting on the couch next to Tagg, the Washington veteran shrugged. 'I don't think it's worth the risk. McKenzie is right, London is still a dead zone. Safety cannot be guaranteed.'

'It can't get much safer,' Zack said. 'If the president says we go, McKenzie will throw an impenetrable protective blanket around him. We go in, we do our thing, then we leave again. Easy. It's a win-win situation.'

Bird shook his head. 'We don't need it. Bob Mitchell is the first president to win a major war since 1945, and sometime between Thanksgiving and Christmas, he's going to announce the dawning of a new energy era to the American people that will transform their lives. We will once again become the dominant global superpower, only this time we use that power – literally as well as figuratively – for global advancement and for the betterment of humanity. What greater legacy can any president hope to achieve than that?'

He turned to Mitchell. 'Sir, by the time you hand the reins over to Curtis, this country will have turned a corner, and you'll bask in that glow until your dying day. Why risk all of that for a few seconds of footage that people will barely remember a week from now?'

'You don't know that,' Tagg said. 'I think it's worth it.'

'Eliot makes a good point,' Zack added. 'But McKenzie will have your back.'

Bird turned to his younger colleague. 'Don't be naïve —'

'Okay, guys,' said Mitchell, heading off another exchange. He put his cup down and crossed to the window, peering around the heavy drapes. Outside, it was pitch black, and there was not a soul to be seen. Mitchell knew there were layers of security reaching out for a couple of miles in all directions, that they protected him from ground assault and missile attack, that every man and woman in uniform within that cordon would give their life to keep him safe. He didn't deserve that level of protection, but it came with the job. He also knew that if he said the word, McKenzie would do everything in his considerable power to ensure that his president returned to the United States in one piece.

And despite Eliot's pragmatism, Sandy painted an attractive picture. Every man wanted to be seen as a hero, but it was more than that this time. Mitchell had seen lots of footage of Britain at war, but he wanted to see it for himself, up close and personal. He'd never been to a war zone, and now he had the opportunity. Yes, there was always an element of danger with these things, but life itself was dangerous. Right now, despite his heart condition, he was still reasonably fit and active. That might change six months from now. *Carpe Diem.* He let the curtain fall back into place and turned to face the others.

'I'm going,' he told them. 'Thousands of Americans have died in this campaign. It's only right that I should be exposed to some risk, even if it's small.'

Tagg unfolded her legs and beamed. 'It's the right decision.'

'Good for you, sir,' Zack said.

Bird said nothing. He folded his arms and bit his lip. Mitchell saw it and knew the man was angry. His national security advisor had been against the idea from the start, and that's why Mitchell respected him. He wasn't afraid to swim against the tide. But Mitchell's mind was made up.

'Zack, inform General McKenzie that I've taken heed of his advice, but I'm going anyway. Tell him to make all necessary preparations.'

'I'll make sure of it, Mr President. You'll be safe, that's guaranteed.'

'That's good, because you and Sandy are coming with me.'

Radanovich stopped in his tracks, and the President of the United States smiled. His advisors didn't. As they swapped a look, Mitchell caught a flicker of fear in their eyes.

[27]

FLY DELTA

THEY STEPPED OFF THE RAMP AT 12,000 FEET AND PLUMMETED towards the drop zone in central London, now 8 miles distant. Each member of the insertion team was wearing a black wingsuit ribbed with pressurised air cells, and they rocketed unseen across the night sky.

Buffeted for several thousand feet by cold air and strong winds, the 16-man Delta Force team broke through a thin layer of cloud, unveiling the streets of London below. Despite a few pools of darkness, most of the city was lit up, and if it wasn't for the absence of traffic, it could have been a normal evening in Old London Town. But nothing was normal, and the Delta Force operators were not on a sightseeing tour. They had a job to do.

They deployed their chutes at 4000 feet, higher than normal, conscious of the noise that unfurling parachutes made. They spiralled down in a well-rehearsed stack, circling above the Westminster School sports grounds in the heart of Westminster. The operators skimmed over the roof of the main building, flaring their canopies over the dark lawn before stepping out of the sky.

They packed and stacked their chutes and suits, and the team moved around the building and out through a gate onto the empty streets of Westminster. As a specialist reconnaissance and surveillance team, their weapons load-out was light, so when they moved, they did so quickly and almost silently. The commander led them north, checking the map unit strapped to his forearm that digitised the live feed from a Global Hawk UAV circling several thousand feet overhead. The streets ahead were clear, but that didn't mean an absence of danger. In fact, the commander expected trouble. There were still plenty of disaffected people armed with guns out there, and many would go down swinging. That was fine by him because Delta was good at fighting – his squadron hadn't lost a single operator since their insertion into Ireland five days before the main assault on its beaches. And the commander intended to keep it that way.

At the junction of Bressenden Place and Buckingham Palace Road, he split his team into two elements, sending one of them east towards the junction of Birdcage Walk and Buckingham Gate, where they melted into the shadows. Half a mile to the north, another team of Delta jumpers were moving into place along the northern perimeter. After several minutes, the radio confirmed that 32 Delta Force operators were in position around the outer walls of the palace, watching and listening from cover. None of them saw the MSS-2 drop from the night sky and land on the grounds of the palace itself.

THE RAMP DEPLOYED AND ANOTHER 16 DELTA OPERATORS exited Vampire One and melted into the overgrown grounds of the palace. With a mild ripple of disturbed air, the stealth aircraft twisted on its axis, folded its insect-like legs up into its body, and lifted off into the night sky. Within seconds, it had disappeared.

On the ground, drone pilots powered up their miniature birds and flew them through open doors and broken windows. The UAVs hummed through the palace's many dark corridors, halls, and reception rooms, but their onboard sensors detected no thermal signatures, no visual movement or audio spikes that suggested danger lurked in the shadows.

The teams followed them inside, splitting left and right, up and down, moving through basement corridors, through ransacked reception rooms and decrepit bedroom suites, their night vision optics revealing a depressing tableau of weather damage and wilful destruction. Fire had burned and blackened several rooms on the upper floors, and the walls were devoid of their artworks, leaving behind patchworks of faded paint and soiled carpets littered with broken frames. A night breeze gusted through the multitude of broken windows, and unintelligible graffiti swirled across walls and doors.

With the interior of the palace cleared and secured, several operators double-timed towards the enormous iron gates, dodging the trail of abandoned furniture and other royal detritus littering the main parade ground. They secured the open gates and went to work, planting their remote cameras and optical tripwires. Overwatch positions were established on roofs and in top-floor windows, and Delta snipers probed the surrounding streets with their high-powered gun sights, using their tactical radios to coordinate with their comrades outside the palace walls. Overhead, an Avenger UAV loaded with Hellfire missiles circled the area at 1500 feet, and far above that autonomous aircraft, a global Hawk interrogated the ground with its advanced platform of high-tech sensors. No threats were detected, not by the humans on the ground or by the robots above them. The night skies were clear, and the streets were quiet.

The landing zone was secure.

A MILE TO THE EAST OF BUCKINGHAM PALACE, EDDIE WAS unaware that Vampire One, the aircraft that had plucked him to safety from that Birmingham rooftop, was moving through the skies above him. Instead, he was focused on his own mission – finding a phone that he could use to contact Scotland and raise the alarm.

He'd tried a couple of buildings already, an insurance company on Kingsway and the ransacked Australian embassy. The former had turned up nothing of use, and the latter was a charred cavern. The Savoy hotel on the Strand had looked promising at first, but the sheer scale of the search task had unnerved Eddie. He'd heard voices too, muted, and unknown footsteps had echoed through the deserted lobby. Eddie and Griff had fled empty-handed.

They found themselves another potential prospect further along the Strand, and now Eddie was searching the third floor of Coutts, a private bank located close to Trafalgar Square. Like most other financial institutions Eddie had seen, it had been pillaged to death. In the basement, his torch revealed an empty vault and a room full of safety deposit boxes, their doors wide open. Moving upstairs, the floors above were littered with the detritus of a good ransacking. Drawers and cupboards gaped open, emptied of their contents. Computers were missing or smashed to pieces on the floor. It wasn't looking hopeful. Eddie lifted the walkie-talkie to his mouth.

'Griff, come in.'

'Go ahead,' Griff's voice crackled back. Eddie had nabbed the walkie-talkie set from a stationary shop along the street. It wasn't state-of-the-art comms by any stretch, but it was good enough. Griff was on the ground floor, watching the street through toughened glass windows that were still intact.

'How are we looking?'

'Clear,' Griff confirmed.

'I've got one more floor to check. Stand by.'

'Roger.'

Eddie headed up the stairwell to the fourth floor. Griff wasn't the same man he'd met in Battersea. The man's general frustration and enthusiasm to get involved had morphed into something else, some kind of pained reflection. Eddie had seen it before. Griff was internalising his exposure to extreme violence and pointless death and was trying to make sense of it all. Back in Ireland, Eddie had found it hard too, but he'd been lucky. He'd had his friends around him and the support of a giant military machine. Griff had no such backing, only

Eddie's quiet words of encouragement. He was no psychiatrist, so he was doing his best to get Griff through it and back home to his family. The man needed time to process everything, that was all. And in the absence of professional help, Eddie's job was to keep him busy and distracted.

Abandoning the third floor, Eddie headed up to the topmost floor. Up here the hallways were carpeted, the office doors solid oak, and his torch beam picked out a fancy reception desk with a large glass panel engraved with the Coutts logo. The looters had left their mark, though. Papers were strewn everywhere, and he saw blood on the pale blue carpet of the boardroom. He moved through the private offices one by one, the MP5 slung across his chest, the Springfield 9mm in one hand and the torch in the other as he swept the dark corners. He found nothing of value, nothing that would help him reconnect with Scotland.

He stepped into another office, and glass crunched beneath his boot. He bent down and picked up a discarded photo frame, the composition taken in happier times. The man in the photo looked like any other corporate exec: puffy face, thinning hair, going soft in the middle. Forgettable. There were two nice looking kids standing in front of him, the youngest one laughing her little head off, and that made Eddie smile. The wife was a looker too, way out of the banker's league, but a lot of things could be ignored for the want of a better life. The office was much the same as every other room he'd checked – empty drawers and empty cupboards, missing computers, and scattered stationery. He turned to leave, took two paces, and stopped.

The door to the office had been wedged open against the wall. Eddie kicked the wedge away, and the door swung closed. Hanging on a hook behind it was a grey suit jacket. He ran a hopeful hand across its glossy grey flanks, and he felt a familiar shape. *No way.* In his stomach, butterflies took to wing. He fished the phone from the inside pocket and saw the manufacturer's name – *Iridium* – and his hopes soared. He holstered his pistol and thumbed the buttons, but the battery was dead. Okay, he was halfway there. A thorough search of the office revealed no chargers of any kind. He went from office to office along the corridor and tried a couple of potential candidates, but the power packs had a different fitting. He yanked the radio out of his tactical vest.

'Griff, how are we looking?'

The answer came back a moment later. 'Still quiet.'

'I need you to go around the floors, grab every charger you see. Gather them up and I'll meet you on the second floor.'

'Roger.'

Eddie spent the next 20 minutes working his way down from the top floor to the second. By the time he got there, he had a waste bin full of chargers and emptied it out onto the pile that Griff had collected. He showed the older man the satellite phone connection.

'That's what we're looking for, a lead that will fit that port.'

They went to work, rooting through the spaghetti of chargers and cables, selecting potential candidates, and gently working them into the phone's power port. They were down to the last four candidates when Griff held up the phone and showed it to Eddie. The power cable dangled from the port, a perfect fit.

'Bingo!' Eddie said. He found a power socket in the floor panel beneath the desk and plugged it in. The satellite phone beeped once, and the network logo glowed on the LCD screen. Eddie unplugged it again and jammed it all in his tactical vest. 'Let's get back to the safe house.'

It took them less than 15 minutes to work their way through the streets to Maiden Lane. In the kitchen, Eddie plugged in the phone and watched the display boot up. The power indicator rose and fell. Eddie dialled the memorised number of 4 ISR, but the call failed as he stabbed the last digit. He had to be patient, wait for the battery to get sufficient power for at least a minute or two of conversation. He didn't want to be cut off in mid chat.

He boiled the kettle and made a couple of coffees. Griff took his and sat down.

'So, what happens now?'

'Now we wait,' Eddie said. 'Once I've spoken to my people, I'll have a clearer picture of what's happening out there.'

'What do you think those missiles are all about, then?'

'Waiting for a target, I'd guess.' He drummed his fingers on the counter. 'How are you holding up?'

Griff shrugged. 'I'm all right. I keep seeing that kid's face, though.'

'What about the man you killed? The one from the truck.'

'What about him?'

'How do you feel about it?'

Griff offered a tired smile. 'You're not going to try and hug me, are you?'

'No,' Eddie said. 'But killing isn't easy, not even when it's justified. I get your frustration about not having done your bit, but trust me, you've stepped up. I couldn't have done this without you, and I certainly wouldn't have taken on that missile crew if you weren't by my side. When all this is done, you'll be able to walk into that pub and hold your head up high. Tell your boys you did your bit.'

Griff looked up at him. 'The funny thing is, I don't care about that stuff anymore. All that matters now is getting home. I've been away too long. Zoe will be going out of her mind.'

'You'll get home soon, don't worry.' Griff didn't look convinced.

Eddie finished his coffee and set his watch timer for 30 minutes. Then he made himself busy, checking his kit, emptying the pockets of his tactical vest, and repacking it. He checked his weapons too, making sure they were serviceable. When the timer went off, he returned to the kitchen and checked the phone – 52% power. It would be enough. Griff was still sitting at the table, the unloaded AK-12 on the table next to him.

'I'm calling my boss. Don't say anything unless I ask you, okay?' Griff nodded, and Eddie dialled the number. He heard a couple of clicks, and then the soft warble of the ringtone. A voice answered after two rings.

'Bradley, 4211. How may I help?'

'Ident alpha-foxtrot-echo, 1 1 7.'

'Confirm ident,' said the voice.

Eddie punched a six-digit code into the phone's keypad.

'Standby.'

The seconds ticked away. If Eddie was operating under duress, he would enter the code in reverse, and the call would end. Instead, the man's soft Scottish brogue came back on the line. 'How may I direct your call?'

'Bradley, zero, one.' That was Hawkins' code number. The man himself came on the line a moment later.

'Wait one.' Eddie heard the familiar tone of the scrambler being activated. Hawkins spoke again. 'Go ahead.'

Eddie wasted no time and gave Hawkins a clear and concise account of his movements and what he'd discovered.

'Were you able to ascertain delivery system type?'

'No, boss. No markings, just a multiple launch box canister with a roof-mounted array. The team were all in civvies and being protected by a mix of cops and militia. Their leader hinted at some kind of organised resistance, but I've seen no evidence of it. Apparently, the missile truck isn't the only one.'

Eddie listened as Hawkins explained about the destruction of the bridges and the city buildings. The theory was wanton destruction, but now Hawkins didn't seem so sure.

'I'm going to have to run this up the chain. Stay close to the phone, Eddie.'

'I've got a civvy with me, boss. He's ex- Fusiliers, and I wouldn't have got this far without him, but he needs to get back across the river. What's the situation like over there?'

'We have drones monitoring the city. South of the water is quiet as far as I know, but that's not where anyone's focus is right now. The southern coastal ports are a mess, and the enemy has pretty much torched every airport between Heathrow and Southend, so the situation is fluid. We'll get to you, but it won't be today. Tell your friend to be patient.'

'I will.'

'And thank him, would you? We owe him a debt of gratitude.'

'Roger that.' Eddie ended the call and set the phone back down on the counter, making sure the battery was still charging.

'Well?' Griff asked.

'We need to be patient,' Eddie said. 'The troops are on their way, but it might take a few days —'

'Days?'

Eddie nodded. 'And he said he owes you a debt of gratitude.'

Griff brightened a little. 'He did?'

'Yes. That's something, right?'

'I suppose so.'

Eddie sat down, and by the light of a candle, they began cleaning their weapons while they waited for the phone to ring.

Both prayed it wouldn't be too long.

[28]

ANOTHER BRICK

HARRY'S HELICOPTER JOURNEY INTO LONDON CAME TO AN unexpected end at a shabby warehouse complex in Batchworth Heath, 16 miles northwest of Trafalgar Square. General McKenzie had grounded all manned flight operations without explanation, yet according to Harry's escort commander, a Parachute Regiment colonel, UAVs were still buzzing across west London for reasons unknown.

Once again, Harry boiled with anger and frustration. Facing him across the bare and sterile office, Wilde sat on an orange plastic chair, tapping away at a smart pad linked to a secure satellite network.

'Anything?' Harry asked, unable to prevent an irascible tone from leaking into his voice.

'Nothing of significance,' Wilde said, scrolling up with his index finger. 'Some of the Cabinet have emailed me asking where you are and what the plan is.'

'I wish I knew,' Harry grumbled. 'I need to see London for myself. That's my priority. And yet I'm frightened to look at it.'

'At least they didn't bulldoze Downing Street.'

'But they flattened everything else for 300 yards around it. I could stand outside Number Ten and see across the River Thames, for God's sake. All that history, gone.'

'I know. It's appalling.'

'So, we rebuild,' Harry said, pacing the bland white box. 'Bigger and better. Grand buildings, reflecting this country's proud history. I won't allow it to be rewritten.'

Wilde looked up from his computer. 'That can't be our priority, Harry. Transport and energy networks, food supply chains, security, jobs – these are the things that will get the country moving again.'

Harry tutted. 'I know that. I'm venting, that's all.'

He stood at the window and looked down into the warehouse. The command element of the 16 Air Assault Brigade had set up their tents inside the warehouse, and soldiers in maroon berets hurried back and forth. The Paras never missed a chance to flash their colours, Harry had learned. He watched as one such Para hurried across the concrete floor and jog up the staircase towards him, his boots ringing on the metal steps. Harry yanked open the office door and met him on the landing. Camouflage cream carved across the young man's face in jagged streaks, and he carried a fearsome-looking rifle across his chest.

'There's a call for you, sir. General Wheeler, in the command tent.'

Harry followed the young soldier down to the collection of tents on the warehouse floor. It was a similar setup to USCENTCOM but on a much smaller scale. A *forward operating combat node*, as the colonel had described it. He ducked into the largest tent and strode past the big combat information screens to the communications officer holding a satellite phone. Harry took it from him and headed for a quiet corner of the tent.

'Nick. Glad you called. How much longer are we going to be held here?'

'Not sure,' the Deputy CDS said. 'Sir David is trying to squeeze some information out of the Americans, but McKenzie is being tight-lipped. Something is going on, but we've no idea what it is.'

'Well, that's a surprise. Kept in the dark once again. It's all rather tedious. Thanks for letting me know, Nick. We'll spend the night here and hopefully be allowed to fly in tomorrow morning.'

'There's something else, Prime Minister.'

Harry lowered his voice. 'Go on.'

'We've received fresh intelligence from an operative on the ground in London. There are reports of enemy anti-aircraft units hidden across the city. We have one confirmed sighting, but the suggestion is, there are others.'

Harry's simmering frustration cooled. 'I see. Well, that explains why McKenzie is holding us here.'

'Actually, this intelligence has yet to be passed to CENTCOM,' Wheeler said. 'It comes direct from the head of 4 ISR Brigade. He bypassed the chain and brought it straight to me. I thought you could share it with the Americans personally, give you some leverage.'

'How solid is this intelligence?' Harry said.

Wheeler's voice was emphatic. 'The operative took out the crew of a mobile unit himself. According to him, there are more.'

'But why haven't we detected them? If these drones can read newspapers from 50,000 feet, why can't they see a bloody great missile truck in the middle of London?'

'The one we know of was parked in a narrow cul-de-sac and shielded from surveillance platforms by its reflective camouflage net. We use the same technology ourselves to hide what we don't want others to see. If it's done right, anything underneath would be very difficult to spot, even with advanced technology. And you know yourself that there are hundreds of public, private, and corporate car parks, loading bays, and event locations where one could easily hide a truck.'

Harry allowed that to sink in. Wheeler was right. London was a maze, a clash of the new and the ancient, where skyscrapers butted up against thousand-year-old stone walls. Hundreds of tunnels criss-crossed the city beneath the ground and hiding places would be abundant. The thought of sitting inside a helicopter while missiles screamed towards him was a sobering one.

'I'm going to talk to President Mitchell directly. Maybe now he'll take my call.'

'Good luck, Prime Minister.'

'Thanks, Nick. It's much appreciated.'

Harry headed back to the office, taking the stairs two at a time. Wilde looked up as Harry closed the door behind him.

'What is it?'

'Fresh intelligence. Apparently, there are enemy anti-aircraft units still operating in London.'

'Credible intelligence?'

Harry nodded. 'According to Wheeler, yes. The Americans are still in the dark. I can bring this to Mitchell personally, build a little cachet.'

'That would be helpful.'

'Set the call up, Lee. Right now, please.'

Harry waited as Wilde worked his phone. He checked his watch – it was late afternoon in Camp David, where the president was staying for the next few days. Hopefully, he would be available to take Harry's call.

The minutes dragged by as comms nodes and encrypted satellite channels knitted together. Harry was sitting in a chair, arms folded, his left boot tapping the floor, when Wilde got to his feet and handed him the phone.

'They're patching you through. The next voice you hear will be President Mitchell.'

But it wasn't. It was the all-too-familiar voice of Vice President Riley. Once again, Harry had to bite his lip and play nice.

'Mr Vice President, how are you?'

'I was told you had some important information,' Riley said.

'I do,' Harry told him. 'Though I'm getting the impression that the president is dodging my calls.'

'Let's hear what you have to say. I have a busy evening ahead.'

For the first time in many years, Harry almost lost his cool. Telling Riley to piss off and ending the conversation would be a cleansing moment but would achieve nothing. He swallowed his temper, and some pride, and repeated everything Wheeler had told him. He waited for Riley to respond, but all he heard was the quiet hiss of the satellite link. 'Are you there?'

Riley spoke after a moment. 'And this comes directly from your intelligence people?'

'We have assets on the ground in London,' Harry told him, pride momentarily restored.

'Thank you for bringing this to our attention,' Riley said.

Harry felt like he was reporting a leaky water main to a bored help desk operator. 'That's it?'

'Good night, Harry.'

The line went dead. Harry squeezed the phone in his hand. He wanted to launch it at the wall and smash it to pieces. Instead, he handed it back to Wilde and poured two coffees from the urn on the refreshment table. He handed one to his chief of staff and sat down, placing the mug between his boots. From the pocket of his combat jacket, he took out a silver flask and emptied a shot of cognac into both cups.

'Not sure we should be doing this, Harry.'

'We might as well because we certainly aren't going anywhere this evening.' Harry put the flask back in his pocket and savoured the sweetened black brew. The alcohol burned its way down into his stomach, fuelling the coals of fury that burned there.

SIXTY SECONDS AFTER SPEAKING TO THE BRITISH PM, RILEY was back on the phone, grilling McKenzie at USCENTCOM. The general declared his opposition to the plan and the determination of the president's team to make it work. Riley sympathised, and for the next 15 minutes, they focussed on the security arrangements. McKenzie announced that an aerial sweep had discovered no missile truck. Either the intelligence was incorrect, or it never existed. But Riley was a cautious man, and he impressed on the general the importance of keeping the president safe.

The next call Riley made was to his boss. When Mitchell took it, the VP made sure the door to his private office was closed and brought the president up to speed.

'Call off your trip, Mr President. It's not worth the risk.'

Mitchell was unconvinced. 'So, some guy in London saw a missile launcher, took out the crew, and then the truck disappeared?'

'That's the story. It's sketchy, but we have to take it seriously.'

'You think Beecham knows I'm in town?'

Riley shrugged. 'How could he possibly? The British element at CENTCOM is working elsewhere. They cannot know you're in-country.'

'Maybe they smell a rat. That being the case, Beecham might be feeding us a line so he can get into town before me.'

'I highly doubt it.'

At the other end of the line, Mitchell took a breath and sighed. 'Me too.'

'So, call it off.'

'Delta are already on the ground,' Mitchell said. 'They've put themselves at tremendous risk, and now the palace and the LZ are secure.'

'That's their job. Believe me, they won't care if you go or not.'

There was another pause on the line. Mitchell spoke after a few moments. 'I'll make you a promise, Curtis. I'll reassess in the morning, and if I don't like the smell of it, I'll call it off.'

Riley sighed, long and deep. 'Thank you, Mr President.'

'But there is an upside. If I don't make it back, you get to be president that much sooner.' Mitchell chuckled down the line.

'Please don't joke,' Riley said. 'You're flying into a combat zone. Your safety cannot be guaranteed.'

'I appreciate your concern, Curtis. You know, I couldn't be

happier handing the presidency to you. You're going to make us all proud.'

Emotion squeezed Riley's throat. Since the death of the VP's parents decades ago, Bob Mitchell had taken care of Riley's education, supported his desire to serve in the military, and had guided his political career. Mitchell's family had embraced him, schooled him, and had welcomed his then-fiancée Olivia into the Mitchell fold with open arms. His firstborn was named Robert as a tribute. Bob Mitchell was the father Riley never had.

'Thank you, sir.'

'Good night, Curtis.'

The call ended, and Riley rested the phone back in its cradle. London was five hours ahead of DC. He'd make sure he spoke to the president again before the sun rose over England.

[29]

FALL BACK

GENERAL BABAN CLIMBED INTO THE BACK SEAT OF THE RANGE Rover and told the driver to head to his temporary headquarters beneath Leicester Square tube station. He'd just left the underground car park off Fenchurch Street, where one of his missile trucks had been moved to after persons unknown killed its crew. Next to him, his 2IC adjusted his pistol belt to a more comfortable position.

'You think they know?' Lieutenant-Colonel Naji said.

'They have the best sniffer drones in the world,' Baban replied. 'If they knew, they would've taken the truck out with a Tomahawk. But to send a couple of guys with guns? Doubtful.' He glanced up through the rain-spattered window. 'They're probably watching us right now.'

Naji said nothing, and Baban watched the world pass outside. Rain swept across the city, and the streets ran red with the dirt of destroyed buildings. The operation had achieved a great deal so far, but Baban thirsted for a more significant victory, to pit himself against an adversary rather than an inanimate object like a bridge or a building. His anti-aircraft assets could deliver that victory, but the target had to come to him, close enough so that escape would be impossible. That's why he had spotter teams on every significant roof top around the city, low-tech assets armed with powerful binoculars and laser lights. When a target presented itself, he would know soon enough. Then his birds would fly.

'Make sure every missile team stays out of sight and powered down until the spotters give us something worth taking out.'

Naji nodded. 'Very good, general.'

'And let's start bringing our people out of the tube stations and up onto the street. I want them all in position in the next 24 hours. I doubt the infidels will wait much longer than that to slobber over their victory.'

'Yes, sir.'

The Range Rover cruised through the empty streets, the rain falling in silver sheets as they headed back to Leicester Square. Baban closed his eyes and let the steady motion of the vehicle soothe his aching muscles. He'd been on the go for days now, visiting the troops, briefing his commanders, poring over maps, and choosing defensive and fall-back positions, ammunition dumps, casualty stations, and last-stand defilades. His army would wreak much havoc, but ultimately, they would all be captured or killed. Baban had instilled in them the importance of the latter.

Last stands were rarely pretty. They were desperate moments of cold fear, savagery, and blood. But there was a certain glory to be found in the aftermath of such actions, and his people had vowed to embrace that glory and die with honour. He looked away from the window and turned to Naji.

'The helicopter. Is it standing by?'

'Fuelled and ready, general.'

Baban nodded. 'Keep it that way.'

He turned back to the window, but not before he caught a trace of a smile on Naji's lips. A glorious death was every soldier's dream, but every general's was a ceremonial procession along the Avenue of Martyrs, with the adulation of a Baghdad crowd ringing in one's ears.

Death is overrated, Baban decided.
Better to live and fight another day.

[30]

DOVER SOUL

'BERTIE, WAKE UP. SOMETHING'S HAPPENING.'

He heard the words cutting through the dull fog of his mind, heard the steady drumbeat of rain on the roof of the Mercedes. He cracked open his eyes and pushed himself off the steering wheel. The windscreen was an opaque rectangle on his side, and he took a rag from his door pocket and wiped it. The view hadn't changed since he'd fallen asleep – he checked his watch – an hour ago. Beneath the falling rain, the traffic stretched for miles into the darkness, solid and unmoving, a river of glass, rubber, and steel frozen in time. Most people had switched off their engines, including Bertie, and the air inside the Mercedes was cool and stale. He cranked the window an inch, allowing a salt-tinged draught to circle around the vehicle.

'Must you, Bertie? We're frozen to death back here.'

He glanced at the mirror and forced a smile. 'Just for a minute, Lady Edith. The fresh air will do us all good.' He turned to Cheryl. 'What am I looking at, love?'

She pointed through the windscreen. 'Militia. Lots of them.'

Bertie saw them threading their way between the stationary vehicles. A couple of big troop trucks crawled along the empty westbound lanes of the M20, shadowing their fellow traitors.

'They're looking for something,' Cheryl said.

'Trouble, I would imagine.' As Bertie said the word, he saw several of the black-clad militia surround a vehicle several cars ahead. It was hard to see what was going on, but through the distorted view of the rainy windscreen he saw arms waving and heard shouts carried on the wind. The car nosed its way out of the jam and through a gap in the crash barriers. Then it drove east along the empty carriageway towards Dover. Bertie watched it until its red lights disappeared far into the distance.

'Lucky bastard.'

'Bertie, please!'

'Sorry, Lady Edith.'

'They let him go,' Cheryl said. 'I wonder why?'

Bertie didn't answer straight away. He wiped the mounting condensation from the windscreen and watched the militia as they approached. They weaved between the cars, vans, and small trucks, tapping on windows, talking to drivers, shouting, waving, pointing their guns. Cheryl was right, something was happening, but right now Bertie was clueless.

They were still ten miles from the docks at Dover, and he tried to imagine how many cars made up such a tailback. A lot, obviously. He did a rough calculation in his head. Maybe a thousand cars per mile, so that was 10,000 cars in front of their Mercedes, with an average of three passengers per vehicle. That meant there were 30,000 people ahead of them, not including those already inside the port's gates. And what about the traffic on the A2, and any other road that led to the port? So, the figure would be more like 60,000, and that was a conservative estimate. All descending on Dover at the same time.

And what about the ferries? How many people could they carry? A couple of thousand? Unless they started using the big cruise liners, they could be trapped in Dover for days, and Bertie didn't like the thought of that at all.

He wiped his door window. In the distance he saw the glow of Folkestone, and beyond that, pinpricks of light that he figured were ships at sea. As they'd slowed at the tail end of the jam, Bertie had thought about turning off and trying to get to Folkestone port, but by the time he'd debated himself to death, he'd driven past the offramp, which was now a mile and a couple of thousand cars behind them. Somewhere in the darkness to the north was the Eurotunnel terminal, but that was a no-go too. No trains were running, and according to The Witch a tunnel had been destroyed by an Allied air strike. So, it was Dover or bust, and Bertie thought it was looking more like bust every minute.

To add to his mounting anxiety, he was still trying to process the events of the last day or so. The passage of time had become blurred, but one thing that was as clear as crystal was their good luck. Caught in that gigantic blast at Southampton, they'd seen cars and people crushed by falling steel the size of terraced houses and yet they had escaped unscathed. At the care home, Bertie knew the scumbags there would've killed them for the treasure buried in the Mercedes. But Mrs H had saved them. There was no doubt about it. That she'd ridden one of them like a bucking bronco to do so still troubled Bertie. The poor bird must've had a breakdown somewhere down the line, but in some bizarre moment of clarity, she'd known what to do and had sacrificed herself so that the rest of them might live.

Maybe it was the shooting in Hampstead that had unhinged her. Al-Huda's brains had splattered all over her. Or maybe it was the journey, the constant tension, the risk of capture, of being dragged out of the van and shot, or hung from a lamppost. Whatever caused her breakdown, they owed Mrs H their lives. And if Judge Hardy could have done so, he would've swapped places with her. He had said little since they'd left the care home and his wife's body by a muddy flowerbed. The Witch, on the other hand, grumbled like an impatient kid on a road trip.

'Here they come, Bertie,' Cheryl said.

'I see 'em, love.'

They funnelled down the sides of the van, wearing black helmets and baseball caps and jackets slick with rain. Bertie glanced at the mirror.

'You folks stay quiet, okay?'

The Witch mumbled something Bertie didn't quite catch, but his focus was now on the armed men streaming past the Mercedes. A black face made eye contact through the windscreen, and Bertie powered down his window. The rain beat a tattoo on the roof, the surrounding cars, the road. The big fella stopped.

'Evening, mate. Any idea how long this will take?'

The man stared at him, at Cheryl, at the old un's in back. Rain dripped off the peak of his black baseball cap with the crossed swords logo. 'Dover's a no-go. Absolutely solid, and a lot of ships are leaving and not coming back. You can either pull off at the next offramp or you can take your chances and wait.'

Bertie's heart sank, but he still had a card to play, a big, fat envelope of cash in his pocket. 'I saw a car pull away a few minutes ago. How did he manage that?'

'That was a VIP and his family.' He pointed into the distance. 'Stay in your lane. The offramp's a mile up the motorway. Good luck, pal.'

Bertie snapped his left arm out, exposing the green rubber ring around his wrist. 'We're VIPs,' he said. 'Look.'

The black man slung his gun around his back and shone his torch at Bertie's uncovered arm. 'Why didn't you say?' He pointed to the empty carriageway beside them. 'There's a gap just ahead. I'll get it cleared. Wait there.'

Bertie nodded, any traces of exhaustion now gone. 'Can you get us on a ship? I can pay you for your trouble.'

The black man lowered his voice. 'I can talk to a mate down in Dover, but I can't promise anything.'

'You get us inside and I'll pay you both. How much is it going to cost me?'

The man didn't hesitate. 'Five grand each.'

Bertie winced theatrically. Then he nodded. 'Okay. You're rinsing me dry, but you've got a deal.'

The man turned and shouted into the rain. 'VIP vehicle here! Let's get these cars moved out of the way!'

The militia swarmed around the blockage, cajoling and coercing the drivers around the Mercedes to move their vehicles with kicks and threats. Bumpers clashed and bodywork crunched. Bertie started the engine. The heater hummed, and the wipers worked the windscreen.

'Don't say a word,' Bertie warned the others. 'I'll do all the talking. Cheryl, climb in the back.'

She squeezed past Bertie and settled in next to The Witch, who tutted and grumbled. Out on the road, the black man waved Bertie through the gap and out onto the empty carriageway. He saw the faces of the other drivers, blurred and envious. He didn't blame them. The black man climbed inside the cab and shook the rain off his cap. He rested the rifle by his side.

'Nice to be out of that weather,' he said. 'Let's go.'

Bertie put his foot down, and they drove in the centre lane towards Dover.

'My name's Leon. What's yours?'

'Dave,' Bertie told him.

'Nice to meet you.' He turned around and smiled. 'Nice to meet you folks too.'

'What's it like down there?'

'Dover?' Leon shivered. 'Chaos. Must be close to 50,000 people down there, and that doesn't include anyone in this traffic jam,' he said, jerking a thumb at the miles of stationary vehicles. 'If we didn't have guns, there'd be a riot.'

'How does the boarding process work?'

'You go in, join a queue, and wait. Right now, there're plenty of shipping agents behind the desks, and they're in touch with the ships' captains. Everyone's making a killing, but it won't last much longer. How much money have you got?'

Bertie stared ahead through the windscreen. The gun was on his right hip, and if he was fast enough, he could shoot Leon before the guy could reach for that big, clumsy rifle. 'Not a lot.'

'Well, they're charging bundles, and the price changes all the time, depending on which clerk you speak to and what boat they can get you on. Can you dump the van? You'll be processed a lot faster if you leave on foot.'

'No!' The Witch barked from behind them. 'Certainly not. I have my clothes, personal things.'

Leon twisted around in his seat. 'That can all be replaced, madam. Your life can't.' He squinted in the dark. 'You look familiar. Have I seen you somewhere before?'

Bertie jumped in before anyone spoke. 'She's been interviewed on the TV news a lot. She's a famous Islamic historian.'

Leon looked disappointed. 'I see.' He turned back and settled in his seat.

The Mercedes ate up the miles. Ahead, Dover was lit up like daylight, a shining beacon of hope, and the white cliffs that towered over the terminal glowed in the reflected light. Bertie saw big ships berthed at several docks and countless vehicles waiting to board them. But that's not what worried him. It was the crowds streaming towards the port on foot, laden down with luggage, bulging against the perimeter fence as the security cordon struggled to cope with the sheer mass of humanity. It was like the fall of Saigon, or Afghanistan. Leon pointed through the windscreen.

'See what I mean? Chaos. This could get really ugly.'

While he despised people like Leon for their choices, Bertie was curious why they were still here. 'What about you?' he asked him. 'Militia, cops, you're all going to be targets for the mobs.'

Leon tapped the side of his flat nose. 'We've got people on the dockside. They'll let us know when to start falling back inside the wire. After that, we'll make a run for a ship. It's all sorted.' He looked at Bertie and smiled. 'You'd better be at sea when that happens, otherwise it's game over for you lot.'

Bertie tried to imagine the scene. Order breaking down. Thousands of people charging through the terminal, across the vast car parks toward the last ship as it blasts its horn and slips its ropes. Every man for himself type stuff. Terrifying.

Red flares burned at the end of the motorway and the entrance to Dover harbour. There were militia and cops everywhere, standing in big groups by the side of the road, moving through the crawling traffic, all tooled up. Some manned big guns mounted on jeeps and trucks abandoned by IS forces, and Bertie got the impression that they wouldn't need too much of an excuse to use them. Beyond them, inside the perimeter fence, the two-lane road became six lanes of nose-to-tail traffic inching forward to a line of control booths manned by more armed militia. Bertie slowed for the flares, and Leon dropped his window.

'Got another VIP,' he shouted to the press of black uniforms, wet weather gear slick beneath the steady rain. He had to shout because the noise was tremendous, a low roar of engines, shouting, ships' horns and the squally conditions. The militia allowed them to pass, and Bertie followed Leon's directions to a seventh lane that ran beside others but was separated from them by a concrete barrier. As they drove past the congestion, Bertie saw broken-down cars and coach engines spewing white smoke. He saw families stamping through the rain, a lot of suitcases and screaming children, and old folks hanging on to railings, fighting for breath as others barged past.

'There's the gate,' Leon said, pointing ahead.

At the end of the lane was a chain-link entrance to the port's inner compound. A short distance beyond it was the departure building. Bertie stepped on the brakes as another militiaman in a baseball cap and rain slicker stepped out of a side gate and waved them down. Bertie brought the Mercedes to a halt. Leon beamed.

'Time to pay the piper, Dave.'

He reached into his jeans pocket and pulled out the envelope of cash. He handed it behind him. 'Babe, count out ten grand, would you?'

Cheryl took it and went to work by torchlight. Leon chatted to his friend out of the window. After a couple of minutes, Cheryl tapped Leon on the shoulder with a thick wad of cash.

'There you go, friend.'

Leon took it, and his eyes lit up. 'Sweet.' He counted it fast, then smiled and waved the fat wedge at his friend outside. The man gave Leon a thumbs up and jogged to the gate, swinging it open.

Leon pointed to the vast building ahead and its adjacent parking area. Bertie saw a few empty spaces.

'Park over there and go in through the side door. Someone will meet you on the other side and direct you into a queue. This is a restricted area, so you won't get caught up with the main mob.' He offered his hand and Bertie found himself taking it. 'Good luck, Dave. To all of you,' he said, smiling at the others. He stepped out into the rain and shouldered his rifle.

Bertie drove through the gate and found a parking space. He reversed the Mercedes back up against the fence and switched off the engine. Then he exhaled a long sigh of relief.

'That was a major stroke of luck,' he said, turning to the others.

'Are we safe?' The Witch asked him.

Bertie shook his head. 'Not yet. Once we get on a boat and sail away, that's when we can relax. Until then, we need to keep our wits about us.' He checked his watch. It was 5 am. 'I'll go inside and find out what's what. Keep the doors locked, okay?'

'I'll sit up front,' Cheryl said.

'We'll be fine,' the judge muttered, the first words he'd spoken for hours. That was a start.

Bertie crossed the car park and entered the building through a set of double doors. Inside, he found himself inside a dark lobby, but the sound was unmistakable. A muted vibration, like he was standing inside a giant bass speaker. It rose in volume as he crossed the lobby and headed towards another set of doors. He grasped a handle, the roar on the other side unmistakable. The flame of hope inside Bertie flickered and died. He pulled open the door.

[31]

FLOCK OF SEAGULLS

Bob Mitchell stepped outside the building and took a deep, cleansing breath of morning air. The sun had not yet risen, and darkness still lingered across the private estate, which was fine by Mitchell because he was a morning person, and nothing inspired him more than watching the sunrise.

He set off walking, his invisible Secret Service detail spread out across the overgrown lawns. Mitchell was in no direct danger, but those dedicated guys and gals did their job anyway, as did the smaller team of Navy SEALs that formed a discrete box around him as he strolled the tree line and the perimeter wall.

The peace of the pre-dawn darkness helped him think. Today was D-Day, which for Bob Mitchell meant decision day. As the song went, should I stay, or should I go? Lying in bed the previous evening, he had considered his position, and he accepted the fact that travelling to London at this point wasn't without risk. And considering the recent intelligence passed on by the Brits, the trip was probably not a good idea. His head said no, but somewhere in his heart, he wanted to say yes. His instinct was to go, to flirt with danger, albeit so briefly that danger would be unaware of his presence until long after his safe return. As for his approval rating, it was meaningless because he was handing over his presidency to Curtis in the New Year, and mentally he already had one foot out of the Oval Office. It had been a privilege to serve the American people, and while checks and balances – and often political interference – ensured that the President of the United States was not the most powerful person on the planet, the job still came with a significant level of authority. There were strings he could pull, and while he was still in the hot seat, it seemed only right to pull them.

And so, he'd slept, and on rising, he'd showered and shaved, and he'd looked into the eyes of his reflection and asked, *Do you want to do this or not?* The answer was yes.

He cut short his circumnavigation of the grounds and headed back towards the dark cubes set against the pre-dawn sky. As he walked up the steps towards the patio, Radanovich and Tagg were waiting to greet him.

'Good morning, Mr President,' they said, almost in unison.

'Morning, guys. Sleep okay?'

Radanovich folded his arms across his jacket. He took a step closer, making sure the SEALs were not in earshot. 'Come on, Bob. The suspense is killing us both.'

Mitchell smiled and spread his hands. 'As they say in the movies, let's saddle up.'

'You're going?' Tagg said, a note of disbelief in her voice.

'Yes, we are.'

His advisors couldn't disguise their concern. Was it reserved for him, or was it more personal? Historically, politicians had no problem sending their young men and women into danger. Often, the folks in DC were the first to demand military action, to applaud the falling bombs and green-light all manner of interventions and invasions, and to hell with the consequences. It was never their sons and daughters learning to walk again on prosthetics. Mitchell reasoned that all politicians should experience a little of what their servicemen and women went through. It wouldn't do his people any harm, and besides, McKenzie would guarantee their safety.

'Zack, tell the general we're ready to move at his discretion.'

His chief of staff hurried into the darkness. Tagg didn't move.

'Sandy, if you don't want to go, that's fine. For me, this is a personal choice. I can't talk about sacrifice if I'm not prepared to take a little risk myself. Do you understand?'

'I do, Bob. You're right, it's important that the American people see their leaders laying it on the line occasionally.'

Mitchell chuckled. 'I don't think it's going to be quite so dramatic, but I believe it's important, don't you think?'

The press secretary nodded. 'I do. Which is why I'm joining you.'

He smiled. 'Only if you're sure.'

Before she could answer, another presidential aide stepped out onto the patio.

'Mr President, I have Vice President Riley on the line.'

Mitchell held up a hand. 'Tell him you just missed me. I'll call him when I get back.'

The aide disappeared back inside the cube. Mitchell clapped his hands together and looked east where the sky had paled.

'It's going to be a helluva day.'

NINETY SECONDS AFTER RADANOVICH SPOKE TO GENERAL McKenzie, a black airship belonging to the 7th Transportation Brigade (Expeditionary) made a final turn in the dark sky and came into land on Eaton Place, the long, tree-lined avenue that connected Sloane Square in Chelsea to Victoria. The stealth airship was an enormous beast, and as it squeezed its massive body between the trees, helium cells popped and blew as branches and streetlights ripped them open, adding pressure on the 12 turbo-lift propellers. The remote operators, ensconced in their flight cabin 20 miles to the west, were unconcerned by the damage, as this was a one-way deal. Their airship groaned as it came down on the tarmac, its landing cushioned by the rubber impact bladder deployed on the final approach. The fat beast rumbled and scraped its way along Eaton Square, snapping branches and streetlights, and crushing cars and traffic signals, until it came to rest half a mile from the walls of the palace. The hydraulic ramp whined down, and cold, pre-dawn air eddied around the compact cargo bay. Inside, eight M5 Ripsaw tanks squatted in the darkness. Once the Ripsaw operators gained control, they powered their charges into life and drove them out onto the street, steering east towards Buckingham Palace. Working in pairs, the Ripsaws headed for their patrol stations on Grosvenor Place, Constitution Hill, The Mall, and Birdcage Walk. Like the airship they'd travelled into London on, these Ripsaws were disposable, fitted with rubber tyres instead of tracks, 20mm guns and 40mm grenade launchers instead of the big, 30mm auto-cannons. They were fast, lean, and carried a decent punch, and with luck, they wouldn't be needed.

The Delta teams outside the palace reported the Ripsaws' arrival on station to CENTCOM, an observation also noted by the UAVs circling above. To the east, the sun appeared above the eastern skyline and flooded the city with its bright autumnal light.

The tables were set, the dance floor ready.

It was time to start the music.

MITCHELL HELD ON TIGHT AS THE DEFIANT HELICOPTER thundered across the city so fast and low that he felt he could reach out and touch the rooftops flashing beneath him. The aircraft rose and fell, banking left and right, and Mitchell wanted to whoop for joy, like a teenager on a theme park ride. This wasn't like any helicopter journey he'd experienced before, especially since becoming president. His trips in Marine One were sedate, controlled affairs that got him to where he needed to be with nary a bump. What he was experiencing now was another world, dangerous yet exhilarating, and he was loving every second.

The other helicopters were performing the same manoeuvres. Two of them were Defiant transports, decoys that would extract the Delta teams already on the ground, and the four others were attack aircraft, Apaches and Vipers, their stubby wings loaded with ordnance. Every few minutes, Mitchell watched them spray bright blooms of magnesium flares that burned with a blinding white brilliance as they tumbled to earth. Mitchell's ride was a Russian doll, inside a bunch of other dolls, impossible to get at.

The aircraft banked hard over and changed course. When it levelled out, Mitchell saw the River Thames, and the jagged edges of the destroyed bridges. He saw a red London bus submerged in the water, and across the grey expanse of slate roofs to his left, a big fire burned unchecked. He caught glimpses of roads littered with debris and burned-out vehicles. This was a city at war. No government, no troops, no cops, no order, and he wondered how the folks on the ground would be feeling. Terrified, no doubt, and he hoped some of them were looking up at the US military aircraft flying overhead and be comforted by the sight.

He glanced at Sandy and Zack sitting opposite him. Both were wearing ballistic helmets and vests over their causal clothes and strapped tight in their seats. Sandy wasn't her usual confident self, and Zack was watching the city outside the window. Mitchell felt a flash of guilt. He'd compelled them to come, he knew that. Sure, Sandy had the chance to sit this one out, but Mitchell stood by his conviction. It was right that they should all experience a little trepidation. It would make them better politicians and give them pause next time angry voices in Congress demanded US military action somewhere in the world. That was the hope, at least.

His headset hissed. 'Three minutes out. Prepare for landing.'

Mitchell's heart beat faster. *Here we go.*

ON THE 28TH FLOOR OF PORTLAND HOUSE, A STONE'S THROW from Victoria Station, a spotter stood deep in the shadows of an empty office and watched the helicopters clatter past the building, close enough to rattle the windows. He noted the size and composition of the flight and saw it pass above Buckingham Palace before banking hard over Green Park and heading back towards the sprawling royal estate. The three transport helicopters – state-of-the-art Defiants – dropped towards the ground, two of them landing on the lawns behind the palace and one descending straight down into the courtyard. Like the others, that aircraft was matte black, but unlike the others, its nose bristled with antenna and other sensors. He noted that detail, too.

The spotter turned his attention to the other helicopters, the gunships that circled low and fast over the area, maintaining their distance from the palace. The speed and intensity of the operation could mean only one thing – someone important was aboard those aircraft. Or maybe there were several VIPs. The spotter moved away from the windows and back into the shadows of the unlit office. He dialled a number on his encrypted satellite phone and relayed his report.

MITCHELL'S HEART RACED, WHICH WASN'T ADVISABLE FOR A man with a condition, but he felt more alive than he had for a very long time. The rooftops of the palace slipped beneath the helicopter, and Mitchell saw a sniper lying prone beneath a parapet, shielding his head as the downdraught of the twin rotors battered him. Mitchell's aides were watching the descent through the windows, and the White House photographer, Gonzales, was snapping the president with his camera. Mitchell caught the eye of the Navy SEAL next to him. The man looked away, but Mitchell thought he saw something there, resentment perhaps, and suddenly he felt very guilty about what he was doing. It wasn't just his life he was risking, he knew that, and now this didn't feel right. He made a promise to himself – as soon as they landed, he would tell Gonzales to get what he needed ASAP, and then be on their way.

The buildings rose around them as they dropped below the roofline and into the courtyard. The noise was tremendous, and then the door flew open and two helmeted soldiers waited, their patterned uniforms flapping in the hurricane of wind and noise. Mitchell took off his headphones and tried his best to leap to the ground gracefully, unsure if he pulled it off. Then Sandy and Zack were beside him, the SEALs folded in around them, and then they were all jogging for the shelter of the palace. As they reached the door, Mitchell looked up. At that moment, he saw a Viper gunship banking over the courtyard, so low that he could see the pilot looking down at them from behind his black visor and the grinning shark's teeth painted on the nose of the aircraft. Mitchell's adrenaline pumped.

Jet engines whined to a low hum, and the twin rotors slowed, but the presidential ride wouldn't shut down. As Gonzales tracked him with his camera lens, Mitchell stepped inside the building and shook hands with the Delta commander, thanking him for his efforts, but his words tailed off as he absorbed the scale of the surrounding devastation. Mitchell had been to the palace many times. He'd dined here, had toured the buildings and grounds, but now blackened, graffitied walls and broken furniture surrounded him. The King's home looked like a crack den, and he waved at Gonzales to stop filming. The Brits wouldn't want to see this. Instead, they'd film outside, where the light would better capture his ballistic vest, the grey/black combat jacket (complete with *MITCHELL* name tag), and his 160th SOAR Night Stalker cap.

He took a final look around the vast reception hall, with its broken windows and once-red carpets that squelched beneath his boots, and he wondered again how the world had turned upside down, and how a royal palace in the heart of London could be considered enemy territory. But the world had, and the palace was.

He turned to the Delta commander.

'Let's take this outside, shall we?'

. . .

In the Transport for London offices on Cranbourn Street, located above one of several entrances to Leicester Square tube station, General Baban and Lieutenant Colonel Naji were debating the veracity of the spotter's report. They had no surveillance footage to refer to, no radar signatures or tracking data to study, only the word of an eyewitness in Victoria. But Baban's gut told him it was a sighting of significant value.

'Must be a VIP,' Nabil said. 'Three transports, four attack helicopters, and the passive array at St James' Park are picking up heavy jamming signals from an airborne platform, probably an orbiting drone. Which means it's a high-value target. You think it could be McKenzie from CENTCOM?'

Baban shook his head. 'Doubtful. A man like that wouldn't risk such a rash move, not while the tactical situation remains uncertain. No, this stinks of political grandstanding. Maybe it's the King himself, on some morale-boosting photo-op.'

'Or a Cabinet secretary. British or American. Or both.'

'Whoever it is, they've got enough clout to whistle up a heavy security envelope. It sounds promising, but the helicopters are operating too low to engage with our missile trucks. Keep them shut down and mobilise the local teams instead.'

'Which ones?'

'The closest. Victoria, St James' Park, Charing Cross. Their mission is to take out as many of those aircraft as possible. And tell them to focus on those transports.'

'Roger.'

Naji barked at a loitering subordinate, who scuttled away. Then he turned back to Baban and rubbed his hands. 'So, the games begin.'

'Indeed,' Baban said, smiling. 'Now let's see if we can flush out their big guns.'

Eddie was asleep beneath a thick bolt of silk when he heard Griff's voice echoing across the room. He opened his eyes, his hand reaching for the pistol hidden beneath the material. He saw Griff in the doorway.

'Something's happening out on the Strand, mate. No idea what it is, but I thought you should know.'

Eddie threw off his makeshift blanket and got to his feet. He hopped around on the wooden floor as he pulled his boots on, then he checked the MP5, chambered a round and flipped on the safety. He followed Griff downstairs to the courtyard door. Griff cracked it open, and Eddie heard it straight away. The rumble of feet; whistle blasts and shouts; and the revving of diesel engines. He yanked on his tactical vest and coat.

'Stay here,' he said. 'I'm going to the end of the alleyway. Get eyes on.'

'Watch yourself,' Griff said.

The surrounding buildings loomed over the courtyard. Eddie crossed it in ten quick strides and slipped through the gate into the alleyway. The sun was still low in the sky, but it was bright, and high above the alleyway, he saw a long ribbon of blue sky. He crept to the end of the narrow passage and checked both ways. Left towards the junction at Kingsway, nothing moved. To his right, across the street, he saw a long line of buses and coaches idling by the pavement. As he watched, he saw hundreds of heavily armed men and women queueing to board the vehicles, cajoled by marshals. Eddie scanned the opposite pavement with his spotter scope. Jihads and militia, hundreds of them, streaming out of Charing Cross Station and from Villiers Street. They'd been hiding in the tube stations all this time, just like the Hag had said. There was an army beneath their feet, and now it was mobilising.

He could see their urgency through his scope, sense the excitement of the combatants, noted the variety of weapons, everything from assault rifles to heavy machine guns, mortars, and anti-tank weapons. His blood ran cold. This was just one station and there were hundreds across London. Where else were they hidden, and what had brought them out on the streets?

A target, obviously. But where? Was the Atlantic Alliance advancing on London right now? Surely their own UAVs would detect this mobilisation? Then again, was it reasonable to assume that every street and district of London was being monitored in real-time? Probably not. But he had to tell Hawkins.

He edged back into the shadows and ran back to the safe house. Griff bolted the door behind him, and Eddie took the stairs two at a time. He heard Griff following behind him and raised a hand, cutting off his questions.

'Give me a sec. I've got to make a call.'

Griff was insistent. 'What was all the noise, mate? What did you see?'

Eddie heard the phone ringing at the other end. He put his hand over the mouthpiece. 'Trouble.'

HARRY HEARD BOOTS CLANKING UP THE METAL STAIRCASE AND got to his feet. He'd slept badly and had crawled out of his sleeping bag an hour ago before the sun had risen. It was bright now, and a shaft of sunlight beamed across the warehouse floor. He put down his coffee and saw a Para officer at the door. Harry waved him in before he could knock.

'Sorry to disturb, Prime Minister, but General Wheeler is on the phone in the comms centre.'

Harry pointed to the satellite phone next to his steaming mug of coffee. 'Patch him through to my personal, would you?'

The Para nodded, relayed the order on his radio and left the room. Thirty seconds later, his phone vibrated across the table. He scooped it up.

'Beecham,' he said. He heard Wheeler's voice on the other end of the line.

'Prime Minister, we've received fresh intelligence from our asset in London. An enemy formation of armed personnel is mobilising along the Strand. Numbers are in the hundreds, no uniforms, but heavily armed and certainly organised. And they're in a hurry.'

'Who else knows?'

'You're the first.'

'Pass it to CENTCOM,' Harry said. 'Right now, please Nick.' He ended the call and put another into the White House. The urgency of his tone ensured he connected to Riley in less than 30 seconds. Harry began talking. Riley slammed the phone down on him in less than five seconds.

THE CONVOY OF BUSES AND COACHES, PACKED WITH JIHADI fighters and die-hard militia, headed south, passing the mountain of rubble that was once Admiralty Arch and through the bulldozed moonscape of Whitehall. They drove as fast as they could because they knew that sooner rather than later, Alliance UAVs would detect their furious movement. Rumbling into the warren of narrow back-streets around St James' Park, the sound of the orbiting enemy heli-copters grew louder as the vehicles stopped and the makeshift army filed out onto the streets, splitting into smaller teams and staying tight to the buildings as they moved closer to Buckingham Palace.

'GENERAL MCKENZIE!'

The urgency of the voice made the grizzled Marine's close-cropped head snap around. A UAV analyst sitting in front of a big screen had her hand raised.

'Speak,' he said, walking towards her.

'Multiple contacts, sir, armed and heading on foot towards the president's location.'

McKenzie and his officers stared at the screen, at the high-defini-tion black-and-white images broadcasting from the Global Hawk. All of them saw hundreds of tiny figures running towards the palace.

'General, we have movement at Victoria Station!'

McKenzie scrambled behind the analysts to another console. A uniformed kid with thick, black-rimmed glasses was pointing at his screen. 'They're coming up from the subway system. Heavily armed and advancing towards the palace.'

The USCENTCOM commander's blood froze in his veins. 'It's a goddam trap!' he yelled. 'Get the president airborne, right now! And light those fuckers up with everything we've got!'

[32]

HURRY UP AND WAIT

THE NOISE INSIDE THE DEPARTURE HALL WAS DEAFENING, A persistent, dull roar of shouting; chattering; screaming and crying children; and the drone of the public-address system that Bertie could barely understand. He didn't know how many people were inside the vast space, but he reckoned there were a few thousand at least, arranged into long queues that snaked around the hall.

The people who made up those queues were a microcosm of British society, with every age and ethnicity represented, all shuffling forward an inch at a time, necks craning to see how far they'd moved and how far they had to go. Bertie knew it would be a long time before he got anywhere near the banks of ticketing clerks seated behind a thick glass panel and the longest counter he'd ever seen. Above each clerk, a huge letter board hung from the high ceiling on thin wires. Bertie was queueing in the 'F' lane, squeezed between families in front and behind, with barely any room between their queue and the 'E' and 'G' lines on either side. The room was stuffy, and the surrounding kids whined and sobbed, prisoners in the crowded room. Bertie had already been queuing for three hours and had barely moved. By his calculation, there were at least five hundred desperate souls in front of him, maybe a thousand. It was going to take hours.

Still, at least Cheryl and the judges could wait it out in relative comfort. Bertie ordered them to stay in the van while he bought the tickets. He'd brought a hundred grand with him, twenty-five in each pocket of his jeans, and despite The Witch's demand that he negotiate hard, Bertie intended to cough up the lot if that's what it took to get them on a ship.

'Hey, where the fuck d'you think you're going?'

'Mind your fucking business!'

Bertie turned around. A couple of queues over, two snarling men were standing nose to nose. People around them backed away as the exchange heated up quicker than a junkie's spoon. Bertie knew it was about to kick off, and then the bald one nutted the other. They tore into each other, and the crowd backed away, sending a ripple through the other queues. People around them began shouting, and then whistle blasts shrilled through the hall and a thick black snake of militia carved through the crowd, guns and clubs raised. They beat the two men to the ground as their families screamed and begged. Bertie saw a lot of pointing fingers and angry militia faces. The bald guy came off worse, and they dragged him back through the crowd as he yelled his innocence.

'That's him done,' said the minister from Manchester, queuing in front of Bertie with his wife Tessa and their two kids. 'Back of the queue, he'll go. No chance of getting to France now.'

'How so?' Bertie asked.

'It's the ships,' Tessa said. 'They're leaving, but a lot of them aren't coming back. That's what we heard.'

Me too, Bertie thought, remembering Leon's words of warning. He shuffled his aching feet and berated himself for not bringing something to sit on. Many people around him were sitting on bags and cases. It wasn't luxury, but it was better than the floor.

'We're supposed to be VIPs,' Tessa complained for the umpteenth time. 'Harvey, speak to someone.'

Her husband pointed towards the scene of the recent tear-up. 'Did the militia ask those troublemakers if they were VIPs? No, they didn't. Besides, anyone of major significance has already left.'

Not all of them, Bertie didn't say.

'We're important, darling. They should give us priority.'

Bertie had kept his mouth shut while these two had chattered non-stop, but now he couldn't help himself. 'What makes you two important?'

Tessa jumped in straight away. 'Harvey is ... *was* the Housing Minister for Greater Manchester. He had a driver, and a bodyguard.' A proud smile cracked her thin face as she patted her husband's arm.

'What about you, Dave?' Harvey asked. 'How did you get here?'

'I'm just a driver,' Bertie said. 'I work for an Islamic historian. She lives in France most of the time, but we couldn't leave sooner because she wasn't well enough to travel.'

'What's her name?' Tessa probed. 'Harvey's a history buff, aren't you, Harv? He answers all the questions on the quiz shows.'

'She likes her privacy,' Bertie explained. Then he steered the conversation away. 'So, what did you do? As Housing Minister?'

Harvey cleared his throat. 'They tasked me with clearing out the ghettos. Places like Salford and Moss Side. Knocked it all down and bulldozed it.'

'He was interviewed on the BBC News,' Tessa said with a conceited smile.

Bertie feigned a puzzled look. 'What happened to the people who lived there?'

'Deported,' Harvey said. 'We're talking about the worst kind of people. Drug dealers, their clients, benefit cheats, problem families, you know the sort. Thank God for the Great Liberation, I say. It gave society the chance to rid itself of those lowlifes.' He frowned. 'Are you telling me you didn't know about the deportations?'

'Of course I did,' Bertie replied. 'But no one really talked about it, did they?' He winked. 'Don't worry, Minister. Your secret's safe with me.'

Harvey lowered his voice. 'That's why we're leaving. No one will understand that we did it for the good of society. Besides, I didn't have a choice. I was following protocol.'

Bertie clicked his heels and put on his best German accent. 'I was just following orders, ja?' He laughed, but the others didn't. Tessa scowled and Harvey tutted. 'That's not very tasteful, Dave.'

'Harvey did what he had to do to survive,' Tessa added. 'Didn't you, darling?'

'With your support, yes.'

She grimaced. 'You were the minister, not me.'

A terrible scream sliced through the clamour of the hall. Bertie spun around, his heart racing. He saw a dozen militia charging through the crowd, using their rifle butts and batons, and knocking people to the ground. Others pushed and shoved to get out of the way, sending more ripples through the tightly-packed hall. The militia surrounded four men, and Bertie saw one of them clutching his face as blood poured between his fingers. The militia dragged them all out of the queue and bundled them towards the main doors.

'Another four gone,' Harvey said. 'Jesus, look at that crowd outside.'

Bertie looked too. Beyond the glass entrance doors to the departure hall, the sun had risen, but the sky was overcast, and rain fell in cold sheets across a vast crowd outside. A thick line of gun-wielding militia barred their entry and corralled them behind steel crash barriers. Those who could, sheltered beneath umbrellas, luggage, and squares of soggy cardboard. The rest looked soaked to the skin, hair plastered to their heads, desperate and miserable. Some of them waved papers and passports at the militia, but their gestures were in vain. All the IDs in the world wouldn't get them processed any faster. It was about reaching a ticket clerk and greasing his palm with readies. That was the only way now to get on a boat. Simple supply and demand economics.

He saw the four men bundled out into the rain and waved off at gunpoint. Harvey stepped closer, his voice low, his beady eyes flicking left and right. 'Perhaps they were resistance.'

Bertie frowned. 'In here? Unlikely.'

'You're wrong,' Tessa said, moving closer. 'They're mingling with the crowds, watching and listening. The rumour is they're looking for people who were high up in the pecking order.'

Bertie couldn't help himself. 'People like you two, you mean?'

'That's right,' she said, without a trace of irony. 'They're pretending they're passengers, but really they're targeting people.'

'They killed a man last night,' Harvey said. 'Found his body in a toilet cubicle. Had a rag stuffed in his mouth. They'd stabbed him multiple times. Blood everywhere.'

'No one saw it,' Tessa added. 'That's why the militia are so jumpy. They're targets too.'

Bertie studied the surrounding faces with fresh eyes. Most of them were families, but then he caught the eye of a man several yards behind him, a tall, thin bloke with grey curly hair and hard eyes. He wore a green Barbour jacket with the collar turned up and he didn't take his eyes off Bertie. Bertie turned away and felt for the gun on his hip. Did the guy recognise him? Or was he just one of those people who just stared? There was no way of knowing, not until he felt a cold steel blade in his back. He raised himself up on his toes and peered above the thousands of heads between him and the ticketing clerks.

'We're not moving,' he said, frustrated.

'You know they're only taking cash, don't you?'

'Yes.'

'They forewarned us,' Harvey said. 'So, we pulled all our money out before things broke down. They'll charge us for the kids too, no doubt. You'll be okay though, travelling on your own.'

'I'm not on my own,' Bertie said.

Harvey frowned. 'I thought you said your historian friend was ill.'

'She's waiting outside. With her family.'

Harvey's mouth dropped open. 'No! She should be here with

you! All family units must check in together.' He raised his hand and tapped it with his other finger. 'They stamp you here. That's how you get on the ship. Without it, they won't let you on board.'

'What?'

Tessa thrust a folded sheet of paper at him. Bertie unfolded it and read the contents. It was true – no stamp, no travel. His stomach churned. 'Where did you get this?'

'They're handing them out as you come in the main door. You should've got one.'

Bertie pointed to the other side of the room. 'I came in through the car park lobby.'

They looked at Bertie as if he had the plague. 'I see,' was all Tessa said and gathered her kids around her legs. Harvey pretended to check his phone.

'If I go get them, you'll keep my place, won't you?'

Tessa spoke before her husband. 'We would, Dave, but look behind you. There's at least a hundred people there, and they won't like it if you leave and come back with a bunch of other people. The militia will probably throw you out.'

'Fuck!'

Tessa turned away, pulling her children in tighter. Bertie looked around the hall. Through the press of bodies, he saw two militiamen nearby, guns held in the crooks of their elbows, the barrels pointing at the ceiling. 'Save my place,' he told Harvey and pushed his way towards them.

'Excuse me.'

Both men turned and glared at him. One had a tattoo on his hand that looked like a very large bruise. The other was taller, thin as a rake and white as a ghost. Beneath the rims of their baseball caps, they looked tired and jumpy. Be careful, Bertie cautioned himself.

'Sorry to bother you. I've been queueing for hours, and I've just been told I need all my family with me. Is that true?'

'Yes,' Tattooed Hand said, scowling. 'Now get back in line.'

Bertie pointed across the hall. 'I've got elderly relatives. They're in my van outside. There's no way they could stand in a queue for long.'

'Look around,' the tall one said. 'Lots of old folks here.'

Tattooed Hand snarled. 'No queue, no stamp. No stamp, no travel. That's the deal. Now get back in your line.'

'I have to get them. Can you hold my place?'

'No.'

Bertie took a step closer, his voice low. 'I can pay cash. A grand each. Get me back in the queue and I'll double it.'

The tall one frowned, his lips moving silently. 'That's four grand,' he said after a moment.

Fucking Einstein. 'Correct.'

They shared a look and Tattooed Hand nodded. 'You got a deal.'

Bertie pointed. 'I came in through the lobby over there. My van's right outside.'

'Stay close,' the tall one said, then he turned and shouted. 'Make a hole there.' He plunged into the crowd, carving his way across the hall, Tattooed Hand beside him, shoving, shouting, and threatening. It took almost ten minutes to squeeze through the crowd, and when they got to the lobby, Bertie already had the money in his hand. He handed the bills over and Tattooed Hand snatched them.

'We can't wait too long. Get your people and meet us back here.'

The door to the car park was now bolted from the inside, Bertie noticed. The tall one dropped the bolts and gestured with his head. 'Go. Be quick, okay?'

Bertie ducked out into the rain and jogged across the car park. The noise from the nearby traffic was deafening, and he saw the access road was an unmoving mass of cars, SUVs, and vans, all desperate to get into the port. He heard a door slam, and Cheryl ran to him, her sneakers splashing through the puddles. She threw her arms around his neck and held him tight.

'Thank God you're okay! The militia came and bolted the doors.'

He eased her away from him and held her hands. 'We've got to go inside, queue up. All of us. We need stamps on our hands. I've got two militia waiting. They'll get us back in the queue, but we have to move fast.'

'What about the van?'

'We lock up and leave it. No choice. Hopefully, it'll still be here when we get back.'

They moved fast, ushering The Witch and Judge Hardy out into the rain. Cheryl had liberated a pair of cataract glasses and made Lady Edith wear them. She refused at first until Bertie told her about the dead man in the toilet. They wore their overcoats and beanies, and they shuffled through the rain and into the lobby. The tall militia bolted it behind them.

'I can't see a thing,' The Witch said, swivelling her head.

'She's got cataracts,' Bertie explained.

'Money,' Tattooed Hand said, holding his out. Bertie dropped another 2,000 in his palm and watched as he counted it.

'More money, Bertie?' The Witch protested. 'You'll have us living in the poorhouse by the time we get to France.'

'Leave the man alone, Edi –' Judge Hardy cut himself off. A few minutes ago, Bertie had warned them about using names. *Auntie* and *Uncle* would do for now.

'We're good to go,' Tattooed Hand said, pocketing the cash.

'I can get you more if you get us to the front of the queue,' Bertie said.

The tall one laughed. 'Nice try, pal, but we ain't that stupid. Last time a couple of our guys tried that, it almost caused a riot, and they got defrocked and thrown out of the port.'

'We'll get you back to where you were,' Tattooed Hand told them. 'That's the best we can do.'

'Fair enough,' said Bertie.

It took almost 20 minutes to make their way back to the 'F' queue. Harvey and Tessa were all smiles again, now that they knew Bertie had a bit of clout. They bowed and scraped when he introduced them to the famous historian, but all The Witch could manage was a nod and a mumbled greeting. The militia made it known by their presence that Bertie and his party were not to be interfered with, and after a while, they drifted away. When he could no longer see them, Bertie felt a twinge of panic, but there was nothing he could do about it. He'd taken more money from the stash in the Mercedes and was now carrying 150,000 in US dollars. He doubted anyone in the hall had that kind of dough on them, and it should guarantee their passage on a ferry. The hardest part would be the wait.

Bertie gave Cheryl a squeeze and settled in. He looked over the heads of the crowd and wondered if it had moved at all. He turned around and saw the mob outside the door; he thought it might've grown bigger since he'd last seen it. Then he saw the grey-haired man in the Barbour jacket in the queue behind him. He was still staring at Bertie.

And then he smiled.

[33]

ATTACK THE BLOCK

WITH A SUBTLE PINCH OF HIS NOSE, BOB MITCHELL CHECKED his watch. He'd been on the ground for 24 minutes, and in that time his walk-and-talk with the Delta commander had helped to calm his nerves. They'd discussed the campaign and Delta's role in it, and Mitchell had pointed here and there, hoping he was looking every inch the commander-in-chief for Gonzales' camera.

They'd stood beneath the famous balcony, where British kings and queens waved to adoring crowds. As he looked down the vast, empty expanse of The Mall, Mitchell had felt more than a little exposed. Zack and Sandy, standing nearby and looking the part in their helmets and ballistic vests, directed Gonzales with subtle gestures. While Zack stepped in and distracted the Delta commander with a question, Sandy moved to the president's side.

'We've got a lot of good stuff,' she said in a muted voice. 'I even captured some footage myself, just to mix it up.' She looked around at the ruined palace building. 'I had some reservations about coming, but I have to say it's been an eye-opener.'

'We'll take the full 30 minutes, then call it a day,' Mitchell said.

The president smiled. 'That's a great idea —'

The sudden roar of a Viper helicopter drowned out his words as it flew over the palace rooftop. Then, to Mitchell's horror, it opened fire, its cannon making a terrifying ripping sound and leaving a trail of white smoke in the sky. Then it was gone, engine screaming, and Mitchell thought he heard gunfire coming from somewhere else.

'We're moving!'

The shout made him jump. Mitchell watched the SEAL team charge him as if he were a fumbling quarterback. They spun him around and propelled him across the parade ground and back into the courtyard. He heard the jet engines of his helicopter spinning up, and the accelerating chop of its twin rotors. He looked over his shoulder and saw Sandy and Zack being bundled towards the chopper by the Delta commander and his people. Ahead, the Defiant crewman was waving at them to hurry, and all Mitchell could see was his mouth opening and closing beneath his black visor, his words drowned by the massive rotors and wailing engines, the deafening roar trapped by the surrounding walls. The downdraught battered him as he climbed aboard, and strong SEAL hands strapped him into his seat. Two of them sat on either side and then Sandy and Zack scrambled aboard and buckled up. The crewman jammed headphones over Mitchell's ears. It was only then that he realised he'd lost his baseball cap.

'What's happening?'

The SEAL next to him spoke into his helmet mic. 'Enemy formations are advancing on our position. We're holding here until the gunships have neutralised the threat.'

'Shouldn't we leave right now?' Mitchell regretted the words as soon as he'd said them.

'We wait,' the SEAL said, turning his head away and listening to his radio.

Mitchell cursed himself. He'd sounded like a frightened child, and what the hell was he doing questioning military protocol?

McKenzie would be all over this. The general would have plans in place, contingency, whatever. Mitchell was in excellent hands, the best, and his heart rate slowed just a little. Opposite him, Sandy and Zack looked shaken up, and Mitchell offered them a reassuring smile. Everything was fine.

They'd be out of this real soon.

THE RIPSAWS STATIONED OUTSIDE THE SOUTH-EAST CORNER OF the palace spun their wheels and headed south along Buckingham Gate in a whirr of electric power. Their operators had orders to engage anything that moved, and rounding the gentle curve in the road, they saw hundreds of Jihadi fighters and black-clad militia piling off coaches and buses and heading north towards the palace.

Driving line abreast, the Ripsaws opened up with their 20mm Gatling guns, raking the vehicles with a storm of lead, shattering windows, shredding tyres, and punching holes through thin metal. The gunfire chopped up scores of fighters, eviscerating bodies and severing limbs, but the Ripsaws didn't have it all their own way. The fighters launched a fusillade of RPG-7 anti-tank rockets, which streaked towards the Ripsaws and exploded in a string of loud detonations, crippling the autonomous vehicles and puncturing their unarmoured bodies. Within minutes, both Ripsaws were out of the fight, and over 200 combatants dodged the burning wreckage and headed for the palace, now less than 300 yards away.

THE DARK BLUE AMAZON DELIVERY VAN CUT ACROSS BIRDCAGE Walk, bounced over the pavement, and drove into St James' Park, the driver steering the Renault through the winding paths, scattering pigeons and clipping fences. Behind the wheel he wore a ballistic vest and helmet, and he bounced in his seat as he cut across a wide stretch of grass, the back-end fishtailing on the soft ground before he got the vehicle under control. He crunched through the perimeter fence and stopped the Renault beneath the huge, ancient trees that lined The Mall. Helicopters buzzed across the morning sky, but the driver didn't see them. Crucially, they hadn't seen him. Yet.

One of his passengers threw open the side door, and all of them climbed out, each of the five men and one woman armed with Stinger missiles. They scattered across the park and The Mall itself, heading on foot towards the palace. When the side door slammed shut, the driver dropped the vehicle into gear and rolled it forward, creeping closer to the palace while staying beneath the trees. Although they were shedding their leaves, there was still enough cover for him to move undetected, or so he hoped. The Americans had technology that the driver could only imagine, but so far, he'd moved into position without being blasted to pieces.

A quarter of a mile short of the main gates of Buckingham Palace, the driver stopped beneath the full canopy of a huge tree and waited for the right moment. It would come soon enough, so he leaned over the passenger seat and flipped the switch on the small plastic box, arming the 1000-pound bomb strapped to the floor of the cargo bay behind him.

VICTORIA TUBE STATION SERVED AS A VITAL INTERSECTION between three tube lines and the mainline train station that transported hundreds of thousands of commuters into the capital. Below ground, the tube station was an extensive network of tunnels, platforms, and concourses, which was why General Baban had positioned a significant force there. Now they were mobilising, and they streamed through the various tunnels and up onto the street. They numbered 500 strong, and despite being laden down with weapons and ammunition, they moved with speed and purpose because their orders were clear.

The enemy was close by. Their mission was to kill them all.

· · ·

THE VIPER PILOT BANKED HIS AIRCRAFT OVER BUCKINGHAM Palace and levelled out at 100 feet, advancing his throttles as he headed straight down Buckingham Gate towards the line of trucks and buses below. The co-pilot/gunner (CPG) opened fire with unguided hydra rockets, and the weapons streaked away in a volley of flame and smoke, detonating along the length of the street and destroying several parked vehicles in a series of flashes and cracks. Then the pilot was banking through the smoke and over St James' Park tube station, where he saw more enemy fighters pouring out of the exits. He radioed the intel back to CENTCOM and pushed his throttles to the stops, racing over the wide-open spaces of Whitehall before banking hard to the west and following The Mall back towards the palace.

IN A BASEMENT STOREROOM BENEATH THE MAIN PALACE building, the Delta commander studied the Global Hawk's real-time feeds on his signaller's hardened laptop and concluded that the tactical situation looked grim. Six of the Ripsaws were out of action and hundreds of fighters were converging on his location from all points of the compass. They were outnumbered and outgunned, and the Delta commander would not risk the lives of his men any more than he had to. And certainly not for a presidential photo-op. He keyed his radio.

'All call signs, this is X-Ray One. Fall back to my position ASAP. Copy.'

His message was acknowledged, and on the screen, he saw his snipers picking up their long guns and leaving the palace rooftops. Outside, the enemy were pushing hard towards the palace walls, racing across the street, dodging the burning Ripsaws, and using the grand old buildings bordering the royal estate as cover. The gunships flew back and forth, carrying out low-level strafing runs, chewing up roads and pavements, their rockets and guns killing scores of fighters and leaving pockmarked and damaged buildings in their deadly wakes. The choppers were dropping bodies, but not fast enough. Sooner rather than later, the mortars would start falling and then it would be over. The Delta commander switched radio frequencies and spoke to McKenzie at CENTCOM. His message was plain enough.

The odds were shrinking. Extract the president.

Now.

THE AVENGER UAV NOSED TOWARDS THE GROUND AT A STEEP angle and fired two Hellfire missiles. The weapons dropped from their hardpoints and streaked away towards their target, the pedestrian entrance to Victoria Underground station on Wilton Street, where armed men and women were still charging up the stairs and running to join the battle at the palace. The missiles screamed to earth and disappeared into the stairwell before detonating, sending a white-hot blast of orange flame and steel fragments through the main concourse of the station, obliterating the tailenders of General Baban's Victoria team and igniting the piles of ammunition crates stacked against the ticket machines.

The Avenger pulled out of its dive and turned towards St James' Park, where more bodies continued to pour onto the streets. In its wake, the ground erupted in a massive blast that threw debris high into the air before the road collapsed onto the escalators and tunnels below, sending a pall of choking dust and smoke reaching into the sky high over Victoria.

THE VIPER MADE A HARD TURN ABOVE THE FLAT DESOLATION OF Whitehall, and the pilot and his CPG observed the fragile skeleton of Downing Street, now propped up by a web of scaffolding. Then it was gone, and the pilot centred his stick and came in low over The Mall. He heard CENTCOM in his headset.

'Outlaw Flight, this is Brimstone. Simba extract imminent. Clear

LZ airspace and initiate cover pattern Foxtrot. Prosecute all ground targets outside LZ perimeter ASAP. Copy?'

'Copy,' echoed the pilot of Outlaw-One-Seven. So, the president was hightailing it out of there, and not before time. The pilot was convinced that the attack was coordinated, and that meant a command-and-control system was in operation. Looks like the ticker-tape parade would have to be put on ice.

'Executing Foxtrot,' he told his CPG. Working with the other attack choppers, Outlaw-One-Seven would continue to saturate the ground with rockets and gunfire. Then, as soon as Mitchell's helicopter was airborne and clear, the entire flight would reform and get the hell out of there. He studied the map, deciding to head over Constitution Hill before swinging around and setting up a strafing run along Buckingham Palace Road, where a sizeable force was now within grenade range of the palace walls.

As the Viper clattered directly over The Mall, two men armed with Stinger anti-aircraft launchers broke cover from behind ancient trees and ran out into the wide avenue. They swung their weapons up onto their shoulders and waited for the targeting radar to screech confirmation of missile-lock. The men were skilled in the art of anti-aircraft warfare, and they fired simultaneously, enveloping them both in a thin cloud of missile exhaust fumes. Then they split left and right, running for cover as their missiles streaked through the air after the retreating helicopter.

The Viper pilot heard the alarm, heard his CPG yell a warning, and reacted in an instant.

'Activate jammers!'

'Launching chaff!'

But there was no time left. Even as the pilot threw his aircraft hard over, the surface-to-air missiles raced in at low Mach speeds and exploded behind the twin-engine exhaust ports, shredding the helicopter's power plant and rotor blades. The Viper fell from the sky in an arc of black smoke, hitting the road outside the palace, where it exploded in a ball of fire. Thick black smoke boiled across The Mall and reached into the sky.

Inside the Amazon delivery truck, the driver saw the Viper sail crash in a ball of flame outside the palace. When he saw the smoke billowing across the front of the palace, he also saw his chance. He slipped the handbrake and accelerated, bumping across the cinder path and onto the road of The Mall itself. He jammed his foot to the ground and headed towards the palace gates as fast as he could.

'Sir, we have an incoming vehicle heading towards the palace.'

General McKenzie watched the live feed on his main screen and saw a van heading towards the palace. 'That's a VIED. Stop him, before he gets to those gates.'

The order went out to the other helicopters and Outlaw-Zero-Five responded, breaking away from its attack run on Grosvenor Place. The Apache gunship flashed over Hyde Park Corner and flew low over Constitution Hill, heading for The Mall. The gunner was already firing, launching two Hellfires then firing bursts from his 30mm cannon, but one missile hit a tree and deflected up into the sky and the other streaked over the roof of the van and exploded in St James' Park, throwing up a fountain of grass and mud. Cannon fire ripped up the road until the pilot realised his quest for revenge made him overshoot his target. He yanked his stick backwards and slammed his foot down on his torque pedal, bringing his tail around to stabilise his motion. As the gunner tracked the fast-moving target, the pilot's headphones screamed a missile warning, and from the

corner of his eye, he saw two fiery streaks of light rising towards him
...

THE DRIVER IN THE AMAZON VAN SAW THE APACHE EXPLODE IN
a bright white blast and flinched as smoking debris dropped from the
sky, raining down around his vehicle. It slammed off the Renault's
bodywork and fractured the windscreen, but the driver was unde-
terred. He slewed past the roundabout where the Queen Victoria
Memorial once stood, seeing the road beyond the wreckage was clear
and nothing was stopping him from hitting his target at speed. The
gates rushed towards him, and he gripped the wheel and stamped on
the accelerator, screaming a cry of victory.

'WHAT THE FUCK IS HAPPENING?'

Mitchell knew he was losing his cool, but he couldn't help
himself. In his headphones, the command net was a mess of garbled,
frantic chatter. He understood little of it, but it didn't take a military
tactician to realise they were all in trouble. He looked to his left
through the arch of the courtyard and saw the other two Defiants
squatting on the open ground, the combined blast of their rotors
lashing the overgrown vegetation. Further away, he saw two small,
black vehicles with fat tyres and guns mounted on their low-profile
turrets. UFVs, he realised, and as he watched, they began firing
smoke canisters from their turret tubes. Mitchell swallowed,
suddenly very frightened. Through the white smoke, he saw more
US soldiers sprinting to the helicopters and piling aboard. He heard
Zack yelling in his headphones.

'The president cannot be here! Let's go already!'

None of us should be here, Mitchell thought.

Beneath her helmet, tears ran down Sandy's terrified face and
Mitchell's heart broke. What had he done?

He flinched as an almighty bang shook the helicopter. Sandy

screamed and debris fell into the courtyard around them, cracking off the spinning rotor blades. Warning tones blared in the cockpit and Mitchell saw the pilots working the overhead switches and buttons. *Please God let the helicopter be okay.* The thought of being trapped on the ground made his stomach churn.

'VIED,' said the SEAL next to him as he listened to the radio traffic. He glanced at Mitchell. 'They've taken out the front gates. If we're gonna move, we need to go now.'

As he said the words, the engines screamed, and Mitchell's stomach was left behind as the Defiant leapt straight up into the air. Clearing the roof, it spun around on its axis. The nose titled, and they were moving. He glimpsed smoke on the ground and saw the other two helicopters rising through the fog, and then they disappeared behind them.

Rooftops passed below, so close now, and what sounded like a hailstorm rattled the airframe.

'Incoming!' the SEAL barked over the net. 'Small calibre. We should be okay.'

The man's composure amazed Mitchell under such intense, dangerous circumstances. The hailstorm faded as the helicopter banked away and gained a little height. Through the window he saw a gunship flash by in the other direction, its rocket pods popping smoke and fire, and the London skyline tilted once more as they changed course. He saw a tower of smoke, but it was receding behind them. Mitchell took a deep breath and sat a little straighter in his seat. It was going to be okay.

He hoped his fear wasn't as obvious as that on the faces of his advisors.

THE BOFORS GUNNER SHOUTED OVER HIS SHOULDER. 'THEY'RE coming back! What's the word?'

'We're green-lit,' said the captain. 'No one fires until I say.'

The anti-aircraft team was one of several dotted across London, and these soldiers were living in the red-bricked high-rises of the World's End Estate in Chelsea. The towers dominated the local skyline, and their rooftops offered lots of hiding places for the SAM teams who'd just scrambled up there on the local commander's orders. He was an IS infantry captain who'd volunteered to stay behind after the main forces had withdrawn to France, and when the flight of aircraft had passed his location earlier, he'd called it in and watched the distant, unfolding battle through his binoculars. Now he was tasked with taking the rest of the flight out. Finally, he would get his chance.

The apartment he occupied was on the 16th floor, just below the rooftop, where four of his men, armed with Stinger missiles, were hiding. The room where they'd set up the 40mm Bofors gun was devoid of furniture and filled with ammunition, and the hope was they'd attack some low-flying transports or passenger planes carrying troops or VIPs into Heathrow. Helicopters were more difficult to hit with a big gun like the Bofors, but they'd give it their best shot.

'Remember, it's the helicopter with the antennae on the nose. You see it?'

The gunner, standing behind the Bofors, squinted through its optics. 'Got it. Range is closing. They're coming right at us. Fish in a barrel.'

'Don't get cocky,' the captain warned. 'Wait until I give the order.'

'Roger.'

He left the apartment and ran two floors down, where more of his men waited. Watching through the window as the helicopters headed towards him, he counted five aircraft, but the captain had two teams on two different rooftops, totalling eight missiles, plus the big Bofors. They'd wing one or two at least.

ON MITCHELL'S AIRCRAFT, NO ONE TALKED. HE WANTED TO SAY something, to express his sorrow at the loss of the two helicopter crews, but he was certain that none of the surrounding people wanted to hear his voice right now. He was the reason those crews were dead, so best to stay quiet. The appropriate words would come later.

He looked beyond the SEAL to his left, to the sky outside the window. It was a beautiful day, bright and blue, but Mitchell's mood was as grey as the London suburbs across the river. In the cockpit, the pilots were going through their in-flight procedures, pushing switches, and checking their big digital displays. Beyond their windshield, west London stretched into the distance, and Mitchell hoped the flight would pass quickly. The question of how he would deal with this disaster was already troubling him, not to mention the tarnishing of his reputation —

He saw a flash amongst a cluster of high-rises, and a moment later, something bright *whooshed* past the nose.

'Jesus!'

A moment later the cockpit exploded in a shower of blood and sparks, and the nose tipped towards the ground. Then another round hit them, bursting Zack's body like rotten fruit, slicing through the SEAL next to him and punching out through the door. Sandy was screaming, but Mitchell couldn't hear her over the wail of the engines. He saw the pilot fighting with the controls as they spiralled out of the sky, spinning faster until Mitchell felt himself losing consciousness. He closed his eyes, knowing death was seconds away. Alarms blared and another explosion ripped through the cabin. Something sliced across his shins, and beyond the plexiglass window, whirling slate and brick shut out the sky.

The helicopter hit hard.

Mitchell's world turned black.

THE CAPTAIN WAS RUNNING DOWN THE STAIRS WITH A DOZEN OF his men, all of them armed with automatic weapons, grenades, and RPGs. Above them, the tower rumbled and shook with repeated missile strikes and strafing runs from the surviving helicopters. They'd only hit two of them because something had screwed with the Stingers' IR seekers – jamming, the captain assumed – but they'd achieved their aim. Now it was time to finish the job.

They charged out of the building, dodging the rubble strewn across the walkway outside, and weaved through the concrete maze of the estate. Above them, the top several floors of the tower burned like a Roman candle and flaming debris fell to earth. A Yankee helicopter flew past, firing its gun from close range, chopping the top floors to shreds. He doubted any of his people up there were still alive.

Down on the ground, they waited in the shadows of a low-rise block, until the voice of a spotter high in another tower told the captain the sky was momentarily clear, and they raced across the King's Road into the side streets. The spotter guided him one block down, then right onto Fernshaw Road. As soon as the captain turned the corner, he saw the crash site.

With a cry of victory, he ran towards it, his men charging behind him.

MITCHELL OPENED HIS EYES AND WONDERED HOW HE WAS STILL alive when everyone around him was dead. The cabin was crushed and tilted at a crazy angle, and bodies still strapped in their seats hung around him like lifeless marionettes. There wasn't much left of Zack, just legs and half a torso, the rest of him was splattered all over the cabin. Sandy's helmet was split in two, and the pink mush inside her skull oozed out of the crack. *What a waste of a good brain,* Mitchell thought. He coughed, the air thick with dust and the stench of aviation fuel. Pain shot through his chest, and when he wiped his mouth, he saw blood on the back of his hand. He heard helicopters overhead and then the engine noise faded, replaced by something else.

Voices.

. . .

THE CAPTAIN'S RPG GUNNERS FIRED AT THE CIRCLING GUNSHIP, the grenade rounds fizzing into the sky and forcing it to turn away. He stood up from behind the parked car and ran, his assault rifle gripped in his hands. The houses along the street were tall with fancy white columns, and the helicopter had fallen on one of them, crushing its roof and stripping away the front of the house. The helicopter's broken tail lay crumpled across the street and its body buried inside the front of the house, pointing towards the sky on a mound of shattered brick and timber. There was no fire, but that might change at any moment. And the cabin, though crushed on one side, was still intact, which meant there could be survivors. If there were, the captain knew he had to finish them before the Yankee helicopter came back. He charged forward as the roar of the returning gunship echoed across the rooftops. He crossed the street and began climbing the loose slope of rubble towards the door of the helicopter.

MITCHELL HEARD SHOUTING, BUT HE COULDN'T UNDERSTAND what was being said. He turned to his left and saw the door had been peeled back by the impact, the street outside tilted at a strange angle. Then he saw them, armed men, all headed his way.

Not American.

He heard gunfire and flinched as rounds cracked around the cabin. He felt a white-hot pain in his leg and looked down. A smoking hole had appeared in his trouser leg, but that didn't shock him as much as the sight of his missing feet. They were gone below the ankle, the mess of gore and trouser material leaching thick blood across the metal deck. His head swam, and with a massive effort, he leaned over and took the gun from the chest rig of the dead SEAL next to him. It was a Glock, a weapon he knew, and when he heard the scrape of brick and the grunting of someone climbing up the slope of rubble, he raised the gun. The man's face appeared, thick curly hair and a dark beard, and Mitchell shot him through the eye. The man fell away, out of sight. Mitchell saw others running towards him, saw them lift their long tubes and knew what was coming. He fired again, once, twice, wild shots, and the rockets whooshed towards the shattered cockpit, trailing white smoke.

President Bob Mitchell died a moment later in a ball of fire, guilt and regret.

[34]

POWER SWITCH

HARRY'S PATIENCE WAS WEARING THIN. FOR MUCH OF THE DAY, he'd remained in the warehouse office, holed up with Wilde as they waited for permission to fly into London. As daylight faded and authorisation from CENTCOM was not forthcoming, Harry had arranged a conference call with his Cabinet. Now, 30 minutes into that call, he found himself to be the target of some consternation from its attendees. Faye Junger, back in Cumbria with her colleagues, was acting as spokesperson and mediator, but Harry felt she wasn't doing much of the latter as she added to the barrage of criticism.

'Harry, the mood around the table is clear – none of us are convinced your trip to the capital is justified. It'll be seen as grand-standing or worse, reckless behaviour.'

Harry folded his arms and leaned over the speaker. 'I need to see the destruction for myself. Surely you must all understand that. And we have no idea of casualty numbers. The uncertainty must be driving Londoners out of their minds.'

'Here we go again,' said Maddox, the Welsh Secretary. 'It's all about London. We agreed to move away from that divisive bubble mentality.'

'Thousands are dead,' Harry snapped back. 'The city has been cut in half and overflowing hospitals are barely functioning. Disease will soon become a factor if it isn't already. They've had it harder than every Welsh town and city combined. Let's park the regional resentments, can we?'

Defence Secretary Chisholm spoke next. 'For the record, I think the prime minister has a point. London is a major world capital with over ten million inhabitants, most of whom must be wondering where the hell we are, given that IS forces have abandoned the country.'

'Thank you, Simon.' *An ally at last.*

'So, what's the holdup?'

'CENTCOM has shut down the airspace over London.'

'For what reason?' asked Shelley Walker, the foreign secretary.

'We don't know.'

'I hope you haven't trod on any toes, Harry.'

Faye, again. 'Do you think I was born yesterday?' he said, his irritation nudging boiling point.

'Calm down, Harry. Losing your temper isn't helping. And it's not good for your health.'

Harry barked into the speaker. 'You're not my bloody doctor, Faye.'

'She didn't mean that, Prime Minister,' said another voice. 'We're all concerned.'

Harry hit the mute button and turned to Wilde. 'Now I've got a health issue? What the hell's going on here?'

'It's Faye. She's working them. You're going to have to keep them onside, Harry. We either fly back to Cumbria and wait until CENTCOM gives us the nod, or the Cabinet can move down here, and we can tour the city together.'

'I like the sound of a joint tour. That'll open a few eyes. Get a few backsides puckering too.'

'Agreed. They've been isolated from the realities of the war. They should see the destruction for themselves, talk to people.'

'Absolutely. Maddox has yet to visit his beloved Wales despite its liberation. He's too worried about his own safety.'

'So, let's run it by them.'

Harry unmuted the mic. He took a breath before speaking but Maddox beat him to the punch.

'We all think it's best if you return to Cumbria,' the Welsh Secretary said. 'Instead of running around down there, playing soldiers.'

Harry fumed. He stood up and was about to give Maddox both barrels, but then he heard the march of boots outside. He went to the window. Deputy CDS Wheeler, flanked by a couple of paratroopers, was crossing the warehouse towards the office staircase. Harry walked back to the table. 'I have a visitor. We'll pick this up later.'

'Before you go, we should —'

Harry ended the call. 'Nick Wheeler's on his way up,' he told Wilde. His chief of staff got to his feet and Wheeler appeared on the gantry a moment later. Harry waved him inside and saw he was wearing full combat gear, a maroon general staff beret, and a look of unease on his face. Something was wrong.

'What is it, Nick?' *Please God, not another nuke.*

'The Americans are running an operation in west London. Sir David overheard a telephone conversation, an American four-star talking to McKenzie. He clammed up when Sir David confronted him.'

'What kind of operation?'

Wheeler shrugged. 'No idea. The four-star mentioned Fulham, but there's nothing of any strategic importance in that sector. It could be a rescue mission. Or perhaps they've discovered one of these rogue missile trucks.'

'So why the secrecy?'

'Sir David has requested a briefing from CENTCOM, but they're not forthcoming. It looks like we'll just have to wait until they're good and ready.'

'Don't we have our own drones? Satellites?'

'Yes, but they're all controlled by the Pentagon. That was the deal.'

Harry folded his arms and sat on the edge of the table, simmering. 'I've a mind to go, anyway. It's our capital city after all.'

'Not sure that's such a good idea,' Wheeler said. 'The mood at CENTCOM has shifted dramatically since this morning. They're razor-focussed on something and it doesn't feel positive. Whatever it is, we're not part of the conversation.'

'Let's see if I can cut through the red tape.' He turned to Wilde. 'Lee, patch me through to the White House, would you?'

He waited as Wilde speed-dialled Washington on his satellite phone. After a moment, his chief of staff frowned, then ended the call. Harry raised an eyebrow. 'Well?'

'It's a recorded message,' Wilde said. 'All lines in and out of the White House are busy. Then I got cut off.' He stared at his phone. 'That's a first.'

'Something's not right here,' Wheeler said.

Harry nodded. 'I agree. And whatever it is, Mitchell better have a bloody good reason for treating us like this.'

Vice President Curtis Riley was chairing a breakfast meeting in his West Wing office when the door opened and Martha, his private secretary, apologised for the interruption and told him she'd routed an urgent call to the phone on his desk. The moment Riley heard the voice of Pat McKenzie, he knew the worst had happened. After the general had spoken, Riley thanked him, told him he would be in touch, and ended the call.

He asked the senators seated on the sofas to give him the room, apologising for the interruption and promising to reschedule. Their discussion concerned the predicted energy sector unemployment spike in the wake of the new power infrastructure rollout. It was an important meeting, but Riley was unable to continue it.

After the door had closed behind the last attendee, Riley's head dropped, and he placed both hands on the desk. His mind whirled, and he found himself unable to breathe as his body reacted to the emotional shock. Those emotions spiked between sorrow and fury and everything in between. Fury won the day, and he hurled a decorative desk lamp donated by the Japanese prime minister across the room, where it shattered against the far wall. The door opened and Martha stepped in. She saw the shattered lamp, the wall painting tilted and damaged, and asked the obvious question.

'Is everything okay ...?'

'Go, please Martha.'

'Sir, I —'

'Get out!'

She closed the door and Riley crossed the room and locked it behind her. He dropped onto a sofa and yanked the tie away from his collar, the fury dissolving, the void filling with overwhelming sorrow.

He'd warned him, pleaded with him, and if he'd been able to speak to him that morning, Riley would've begged Bob Mitchell not to go. It was a bad idea, and now that others had been killed – Zack and Sandy, the SEAL detachment, the Defiant crew – Riley knew that decision would be an indelible stain on the man's legacy. Bob Mitchell, the commander-in-chief who went against all sound advice and got himself and his own servicemen killed. That's how they would remember him.

But not Riley. He'd lost a mentor, a friend, and a man who'd been a father to him, the kind that every boy growing up should have. Riley had been lucky, honoured to have known the man. But now he was gone, and that reality sliced through Riley's heart like a dagger of ice.

For the first time since he was a boy, Curtis Riley hung his head in his hands and cried.

FROM THE DARKNESS OF AN OFFICE ON THE TOP FLOOR OF THE Peter Jones department store in Sloane Square, General Baban watched the ongoing military action through his binoculars. Just over a mile away, another explosion lit up the darkening sky as it ripped through the tower block at Fulham, reducing its height by several more floors as debris rumbled to the ground. American A-10 aircraft had pounded the building with guns and rockets for the last 20 minutes. They'd already destroyed one suspected launch site, and now they were severing the top floors of another block, sending them crashing to the ground. There appeared to be no consideration for collateral damage, and Baban found that fact most intriguing.

He switched his focus to the crash site. Above the flames, gunships buzzed back and forth, and the surviving spotter reported that a battalion of armoured vehicles had sealed off the entire area. The crash site itself was an inferno, and it engulfed the surrounding houses in flames, spewing black smoke across the London skyline. The sun had set behind the horizon, but the sky was still clear and bright. Baban handed the binoculars to Naji, who whistled through his teeth.

'Must've been someone high up the chain,' he said.

'No doubt. Dismantling and reassembling that Bofors gun was a good move. Shame we can't congratulate the team.'

'So, what's the plan now?' Naji asked, the binoculars still pressed to his eyes.

'Deploy everyone to their battle positions. Whoever was on the chopper, they'll want revenge. When they attack, we'll deploy the missile trucks.' He slapped Naji on the back. 'Come on, let's get back into town.'

Escorted by two IS special forces soldiers in civilian clothes, they took the stairs to the ground floor and drove off in a London Underground crew van. As they circumnavigated Sloane Square, Baban considered his next move. The deployment of the rest of his subterranean army would not go unnoticed, and the Americans would make plans against them. The general suspected it would come as a *shock and awe* campaign, a mass bombing of his forces, but that could prove ineffective given that his people would deploy into residential homes, shops, and businesses around the West End. Once the storm was over, they would send in the troops, mechanised formations that would engage anything that moved. The fight would spread into the very heart of the city, and his *mujahideen* would make them pay for every square inch.

'Look at that thing,' Naji said, pointing through the windscreen.

Baban saw the monstrous black airship ahead, partly deflated and wedged between the gated parks on either side of Eaton Square, forcing them to divert. As the van threaded a path through the carnage at Buckingham Gate, the aftermath of the palace battle revealed itself. A truck bomb had shattered the front of the building, blasting away the surrounding wrought iron fences and stone plinths, ripping the façade from the front of the palace itself and scattering debris all over the roads and pavements. Baban saw the blackened wreckage of crashed helicopters, still smoking on the road outside the palace. The Americans had yet to recover the bodies. Baban would beat them to it.

'Get a message to what's left of the Victoria team. Tell them to torch the palace, every building. And drag those helicopters out of the way. Dump them in the park.'

Naji smiled. 'You're poking the bear.'

'He's already been poked. Let's see what else we can make him do.' He slapped the driver on the shoulder. 'Let's go. The quicker we get underground, the safer we'll be.'

Baban leaned back in his seat as the driver floored the accelerator and the van raced along The Mall.

EDDIE AND GRIFF CROUCHED IN THE BLACK SHADOWS OF ST Martin-in-the-Fields church, on the eastern edge of Trafalgar Square, and watched a long line of dark figures cutting across the famous quadrangle and disappearing into Pall Mall. To his right, somewhere up Charing Cross Road, he heard glass breaking, engines revving, and the rumble of boots on tarmac. The enemy forces that had lain in wait beneath the streets of London were now on the move and preparing for combat.

Something had happened that morning, something that had triggered this nocturnal mobilisation. Just after sunrise, Eddie and Griff heard helicopters and explosions, but it was too dangerous to go out onto the streets and investigate. Griff had suggested climbing up onto the roof, but Eddie explained buildings on The Strand overlooked them, and if spotted, they could be in serious trouble. So, they'd sat in silence close to an open window and listened to the engagement somewhere to the west of their position. Eddie had recorded details of the audio battle, noting the times of the major explosions, and had passed it all to Hawkins. For the rest of the day, they'd taken turns at the window, but the distant, unseen conflict that had rippled across the morning sky had stopped shortly afterwards. The rest of the day had passed in relative silence, except for the odd rumble and the faint roar of aircraft. As the sun dipped behind the rooftops, Eddie and Griff noticed another occurrence – power to the city had been cut. The streetlights outside had failed to blink on and the narrow lane below transformed into a dark trench where nothing moved. Eddie had taken the opportunity to recce the local area. Griff came too, and Eddie had led them west towards Trafalgar Square, hoping he might find some evidence of the unseen battle of that morning. Slipping into the shadows of St Martin's church, it wasn't long before they observed activity on the streets. They found a good spot, with views across the wide-open spaces of Trafalgar Square. Eddie saw Admiralty Arch lying across the entrance to The Mall and wondered how much damage England's other cities had suffered. The scale of the destruction must be enormous. He felt a tap on his shoulder.

'We've got movement behind us.'

Eddie signalled with his hand, and they crept down a stairwell by the side of the church. They crouched in the dark, Eddie squatting above Griff on the smooth stone steps, his eyeline level with the pavement. He gripped the MP5 a little tighter as the sound of footfalls rose, echoing off the ancient walls of the pedestrian passage that ran beside the church. Eddie peered through the eye-slit of his makeshift mask that Griff had fashioned from a bolt of black cloth. Then he saw them, filing out of the dark and past their hiding place, a long line of men and women, their weapons slung, their hands filled with ammo cases. Some struggled with heavy belts of ammunition, while others carried RPG rockets. Like the other groups they'd observed, this one moved with purpose, and Eddie's heart sank. He'd started to believe this war might end soon. Now it looked like it would continue for some time. He wondered whether it was a coordinated effort. Were there other Jihadi groups mobilising in other towns and cities across the south-east? The last figure jogged past their hiding place, crossing the road and following the others into the black void beyond the National Gallery.

'We're heading back to the safe house,' he whispered.

Griff's shrouded head nodded. They set off, watching and listening at every corner, and they returned to their base without further incident. Slipping inside the building, they worked in silence as they secured the main door before heading upstairs. Neither man used his torch, just in case.

While Griff watched the street from an upstairs window, Eddie called Hawkins on the satellite phone. He spent five minutes relaying the intelligence gathered during the day and from their recent excursion. It was thin, but it might be useful to someone.

'This is good stuff,' Hawkins said. 'We've lost access to the UAV feeds, so we're blind right now.'

'What's happened, boss?'

'The Yanks are running some sort of op over in west London. CENTCOM is keeping us out of the loop. Not sure when they'll take the blinkers off.'

Eddie saw a match flare in a window across the street. A moment later, a candle glowed. 'One other thing, boss. The power is out. Streetlights, domestic supplies. Nothing's working.'

Hawkins considered the intel. 'Shutting down the grid might be a precursor to military action. I'll try and find out what's going on. In the meantime, if there's a gas supply at your location, knock it off at the mains.'

'Already done.'

'Good lad.' Hawkins paused, then said, 'How's your friend holding up?'

'He's got my back, and his local knowledge has been helpful. He's been an asset, boss.'

'Glad you got somebody to bounce off,' Hawkins said. 'I want both of you to keep a low profile. No more midnight strolls, understood? Not until we know what's happening.'

'Roger, boss.'

'Stay close to the phone.'

Hawkins ended the call and Eddie checked the power indicator – 40%. Even on standby, the phone was sucking juice, and they had no way of charging it. He went back downstairs and asked Griff to join him in the kitchen. They sat at the table in the darkness.

'Any news?' the older man asked.

Eddie shook his head. 'Nothing.' He didn't elaborate.

'After that tear-up this morning, I thought we were going to see American tanks rolling down The Strand.'

'I guess we'll have to be a bit more patient.'

'I guess we will,' Griff echoed, the AK resting across his legs.

He looked tired. Eddie was beat, too. 'It's too dangerous to go out and there's nothing to add to the intelligence picture by sticking our heads out of the window.'

'Agreed,' Griff said.

'So, I suggest we cook up some rations, have a brew or two, then get our heads down for the night. Downstairs is secure, so we can relax a bit. What d'you think?'

'I think it's a good idea,' Griff said. 'I could do with a decent kip.'

'That's the plan, then. We'll see how all this looks in the morning.'

Griff stood up and stretched. 'With any luck, that lot out there will come to their senses and wave the white flag.'

'Maybe,' Eddie said.

They shared a look in the darkness. Neither man was convinced.

'... THAT I WILL FAITHFULLY EXECUTE THE OFFICE OF THE President of the United States, and will do to the best of my ability, preserve, protect, and defend the constitution of the United States. So help me, God.'

'Congratulations, Mr President,' said the federal judge, concluding proceedings. The salutation was muted, as was the mood in the Oval Office. President Curtis Riley lowered his hand, and for a moment, his head. He had expected to take the oath of office at the proper time – not now, and not under such tragic circumstances.

None of the assembled witnesses said anything. Eliot Bird stood to one side, stony faced. His wife, Georgia, smiled at him, but she knew how much he was hurting. So did his press secretary, and the representatives from the states of Texas, Connecticut, and Arizona, and Martha, his personal secretary. Riley's newly-appointed military advisor, General Chester Schweitzer, and the head of the White House secret service detail, stood behind them, impassive, their expressions set in stone as they waited for the president's next words. At momentous occasions such as this one, those words were often poignant and set the tone for the forth-coming presidency. But Riley was unconcerned about tradition. They were still at war, and he intended to finish it fast. He cleared his throat.

'You are among the first people to learn of the president's death, and it will remain that way for the next 24 hours. You are to say nothing to anyone. If news of the president's passing leaks out, it will have come from someone in this room, and if that happens, the person who leaked it will regret the day their mother gave birth to them. That I will promise you. Do you all understand?'

There was a subdued murmuring of, *Yes, Mr President.*

'Twenty-four hours, that's all I ask. The president was killed on the battlefield, and that battlefield is still in play. Until it's been neutralised, I expect you all to stay silent. Thank you, you're dismissed.'

The room emptied quickly. Only two men stood their ground. One was Bird and the other wore a US Air Force uniform with stars on his shoulder tabs. Riley walked around the Resolute desk and sat in the chair recently and so tragically vacated by the man he'd called *Mr President* in public and *Pops* in private. His heart ached, but this was no time for tears and fond memories. Now was a time for retribution. He pulled the chair into the desk and looked up at General Schweitzer.

'Where are we with the response?'

Schweitzer, his service tucked beneath his arm, cleared his throat. 'One squadron is already airborne. The rest will assemble in Ireland over the next three days.'

'Will they be ready in time?'

'Yes, Mr President. We've maintained a comprehensive arsenal of ordinance both in Scotland and in Ireland. We'll have the tools to do the job, sir.'

The president leaned back in his chair and nodded. 'And this type of operation has never been attempted before, correct?'

'Not in these numbers, and not on a combat mission. If the missile threat pans out, there will be losses.'

'What are we looking at?' Bird asked him.

'It's hard to say.'

'Best guess,' Riley said.

'Up to 50%, sir. Maybe less.'

Riley thought about that and nodded. 'So be it.' He stood up and held out his hand. Schweitzer took it. 'Thank you, Chester. Keep me posted.'

'Yes sir, Mr President.'

Bird walked him to the door and closed it behind the general. He stood in front of the president's desk.

'If you change your mind, we have a significant window.'

Riley shook his head. 'We need to retaliate. The people will demand it.'

'Yes, they will.'

'Thank you, Eliot.'

Bird left the Oval Office and the president leaned back in his chair. He was a warrior at heart, but Curtis Riley was tired of war. It had cost him many friends, and now it had taken the man he considered to be his father.

It was time to end the conflict in Britain and move on.

[35]

NIGHT BOAT TO CALAIS

BERTIE WAS EXHAUSTED, DEAD ON HIS ACHING FEET. BEHIND him, Cheryl was helping The Witch and Judge Hardy to theirs. They'd been sitting on the floor, huddled in their coats, for the past 16 hours. The judge was a crumpled mess, his eyes red-rimmed and watery, his white hair sticking up off his skull. Bertie stepped in, taking the judge's arm, and helped him up. The Witch looked no better, wrapped in an old rust-coloured coat, and wearing oversized cataract glasses, both items liberated by Cheryl from the care home. No one would ever recognise them, and even Bertie struggled to remember them wearing their judicial finery. Instead, they looked like refugees, exhausted, frightened, but the only difference was, these two weren't penniless. And that was going to make the difference.

Bertie's hopes had risen with the dawn but faded as the day passed agonisingly slow. The couple in front of them, Harvey and Tess, had given up trying to make conversation with Bertie's 'family' and had passed the time fussing over their children and taking turns to sleep. Across the hall, others were doing the same, curled up on the floor because nobody wanted to lose their place and the chance to escape. But sleep was hard, as Bertie had discovered. As the hours passed, the noise in the hall increased, a relentless cacophony of chatter and shouting; kids crying and screaming; blaring PA announcements and militia whistles. And when Bertie had the chance to find a spot on the floor and close his eyes, the queue would move forward, forcing him to move with it. So, he gave up trying.

They'd eaten the last of their sandwiches, and the only refreshment they had left was a single bottle of water between the four of them. Cheryl had escorted The Witch to the toilet, a mission that had taken over an hour, and Cheryl had returned with tales of pushing and shoving; arguments and threats; men urinating in the sinks of the ladies' toilet; shit-choked cubicles; and lakes of piss on the floors. No wonder The Witch had returned in a state of shock.

Conditions in the departure hall were deteriorating fast, so when Harvey's family reached the steel barrier at the head of the queue, hope blossomed once more. All that stood between them and a place on board a ship was Harvey and his brood. Bertie watched them as they gathered at the glass partition. They spent several minutes talking, pointing, and what looked like pleading. Bertie turned to face the others.

'Is everyone ready?'

'Of course,' snapped The Witch. 'Let's put an end to this ghastly experience.'

Cheryl rolled her eyes, and the judge looked down at his scuffed brogues. Bertie smiled. 'Okay, they'll call us forward any minute now.'

The smile faded as he caught the eye of the tall man with grey curly hair. The first time he'd seen him, the man had smiled, but his dubious affability was no longer clear, and Bertie had observed two things since then. Number one, Curly Top had been joined by a friend, a short, squat, shaven-headed bruiser with a thick neck and a square jaw. A man of violence, Bertie recognised. Observation number two was equally worrying – the men had moved up several places in the queue and now loitered a couple of groups behind their own. That was troubling. There had been several disturbances during the day, as tempers frayed and the crowd swelled outside the main doors, and yet no one had challenged the men behind him, and that meant they'd made threats. Bertie wasn't too worried, though. They were almost out of here, and if the dodgy pair followed, he'd stick the militia on to them.

Militia policed the head of each queue, making sure the crowd stayed back behind the barriers separating them from the ticket counter. Bertie was watching Harvey and Tess when he heard the shout.

'Spencer!'

Then another voice, a sharp bark. 'Governor Spencer!'

Bertie tried to stop her, but it was too late. The Witch turned around, lifting the dark glasses off her face.

'Yes? Who is it?'

Curly Top and his buddy had made her. They glared from behind the other passengers. Bruiser stared at Bertie and drew a finger across his unshaven throat. Bertie turned away.

'Fuck!'

'Bertie, please!'

He grabbed The Witch by the arm and moved her in front of him. He hissed in her ear. 'People behind us have recognised you. Now they want to hurt you, d'you understand?'

She pulled her arm away. 'Don't talk to me as if I'm a child.'

'Put your glasses back on. Please, Lady Edith.'

She complied, and Bertie felt for the gun beneath his hoodie. He didn't want to use it, not in here, because the militia would shoot first and ask questions later. What he needed was to get out of this building.

As Bertie watched, Harvey and Tess slipped their hands beneath the glass partition and had them stamped by the clerk. The kids reached up, giggling, and the clerk did the same. Harvey thanked him, and then they were moving, hurrying past the other ticket windows towards the dockside doors. He saw Harvey turn and wave.

'Good luck, Dave!'

Bertie cocked his chin in response and watched them as they approached a phalanx of black uniforms guarding the exit to the ships, thrusting their hands out for inspection. The uniforms parted and swallowed the family.

'Who's Dave?' The Witch said. 'Was he referring to you, Bertie?'

'Yes. Don't worry about it, it's a long story.'

'Why aren't they calling us forward?'

'Just be patient.'

But Bertie felt anything but as he watched the clerks behind the counter. That morning he'd counted 30, or thereabouts. After lunch, there were 20. Now he counted 13, leapfrogging each other behind the counter as they battled to service the queues. Everyone was handing over cash, but from where Bertie was standing – a good 15 feet from the counter – it was impossible to hear the negotiations. Five grand, that was the going rate buzzing through the people around him. Bertie had 20 g's in an envelope to cover all 4 of them. In another envelope, he had 40, in case the price doubled. Cheryl had another 10 in her rucksack, but that was for emergencies.

'Next group to Window F! Window F!'

Bertie's heart raced. The militiamen blocking their path stepped aside and growled. 'Come on, you lot. Move!'

Bertie ushered everyone into the no-man's-land between the barriers and the counter that stretched away across the hall. Cheryl shepherded The Witch and the judge towards the glass partition where the clerk waited. Bertie noticed that most of them were younger kids, in their twenties, but this one was older, and he wore a curly earpiece looped over his ear. He was stick-thin, with a mop of dark, greasy hair and pockmarked skin. His black tie was loose, and the top button of his white shirt undone, revealing a stained t-shirt beneath. The name tag over his pocket said, *Darren – Senior Customer Liaison*. Bertie reckoned Darren had been working non-stop for days. As he watched, another clerk approached him, holding open a large Royal Mail sack. Darren dropped Harvey's envelope into it and the sack carrier moved on down the line. Bertie did the calculation – five grand a pop, times a couple of thousand – call it three – equals ...

He gave up. Maths was never his strong point.

'Just the four of you?' Darren asked.

Bertie leaned over and spoke through the gap beneath the partition. 'That's right. Just four.'

'It's 15,000 per person,' Darren said, his eyes flicking towards the throng behind them, his large Adam's apple bobbing up and down as he spoke.

'I was told it was five each.'

The man stared without blinking. 'That's when we had enough ships. Now it's 15. Take it or leave it.'

Bertie was about to dig into his pockets when another clerk hurried over to Darren. They had a whispered, intense conversation behind the thick glass. The younger clerk turned away, and Bertie saw him grab his coat off a chair and disappear behind a door at the back of the ticketing office. Darren tapped the glass with his pen.

'Pay the money, or I'll ask security to move you on.'

'For God's sake, pay the man,' the judge said, exhaustion grinding his words.

Bertie pulled out both envelopes, then he frowned as he heard a growing commotion, a rumble that was growing by the second. Across the hall, the vast crowd was turning this way and that, as skittish as a herd of deer. Something was coming their way.

'Bertie, what's happening?' It was Cheryl, and beneath her baseball cap, her wide eyes were frightened.

'I don't know. It's –'

A terrible thunder drowned his words, and the building shook as an unseen, low-flying plane screamed overhead. Bertie flinched. Outside the main doors, night turned to day as burning flares drifted to earth, bathing the port in flickering white light and illuminating the sea of faces outside. The panic was immediate, and the militia line crumbled as the crowd stormed the main doors. The hall filled with screams as the glass shattered and hundreds of bodies piled inside. Bertie knew he had only seconds to act. He spun around.

Darren had vanished.

After a frantic search, Bertie saw him having an urgent discussion with another clerk, who was waving her arms around. Bertie yelled his name as he banged on the glass.

'Darren! DARREN!'

He spun around, and Bertie waved two envelopes at him. Darren hurried over to the counter, his eyes watching the surging crowd. He was ready to bolt. Bertie could see it in his face. He turned around, grabbed The Witch by the arm, and dragged her to the counter, snatching the cataract glasses off her face.

'This is Lady Edith Spencer, governor of the British territories. Get us on a boat to France, and I'll double that 60 grand when we get there. And the governor here will make sure you're set up for life.'

Bertie shoved the envelopes beneath the glass partition, then flashed his badge like a veteran cop.

Darren stared at The Witch, then at Bertie's credentials. He pointed to the phalanx of militia guarding the dockside doors. 'Give me your hands, then meet me outside that door in 30 seconds.'

One by one, they shoved their hands through the gap and Darren stamped them with an ink motif of a ship. As Bertie whipped his back, the crowd roared, and at the other end of the hall, the barriers gave way.

'Go!' Darren yelled.

Bertie grabbed The Witch's arm and hurried towards the other side of the hall.

'Bertie, you're going too fast! I can't keep up!'

'Please, Lady Edith, try, otherwise we won't make it!'

He turned around. Cheryl was right behind him, her arm linked through the judge's. Then he saw Curly Top and Bruiser struggling with the militia. He increased his pace, almost jogging now, dragging The Witch past the 'E' window, then 'D', then 'C'. Shots rang out, and people ducked and screamed. More barriers collapsed, and a wave of humanity rushed forward and crashed against the counters.

'We're stamped!' Bertie yelled at the scrum of militia blocking the exit. 'Let us through!'

The black uniforms parted, their guns held ready, their faces white and sweaty. It was breaking down, and Bertie knew people were going to get killed. They pushed through to the lobby on the other side and out into the car park. The rain had stopped, and a glorious wave of fresh air washed over Bertie. Darren was waiting, a rucksack on his back. Bertie looked across the car park and saw the Mercedes.

'I've got a vehicle,' he told the clerk.

'Let's go then!'

Bertie put his arm around The Witch's shoulder and urged her forward. 'Come on, Lady Edith, you need to pick up the pace.'

'Don't let anything happen to me, Bertie.' She was breathless and her voice sounded small, like a child's.

'I won't, don't worry.' He turned around and waved to Cheryl. 'Come on, love. Hurry!'

Bertie heard more shots from inside the hall and then he saw the militia spilling out of the side entrance. Some stayed on their feet, but the solid wall of fast-moving panic trampled many others underfoot. Hundreds streamed outside and disappeared around the building, heading for the ships. But not all of them. Bertie saw Curly Top and Bruiser break away, searching left and right.

Bertie pulled the key out of his pocket and unlocked the Mercedes. Orange lights flashed.

Curly Top saw Bertie. 'You! Stand still!'

Bertie tugged open the side door. 'Everybody inside, quickly!' They piled aboard. As he ducked around the front of the vehicle, Curly Top yelled again.

'Governor Spencer!'

They were ten yards away.

Curly Top was pointing with a big kitchen knife. 'Governor

Edith Spencer, I sentence you to death for the murder of thousands of British people.'

Next to him, Bruiser snarled, a knife in one hand, a claw hammer in the other.

'Bertie!' Cheryl screamed. 'Get in the van! Now!'

Then both men charged, teeth gritted in murderous rage. Behind the open driver's door, Bertie raised the gun and shot Curly Top first. He grunted and fell to the ground, and Bertie ducked as Bruiser rushed him, raising the hammer, and shattering the window. Glass exploded over Bertie. He straightened up and grabbed the man's wrist, trapping his arm through the broken window. Then he shot him through the temple at point black range, and Bruiser collapsed at his feet, his mouth frozen in a perfect oh. Curly Top was on his knees a few yards away, clutching his side and screaming obscenities. Bertie climbed behind the wheel and started the Mercedes, dropping it into gear.

'Go, Bertie!' Cheryl yelled.

He yanked the wheel left, accelerating past the stream of humanity pouring out of the hall. Clearing the edge of the building, he turned right and drove towards the ships still tied to the dock. The mob was running towards them too, and many were abandoning their luggage as they ran. As he weaved past them, Bertie saw young men and women dashing ahead, pushing buggies and bouncing screaming children in their arms. He saw old people stumbling and falling to the ground. Some stood motionless, just watching, knowing they would never make it. The ships were hundreds of yards from the departure building, but already there were thousands of people converging on them. Bertie saw cars too, weaving recklessly around the runners, the immobile, and the piles of abandoned luggage. One car drove straight, knocking people over as it sped towards the loading ramps.

'We're never going to make it,' Bertie said.

'Forget those boats!' Darren leaned between the seats and pointed. 'Go that way!'

Bertie looked to his left, at the vast expanse of empty quays and docks. 'There's nothing there!'

'Do as he says!' Cheryl shrieked.

Bertie obeyed, reminding himself that Darren was just as desperate to leave as they were. He put his foot down and drove as Darren explained.

'Those two ships back there? One's got a broken boiler and the other one has already pulled up its gangways. No one's getting on either of them. They're decoys.'

'And yet you still took money from people,' Judge Hardy said. 'That's fraud by false representation, a failure to disclose information, and an abuse of your position.'

'What?'

'Forget it,' Bertie told Darren. 'Judge, you're not helping.'

Darren pointed to a route ahead, bordered by thick white lines. 'Follow that lane there.'

Bertie obeyed, keeping his speed in check, wanting to go faster but afraid that an accident might render them without transport. To the right of the lane, shipping containers towered above the road. To his left, huge concrete barriers, and a high chain-link fence. Beyond it, the lights of thousands of vehicles still queuing to get into the port. 'Where are we going?' Bertie asked.

'Eastern Arm North,' Darren explained. 'It forms one jaw of the harbour wall. There's a ferry there, the *Dunkerque Seaways*. She's a smaller vessel, and it's waiting for us – for the workers and militia.' He pointed. 'Look! There she is!'

As they cleared the container towers, Bertie saw it in the distance, a dark hulk silhouetted against the night sky with white steam drifting from its stack. It was unlit, which was why Bertie hadn't seen her.

A car overtook them, and then another, both heading for the ship. Cheryl yelled.

'Bertie! Look!'

He followed her pointed finger and saw a crowd massed against the fence, clambering up and over the chain-link ahead of them. Hundreds of people – men, mostly – were scrambling over and dropping onto the road ahead.

'It's people from the vehicle queues!' Darren said. 'They've seen the ship!'

Bertie put his foot down, hitting his horn and veering away as people spilt across the road in front of him. A man staggered and fell in front of the Mercedes. Bertie swerved right, clipping the concrete barrier by the side of the road. Something blew, and he felt the steering turn to mush. The Mercedes fishtailed left and right, and Bertie struggled to control it.

'Shit! She's all over the place!' He checked his side mirror. 'The back tyre's blown!'

'Don't stop!' Darren said. 'The ship won't wait!'

'Look out!' Judge Hardy yelled, and Bertie's head snapped to the left. He saw an articulated lorry heading towards the fence at full speed. He put his foot down, and the back end swung wildly before correcting itself. Behind them, the truck crashed into the concrete barrier and mounted it, hurtling through the fence before tipping over on its side, dragging a long length of chain-link behind it. Bertie glimpsed dust and sparks, but he ignored it, steering the crippled Mercedes towards the harbour wall.

'Jesus Christ!' Darren said. 'They're pouring through the fence! Thousands of 'em!'

Bertie didn't look. He kept his speed steady and gripped the steering wheel as if his life depended on it. Because it did. All their lives.

The *Dunkerque Seaways* blasted its horn, a warning that it was about to depart.

'Hurry, Bertie!' screeched The Witch.

He slowed for the bend, and then he was rumbling along the harbour wall's eastern arm. He saw the twin towers of the gantry ahead and a small queue of cars bumping up the vehicle ramp.

'We're the last ones,' Darren said, looking behind them.

Men and women in yellow vests waved them forward and Bertie drove up the metal ramp. The wheel screeched in protest, and sparks flew, but Bertie kept driving. The ramp rose, then fell, and the ship's gaping hold waited to receive them. He drove onto the vehicle deck, showering sparks, and another yellow vest waved him into a lane. He stopped behind a car that had its doors open. Militia climbed out, laughing and hugging each other.

'I need to check in with my people,' Darren said. 'You should stay in the vehicle until we get underway.'

Bertie twisted around in his seat and held out his hand. 'Thanks, pal. I meant what I said about the money. Come and find me before we get to Calais.'

'You bet.' Darren turned to The Witch. 'I'm just glad you made it okay, Governor Spencer.'

She nodded without looking at him. 'Thank you, young man.'

Darren disappeared between the parked cars. Bertie exhaled a long sigh of relief. 'Well, that was bloody close, wasn't it?'

Cheryl reached out and squeezed his hand. 'You did great, Bertie.'

Klaxons echoed across the car deck and the enormous doors closed. 'Everyone wait here.'

'Where are you going?' Cheryl asked him.

'I just need to see this, that's all. I'll be back in a minute, I promise.'

He threaded his way through the parked vehicles and felt the ship rumble beneath him. The stairwells and gangways were using red emergency lighting, and people hurried back and forth, a mix of crew, civilians, and militia. He found a doorway out onto the deck, and the strengthening sea breeze whipped around him. He went to the rail and looked over the edge. They hadn't cleared the harbour wall, but people were still running alongside it, waving at the ship, as if it would stop and pick them up. Bertie felt sorry for them. Almost.

He walked to the stern, where scores of people gathered along the rail. It was a bizarre sight, frightening, Bertie thought. In the distance, he saw a vast crowd besieging the broken ship, and beyond the entrance to the port, thousands of headlights snaked all the way out of Dover. So many people, so desperate to leave. Why? It baffled Bertie.

As they cleared the harbour wall, he heard another rumble, and a plane thundered low over the docks, spitting out flares that shimmered against the backdrop of chalk cliffs. Bertie watched its blue flame exhausts disappear into the night sky and cursed the pilot. What was the point? It would only terrify everyone.

He stood with the other spectators for a while, watching those famous cliffs shrink and fade. The darkness wrapped its cloak around the ship, and Bertie wondered how long it would be before he returned. Months, certainly. Probably years, but he could live with that prospect. His nerves were shot, and exhaustion had become a permanent state of being. What he needed was rest, good food, the sun on his back, and Cheryl by his side. And he would live far from any city and under The Witch's protection. Then, one day, when things settled, he would return home.

He looked down at the stern and saw the water churn to white foam as the ship pushed out into the Channel. Above him, the wind whistled through the lines, snapping out the French tricolour. Bertie smiled.

They'd made it.

THE FIRST OF THE B-52H(A) BOMBERS CROSSED THE WIDE, muddy estuary at Barley Harbour and touched down at Shannon International Airport in southern Ireland. Behind it, seven more of the venerable aircraft landed on runway zero-six – the longest in Ireland – and taxied around the airport to the large apron outside the terminal building.

Turbofan engines wound down, and in the darkness of the blacked-out airport, ground crews drove out to the planes, chocked the gigantic wheels, and began preparing each aircraft for the mission ahead.

A mobile staircase was driven up to the bulkhead door of the lead B-52, and a team of US defence contractors from Boeing's Defence, Space, and Security Division jogged up the steps and opened the pressure door from the outside. Stepping into the aircraft, the lead technician turned left into the pilotless cockpit and plugged his laptop into the small server rack bolted to the floor where the captain's seat once stood. He downloaded the flight data from the servers while the rest of his team ran their physical checks on the flight systems, ensuring that connections hadn't failed or worked themselves loose during the turbulent transatlantic flight.

They would check every plane in the same way and the down-loaded data would be analysed by other Boeing contractors. Of the eight planes now sitting on the apron, none of them had experienced any major flight system failures and that information was passed to USCENTCOM, where the mission status board was updated, and the order sent across the Atlantic to Global Strike Command. That order would be passed to the Strategic Bomb Squadrons in North Dakota and Louisiana, who would launch their fleets of ageing, yet still highly effective B-52, subsonic, long-range bombers.

The forces of vengeance were gathering for war.

'NEED A HAND DOWN THERE?'

Bertie looked over his shoulder. Judge Hardy was standing over him, a half-smile on his face.

'No, thanks, Judge. It's all done.' Bertie got off his knees and stood up, wiping his hands on a rag. He kicked the replacement tyre, now fully inflated. 'We're good to go.' He started packing away the tools. 'Did they find Lady Edith a cabin?'

The judge nodded. 'The last one. It's down in the bowels of the ship, and she's not too happy about it. Mrs P is settling her in.'

'Hopefully we won't be at sea for too long.'

'You heard that purser. The French ports are jammed with vessels, and the registration process isn't helping. They could hold us at anchor for some time.'

Bertie heaved the shredded tyre on top of the roof rack and started tying down the waterproof sheeting. 'It's better than being stuck at Dover. I dread to think what it's like there now.'

The judge nodded. 'Ghastly, I would imagine.'

Bertie slapped his hands together. 'Fancy a drink? The bar's open.'

'Do you think it's a good idea? They'll be pretty jumpy in France, and we don't want to be smelling of booze. Not sure I could cope with 50 lashes in a Calais square.'

'We'll stick to the orange juice.' Bertie smiled and patted his pocket. 'Her Ladyship's buying.'

They made their way up a couple of decks to the bar, and Bertie had to wait for the judge twice as he puffed his way up the steps. The bar was busy but subdued, and people huddled in groups, chatting quietly. Bertie bought a couple of orange juices and four miniature vodkas and set them down in a corner booth.

'Here we go,' Bertie said, sliding the judge's drink in front of him. 'I got you vodka, just in case.' Bertie emptied two miniatures into his juice and stirred it with a straw. The judge watched him, smiled, and then did the same. Bertie raised his glass.

'Here's to Lady Luck for getting us this far.' He winced. 'Shit. I'm sorry, Judge. That was a stupid thing to say.'

'That's all right.'

Bertie took a sip of his drink and felt the vodka kick immediately. It was glorious. 'She really saved us, you know.'

The judge swirled his glass, his eyes downcast. 'It's the circumstances I'm struggling with. She was like a different woman. But you're right, without her, we wouldn't have made it. The thing is, I'm not sure if I want to be here without her.'

'Don't be silly. You've got years ahead of you and a comfortable life in the sun. The grief will pass, you'll see, and then you'll only remember the good things.'

Hardy took a long pull of his drink and set it down. He looked at Bertie, his face like stone. 'Don't get complacent.'

Bertie's glass froze halfway to his lips. 'What d'you mean?'

'You and Mrs P need to get out from under Edith's shadow.'

'Why?'

'Because she cannot be trusted,' he said, glancing over his shoulder. 'After her run-in with Al-Huda in Bloomsbury, she wanted to give you up to him. Sacrifice you. I persuaded her otherwise.'

Bertie's stomach lurched. 'She what?'

'Don't be naïve, Bertie. Edith Spencer sold her soul a long time ago. As did I.' He looked over his shoulder, then leaned across the table. 'You must leave her, at the earliest opportunity.'

'Why? Al-Huda is dead, and the Alliance will march through London any day now. It's over. No one will come looking for us.'

'Perhaps no one in the caliphate. But the governor has blood on her hands. Mass incarcerations, deportations, grisly executions. She ordered most of those programs. You know that.'

'So?'

'So, the Atlantic Alliance will demand its pound of flesh, and when they do, great pressure will be brought to bear. Deals will be made at the highest levels, and Wazir will order the arrest and extradition of the perpetrators so they may be brought to account. And when they come for her, she will bring down as many people as she can, and that will include you and Mrs P. You need to be gone before that happens.'

Panic fluttered at the edge of Bertie's consciousness. The cushy life he'd imagined was already crumbling. 'Where would we go?'

'Switzerland. I have friends there, influential people who will help you settle, get you papers. It won't be Provence, but you'll be safe.'

Bertie imagined him and Cheryl shivering in a drab block of flats, staring out the window across a snowy, soulless Swiss city. Still, it was better than being shipped back to England in chains.

'How long d'you think we've got?'

Judge Hardy took another sip of his drink. 'The victory parades and speeches won't last long. Triumph will soon turn to anger and vengeance. My guess? Less than six months.'

The PA system crackled, and a voice boomed across the bar. 'Your attention please, this is the first officer speaking. We've been informed that all French ports are no longer taking any new arrivals due to the sheer weight of traffic, so they've diverted us to Zeebrugge. Disembarkation should begin at midday. The restaurant will be open in one hour for hot food. Thank you.'

The PA system thumped, then fell silent.

'As I suspected.' Judge Hardy got to his feet. 'I'll go down to the cabin, send Mrs P up here. You could both do with a little relaxation.'

Bertie forced a smile. 'Thanks, Judge.'

He went to the bar and bought four more vodkas and a couple of bottles of orange juice. If they weren't getting off the ship until midday tomorrow, they'd have plenty of time to freshen up. Cheryl appeared a few minutes later. Bertie stood and waved, and when she got closer, he opened his arms. They held each other for several moments, then he kissed her and sat down.

'I got you a couple of vodkas,' he said.

Cheryl beamed, taking off her baseball cap and setting it on the seat beside her. 'You're an angel.' She sipped her drink and closed her eyes. 'God, that tastes divine.' She took another sip. 'How's the judge?'

Bertie shrugged. 'Better. Broken-hearted of course, but he's coping.'

'We'll have to take care of him when we get to Provence.'

'I think that's a good idea.'

There was no point in breaking the bad news yet. That would be a conversation for another day, after they'd found their feet and settled in. In the meantime, they would enjoy a couple of drinks and a meal, and maybe later, they would take a stroll out on deck. It wasn't exactly a Mediterranean cruise, but he felt the stress of the last few months lifting off his shoulders. Provence might be temporary, but at least they had options.

So, for now, they could both relax and maybe find a little peace and happiness. Bertie raised his glass.

'To the future.'

Cheryl kissed him on the cheek. 'To *our* future.'

THE SENTINEL WAS FINALLY FREE. THE SEA HAD TRAPPED IT beneath the waves for some time, twisting in a vast, slow-moving vortex, its heavy chain holding it beneath the surface, where light turned to darkness repeatedly as it revolved, a prisoner of the tidal whirlpool.

And then, as the light faded again and the undersea world became a realm of swirling, grainy darkness, the Sentinel was dragged from its icy prison by the undertow of a passing vessel and set free. Drifting into the path of another subsurface stream, the Sentinel continued its journey east, picking up speed as the current strengthened, hurtling through the darkness, drawn by the undertow and now by something else – the steady, rhythmic heartbeat of another travelling mariner.

The end of the Sentinel's purgatory drew near. The water throbbed with the force of the mariner's heartbeat as it thumped ever louder. And then it took form just ahead, its gigantic, rust-coloured belly looming out of the abyss like a prehistoric behemoth. The Sentinel was on a collision course, unstoppable, reaching out for the mariner, desperate to make contact, to deliver its deadly kiss, and trigger the 200 pounds of RDX explosive inside its belly ...

BERTIE GRABBED THE TABLE AS A METALLIC BOOM FILLED THE ship, and the *Dunkerque Seaways* shuddered, the glasses and bottles behind the bar rattling violently. Across the room, people staggered, and glasses smashed on the floor. Through the windows, Bertie saw a torrent of seawater crash down on the deck outside. Cheryl grabbed his hand. 'What was that?'

Bertie swallowed. 'Don't know. It sounded like an explosion. Maybe a gasket blew. Or something.'

'Do boats have gaskets?'

'I suppose.' People were leaving the bar and streaming out on deck. 'Wait here. I'll see what's happening.'

Cheryl got up. 'I'll come with.'

'No, stay there, please.'

She retook her seat and Bertie followed a couple of militiamen out onto the deck that was slippery with seawater. Everyone was crowding at the rail, so Bertie moved further along the deck. Squeezing through the crowd and leaning over the rail, he felt the blood drain from his face.

The boat was still moving, but Bertie knew it wouldn't be for long. The hole in the ship was huge and as seawater rushed in, steam rushed out. 'Jesus Christ,' he whispered.

'We hit a mine!' someone shouted, and then alarms blared across the ship. As Bertie ran back towards the bar, an explosion knocked him off his feet and he fell to the deck. The ship shuddered beneath him. He picked himself up and barged his way back into the bar. Cheryl was already on her feet. Bertie grabbed her hands.

'We've hit a mine —'

'What?'

'Grab a lifejacket, just in case.'

'Are we going to sink?'

Bertie looked around, saw a couple of crewmen in maintenance overalls running across the bar. 'I don't know. These things have watertight doors and stuff, don't they?' He saw a bottle of beer rolling across the carpet. 'We're listing,' he whispered, unable to believe what he was seeing. 'That's not good. Go to the back of the ship, find a lifejacket, and wait for me there. I'll get the others.'

'No, Bertie! It's too dangerous!'

Bertie squeezed her hands. 'I have to try.'

'They're in G6,' Cheryl said, slapping her baseball cap on her head. 'I'm coming with you as far as the car deck. I need my rucksack.'

'Don't hang about. Get to the back of the ship as fast as you can. If they tell you to get on a lifeboat, don't wait for me. I'll find you.'

The PA system crackled into life. 'All passengers, this is the first officer. Make your way immediately to the nearest muster station on A Deck. Do not bring your luggage. Life jackets will be issued on deck. All passengers ...'

They hurried down the stairs as people were streaming up. Everyone was shouting, pushing, and shoving. He let go of Cheryl's hand when they reached the car deck and he continued down into the bowels of the ship where the staircase became narrower and steeper, the ceiling lower. People struggled past him, ignoring the calls to leave luggage behind. Bertie was scared. He didn't like confined spaces, and the thought of being trapped terrified him, but he pushed on, following the signs to G Deck.

The terrible noise was much louder now, and the screech and groan of metal hurt Bertie's ears. The ship was dying, he knew that now, and when he reached G Deck, he saw the far end of the corridor half-submerged in green water.

'Lady Edith! Judge Hardy!' They're in G6 ...

He looked at the nearest door – G34. He ran down the corridor, plunging into the water that lapped around his shins, then his knees. 'Edith!' he yelled. 'Victor!' He waded deeper, the cold taking his breath away. G6 was two doors down on his left. As he pushed on, the water rose above his waist. He tried the handle, but the door wouldn't open. He thumped on it.

'It's me, Bertie! Open the door!'

'Bertie, help us!' he heard The Witch cry. 'There's water in here. Get us out!'

'Stand back!' He shouldered the door, but it wouldn't budge. Then he heard the judge's voice.

'Bertie, listen to me. I can't unlock the door. Is there something around you, an axe, anything like that?'

His voice was calm, and Bertie wondered how that was possible. If he was on the other side, he'd be chewing through the wood right now. Across the corridor, he saw a half-submerged fire extinguisher and yanked it off the wall. His hands were freezing, and the metal extinguisher was icy to the touch. 'Stay away from the door! I'm going to smash the lock!' He didn't wait for an answer. Instead, he lifted the extinguisher high above his head and brought it down on the submerged handle. It sheared it off, and he watched it sink below the green water.

The door stayed shut. He shouldered it again, using all his strength. It didn't budge. 'Fuck!'

The overhead lights flickered, and Bertie leaned against the door. The corridor was filling fast, and its angle had shifted. He heard the judge's muffled voice on the other side.

'The ship is listing, Bertie. Get out, before the lights blow. Find Mrs P, get to a lifeboat. Save yourselves. Please.'

The Witch screeched like a banshee. 'Don't you dare leave us, Bertie! I forbid it! Do something!'

The lights flickered again, and Bertie stopped breathing. The water was up to his chest now, and he could barely feel his legs. Back up the corridor, the water was lapping at the staircase. If he didn't go – right now – he'd die. He thumped on the door.

'I'm sorry, Judge. I'm so sorry.'

The voice on the other side of the door was somehow calm. 'Thank you, Bertie, for all you've done. Now go.'

Bertie turned and waded through the water. The ship groaned, and then he heard The Witch's voice behind him, filled with anger and fear.

'Bertie, get back here! Bertieeee! Answer me!'

He kept moving, sloshing through the flood, finally escaping its icy grip as he reached for the staircase handrail —

The lights went out.

Bertie's hand found smooth cold steel, and he dragged himself up the stairs, the blackness so thick he was blind. He gripped the rail, moving hand over hand as his feet found the stair treads. He heard rushing water below and felt a deep concussion run through his hands as the ship shuddered once more. Bertie ignored it, swallowed his terror, and kept moving upward.

Shapes came into view, and light falling from the landing above restored his sight. He increased his pace, taking the stairs two at a time now, but the ship was leaning over. Soon it would capsize.

As he passed the car deck, he saw a vehicle slide into another and crunch against the bulkhead. He climbed another four landings and burst through a door onto a deck that was tilted at 45 degrees. The wind whipped and gusted, and he heard shouts and whistles, all coming from the darkness beyond the ship. Lifeboat stations stood empty, and that gave Bertie hope. Cheryl would be on one for sure. He staggered to the back of the boat, hanging on to the rail as the slope deepened. There were others there, a dozen souls scrambling over the rail, and then he saw a Spurs baseball cap —

'Cheryl!'

She saw him and waved. 'Bertie! Quickly!'

He staggered towards her. Over the rail, a lifeboat dangled from its stanchions, filled with terrified faces, all screaming and waving at him.

'Hurry!'

'Get in!'

He helped Cheryl over the side, then followed her, dropping a few feet into the fibre-glass boat and squeezing in at the side. Two crewmen worked the winch, and they hit the water 30 seconds later. Cheryl hugged him.

'You're soaking.'

'I couldn't get them out, Cheryl. The door wouldn't budge. I tried, I really did.'

She stroked his face. 'It's okay, Bertie.'

The ship roared as the sheer weight of water dragged the bow beneath the waves. With a terrifying hiss, a huge propeller lifted out of the water above them, the ship rising like a hulking sea monster, blotting out the stars. The shadow of a man loomed over Bertie and thrust a plastic oar in his hands.

'Start paddling, before she drags us down with her!'

Bertie snatched the oar, plunged the paddle into the sea and began pulling with what little strength he had left.

EDITH STOOD ON THE SINGLE BED AND WATCHED THE WATER spraying through the gap around the door. It was the pressure, she knew, which meant the passageway beyond was submerged. Victor stood next to her, both of them pressed against the cabin wall as their underwater prison tilted, the filthy water sloshing around their legs. A small green emergency light glowed overhead, and a torrent of seawater ran down the shadowy walls. In her whirling, tortured mind, Edith remembered an overgrown Victorian crypt in the grounds of her old school, a damp and depressing place where one could enjoy a furtive cigarette before scampering up its mossy steps and re-joining the world of the living. But there would be no leaving this water-logged tomb and that infuriated her.

'Do something, Victor!'

He looked at her, his white hair plastered against his forehead. 'There's nothing to be done, Edith. The ship is already underwater. It won't be long now.' He pointed to the life vest around her neck. 'That's rather futile, you know.'

'Shut up!'

'At least you'll be buried with your treasure. Rather like an Egyptian pharaoh.'

The thin spray of water blasting through the doorframe was

whistling like a kettle now, and Edith watched it in fascination. The door would give way at any second. She railed against her imminent death. It was so unfair.

'At least we made our mark, Victor. Our names will be remembered. And feared.'

'Not quite the legacy I had in mind when I left Oxford.'

Edith turned on him. 'What's this? Regret?'

'Something like that.'

'What a hypocrite you are, Victor. You deserve this.'

The pressure increased, the water screeching through the door frame.

'We both do. After all the lives we've destroyed.'

Crack!

The door split and water roared through the fissure like a fire hose. The frame creaked and buckled.

Edith braced herself. 'I'm proud of everything I've done, Victor. I have no regrets.'

'In that case, I'll see you in hell.'

Edith smiled. The concept of an afterlife had always been an absurd one, but now it comforted her. 'I do hope so, Victor.'

The door groaned then exploded inwards. Water filled the void, and Edith floated in the blackness. The air in her lungs ran out. Seawater ran in.

A second later, she was dead.

[36]

MIGRANT CRISIS

THE ARMOURED JLTV SLOWED AT THE JUNCTION OF
Connaught Place and Edgware Road and parked between two mud-
splattered Stryker armoured vehicles. The Parachute Regiment
colonel, sitting in the front passenger seat, turned around.

'This is as far as we go, Prime Minister.'

Harry climbed out, adjusting the strap of his ballistic helmet, the
significance of the moment not lost on him. It was the first time he'd
set foot in London after being plucked from that Knightsbridge
rooftop over three years ago, and he felt a strange mixture of
emotions. Elation, sadness, doubt, and trepidation for what lay ahead
in the coming years. He looked up at the surrounding buildings, at
the mixture of architecture, the jarring clash of old and new, and
noticed the scars of war and occupation everywhere. The cold
autumnal breeze snatched at open windows, where ragged curtains
rose and fell, whipping black dust from scorched brickwork and
burned roof timbers. It was a familiar scene to Harry and his journey
into the city had revealed much the same, passing mile after mile of
looted shops, burned-out cars, and rubbish-strewn parks patrolled by
packs of stray dogs. He saw people too, streaming in and out of shops

and supermarkets, their arms and trolleys laden with looted goods. They'd stared in bemusement and then hurried away as the JLTVs, Strykers, and Abrams tanks had rolled through their neighbourhood. Only the old and the young waved.

As a huddle of helmeted paratroopers stood guard, Lee Wilde, also kitted out in a helmet and ballistic vest, climbed out of the JLTV and joined Harry. Wilde looked around and grimaced.

'I was never very fond of this part of town,' Wilde said. 'Too touristy.'

Harry pointed back up the Edgware Road. 'I remember smoking a pipe in a shisha bar just up there. Before I entered politics, of course. The food was wonderful.'

Wilde raised an eyebrow. 'Drugs, Harry?'

'Hardly. Still, the hope remains that one day things will return to the way they were.'

'Isn't that what got us here in the first place?'

The Parachute Regiment colonel – a man named Fletcher – escorted them through a maze of vehicles towards the enormous American tanks blocking the junction of Edgware Road and Marble Arch itself, their enormous guns trained towards Hyde Park. Everywhere Harry looked, there were soldiers, moving in formations or standing in small groups watching the area to the south with binoculars. Military vehicles filled the side streets, and the sight of it all lifted Harry's spirits. CENTCOM was still prohibiting manned flights over the city, but the order to advance south had finally come through and the King's Continental Army was right where it should be – at the spearhead of the push into London. But right now, this was as far as they went.

Like his soldiers, Fletcher had painted his face with war stripes, and he carried a compact sub-machine gun across his chest. He led them between two huge Abrams, where they could see... not very much, Harry realised. Despite the occasional flutter of drifting leaves, the trees were still in bloom and blocked any significant views to the south. Fletcher was explaining the tactical situation.

'So far, the operation to encircle the West End and The City of London has encountered little resistance, and where it has, we've dealt with it robustly.' He pointed to the surrounding buildings. 'We've got spotter teams positioned on several rooftops across the area and ground units are pushing east towards King's Cross, where they'll link up with elements of the 2nd Armoured Division. Across the Thames, the 4th and 7th Divisions are moving into position around the South Circular. By midnight tonight, Alliance forces will have formed a ring of steel stretching from Hammersmith to Canary Wharf.' He pointed to the ground. 'This point here is the closest anyone from the Alliance has got to the centre of town.'

'What about the locals? Civilians?'

'Most are heeding the radio warnings to stay inside. It must be difficult for some, given that the power is out from here to the Thames.' He turned to Harry. 'We're ready to advance and take the rest of the city. Do you know when we can expect that order?'

Harry could sense the frustration in the man's voice. He shook his head. 'I don't, I'm afraid.'

'What's the delay? We're hearing a lot of rumours.'

'Unless you hear it from CENTCOM, I would disregard anything else.' That was Harry's way of saying, *I'm as clueless as the next man.*

'The regiment has fought long and hard,' Fletcher said. 'I've lost a third of my battalion, and I'm tired of writing letters of condolence. I suppose I need to know that we're not walking into a trap here. Perhaps another nuke?'

Harry shook his head. 'Wazir knows that such a move would signal the end of his caliphate.'

'So why are we being held back?'

'I don't know. The Americans are playing this one close to their chests. It's their show, Colonel Fletcher, and they'll tell us what's happening when they're good and ready. Until then, we wait.' Harry looked to the east, along Oxford Street. 'Looks like quite a mess down there.'

'The looting has been wholesale,' Fletcher said, handing Harry a set of binoculars.

He squeezed them against his eyes and spun the focus ring, bringing the scene into sharp relief. As far as he could see, Oxford Street was a landscape of ransacked stores and businesses, where the roads and pavements were buried beneath a carpet of abandoned goods and rubbish, and almost every window Harry saw was broken. His spirits dipped. The sheer scale of destruction and vandalism was beyond anything he'd imagined. He swung the optics south to Marble Arch square, and something pale caught his eye. He readjusted the focus. Above the trees, black birds cawed and swooped, rising, then settling back down on something pale, something veiled by the foliage around the square. 'What is that?'

It was Wilde who solved the mystery. 'It's people, Harry. The crucifixions, remember?'

Harry remembered the briefings, the satellite images. He turned to Fletcher. 'Take me over there.'

'We're not supposed to advance past this line,' said the soldier. 'I've got a burial team on standby. In the meantime, thank God for those trees.'

'I'm going,' Harry said.

'They're dead, Prime Minister. There's nothing anyone can do.'

'I can bear witness,' Harry said. 'I'm going, with or without an escort.'

Fletcher bobbed his helmet and called up an MRAP. The mine-resistant armoured vehicle squealed to a stop on the road beyond the Abrams a few moments later.

'Let's go, Lee.'

His chief of staff shook his head. 'I'm going to sit this one out if you don't mind.'

Harry understood. Fletcher and half a dozen paras escorted him into the vehicle. The steel door clanged shut and then they were moving, racing across the five-lane road and bouncing onto the square. It stopped beneath the cover of a large oak and the paras deployed. Fletcher waved him outside.

'Sixty seconds, Prime Minister.'

'Understood.'

Wrapped in a cocoon of uniforms, Harry strode across a patch of churned up grass, the line of crosses planted around the square. He counted a dozen of them, as tall as telegraph poles, and on four of them, semi-naked corpses hung from thick crossbeams. As they got closer, the scavenging blackbirds clattered into the air, screeching in protest. Harry stopped beneath the poor wretches, the flesh on their bodies pecked to raw meat. Their eyes were missing, and their legs hung free, dangling in death as blood and other fluids pooled on the ground beneath them. Their elbows were bound by ropes to the thick crossbeams, and their executioners had driven huge bolts through their wrists.

'We're moving,' Fletcher said, and Harry was grateful. Climbing back into the vehicle, he ground his teeth in quiet anger. The cruelty was bad enough, but to see it enacted on a London landmark was difficult to comprehend. He'd never see Marble Arch in the same way again.

'Hard to believe that people came to watch this,' Fletcher said. 'They were popular spectacles, if one can believe the rumours.'

'Like ancient bloody Rome,' Harry replied. He wondered who the victims were and what they had done. The quislings who'd ordered such barbarity would pay for their crimes, he vowed. 'I want those bodies removed at the earliest opportunity,' Harry told Fletcher.

Back behind the safety of the cordon, Harry and Wilde spent the afternoon meeting the troops and officers and touring the nearby streets. From the roof of the Hard Rock Hotel on Great Cumberland Place, Harry saw the vast emptiness of Park Lane stretching towards Hyde Park Corner. Nothing moved except rubbish and windblown leaves. Black smoke rose into the sky somewhere to the south.

As the sun set, Harry and Wilde sat down for dinner in the

Victory Services Club on Seymour Street, which, to Harry's surprise, had suffered only minor damage. They ate a meal of MREs with some British officers, and afterwards, Harry and Wilde took coffee in the lounge as they discussed their next move. As Harry spoke, Wilde scrolled through his phone.

'Where's the Cabinet right now?' Harry asked.

'Still travelling,' Wilde said. 'They should be in Northwood by midnight tonight.'

Harry smiled. 'They won't enjoy exchanging the comforts of Cumbria for a ransacked military base. Still, that's what they wanted.'

'You've kept them onside, which is the main thing.'

Harry stood and went to the window. Through the thick net curtains, he could see an anti-aircraft vehicle parked nearby in Connaught Square, its missile tubes pointed up at the sky. Yet as he sipped his coffee, all he could think of were those bodies in the square nearby.

'Why d'you think they did it?'

Wilde looked up from his screen. 'Who?'

'The collaborators. Like Edith Spencer, for example. I met the woman several times before the invasion. She was at the top of her game and well-respected both at home and in Europe. She even mixed with royalty, for God's sake. How does someone go from being a distinguished member of the establishment to a butcher capable of such atrocities? I'm struggling to understand it.'

Wilde lowered his phone. 'This came up a couple of times during my post-grad studies. The question was, where had all the psychopaths gone? They didn't simply die out after Hitler and Stalin.'

'So, what was the answer?'

Wilde shrugged. 'They hide in plain sight. Amongst the political class primarily, and health care too. Executive power can provide opportunities to carry out their murderous fantasies. And the medical community too. Often, they're restrained by prevailing political winds and bound by the laws of the land, but in times of crisis and war, those shackles are removed, giving them free rein to do as they please. Many high-ranking Nazis and Communists were very dull people before the war.'

'Intriguing,' Harry said, sitting back down. 'When this is over, I want Spencer found. We must bring her and her ilk to justice.'

'Absolutely.' Wilde's phone pinged with an incoming message. 'Faye's helicopter just landed at Northolt. The others should arrive in the next couple of hours. Then they'll transfer to Northwood.' He put the phone on the table between them. 'Maybe you made a mistake with Faye. Making her deputy PM, I mean. She wasn't exactly on your side during that last call.'

'The thought had crossed my mind,' Harry said. 'But she's a smart lady and strong enough to keep the Cabinet in line. If she can do that for a few more days, then she will have done her job. For now. Once hostilities have ended, and everyone is busy with their departments, we'll see how well this Cabinet works.'

'So, you're not ruling out an early reshuffle?'

Harry was adamant. 'Not at all.'

Wilde's phone rumbled across the table, and he scooped it up. He listened for a moment, then passed the phone to Harry. 'It's Eliot Bird, Mitchell's NSA.'

Harry had never taken a call from Bird. He took the offered phone. 'Eliot, how are you?'

'Fine, thank you, Prime Minister.'

He sounded reserved. 'How may I help you?'

'The president would like to see you as soon as you can.'

'That's good news.' Harry winked at Wilde. 'When and where?'

'Here, tomorrow. He's sending Air Force One to collect you and one of your team. Your choice. General McKenzie will make the arrangements. I look forward to seeing you.'

The call ended, and Harry handed the phone to Wilde. 'Mitchell wants a meeting. He's sending Air Force One.'

'Progress, at last. When's the meeting?'

'Tomorrow morning.'

Wilde got to his feet. 'I'll find Fletcher, organise transport back to Northwood.'

Harry watched him walk away, and his spirits lifted again. If Mitchell was laying out the red carpet, Harry could ignore the recent snubs and his own frustration. He had to remember that America wanted this war over with as much as he did. The sooner they could get around the table and hammer out an endgame, the better for everyone.

Then he could begin the job of building back Britain. I like that, Harry mused. *Build Back Britain.* It was catchy. He'd run it by Wilde, get some feedback. It might just become his new slogan.

And after what he'd seen so far, it was exactly what the country needed.

BERTIE HUDDLED NEXT TO CHERYL, SHIVERING IN THE DARK beneath the stars. Behind them, the promise of dawn was nothing more than a thin band of yellow on the horizon. They'd drifted in the Channel for two nights, assaulted by rain, by a period of frighteningly rough seas, and a fog that had trapped them for most of the previous day, masking the last of their emergency flares, muffling their whistles, and cloaking the invisible vessels that passed them by. Bertie and Cheryl had nestled together, and Bertie's body ached with cold. The life raft had space blankets, and Bertie used a couple to keep them both warm. When the rough weather had hit their boat, they'd lost an oar, but still they'd paddled, trying to capture currents they knew existed yet remained elusive. The coastal lights of Europe were invisible, and they argued constantly about course, wind, and tide. There were no sailors aboard, only a couple of young militia lads with no weapons and plenty of gob. After 24 hours, they too lapsed into a sullen silence.

They were adrift in the busiest shipping lane in the world, and as night turned to day, then night once more, the miserable survivors of the *MS Dunkerque Seaways* took fate in their hands and paddled, vowing not to stop. France or Belgium was the target, and when it was his turn, Bertie had worked his oar as hard as the others, grateful to be moving his cold, painful limbs. Cheryl had tried to keep his spirits up, but she wasn't a miracle worker, and as the second night dragged on, Bertie's hopes of surviving waned. He wasn't the only one.

And so, the oars moved from hand to hand, and the fibreglass boat turned and twisted and made headway, assisted by a strengthening wind. When Bertie wasn't rowing, he held Cheryl tight for warmth and to hear her whispered words of hope, and yet those words grew faint as he felt himself slipping away. He wanted to close his eyes and sleep forever.

The shouting dragged him back to life. Cheryl was shaking him awake and pointing. Then Bertie saw it too, a thin white line on the horizon, distant waves breaking on a distant shoreline. After two more hours of paddling, the sound of the surf was clear. After another hour, the sky behind them paled, but nobody cared that the sun was rising on the wrong horizon. None of them had eaten for two days and there was little bottled water left. They were cold and tired and frightened, and all they wanted was to get off the life raft.

Bertie dug deep, slapping the paddle into the waves, dragging it backwards, his head down, his mind frozen, the wind slicing through his sodden clothes. The boom and hiss of the waves grew louder, and then they were riding the surf onto the shore. Bertie's oar hit the seabed, and the others scrambled overboard, dragging the boat into shallow water. The lifeboat finally grounded, and Bertie clambered over the side and carried Cheryl up a steep bank of pebbles. As the sun broke the horizon, the other passengers headed for the dunes that overlooked the beach, desperate to escape the area before someone alerted the authorities.

But Cheryl didn't move. Bertie tugged her hand, his teeth chattering. 'Come on, love. We have to get out of here.'

Cheryl stood her ground, looking along a beach that stretched for miles in either direction. 'Are you sure, Bertie? Maybe they made a mistake.'

He shook his head. 'I wish that were true, but it isn't. This is England, and if they catch us here, they'll know we were trying to escape. We have to go. Now.'

So, they ran, up over the shingle, through a maze of dunes where the sand gave way beneath their feet, chased by the sun that threatened to expose them. Beyond the dunes, they found a road, and Bertie watched the others head off in a large, disorganised group. He squeezed Cheryl's hand, and they jogged in the opposite direction.

The irony of their circumstances wasn't lost on Bertie. He'd sailed across the Channel in a lifeboat and landed on an English beach. Now he was trying to evade the authorities. He hoped the day would come when they could laugh about it.

For now, his only thought was escape.

[37]

DANGER CLOSE

'*THIS IS A RADIO FREE BRITAIN BROADCAST ON BEHALF OF THE Atlantic Alliance. Citizens of London, you are ordered to remain in your homes until further notice. Ensure all water, gas, and electricity supplies are shut off. Stay away from doors and windows, and close curtains and blinds where possible. Remain tuned to this frequency. Share this message with your neighbours. Remain calm. Conserve food and water. Atlantic Alliance forces will be with you shortly. Thank you for your courage and patience. This has been a broadcast on behalf of Radio Free Britain and the Atlantic Alliance.*'

Griff clicked off the portable radio. 'What's taking them so long?'

'They'll be here soon,' Eddie said.

'That's what you said yesterday. And the day before that.'

Eddie shrugged. 'There's still a threat.'

'Your boss said there's a mechanised division at King's Cross. That's a mile away. Don't tell me they're worried about those Jihadis we've seen. They don't even have heavy weapons.'

'You're forgetting the missile trucks.'

'Fuck the trucks! They can't take out tanks, can they? All the

358

Alliance has to do is roll into town with an armoured division and it's over.'

There was no denying the logic of Griff's words. 'Maybe we should put you in charge,' Eddie said.

He saw Griff's face darken and knew his joke had backfired. The older man pointed into the distance. 'I've got a wife and two kids out there, and they'll be thinking the worst. I've got to get home, Eddie!'

'It's too dangerous. You know that. You've seen them out there.'

Griff turned away. Despite orders to the contrary, Eddie and Griff continued to venture outside after dark, though never drifting far from the safe house. Both of them had seen the red London bus parked outside Charing Cross train station, had watched as Jihadis loaded boxes inside and ran wires across the station forecourt. They'd seen torches waving around the upper floors of buildings along the Strand, and armed groups of men and women continued their nocturnal movements around the area. There was no question the enemy was preparing for a fight. Griff knew it too, but he had other priorities.

'So, they're rigging IEDs and digging in. So what? The Alliance has kicked their arse from Donegal to Dalston. Now they've circled the city, shut off the power. It's game over for that mob out there.'

'I know you're frustrated,' Eddie said. 'I know the waiting and uncertainty is eating you up, and I know what that feels like. My brother Kyle was killed up on the Scottish border three years ago, but it was months before we knew he was dead. That was a terrible time for me and my folks. So, I get it, I really do, but like you said, this stand-off can't last. If the armour isn't moving, there'll be a good reason. We'll know soon enough.'

Griff raised an eyebrow. 'Really? Your phone has got less than 10% battery. Another couple of messages and that's it. We go dark. Then what?'

'Then we make a plan. Take our chances. Until then, we need to be patient. We don't want to end up like those people outside The Savoy.'

Griff bit his lip and stared at his trainers. They'd heard shots and screaming last night. A dawn recce had revealed three bodies lying out on the Strand – a man, a woman, and a young girl. Pigeons plucked at the contents of their bags spilt across the road. Eddie guessed they'd been holed up in The Savoy Hotel and made a run for it. Snipers had done the rest.

'I'll make you a promise,' Eddie said. 'When this is over, I'll help you get back to Zoe and the kids, even if I have to commandeer a helicopter to do it, okay?'

Griff stared at him for a moment. Then he shrugged. 'Sure. Whatever.'

Eddie watched him walk away.

[38]

AIR RAID WARNING

THE RECENT FRUSTRATION THAT HAD PLAGUED HARRY GNAWED at him once again. As a national leader, he wasn't used to being kept waiting in anterooms and fobbed off with tea and biscuits. Wilde sat on the opposite chair, his head buried in his phone, aware of Harry's impatience and ignoring it. He knew Harry's temper was bubbling, and yet the trip to Washington had started so well.

A Defiant helicopter had picked them up from Northwood and flown them a short distance to a dark, disused airfield. The wait there had been brief and spent inside a dusty, abandoned building along-side a concrete apron and a row of weather-beaten light aircraft. A squad of American soldiers in black helmets and uniforms had entered the building and escorted Harry and Wilde to the aircraft waiting on the runway. It was the same one they'd seen in Iceland, only this time its skin was black and seemed to absorb the surrounding darkness. The interior of the aircraft was markedly different from the Air Force One 747 he'd travelled on in the States. It was wide-bodied and half the size of the big Boeing, but no less comfortable. Harry sat beside Wilde in big leather seats and the aircraft lifted off a few moments later. They weren't visible from the outside, but inside the aircraft, the extra-large window panels curved around the fuselage and gave passengers an unprecedented view of the world outside. In Harry's case, there wasn't much to see as the night was dark and unlit, but the ride was as smooth as a limousine, and they'd barely had time to enjoy their in-flight refreshments and marvel at the view of America's glittering eastern seaboard before touching down at another small, dark rural airfield. Climbing into the waiting black sedan, Harry noticed that the flight had taken less than 90 minutes.

The ride to his Palisades home on the outskirts of Washington DC took almost as long. After dinner, Wilde set up a conference call with the Cabinet and they discussed potential talking points with Mitchell. As usual, Faye dominated the conversation and was keen to press the president hard, and Harry realised he was beyond taking advice from his deputy PM. Her tone was more *instructive* than constructive, and his foreign secretary, Shelley Walker, made clear her disappointment that she'd been overlooked for the trip. Harry was tempted to remind them all that if it wasn't for Mitchell and the might of the US Armed Forces, they wouldn't be having a conversation at all, but he kept his powder dry. Somewhere down the line, he thought he might need it.

Wilde spent the night in Harry's guest suite, and the next morning another two-sedan convoy whisked them directly to Pennsylvania Avenue. And that's where Harry's frustration began. Instead of being escorted into the Oval Office, they'd been forced to wait in the Roosevelt Room and mollified with tea and biscuits. Now, even the ticking of the carriage clock above the fireplace grated on Harry's nerves. He got to his feet and paced the room, stopping to study the paintings of the former president and hoping the distraction would soothe his brewing irritation.

'Everything all right, Harry?'

He didn't bother turning around. 'Do I need to spell it out? We've been here for almost an hour.'

'Perhaps something's come up.'

'Then why doesn't someone tell us?' He continued his pacing, impressed by the impeccable surroundings. By stark contrast, Downing Street was a collection of shattered buildings propped up by scaffolding and surrounded by a compacted wasteland, and he wondered how things might look in five or ten years. He had some ideas, but it was important they maintained tradition. The renovation of Downing Street would be part of that continuation. It was also the spot where his wife had died, and he wouldn't allow that event to be bulldozed into history. Wilde's voice snapped him out of his reverie.

'What?'

'I said, d'you think everything's okay?'

Harry sat opposite his chief of staff. 'Why d'you ask?'

Wilde leaned forward and spoke in a low voice. 'It might be my imagination, but I'm sensing an atmosphere. Secret Service, secretaries, aides, they all appear subdued, don't you think? And this place isn't its usual bustling self. It feels empty.'

Harry thought about it and decided Lee had a point. The greeting had been cordial and handled by an aide who'd escorted them through empty corridors to the Roosevelt Room. Even the catering staff who'd delivered refreshments seemed unresponsive.

'Maybe it's us,' Harry replied. 'Maybe we're being oversensitive.'

Wilde was about to respond when the door opened and the Latino aide who'd greeted them, entered the room. 'The president will see you now.' They got to their feet. The aide smiled at Wilde. 'Just the prime minister.'

There was no apology, no explanation. Harry was about to protest, but Lee beat him to it.

'Of course,' he said and sat down again.

Harry followed the woman to the Oval Office, where stone-faced Secret Service agents framed the doorway. Harry was ushered in, and the thick door closed behind him with a soft thump.

He registered the empty desk. Mitchell was nowhere to be seen, just VP Riley and NSA Bird standing by the sofas. Hands were shaken, and Riley offered him a seat. Harry unbuttoned his jacket and sat opposite Bird. Riley took the chair at the head of the coffee table between them. He crossed his legs, smoothed his tie, and opened the conversation.

'How was your trip?'

So, the meeting was underway, and that told Harry all he needed to know. Snubbed again. He glanced towards the empty desk and failed to contain his petulant tone. 'I take it President Mitchell is too busy to join us?'

Riley looked down at his tie. It was Bird who spoke next.

'President Mitchell was killed in London, three days ago —'

Harry's jaw dropped. 'What?'

'A clandestine trip to meet and greet a detachment of US troops. His helicopter was shot down shortly after leaving Buckingham Palace.'

The news stunned Harry. Bob Mitchell had done more for Great Britain and Ireland than any other president, and despite the recent cooling of their relationship, Harry had considered the president a friend. He turned to Riley. 'Please accept my deepest condolences, Mr Vice President. I know how close you were.'

'Thank you.'

Harry grimaced. 'I'm sorry, I mean, Mr President.' And suddenly everything made sense. 'That explains the no-fly zone over London.'

Bird tapped the table between them. 'We're keeping the news under wraps until the necessary action has been taken. We expect you to do the same.'

Harry nodded. 'Of course. What necessary action are you referring to?'

'Military action,' Riley said, clearing his throat. 'Significant enemy forces are dug in deep from Victoria to Liverpool Street. We're going to neutralise that threat.'

'And the King's Continental Army stand ready to assist in any way possible.' Hollow words, Harry knew, because the British Army operated under the control of the Pentagon. Still, he hoped it came across as intended, as a gesture of support.

Riley toyed with the heavy class ring on his finger. 'This will be an aerial operation, Harry. Precision and strategic bombing.' He looked at his watch. 'By midday today, the threat posed by those enemy forces will be degraded. CENTCOM will carry out a post-raid analysis and surveillance platforms will monitor events on the ground. If the threat to Alliance aircraft has been drastically reduced, the order will be issued and ground troops – including British units – will move in and secure the rest of the city.'

Harry shuffled forward in his seat. 'What do you mean *precision and strategic bombing?*'

Bird answered him. 'Exactly what we say. Guided munitions will take out their hiding places and strategic bombing will liquidate their ground deployments. After that, it's a mopping-up exercise.'

Harry was struggling to understand. He turned to Riley. 'Am I hearing this right? You're talking about bombing my capital city. Reducing it to rubble.'

'They're not going to surrender,' Riley said. 'And enough American lives have been sacrificed during this campaign, a death toll that now includes the president himself, not to mention the civilians and military personnel also killed. Steps must be taken to ensure that no more lives will be lost unnecessarily.'

'But a bombing raid will kill civilians.'

'The radio announcements will keep them off the streets.'

'Did you explain they were about to be bombed?' Harry said, struggling to control his temper. 'And not everyone has a bloody radio.'

'We're talking about precision weapons,' Bird said. 'Surgical strikes. Collateral damage will be very limited.'

Harry turned on him. 'That's bullshit, Eliot, and you know it. There are still tens of thousands of people living in central London. The death toll could be horrendous.'

Riley snapped. He shook his finger at Harry. 'Those fighters on the ground, they've dropped entire buildings, blown up Admiralty Arch, destroyed every bridge across the Thames, and torched Buckingham Palace. They're armed with missiles and heavy guns, and they killed the President of the United States. They've made it clear they want to fight. We're going to finish it.'

Harry stared at them both. 'This is a revenge mission, pure and simple.'

Riley waved his hand. 'Americans were killed. I can't let that stand.'

'I know this is personal for you —'

'Personal or not, this country has sacrificed enough to free yours. That sacrifice ends now. We're doing this our way.'

Harry swallowed his temper. 'Then send in the King's. Let them deal with the problem. Keep your people out of it if you must. Just don't do this. Please.'

'And what will that achieve?' Bird asked. 'Those fighters are dug in like ticks on a mule. Your people could be tied up for weeks in house-to-house fighting. How many troops will die trying to defeat a couple of thousand well-armed, committed maniacs? And what about those civilians? They'll be trapped by the fighting, caught in the crossfire.' Bird leaned forward. 'Many have tried to leave already. Snipers are discouraging that option. There are a lot of bodies on the streets.'

Harry sat back in his chair, deflated but not yet defeated. 'There must be another way. You've got all these autonomous vehicles, tanks and things. Can't we use them?'

'These *things*, as you call them, cost millions of dollars to produce.'

Harry spread his hands. 'What's a few million dollars compared to the lives that will be lost? You're about to transform the world with your new power technology. The US stock market will go stratospheric, permanently. Why the hell are you talking about money? If it means that much, bill me.'

Riley got to his feet and buttoned his jacket. Bird did the same.

Harry remained seated. 'What's this? The meeting's over?'

'Yes,' Riley said. 'And we held it as a courtesy to you. To keep you in the loop.'

Harry stood and looked at them both. 'Please, reconsider. You don't have to do this.'

Riley checked his watch. 'The planes are already flying. I'm sorry, Harry. I wish there was another way —'

'We'll find one. Just turn those planes around, for God's sake.'

The door to the Oval Office opened and the two agents stepped into the room, their hands folded in front of them, their hard eyes boring into Harry's.

'Thank you for coming, Prime Minister. We'll speak again soon. Air Force One will take you back home.'

Harry's shoulders slumped. No handshakes were offered, and Harry buttoned his jacket and left the room. Wilde was waiting further along the corridor. He had his phone in his hand. 'Harry, I've just had a call from Sir David. He says it's urgent.'

Harry took the phone from Wilde's hand. They left the building and Harry peeled away from the waiting sedan. He dialled the last number, knowing what he was about to hear. Chief of Defence Staff General Sir David Roland-Jones answered after one ring.

'Prime Minister, CENTCOM has just informed us that —'

'I already know. I'm still at the White House, so if we have anyone in that area of London, send word. Tell them what's coming, Sir David. Tell them to find shelter, to go as deep as they can. Do it now, please.' He handed back the phone to Wilde, who looked at him with utter bemusement.

'Harry, what the hell's going on?'

'President Mitchell was killed three days ago, and Riley has decided that London is going to pay for his death. The bombers are already flying.'

Wilde's face paled. 'They can't do that.'

'They just did. There's nothing more to be achieved here. Let's go home,' Harry said, and climbed aboard the waiting sedan.

[39]

DEATH FROM ABOVE

THE US ARMY INFLATABLE STEALTH PLATFORM WAS A MUCH smaller blimp than the giant black monster still blocking the road in Eaton Square. It was smaller, sleeker, and stealthier than its super-sized cousin. Its skin was an IR and light-absorbing matte black material and its carbon fibre, battery-powered engines incorporated the latest sound reduction technology that made the aircraft almost silent and invisible at night.

From the pitch at Chelsea Football Club, the 45-foot blimp rose above the dark, empty stands and turned east, climbing to 200 feet as it glided low across the west London suburbs. It flew over the collapsed walls and charred timbers where President Mitchell had died, and past the severed towers of the World's End estate. It continued eastwards, skirting the enemy heat blooms downloaded to its navigational software by orbiting Global Hawk UAVs. As it flew above The Mall, the black horizon behind it paled to a deep blue. It slowed, drifting above Trafalgar Square, unseen by enemy fighters lurking behind the windows of the National Gallery, using the predawn breeze to float into position above the streets of Covent

Garden, where it activated its specially-mounted public address system.

A little over three miles to the west, sitting at the blimps' controls in a truck parked behind Chelsea's famous 'Shed End', the pilot, a female Air Force sergeant named Krystal, hovered her mouse control over the software's 'PLAY' button.

And clicked it.

THE SOUND WAS FAMILIAR, EVEN TO THOSE WHO'D NEVER HEARD it played in anger, but its ghastly howl was as familiar to Londoners as Churchill's voice or the roar of a Spitfire's Rolls Royce engine. Nothing spoke of impending danger more than a World War II air-raid siren. The sound echoed across the dark sky, punctuated every 20 seconds with a computerised female voice ...

'This is a message from the Allied Alliance. Emergency warning. Danger imminent. Stay off the streets. Remain in your homes. Seek cover where possible.'

The siren wailed again for another 20 seconds, and the message repeated.

'This is a message from the Atlantic Alliance. Emergency warning. Danger imminent ...'

For the next 40 minutes, the blimp tracked across the sky from Trafalgar Square to the remains of London Bridge and back to Victoria, broadcasting its message down onto the streets below where General Baban's fighters broke cover and blasted the sky with small arms fire, unable to locate the source of the terrible siren and the cold voice of warning. As the sky to the east brightened, the sun's light revealed the black dirigible drifting above the rooftops of the West End, and finally Baban's people had a target.

Punctured by hundreds of rounds, the blimp nosed out of the sky and crashed into a crane towering over the flattened suburb of Soho. Wrapped around its rusted metal arm, the wailing siren continued to blare until the electrics fried and the computerised voice stuttered and fell silent.

The blimp was dead, but its message was very much alive.

'IT'S STOPPED,' GRIFF SAID.

Standing at the window, Eddie nodded. 'That'll be the gunfire.'

The wailing siren and the booming message had woken them both. Griff should've been keeping an ear out for trouble, but he'd fallen asleep in the chair by the window. Both awake, they'd listened to the broadcast as it grew louder, before fading away, then returning. It was spooky, they both admitted, a God-like voice booming from the night sky, spouting biblical warnings of danger. Except it was probably a drone, and as daylight flooded the city, gunfire rattled across the West End, an obvious attempt by the Jihadis to silence the voice and the creepy siren. And it appeared they'd achieved their aim because the clear blue sky was now silent.

'How imminent is *danger imminent?*' Griff asked, a note of fear in his voice.

'Let's find out.' Eddie took the phone out of his pocket and powered it up.

'Maybe we should take cover, like the voice said. Get down to the basement.'

Eddie thumbed the phone's power button. 'Standby.'

He watched the screen as it booted up. He'd struggled with keeping it on 24/7 or switching it off and powering it up only when required. Eddie had decided on the latter. Looking at the screen, his heart sank when he saw the phone had 3% battery life, which meant this could be his last call. Unless the city's power came back on. Which was unlikely, given that danger was imminent.

On the display, the signal bars crept up and Eddie was about to call Hawkins when he noticed the flashing voicemail message icon. He keyed the pad and pressed the phone to his ear. A nice computer lady told him he had one message and to *press one* to hear it. He stabbed the button ...

And heard Hawkins reeling off the date and time, rapid fire. Then he said, 'Eddie, if you can't evac the area, get to deep cover. The Americans are going to bomb the city. And whatever you do, avoid the —'

The screen went blank. 'Shit!' He held the power button down, but the unit was dead.

'What happened?' Griff asked.

Eddie stared at the phone in his hand. Hawkins had left the message over an hour ago. Outside the window, the narrow road was still gloomy, but the sky above was bright blue. Moving in daylight was bad enough, and the snipers would make it deadly. Unless they'd heeded the message too and had already gone to ground.

'Eddie! Answer me. What did the message say?'

Eddie looked at him. 'They're going to bomb the city.'

'What? Who?'

'The Americans. The boss says we have to find somewhere deep.'

'Maybe the cellar —'

'It's not deep enough. We should head north, make a run for our lines.'

'That's over a mile away. Fuck that. It's a shooting gallery out there.'

'Unless the Hajis are under cover already.'

'You want to take that chance?'

Eddie didn't. 'The boss said we needed to avoid something, but the phone went dead before he could finish.'

'Avoid what?'

Eddie grimaced. 'Mate, if I knew that, I wouldn't ask.'

Griff pulled on his hoodie and his backpack and slung the AK-12 over his head. 'Then let's get the fuck out of here.'

'We should find cover.'

Griff nodded. 'We will. In Embankment tube station.'

'Don't be stupid. That's where the Hajis are hiding.'

Griff shook his head. 'They've deployed all over the place. No one's hiding anymore. I say we take our chances.'

'It's too risky.'

'So's staying here. I'd rather die trying to get home than be buried alive in some dirty basement. Besides, if we can get down to the platforms, the Northern Line will take us right under the river and into Waterloo.'

Eddie weighed it up. He didn't know what form the attack would take, but he suspected it would be a tactical strike, cruise missiles and suchlike, which was why Hawkins was adamant about going deep underground. Griff had already made his mind up, and he had a plan. Right now, it was a better one than anything Eddie could come up with.

'I'll grab my gear. See you downstairs in five.'

'Roger that.'

Eddie took the stairs two at a time.

THE SPOTTER'S NAME WAS RIZ, AND HE'D BEEN A SECURITY guard at the Sky television centre in Isleworth, west London, for more than a decade. His was a familiar face, and as head of his own security shift, Riz had access to almost every room in every building across the estate. Since the collapse of the government and the impending arrival of the Atlantic Alliance, many people had made themselves scarce around the studios, especially the presenters and news anchors. Before the *Great Liberation*, they'd sucked up to Wazir while slagging off their own government. After the caliphate had taken over, the Sky bosses had sided with the new regime, reporting from docks and prisons as the deportations and executions took place, and doing softball interviews with members of the Islamic Congress. Now that the shoe was on the other foot, those same, self-important anchors (Riz had a more fitting name for them), had run for the hills.

Now, nothing was being broadcast, but people were still showing up for work because they knew, eventually, the station would be back in business. Riz would stay put, too. He liked England, and the last place he wanted to go was the Middle East. The Hajj had been tough enough, but though he was of Yemeni descent, Riz preferred to live in cooler climates. And life before the *Great Liberation* wasn't bad at all. He had a good job, with decent benefits, and he enjoyed taking the kids to see Brentford on Saturday afternoons. What would he do back in the caliphate?

But right now, he had another job to do, and a satellite phone to do it with, so when he saw the contrails streaming across the sky, he'd climbed up onto the roof of the main studio and dialled the memorised number.

When the phone was answered, he reported the size and composition of the aerial armada winging its way across west London. The first ten planes were flying in a 'v' formation directly overhead. A few miles behind them, there was another formation – Riz counted another eight planes – followed by a third formation of the same number of aircraft. Twenty-six planes in all.

He had no idea what type of aircraft they were, but he knew that many brothers and sisters were still in London, preparing to fight to the death. Riz was glad he wasn't with them, because if they were American bombers up there, those fighters were probably going to have a whole world of pain dropped on their heads.

EIGHTEEN THOUSAND FEET ABOVE THE SKY STUDIOS, THE FIRST flight of B-52s – Alpha Flight – rumbled through the cold, thin air in a mile-wide arrowhead formation. The target corridor was tight, with the winding river Thames on one side and the densely-packed streets of London on the other, but their specific mission had allowed for considerable overlap to provide maximum protection for the following flights.

Far below, central London was bathed in the golden light of another beautiful autumn day, and in the distance, gleaming towers rose out of the earth. On-board threat detection systems remained silent, but the pilots, seated in their flight operations command centre in a secure hanger at Shannon International Airport, knew those systems wouldn't stay quiet for long.

And the B-52s had come prepared.

IN THE STATION MANAGER'S OFFICE OF LEICESTER SQUARE underground station, General Baban sat with his feet up on the desk and his hands behind his head, wondering when it would begin. The infidels had sealed off much of the city and their eyes in the sky watched every move his people made. Sooner or later, their armour would push towards the West End and the City of London. Through the window, he saw his people ferrying boxes of ammunition from the concourse to a van parked on the pavement outside the main gates. Then he saw Naji trotting towards the office. The look on his face had Baban swinging his legs to the floor and getting to his feet. His 2IC entered and closed the door behind him.

'What is it?'

'American B-52s are heading for the city. A spotter counted 26 aircraft.'

Baban whistled. 'They're going to bury us.'

'That looks likely.'

'Deploy the missile teams. Tell them they are weapons-free.'

'Already done. They'll go live in the next five minutes.'

'Good.'

Naji turned his back to the window and lowered his voice. 'If we're going to go, we need to go now.'

Baban looked beyond his subordinate and watched his volunteers as they hurried to and from the van. The pre-dawn sirens and Yankee warning messages were precursors to what he knew would be a historic day. He was proud of his fighters, of their courage and their loyalty; he would make sure they were remembered, and their sacrifice cast in stone on the Avenue of Martyrs.

'Let's get to the car, nice and easy.'

They left the station manager's office and crossed the concourse to the street entrance. On his way out, Baban picked up a case of 7.62mm ammunition and loaded it on the van outside. He slapped a couple of backs and then walked around the corner to Cranbourn Street where his Range Rover waited. Yani, his driver and bodyguard, started the engine as Baban and Naji climbed in the back.

Yani looked in his rear-view mirror. 'Where are we going, general?'

'The helicopter. As fast as you can if you want to live.'

The car powered away from the curb and headed east towards Blackfriars.

FOUR HUNDRED METRES AWAY, THE DRIVER OF ONE OF BABAN'S missile trucks started the engine, crunched the gear stick, and pulled out from beneath the plywood hoardings concealing the alleyway where the truck had been parked for ten days. He drove in a straight line out onto Haymarket, obeying the hand signals of another comrade who waved him out onto the deserted thoroughfare. The driver eased the truck forward, watching the cables in his mirror, the ones connecting the missile canisters on the back of his flatbed to the radar array on the roof of the building. His comrade held up a hand, and the driver stepped on the brakes, shutting off the engine. He climbed out, and the three-man team went to work, two of them ducking back into the alleyway and into a commandeered graphic design office. While they powered up the missiles' pre-flight systems, the driver raced to the roof and extended the pole-mounted radar as high as it would go. Via radio, the technicians below instructed him to make some adjustments, and then they were good to go. Before he left the roof, the driver looked up at the sky and saw white contrails far above, tracking towards central London. He raced downstairs.

On the ground floor, the targeting software was already running, calibrating the Arabel radar and sending test packets of data to the missiles. Pre-flight checks returned green lights, and on the back of the truck, 12 Aster-30 anti-aircraft missiles were set to automatic guidance and tracking. Already, the missiles were receiving data from the radar array. Satisfied that everything was set, all three men grabbed their gear and weapons and headed to their prearranged defensive positions, a former gentleman's club on Pall Mall.

Across the West End and into the City of London, 17 other missile trucks went through the same procedure, moving to their launch positions and firing up their anti-aircraft radar. Supporting them, more fighters with man-portable Stinger missiles scrambled to high roofs across central London. They looked to the west, saw the contrails, and prepped their weapons. The enemy planes were already within range, and while their defensive systems were no doubt formidable, there would be leaks in their electronic armour, and some missiles would get through.

Soon they would find out just how many.

IN THE FLIGHT OPERATIONS COMMAND CENTRE AT SHANNON International Airport, the lead element of B-52s was picking up tracking signals from all over central London. Above the bombers, two Global Hawk surveillance platforms were pinpointing the signals and feeding the information via CENTCOM to the weapons technicians back in Ireland. Those techs then armed the AGM-90 high-speed, anti-radiation missiles carried by all three flights of BUFFs (an affectionate nickname for the ageing bombers – Big Ugly Fat Fuckers). They did all this in relative silence, as everyone involved in the raid worked unobtrusively, talking in hushed tones beneath the low lights, their faces lit by their multiple control screens. Air Force commanders moved between the rows of pilots; engineers; weapons and navigation specialists; and supporting technicians, watching and listening, ready to head off potential problems, because everyone in the hangar knew they were making history. Of the 26 planes in the air, not a single human being was aboard any of the aircraft. And as everyone in the room knew, it was the shape of

things to come. What none of them knew, was where it would ultimately lead.

The command net hissed, and a pilot's voice spoke. 'Alpha Flight
now passing the ten-yard line. Sixty seconds to release.'

Another voice. 'Alpha flight is weapons-free.'

'Roger. Weapons free. Opening bomb bay doors...'

As the deadly arrowhead passed above the suburb of Pimlico,
their huge bomb bay doors hummed open, revealing the city below.
The streets of Victoria slipped beneath the nose of the lead aircraft,
and pockets of white smoke blossomed on the ground.

The fight had begun.

ON THE STREETS OF VICTORIA, WESTMINSTER, AND ST JAMES'
Park, target tracking radars lit up with multiple contacts, and the first
trucks shuddered with the force of multiple launches as missile after
missile sped away, blasting white smoke across the streets. Inside
their homes, civilians huddled in terror as windows rattled and walls
shook. The streets of London trembled in the wake of the rockets that
roared and streaked into the clear blue sky.

FAR ABOVE THOSE TERRIFIED CITIZENS, ALPHA FLIGHT BEGAN
dropping their munitions. First to launch were the AGM-90s, dropping from their wing-mounted hardpoints and firing their solid-
propellant motors. The anti-radar missiles accelerated to Mach 2 and
raced towards the earth, and the launch points of the SAM swarm
rushed up towards the B-52s. Inside the aircrafts' bomb bays,
hydraulic rails rattled and clanked as they fed munitions out through
the bay doors. A thousand feet below the planes, plastic-cased bombs
detonated, filling the sky with millions of aluminium-coated, glass-
fibre chaff fragments, the cloud blooming so large that the rising sun's
rays reflected off the twirling aluminium, creating a living, sparkling
display that was as beautiful as it was terrifying. Within the

expanding cloud, infra-red decoy flares exploded and blazed, calling to the incoming missiles' seeker heads.

Like boxers in a ring, the weapons converged and began trading blows.

THE FRENCH MISSILES ROARED THROUGH THE SKY, STREAKING towards the B-52s, but their seeker heads were now confused. One target had become four, then ten, then a hundred. Sensors locked on, dropped out, then locked on again. On-board computers reset and reprogrammed for the nearest target. Above the rising missiles, a solid wall of chaff and IR decoys beckoned them to their deaths, and the missiles were happy to oblige. Explosions rippled across the sky as the first wave of missiles destroyed themselves in that glittering cloud drifting thousands of feet above the city. The BUFFs continued onwards, now launching their CBU-110s, precision-guided bombs programmed to fall across the launch sites and obliterate the missile trucks, their crews, and anything else that came within range of the deadly submunitions packed inside each cluster weapon. The goal was to eliminate the threat entirely.

No one at CENTCOM was taking any chances.

THE AGM-90S CONVERGED ON THEIR TARGETS, THE MISSILE trucks that had revealed themselves, that had emptied their missile canisters and now stood abandoned and exposed. The American missiles streaked to earth and exploded, destroying radars and masts and a dozen rooftops in Victoria, Westminster, and St James' Park. Less than a minute later, the cluster munitions began falling across the streets of London, spilling out submunitions across roads and rooftops, annihilating the trucks, parked cars, nearby buildings, and the people cowering inside, be they friend or foe. The blasts rippled like a storm of deadly firecrackers across London's famous streets until there was nothing left of the missile trucks, nothing except smoking craters surrounded by burning, crumbling buildings.

The first punches had been thrown, and the enemy was reeling, but the fight wasn't over yet.

As Alpha Flight cleared the West End and began dropping bombs over the City of London, the rooftop Stinger teams launched their own weapons into the sky. Clear of the chaff clouds still falling across the West End, the supersonic missiles raced at Mach 2.5 towards the huge bombers, 32 high-altitude warheads against 10 bombers that were now bereft of chaff bombs. Detecting the incoming missiles, autonomous, onboard defence systems began jamming the missiles' seeker heads, scrambling the brains of 20 inbound weapons. But it wasn't enough. Twelve missiles punched through the jammer waves and exploded amongst the flight, shredding wings and igniting fuel tanks, eviscerating cockpits and frying the flight controls inside.

One B-52 exploded, severely damaging two more on either side of it. With wings and engines shredded, the planes nosedived towards the ground, trailing black smoke. Another plane took a direct hit, the Stinger warhead ripping off the wing and causing it to flip over, smashing into the plane flying behind it. Locked in a death embrace, the aircraft twisted and tumbled out of the sky. From Blackfriars to Aldgate East, eight stricken B-52s screamed to earth like falling meteors, crashing through skyscrapers and impacting on roads and buildings below, shaking the earth and leaving ugly black smoke trails across the sky.

[40]

TUBEWAY ARMY

EDDIE AND GRIFF RIPPED THE BARRICADES FROM THE FRONT door. They'd packed their gear, prepped their weapons, and were now good to go. Both men wore their homemade head coverings, a detail that might give the snipers pause, but getting shot at was the least of their worries now. The floor beneath their feet shook as the thunder of detonating bombs grew closer and closer. The narrow slice of sky above Maiden Lane shimmered with chaff and was slashed by white smoke and contrails. As far as Eddie was concerned, Embankment tube station was now their only option. He slapped Griff on the back.

'Ready?' Griff nodded. 'If we move fast, it shouldn't take us more than five minutes.'

The building shook. Griff looked up at the ceiling. 'If we don't get out of here now, we'll be dead in less than two.'

Griff was scared, but his eyes were alive with hope. His journey home was about to begin.

'Let's go.'

Eddie ducked out into the street, turning left, then left again into the alleyway that led to the Strand. There, they paused. The road was empty, except for rubbish and the snipers' dead victims. Beyond Trafalgar Square, rising columns of smoke stained the sky, and far above, he saw contrails of high-flying planes.

'Jesus Christ.' He looked over his shoulder. 'Move!'

The ground shook as they reached the other side of the road and disappeared into a side street. Debris fell around them and the sound of a thousand windows breaking chased them into John Adam Street. As they turned the corner, Eddie almost collided with a group of Jihadis going the other way. Like Eddie and Griff, most of them had their faces covered and carried belts of ammunition and RPG rounds. He counted ten of them, and Eddie was the first to speak as he backed away.

'Yankee bombers are right above us! Get off the streets!'

'What do you think we're doing?' a big, bearded guy snarled, pointing to a car park ramp across the road. 'We're headed down there. Come on!'

'Not deep enough,' Eddie said, shaking his head. 'We're going to the tube.'

'Good luck, brothers!'

Eddie and Griff kept moving, skirting a small park that over-looked the river. Turning left onto a deserted Villiers Street, they ran towards the entrance of Embankment station. As they neared the half-open concertina gates, Eddie saw the twisted steel girders of the adjacent Hungerford railway bridge jutting into the sky like rusted teeth. Debris from the bridge was scattered all over the street, and Eddie swerved his way through it and ducked inside the station.

He slowed, and Griff slipped inside, raising his AK. The ticket hall was shadowy and devoid of life, but everywhere Eddie looked, there were empty crates and cardboard boxes across the floor. They'd stockpiled ammunition in the stations, he realised. Someone had gone to inordinate lengths to ensure that the Atlantic Alliance paid for every inch of pavement in the capital. Which explained the bombers in the sky.

'The Northern Line's that way,' Griff said, puffing and pointing to the signs on the wall and the escalators beyond the ticket gates. As they squeezed through the gates, a door on Eddie's left flew open. He saw a shadowy figure, a gun, and he heard a shout, a warning or a challenge, Eddie wasn't sure. Instinct kicked in, and he fired a two-round burst and ran towards the door. The man staggered back into the shadows, and he heard people scrambling inside. Eddie crouched and swivelled around the door frame. Two targets, lit by a camping light, reaching for their weapons. The man was faster, and Eddie shot him first, the bullet taking him high in the chest, just below the throat. The woman screamed, fear and fury all rolled into one, and Eddie dropped her with a double-tap to the chest. She stumbled backwards and hit the wall, landing on her arse. She looked up at Eddie, chest rising and falling, and then her eyes rolled up into her head and she slumped sideways, lifeless.

Eddie felt reassured by the speed of his reactions. Three targets down and not one of them had got a shot off. He saw a box of grenades and checked them, making sure they were primed. Then he slipped four into his tactical vest. Griff appeared in the doorway.

'Jesus. Nice work, brother.'

The ground shook as a ripple of explosions rattled the room. Eddie nodded outside. 'Northern line, yeah?'

'That's the one,' Griff said.

Eddie pushed past him and back out onto the station concourse. Dead escalators stretched down into the darkness below. 'Torches,' he said over his shoulder. He snapped his barrel light on and crept down the escalator, his ears alert for any sound at all. The walls rumbled as bombs fell above them. Reaching the bottom step, he swept his torch-light around a large open concourse. Signs on the wall pointed towards the District, Circle, and Bakerloo lines. A benevolent Wazir stared at Eddie from a poster. He shone his torch at a tube map. 'Bakerloo runs beneath the river too.'

'It's not as deep as the Northern Line,' Griff said.

As if to emphasise the danger, the ceiling trembled and dust filled the air, swirling through their torch beams. Eddie opened his mouth to speak but then stopped himself.

Voices drifted down the escalator. They grew louder, echoing through the concourse above, angry, urgent voices. Someone had found the bodies, and they weren't happy. Eddie covered the torch with his hand. Standing next to him, his back against the wall, Griff did the same. Both of them watched the escalator, listening to the voices grow louder. Torchlight probed the darkness at the bottom of the lifeless metal stairs. Boots stamped on the stair treads. The beams probed deeper into the concourse, creeping across the walls, sweeping towards them...

Eddie leaned into Griff's ear. 'When I say go, head for the Northern Line platform.' Griff nodded, and Eddie pulled a grenade from his tactical vest. The voices were louder now, and more boots pounded the stairs. He saw the first shadow on the escalator, an AK barrel, its torch turning towards him —

'Go!'

Griff ran, torch waving through the dark.

Eddie took two steps and lobbed the grenade onto the escalator. He turned and followed Griff, and then the weapon exploded, the bang deafening. Eddie heard screaming and gunfire, and the sound of ricochets. Another grenade exploded on the concourse behind him. Safety lay ahead.

Griff's torch bounced in the darkness. Eddie followed him, sprinting across a tunnel interchange, then Griff was twisting around a rubber handrail and disappearing out of sight. Eddie turned and chased him down another dead escalator. Griff waited at the bottom, breathing hard, his headscarf around his neck. Eddie pulled his down too. They were deep beneath the station, and there were platforms to Eddie's left and right, north and southbound tracks. 'Switch off your torch.'

Griff obeyed, and Eddie did the same. 'Where's that light coming from?'

They stepped onto the southbound platform. It was gloomy, but they could see all the way along the platform to the black mouth of the southbound tunnel.

'Emergency lights,' Griff said. 'Must be battery-powered. Some are brighter than others.'

Eddie hurried back to the bottom of the escalator, listening to the sounds from above. He heard shouting and the screams of the wounded. He heard radios blaring, and then he heard something else, a growing rumble – pounding boots and rattling weapons. Now they were being hunted. Griff heard it too.

'They're coming after us.'

'Start heading south.'

'What about you?'

'I need to slow them up.'

Griff disappeared onto the southbound platform. Eddie heard his running feet echoing off the tunnel walls. He headed up the escalator, tugging a roll of fishing wire out of a pouch. He strung it across the steps halfway up, cut it with his knife and tied it off around a grenade pin now taped against a stair tread. Above him, the sounds of pursuit grew louder and shouted commands echoed from all directions. They didn't know where Eddie and Griff had gone so they'd be checking the District and Circle Line platforms first. Central London's tube stations were a maze of tunnels, stairs, and concourses, and it was dark down here. He had time, but not much.

At the bottom of the stairs, he rigged up another booby-trap, easing the pin from the grenade almost all the way out. What he really needed was a claymore, but beggars couldn't be choosers.

He stood and looked up the escalator. A light blinded him, and Eddie fired his MP5 in a reflex burst. He heard a grunt, then a warning shout.

He turned and ran.

The platform stretched away towards the tunnel. Halfway down it, the other grenade exploded, but the screams of the wounded now competed with bellowed orders and cries of revenge. The train tunnel loomed ahead. Behind him, grenades cracked and banged as his pursuers took no chances. Grenade fragments pinged off the curved walls, but they were too far away to do any damage. Their guns, however, could. The roar of them was deafening as the hunters spilt out onto the platform behind him and opened fire. Eddie threw himself to the ground and crawled over the edge of the platform, dropping onto the tracks. He crouched low and ran forward into the tunnel. A storm of bullets chewed up the wall to his right, exploding the brickwork and ricocheting off into the shadows. He switched on his torch and saw Griff ahead, and Eddie had to remind himself that the rail brushing against his right leg was dead.

Griff stumbled on, his torchlight bouncing in the dark, but the emergency lights extended all the way along the tunnel and Eddie could see the slight left-hand curve ahead. That would give them some protection, but they needed to move as fast as possible. Waterloo Station was over half a mile away by Eddie's reckoning, and that was a lot of ground to cover in a tunnel. With armed men in pursuit, it would be almost impossible to survive.

'Come on, Griff! Move your fucking arse!'

ONE BY ONE, A STEADY STREAM OF AGM-90 MISSILES FELL upon the enemy radars like a volley of medieval arrows, followed by swarms of cluster munitions that transformed the missile trucks and everything around them into smoking craters. Across the city's rooftops, the Stinger teams fared better but outlying Viper and Apache gunships targeted their launch sites, obliterating them with 30mm canon and hellfire missiles, sending showers of glass, steel, and human remains tumbling to earth. Across central London, columns of black smoke boiled into the bright blue sky from the shattered towers.

The major air threat now neutralised, Bravo Flight began launching their own missiles, High Velocity Penetrating Weapons – HVPWs – a rocket-propelled, 2000-pound smart bomb that could drill down through 12 feet of concrete before detonating in a massive explosion. The eight aircraft of Bravo Flight launched two HVPWs each from their rotary launchers, one munition targeted at each nest where the enemy had hidden and from where they had emerged to attack and kill the President of the United States. Sixteen such nests had been identified after days of surveillance, and now they had to be destroyed.

The HVPW missiles fell from the B-52s and hurtled to earth towards the unfortunate tube stations, now designated as strategic targets and a continued threat to the forces of the Atlantic Alliance.

Embankment tube station was one of those targets.

THE OLD MAN HUFFED AND PUFFED AND KICKED THE DOOR down, squinting as the sun blinded him. He turned the corner of the rooftop fire escape and saw London laid out below him. He saw the billowing smoke and the fires that clawed above the rooftops of the West End, and above him he saw the infidel planes and their contrails. There was still a chance.

He dragged the cursed Stinger missile launch tube up onto his shoulder, grunting with the effort. He'd already carried the thing up 36 floors to the roof of The Heron tower in Moorgate, a mission that had taken almost 3 hours, during which he'd cursed every cigarette he'd ever smoked during his 62 years. And that was a lot of smokes, he knew. But he'd made it, and he wished the youngsters could see him now. They'd abandoned him for pastures new, eager to engage the infidels on the ground. A pity.

The targeting system warbled and settled into a steady tone. The old man hadn't selected a specific aircraft to target, but it seemed the weapon resting on his shoulder had made that decision for him. He aimed it above his head and squeezed the trigger, closing his eyes as the thing hissed and roared in his hands, engulfing him in a haze of bitter white smoke. He threw the tube away, wracked by a painful spasm of coughing, and then he watched the missile zoom into the sky. There were still fragments of chaff drifting on the morning breeze, but the earlier clouds had dissipated and now the weapon was arching up almost directly overhead, racing towards the contrails above.

'Go, baby, go!'

His eyes weren't so good either, but they were in better shape than his lungs. He saw a tiny puff of black smoke, and one of the Yankee planes broke formation, tipping over and trailing dark filth from two of its engines as it fell from the sky. The old man punched the air with his fist.

'I got you, you sons of whores! I got you!'

But there was nothing wrong with the old man's ears. What started as a distant thumping became a deafening roar and the familiar *chop-chop-chop* of a helicopter. He lowered his arm and turned around. An infidel gunship hovered in the air close to the edge of the rooftop. It bounced and swayed as it held its position, buzzing like a giant, angry wasp. The old man smiled and scratched his grey beard. If he could take out a big bomber, why not a helicopter too? He reached for the rifle slung over his back. The last thing he heard was the whine of the cannon beneath the helicopter's nose, and a moment later the old man's eyes, lungs, ears, and much of the rest of his body steamed in wet, bloody chunks all over the rooftop.

THE MOMENT THE OLD MAN'S MISSILE EXPLODED, THE B-52 he'd killed was launching its third HVPW. Caught in the shock wave, the munition accelerated towards the ground, its laser guidance system damaged. Its on-board computer tried to correct the problem and failed. All it could do was keep the weapon on course towards the general strike area. It hurtled towards the ground at terminal velocity, the air whistling through its fins as it tried to correct its course and strike its target – the London Underground station at Embankment.

. . .

As Eddie rounded the bend in the tunnel, his hopes faded. Instead of a series of slight curves that would offer some protection from their pursuers, the Northern Line ran straight as an arrow. As gloomy as the tunnel was, the emergency lights would ensure they were seen, and when their hunters rounded that same curve, they could take their sweet time picking them off.

Options, that's what Eddie and Griff needed. They could get down on their bellies and crawl beneath the rails, but the Jihadis would just keep running and catch them in no time. Surrender was not an option either, not after the booby traps.

Vengeful voices echoed off the curved walls behind them, then drowned by thunderous gunfire as bullets cracked and ripped through the stale air, pinging off the walls. A round ricocheted off a rail ahead in a flash of sparks and a crack of dust as it hit the tunnel ceiling.

'Faster, Griff! Once they round that bend, we're fucked!'

'I'm trying!' the older man said, puffing and wheezing. Griff was out of shape, and that could get them both killed. The narrow channel they were running along was too tight to overtake him, and the knee-high rails were bolted to concrete stanchions, making it impossible to run fast without the risk of tripping and injury. All Eddie could do was push Griff on and pray that the men behind them were terrible shots.

The HVPW fell to earth, whistling past its target and missing the roof of Embankment station by a hundred yards. It also missed the destroyed Hungerford Bridge by less than ten, before landing in the Thames and drilling its way through the rising tidal flow into the riverbed itself. The 2000-pound penetrator bomb, encased by thick mud, exploded, the force of the blast directed down through several feet of sludge, mud, and clay, through layers of concrete linings and blasting a hole in the roof of the southbound tunnel of the Northern line 100 feet long and 20 feet wide. The

Thames River, now in full flood, rushed in through the hole in a deluge of concrete, mud, and brown water, swamping the platform, then turning to stream along the least path of resistance, the south-bound stretch of the Northern Line that fed into Waterloo Station.

YANI STEERED THE RANGE ROVER THROUGH THE BACK STREETS of Covent Garden and out onto Kingsway. Buckled up in the back seat, Baban could feel the earth shaking as missiles struck the surrounding city. On Aldwych, a shower of masonry rained down onto the road, cracking the windscreen and causing Yani to swerve the vehicle to avoid the bigger chunks that rolled in front of them.

'The Americans aren't fucking around,' Naji said, hanging on as the car weaved in a violent arc.

Baban grunted in agreement. The ferocity of the bombardment surprised him. And made him a little nervous.

Reaching the Thames embankment, Yani turned left onto the dual carriageway. Through the cracked windscreen, Baban saw Blackfriars station bridge ahead, now severed in two by the explosive-filled barge his engineers had moored to its central support. The operation had been an immense success, Baban realised. Planning it was one thing, executing it another, but seeing the results was satisfaction indeed.

Yani stamped on the brakes and yanked the wheel to the left, driving through open wrought-iron gates into the grounds of Inner Temple, one of England's former legal associations. They drove up towards the main building, then veered right onto the grass. Beyond a line of trees, a black Airbus ACH-175 helicopter beat the surrounding shrubbery with its running rotors. Next to Baban, Naji breathed a sigh of relief.

'I had a bad feeling it wouldn't be here with all that debris flying around. I thought the pilot might've had second thoughts.'

'Lucky for him he stayed.'

The Range Rover stopped 50 yards short of the chopper and the three men bailed out. Through the cockpit window, they saw the pilots wore dark glasses and were flipping switches. Standing by the passenger cabin door, a helmeted crewman was urging them on with a frantic wave. They ran across the grass, ducking beneath the rotors. Baban climbed in first, strapping into the soft leather seat. Naji sat next to him and Yani behind. The crewmen slammed the door shut and twisted the handle. Baban slipped on headphones and dialled into the cockpit.

'What's the plan?' he asked the captain. The sky above them was full of white missile tracks. Not a good place to be in a helicopter with hot engines.

'We'll follow the river, all the way out to the estuary and into the English Channel. We'll be flying low for a while, just until we clear the city, so make sure you're all strapped in back there. It's going to be bumpy.'

'Just get us in the air,' Baban said.

He watched the pilots work the controls and felt the aircraft vibrate as they prepared to lift off. He looked outside, saw the grass beaten down by the rotor blades, the sunlight falling across the gardens.

And then it wasn't.

Shadows rushed over the grass towards the aircraft, blotting out the sunlight. Next to him, Naji looked puzzled.

'What's that noise? Is it the aircraft?'

He heard it then, a wailing sound. He spoke to the pilot. 'What's wrong?'

The pilot turned in his seat. 'No idea. We're green across the board, but there's something —'

He saw the pilot look up. To Baban's surprise, the man scrambled out and sprinted away from the still-running helicopter. The co-pilot ran behind him, and Naji was unbuckling too. He threw open the cabin door, and a terrible screaming filled the air. Baban unbuckled his seatbelt and stumbled out of the helicopter, falling to the grass. He felt it tremble beneath his hands, and a rising, terrible screaming assaulted his ears as if the unleashed demons of hell were charging unseen towards him. The sky darkened. Baban looked up through the spinning rotors.

And then he knew.

A giant B-52 was heading for him, spiralling through the air on a single wing, hurtling towards the ground in a rush of air and a growing roar. It bore down on him like a monster, blotting out the sun, and Baban was frozen in fear and fascination. The demons roared. The general closed his eyes and slapped his hands over his ears.

The giant aircraft slammed into the ground at terminal velocity, crushing the helicopter beneath it and detonating the remaining missiles in its belly. The explosion was devastating, demolishing the buildings around it and sending a shock wave that rolled across the surging Thames, rattling every window south of the river for half a mile.

THE SHOCK WAVE RIPPED THROUGH THE TUNNEL LIKE LEAD through a shotgun barrel. It threw Eddie forward, and he careered into Griff, knocking him to the ground. Eddie fell on top of him, and Griff cried out. The tunnel shook and dust swirled around them. Eddie's head was spinning, and he pushed himself off Griff. He remained on his knees, keeping low. At least the shouting and the shooting had stopped. A moment later, he knew why. He could hear rushing water —

And then it was shooting past him – cold, black water washing around his hands and legs. He yelped and scrambled to his feet, dragging Griff up by the arm. The older man coughed and spluttered, his clothes drenched. Eddie held on as Griff swayed in the gloom.

'Are you alright?'

Griff had a hand on his chest. 'I fell on a stanchion. Knocked the wind out of me.' He looked down and saw water swirling around his trainers. 'What the fuck?'

Eddie shoved him forward. 'The tunnel's breached! Go!'

Griff staggered on, the water sloshing around their ankles. It was cold and sooty as it washed through the rat-infested tunnel. All Eddie could hear now was the roar of water. It must've been a bomb, he figured. And the water wouldn't stop coming.

'Keep moving,' he told Griff, and the man splashed on without answering. Eddie turned around and brought his weapon up. He could hear voices and shouting, but it wasn't in anger. It was fear. He flinched as an almighty boom echoed down the tunnel. As he watched, a surge of water rushed towards them, washing up the curve of the wall. Another collapse, and now the river was thundering inside. The fast-moving stream was now a dangerous tsunami. He turned and ran, catching Griff up in seconds. Their feet threatened to collide.

'Griff, move your arse, for fuck's sake!'

But Griff was staggering left and right, clutching at the wall, bouncing off the rail. If he tripped, they could both go under. Eddie grabbed his shoulder, pushed him against the wall, and waded past him. 'There's a fucking tsunami coming down that tunnel behind us!' he yelled. Already the water had risen above their knees, and Eddie could feel the current pulling at him. This was bad, very bad.

'I can't breathe,' Griff gasped. He kept lifting his chin, trying to take deep breaths. Eddie looped the AK over his head and threw it in the water along with his backpack.

'You don't need that shit now! Just keep up, okay? We're nearly there.'

Eddie turned and ran, splashing through the filthy water, picking his knees up, terrified he would trip over and disappear beneath the surface. The tunnel stretched ahead of them, and Eddie thought he glimpsed something, a lighter shade of darkness, a shadow.

'Eddie!'

He turned and saw Griff struggling through water that was now above his waist.

'Wait for me ... please.'

He ran back, the surging water dragging at his legs. Griff was too heavy to carry, the channel between the wall and the rail too narrow to support him. He grabbed Griff by the neck of his hoodie and pulled him close. Water roared, echoing off the tunnel walls, black and freezing as it swirled around them.

'Keep up!'

'I c-c-can't ... b-breathe.'

Griff coughed, and Eddie saw blood on his chin. *Oh fuck.* He'd fallen on one of those stanchions with the big, protruding bolts. Maybe a broken rib had punctured Griff's lung. 'Listen to me, just hold my hand, okay? I won't let you go. Open your stride and stay with me, one foot in front of the other. Just focus on that!'

Griff nodded and wheezed, unable to speak. He was pale and frightened, and Eddie didn't blame him. Neither of them wanted to end their days in a stinking underground tomb filled with water. He gripped Griff's greasy hand and pulled him along, wading through the deepening water. Up ahead, the shadows shifted; he could see a pale cavern and advertising posters on the curved walls. He shouted over his shoulder.

'I can see the platform! Keep going!'

The current was helping, pushing them forward, but the tunnel was also filling fast. White water broke over the rails, and Eddie felt his feet lifting off the floor as the water reached his chest. In a few seconds, it would be easier to swim than walk. Behind him, Griff had his bloody chin lifted out of the water, but his eyes were wild, and his other arm flapped and splashed in the water.

'Help me ...'

The platform loomed ahead, and Eddie saw the distinctive London Underground station sign on the wall – *Waterloo.* He saw the platform ramp rising out of the water just ahead. The water surged around them, like white water rapids, and he felt Griff's hand slipping from his.

'Hang on, mate! We're almost there!'

A momentary flash of panic seized Eddie. If he missed the ramp, the flood might wash them both through the station and into the blackness of the tunnel beyond. He couldn't let that happen. His body bumped along the rail, and he used his left arm to pull himself across the torrent. The ramp was yards away and Eddie gritted his teeth and pushed towards it, but he wasn't close enough.

He let go of Griff's hand and used both arms to swim to the ramp. His body hit the edge, and he reached out and grabbed a thick cable running along the wall. He caught Griff with his right leg to stop him from floating past.

'Climb up my body, Griff! Do it!' He felt Griff's hands pawing at his back, but there was no strength there. He craned his neck and saw Griff's head bobbing in the water, his mouth open, his head tilted back, desperate to stay afloat but not strong enough to climb over Eddie. 'Come on, Griff! You're almost there! You're almost home with Zoe and the kids!'

The water turned to foam as it battered the bottleneck of their bodies. Eddie's thigh muscle screamed as Griff's weight pressed against it. Then he couldn't hold him anymore, and Griff gurgled and choked as he floated past, his fingers scrabbling for a hold on Eddie's jeans. He flipped over and grabbed Griff's hood, dragging him backwards towards the ramp. Surging water washed over their heads. Eddie held on, the cable gripped in his left hand, Griff's hood in his right. The water roared, a terrifying sight in the near darkness of the empty tunnel. Eddie could barely hear Griff's voice.

'Help me ... Eddie ... d-d-don't let me go!'

'I won't! But you have to move! I can't hold on much longer! Grab something! Anything!' His arm was being pulled out of its socket. 'Please, Griff, you have to try!'

Griff's arm flapped in the water. The hood slipped from Eddie's fingers.

'Eddie ...!' The current snatched him away, his head bobbing, then going under.

Eddie dragged himself up the cable, hand over hand until he was on dry concrete. He staggered to his feet and stumbled up onto the platform, barely lit by the emergency lights. He had to get ahead of Griff.

He ran along the platform edge, flipping on his barrel torch and sweeping it across the raging torrent beneath his feet. Something pale caught his eye, and he stopped, shining the torch below. A few inches beneath the water, Griff's face stared back at him, his eyes and mouth wide open in death, his body trapped by a rail stanchion. Eddie sank to his knees, but before he could reach into the flood, the current dislodged Griff's body and swept it away into the darkness of the tunnel beyond.

'No!'

But he was gone. Eddie crawled away from the platform edge and sat with his back against the wall, the MP5 across his lap, soaked to the skin but alive. He stayed that way for some time, unmoving, exhausted and alone, sitting in the darkness as he mourned the loss of another comrade.

ABOVE THE SKIES OF CENTRAL LONDON, CHARLIE FLIGHT began unloading their bombs. Hundreds of cluster munitions fell from the sky, targeting the concentrations of enemy fighters who'd dug themselves in at strategic road junctions and traffic bottlenecks. Some munitions were primed with altitude fuses that detonated above ground, shattering glass, steel, and brick, and killing the fighters hiding in buildings.

Buckingham Palace, already a blackened and ransacked wreck, was cut in half by a string of 1000-pound bombs that killed the enemy fighters who'd set up defensive positions inside. The munitions continued to fall, tracking across Pall Mall, Trafalgar Square, and Charing Cross, across Blackfriars and the City of London itself, screaming out of the clear blue sky and punching holes across the target area. No pocket of resistance was left untouched, and surveillance drones continued to hunt for thermal signatures that showed concentrations of enemy fighters. Not a single B-52 from

Charlie Flight suffered any damage, and as they cleared the skies over east London, the mighty planes turned as one as their courses were set for Shannon International Airport.

Behind them, central London lay in ruins beneath a pall of dust and rising smoke. Victoria station had been destroyed, along with the mainline stations at Liverpool Street, Cannon Street, and Blackfriars. The targeted underground stations fared no better, the penetrating munitions obliterating 15 of the city's subterranean terminals. Falling planes had also inflicted heavy damage, and the subsequent fires and rising smoke blotted out the morning sun.

A tomblike silence descended over the ancient city. As dust swirled and settled across the streets, the circling drones registered enemy fighters staggering from the ruins of buildings, crawling from the rubble of their hiding places, their clothes and skin caked in dust, their eyes wide with shock and their hands raised in defeat. There were no martyrs left, only those who'd had enough of war. CENTCOM finally issued the order that the Atlantic Alliance was waiting for, and at the stroke of midday, heavy armour began moving from all points of the compass towards the smoking ruin that was central London.

The battle was finally over.

[41]

BARNEY RUBBLE

EDDIE CREPT ALONG THE BALCONY, THEN PAUSED OUTSIDE Griff's flat. There were no sounds coming from inside, no mad rush of playing kids, no Zoe shouting at them. He could hear no voices, no radio, and he saw no lights behind the kitchen blind. He ducked beneath the window, knowing it was a cowardly act but doing it anyway. It was too soon, his emotions too raw. Like a cat burglar, he unlocked the security grille, then the front door, and eased it closed behind him. He was home, after a fashion.

He unpacked the satellite phone and charger and plugged it in. He dropped his filthy, sodden clothes on the kitchen floor and took a long hot shower, washing every scratch, scrape and bruise he'd picked up on the way. He cleaned his weapons and placed the MP5 back in the covert equipment store, keeping the Springfield 9mm close by. He cooked a bowl of pasta and watched a convoy of M1 tanks flying enormous Stars and Stripes flags rattling their way across the junction of Battersea Park Road and Queenstown Road. When the phone had charged sufficiently, he called ISR. He couldn't reach Hawkins, so he gave a full report to a transcriber, emphasising Griff's contribution and sacrifice.

As the sun set below the horizon and the blue sky darkened, a dispatcher called him back and told him that a transport helicopter would collect him from a temporary airfield at Battersea Park and transport him to the King's Continental Army divisional HQ at Northwood. The codeword of the day was *Achilles*, the flight would lift off at 20:00, and the dispatcher ordered Eddie to arrive no later than 19:45.

He was napping on the bed when he heard someone banging on the grille outside.

Eddie stepped out into the hallway. A shadow stood at the kitchen window, hidden by the drawn blind. Then he heard her voice, muffled through the double glazing.

'Eddie, are you in there? It's Zoe from next door.'

He swore under his breath and unlocked the front door. She stood outside the grille, wearing jeans, sneakers, and a light blue puffer jacket. He opened it, and she barged past him.

'Billy!'

Eddie said nothing as she marched from room to room.

'Billy! Where are you?' No answer. How could there be? Zoe swore, then stood in front of Eddie. 'Where is he?'

Eddie opened his mouth to respond, then closed it again.

'What is it? Speak!'

He found his tongue. 'They destroyed the bridges. We couldn't get back.'

'I know that, for God's sake. They bombed half of London. Where is he?'

Eddie studied her face. The lines around her bloodshot eyes were deeper, the circles beneath them a little darker. She screamed —

'Tell me where he is!'

The shriek startled him. The words came out before he could stop them. 'He didn't make it, Zoe. A bomb flooded the Northern line and we —'

'Stop!' she yelled, holding up her hands. She took several deep breaths before she spoke. 'What d'you mean, *didn't make it?* You mean he's still there? Trapped?'

Eddie bit his lip and shook his head.

'What, then? What is it?'

He couldn't find the words, so he just stared at her. Her angry frown melted as she read his face. 'Are you telling me my husband is dead?'

'He was injured. I tried to save him, but I couldn't.'

'You're lying.'

'He's dead, Zoe.'

Tears fell from her glassy eyes, but she never looked away. She stared at Eddie, shaking her head, not wanting to believe his words yet knowing they were true. Her bottom lip trembled as she caught her breath.

'This is your fault.'

'I'm so sorry —'

The slap cracked against his face. He didn't react, and Zoe bolted from the flat. He heard her front door slam, then the terrible wail of her voice. Eddie closed his own door and locked it.

Outside, the sun had set, and the flat was dark. He went back to the bedroom and lay down, ashamed of himself and struggling with more guilt than he'd known in his life. He tried to justify his actions, knowing that Griff wanted to get involved, but Eddie had used that desire to his own ends. Griff had proved himself, too, but ultimately, he was a civilian, a husband and a father. Eddie should've cut him loose in Victoria.

The intelligence game was a brutal one, and Eddie wasn't sure if he was cut out for the human aspect of it. Put him in an OP, get him to count troops, tanks and planes. Fine, he could do that. But embroiling himself in people's lives and manipulating them — especially when they had wives and children — not so much.

He lay in the dark, his mind drifting, and then his watch alarm beeped, snapping him out of his troubled thoughts. He dressed, packed his still-damp daysack, and clipped the Springfield to his waist. From the equipment store, he took the rest of the money – $4,500 – and snapped an elastic band around the plastic packet. He took the sat phone, turned off all the lights and locked the external grille. On the balcony, he stood still and listened, but there was no noise from Griff's flat, and no lights to be seen. Maybe Zoe was alone, crying in the dark. Or maybe she'd gone back to wherever she'd left the kids. It didn't matter because Eddie didn't think he'd see her again. He lifted the flap of Griff's letterbox and dropped the money inside.

The entrance to Battersea Park was less than a ten-minute walk away. JLTVs mounted with mini-guns guarded the gated entrance, and watchful troops challenged Eddie as he approached. He offered his ID for inspection and another JLTV drove him around the park to an area of artificial football pitches surrounded by high chain-link fencing. Behind it, three helicopters loitered in the dark. Eddie was processed in a nearby office and directed back onto the football pitches, where the massive tilt rotors of a M-22 Osprey were turning.

After the ramp was lowered, Eddie filed inside with a dozen others. Most of his fellow passengers wore uniforms, and Eddie was thankful that no one was in a talking mood. With the ramp still partially open, the helicopter took off, rising over the football pitches before tilting its rotors and heading across the park. Treetops flashed beneath the ramp, and Eddie glimpsed the buckled remains of Albert Bridge and the foaming waters beneath it.

The ramp sealed shut, and the aircraft climbed into the night sky. Eddie settled in and closed his eyes, grateful to be leaving a broken city and its countless shattered lives behind him.

'THIS IS THE 6 O'CLOCK NEWS, BROUGHT TO YOU BY RADIO FREE Britain on behalf of the Atlantic Alliance. Efforts continued today in the search for survivors after last week's military action in central London. Specialist military and civilian rescue teams have been working around the clock for several days, but hopes are fading that *anyone else will be found alive. Despite the mounting death toll, Prime Minister Harry Beecham has expressed his gratitude to President Curtis Riley and praised the US military for heading off what intelligence sources are saying was another potential catastrophe, prompting speculation that a nuclear weapon was to be detonated in London...'*

'DINNER TIME.'

Through tired eyes, Bertie saw Cheryl click off the radio and set a steaming cup of soup on the bedside table. 'It's tomato,' she said. 'And the doctor is on his way up.'

'Okay, love.' He struggled upright and leaned forward as she plumped up his pillows and fixed the top button of his pyjamas. 'That smells good.'

She kissed him on top of his head. 'Glad to see you getting your appetite back.'

'You can't get rid of me that easily,' he said, smiling and squeezing her hand.

She stood back and inspected him. 'Presentable. I'll let him know.'

She left the room and the door ajar. It was a comfortable room too, with an enormous bed, a private bathroom and thick carpet underfoot, although Bertie hadn't been on his feet much lately. In fact, since the doctor had given them refuge, Bertie had yet to leave the room. And if Cheryl hadn't called him in the first place, he'd be dead. Cheryl too, most likely.

His memory was hazy, but he recalled being washed ashore and heading away from the beach. They'd kept to quiet footpaths and country lanes, doing their best to look as if they were out on a stroll, but Bertie's clothes were soaked through, and Cheryl's jeans were dark and wet from the knees down. An hour after making land, the heavens had opened, and they took shelter in a leaky country bus stop, where Bertie had shivered violently and slurred his words. He remembered little after that. Cheryl had told him the rest.

The bus stop was on the edge of a village called Finglesham and the B&B was owned by a sour-faced, suspicious woman called Pauline, who'd shown little sympathy until Cheryl handed her a wedge of cash. In the privacy of their small, draughty room, Cheryl had stripped Bertie naked, wrapped her arms around him beneath the thin duvet, and held him tight as he trembled. For two days Bertie had struggled to warm up, and Pauline had interrogated Cheryl, clearly not buying their cover story. *Yes, their car had broken down and no, she couldn't remember where they'd left it.* Pauline had pressed. *Where were they going? Where were they from? Why did they disobey the radio broadcasts?* Another guest had told Cheryl that refugees were washing up on local beaches, traitors who'd sided with the caliphate, so Cheryl had paid him to find a doctor.

Bertie remembered the man leaning over him, blinding him with his pen torch, pumping the strap around his arm, and telling Pauline that he was to be hospitalised immediately. He remembered riding in a car, wrapped in a blanket, and Cheryl holding him tight. But they never made it to the hospital.

Instead, the doctor drove them to his home, a big, six-bedroomed house hidden behind high, unkempt hedges, and he treated Bertie in one of his several warm, spare rooms, complete with fresh bedding and clean pyjamas. He put Bertie on a drip of warm salt water, and within 24 hours, his recovery was noticeable. His fever broke after three days, and he took a bath on the fifth day, a glorious experience. But he was still weak and their future was uncertain. They had to be careful.

He heard the stairs creak and voices on the landing. Bertie sipped his soup as Cheryl walked in, accompanied by Dr Ruskin, a round-faced man in his late sixties. He wore brown corduroys and a plain blue shirt, and he placed a stethoscope against Bertie's bare flesh. He liked what he heard and smiled.

'You're making excellent progress, Bertie, but you must continue to rest and get lots of sleep. We'll increase your calorie intake over the next few days, then try a few laps of the garden. How does that sound?'

'I don't know how to thank you, doctor. Stupid of me, getting caught out by the weather.'

The smile faded. 'Cheryl told me everything.'

Bertie's eyes flicked to Cheryl, and she held his disapproving stare. 'The doctor's not a fool, Bertie, and I won't lie.'

Ruskin pulled up a chair and sat by the bed. 'Bodies have been washing up along the coast for days. The woman at the B&B suspected you both and told me so. I said I'd report the fact when I took you to the hospital.'

'People have been murdered,' Cheryl said. 'People like us.'

Ruskin nodded. 'We've had it pretty easy out here in the sticks, but there's a nasty element in some of the villages and nearby towns. They've started patrolling the roads and beaches. You were lucky.'

'We're not traitors,' Bertie told him. 'The truth is, me and Cheryl were caught between a rock and a hard place. Yes, we tried to leave, but we were always going to come back.' Bertie shrugged. 'It's complicated.'

'I'm sure it is, and perhaps one day you'll tell me the story. I myself was forced to wait hand and foot on the local administrator and his friends and family. Ghastly people. Dangerous too. It didn't stop some thinking the worst of me.'

He patted Bertie's leg and stood up.

'Don't feel too indebted. Cheryl has compensated me handsomely, and I'm glad for the company, too. My wife died 18 months ago, and the place is empty without her. I would've left long ago had it not been for the occupation. So, we're helping each other, yes?' He pointed to the medication on the bedside table. 'Take your pills before you sleep, and I'll see you in the morning. Good night to you both.'

'Good night, Doc.'

Ruskin closed the door behind him, and Cheryl took the seat next to the bed. Bertie drained his soup and set the mug on the bedside table.

'Okay, break it to me, love. How much did you give him?'

'Five thousand,' Cheryl said, without hesitation.

'What?' Bertie felt his temper rising. 'But that's half of what we've got left.'

'Actually, it's more than that. Some notes were damaged while we were at sea. I couldn't dry it out at the B&B because that woman kept nosing around. When we got here, a lot of them just fell apart.'

Bertie felt sick. 'How much is left?'

'$2,850.'

Bertie closed his eyes. 'Oh, Jesus. We're so screwed.' He opened them again. 'Five grand, love? Why?'

'Because he took us in and saved our lives. And since then he's been protecting us.' Cheryl grasped his hand and squeezed his fingers. 'We can stay here as long as we like. He's buying the food and I'm cooking and cleaning.'

'You're not a bloody skivvy anymore.'

She smiled. 'He hasn't had a home-cooked meal for almost two years. Last night I made him beef wellington and all the trimmings. He's putty in my hands.'

Bertie laughed. 'No wonder. That's your signature dish. Even Chef loved it.'

'So, we stay until you're back on your feet. This house is warm and dry, and we're not overlooked by the neighbours. It could be so much worse, Bertie.'

'I'm not so sure. How long before someone sees us, mentions it to someone else. Next thing we know, there's a mob at the door.'

'You're too weak to go anywhere.'

Bertie felt it too. 'When I can, we need to leave. If we stay, they'll come for us.'

'Let's not worry about it now.'

'We'll need papers, ID cards. And we can't use our own names.' He swore and shook his head. 'All that money in the van, the millions in cash and jewellery, not to mention those paintings. All at the bottom of the sea.'

'Put it out of your head, Bertie. It won't do you any good.' She got up and placed the chair back against the wall. She took his empty mug and walked to the door. 'I'm going to wash up, then take a long, hot bath. Get some rest. I'll see you soon.' She blew him a kiss and closed the door.

Bertie lay back and pulled the quilt up beneath his chin. Cheryl was right, the treasure was now well and truly buried, and he imagined someone in the future, diving on that wreck and hitting the jackpot. As for Bertie, well, he would have to start all over again, but that was no big deal. He would have Cheryl by his side, and together they would work it out, carve out a life somewhere else. Not London, though. He'd stay well clear of that place for a long time. Maybe forever.

His eyes felt heavy, and he turned over, curling up beneath the warmth of the quilt. He would sleep for a while, until Cheryl came to bed, and then he would hold her and tell her he loved her. She was all the treasure he would ever need.

He closed his eyes and sleep rushed in. The darkness turned to bright sunlight, and Bertie found himself perched on that same rock, sitting above that same sparkling river, a rod in his hand.

Only this time no fish darted beneath the surface of the crystal-clear water. What he saw instead was a treasure chest overflowing with cash and jewels.

HARRY STOOD OUTSIDE THE BANK OF ENGLAND ON Threadneedle Street, numbed by the scale of the destruction before him. The West End had been bad enough, but the devastation caused by the controlled demolition of one of the city's major landmark buildings was staggering. The collapse of 22 Bishopsgate had destroyed an entire city block and flattened a corner of the Bank of England itself. Rubble stood 50 feet high, creating a mountain range of twisted steel, brick and concrete that rose and fell all the way back to Bishopsgate. Around him, he heard the gasps and groans of his Cabinet as they absorbed the depressing tableau before them. This was the first time they'd seen London with their own eyes, and their shock was palpable. Harry had already seen it from a helicopter over-flight a couple of days ago, but nothing had prepared him for the view from the ground.

So far, the tour had been a long and macabre one. Harry and his Cabinet had landed by helicopter in Hyde Park, and from his window seat, he saw that the crucified bodies at Marble Arch had been removed. The crosses were still there, though, and were to remain untouched on Harry's orders. It was a crime scene, and inves-tigations would need to be carried out.

From the leafy grounds of Hyde Park, Harry and his team had boarded a convoy of sedans bookended by truck-mounted troops and armoured fighting vehicles, and they set off on their tour of central London. They'd driven south to the embankment, where they'd watched the Thames foaming over the rubble of destroyed bridges. They'd crawled past the smoking ruin of Victoria train station, and gasped at the sight of Buckingham Palace, blackened by fire and brutally dissected by cluster munitions. Across Horse Guards Parade they stopped and gathered at the forlorn shell of Downing Street, still supported by steel poles and cocooned in plastic sheeting. They'd all seen the satellite footage many times, but it failed to capture the sheer brutality of the destruction around them. Everything was gone, the Cabinet Office, the MOD, Richmond House, Big Ben, the Houses of Parliament, Westminster Abbey, all replaced by a vast, empty building site. The scene rendered them silent as they struggled to absorb the jarring transformation to London's famous skyline. Harry ushered them back aboard the vehicles.

Beyond the rubble of Admiralty Arch, the National Gallery was a smoking ruin, and some of Harry's more culturally-minded colleagues mourned the loss of its artworks. The convoy weaved its way eastwards through the streets, diverting around fallen buildings and collapsed roads. Everywhere they looked, grey dust clung to buildings and pavements.

In the City of London, they saw the famous 34-storey 'walkie-talkie' building on Fenchurch Street torn in half by a falling B-52 bomber, and at Liverpool Street station, the tailplane of another aircraft protruded from the rubble and twisted train tracks. They stood behind safety ropes and inspected giant holes that used to be busy tube stations, the tunnels and walkways beneath the ground now exposed to daylight, and where falling water from fractured mains collected in deep, oily reservoirs. They watched army engineers on the river, toiling like ants as they constructed a temporary road section to replace the central span of London Bridge. They saw the muddy whirlpool near Waterloo, where the River Thames continued to empty into the tunnel below, and where more engineers were working to seal the Northern Line and stop the river forming a new tributary beneath the streets. And they saw people huddled in groups behind barriers and cordons, watching with suspicion as another army descended on their broken capital. Harry could understand the furrowed brows and nervous faces.

As he stared at the mountain of rubble on Bishopsgate, he heard Junger's voice break the shocked silence still gripping the Cabinet.

'When does the clear-up operation begin?' she asked no one in particular, but all eyes turned to Harry.

'It's started,' he said, as the other Cabinet members turned away from the destruction and formed a huddle around him. Further out, British troops from the 216th Pennsylvania Battalion formed a protective cordon around them. Harry noticed some of them squinting through their rifle optics, but he figured they were inspecting the destruction rather than looking for any of the rebels who'd stood ready to fight them. Those people were still in the rubble or languishing on the prison ships at Gravesend. Harry continued.

'Army engineers are working with utility companies to plug the leaking gas and water mains and restore disrupted electricity power supplies. Then they'll start work on road clearance and salvage.' He waved an arm at the surrounding devastation. 'At least the destruction is confined to a relatively small area of London.'

'Small, but significant,' Junger said. 'They've ripped out the heart of the city. Cultural sites, commerce, finance, transportation – much of it is gone. Perhaps you should've pushed back harder, Prime Minister. After all, they still haven't found a nuclear weapon.'

'Would you rather we'd left that to chance?' Harry said. His response was sharp, partly because Faye was getting under his skin and because he was forced to tell a lie. No one except Harry and Lee Wilde knew the truth, that the nuke cover story was a face-saving exercise for both countries. America had avenged the death of its president in a show of military force, and the footage, which had played endlessly on American news channels both before and after Bob Mitchell's funeral, had appeased the US electorate. And Harry could justify the destruction in order to avert another nuclear disaster on English soil. Even Faye couldn't argue with the logic of that one. In another few weeks, suspected nuclear bomb materials would be 'found' in the rubble, further underpinning the official narrative, and then the subject would go away, and people would move on. His chief of staff's voice interrupted his thoughts.

'Skyscrapers and bridges can all be rebuilt,' Wilde was saying to the others. 'That's why we're here today, not only to absorb the scale of the challenges that face us but to see how we can improve things as we move forward.'

'We have an opportunity to build back Britain,' Harry said, injecting his new mantra into the conversation.

'Are you actually going with that slogan?' Junger said, swapping amused looks with some of her colleagues.

'Do you have a better one? I'd love to hear it.' Harry waited.

'Why do we need slogans at all?' Shelley Walker asked.

'Because people rally around them. It's apolitical. And it's what we intend to do, as a country, and as a government.' He looked at the blank faces around him. Defence Secretary Simon Chisholm came to his rescue.

'I think it works. My team like it.'

'We should run it by some focus groups,' Welsh Secretary Maddox said.

'Can we forget the bloody slogan for now?' Harry said, thrusting his hands in his pockets. 'We have many challenges ahead, aside from physical reconstruction. The first of those is demanding our deportees are sent back to us, the hundreds of thousands – possibly millions – of men, women and children who were shipped abroad. And we'll demand the extradition of the criminals who sent them there. That's our priority from this point on. And the priority of our new Justice Ministry.'

'And where will we govern from?' Junger asked. 'Northwood is a military camp. It's a very oppressive and difficult atmosphere to work in.'

Harry broke the news. 'Which is why, until further notice, the British government will reside in Winchester, Hampshire. A former boarding school on the outskirts of the city is being made ready for our use. As England's ancient capital, I believe Winchester will make a fitting substitute until further notice. And London is just an hour away.'

He looked around their faces, but he saw little enthusiasm there. Their attitudes depressed him. *Maybe it's me,* Harry thought. Maybe he'd lost his ability to bring people together. Or maybe he'd chosen poorly, and the people around him were already forming factions and plotting in quiet corners. *Now you're being paranoid.* Still, Harry felt depressed, and the weight of the political task ahead was already heavy on his shoulders.

The wind picked up then, gusting through the rubble and whipping clouds of grey dust around them. Harry squinted and coughed. 'I think we've all seen enough,' Harry said. 'Let's call it a day.' Whistles blew, and the soldiers folded in around them as the Cabinet headed for the line of black sedans waiting nearby. Harry climbed into the back of his designated vehicle and Lee Wilde joined him.

Tom Fuller, Harry's newly appointed bag carrier, sat behind them in the jump seat.

'Trying to get a consensus from that lot is like trying to herd cats,' Wilde said, as their vehicle pulled away behind the mud-caked armoured vehicle ahead. He turned towards Harry. 'She's going to be trouble, you know. She's working her way through the Cabinet, sounding people out.'

'You know that for a fact?'

'No, but it's obvious. Shelley used to be a fan. Now she's in lock-step with any position Faye adopts.'

'So, what are my options?'

'Cut her loose. She won't be tamed.'

Harry coughed into his hand. 'Tom, hand me my water, please.'

The young Harvard graduate and only son of David Fuller, Harry's chief of staff who'd died in the garden of Downing Street on that terrible evening, handed him a bottle of mineral water.

'Infighting is the last thing any of us need.' Harry told Wilde. 'In some respects, I actually envy Wazir. No arguments from his government, no backchat from subordinates. It's his way or else. Dictator-ships are underrated.' He saw Wilde's expression and smiled. 'For the benefit of the tape, I'm joking.'

'That's a relief.' Wilde grinned. 'Although I do see your point.'

Harry unscrewed the cap off his bottle and took a long pull, watching the depressing tableau of destruction pass by as the vodka burned a path to his stomach.

[42]
REGIME CHANGE

THE CALIPH WAZIR STOOD AT THE GLASS WALL OF HIS PRIVATE quarters and gazed down across a pre-dawn Baghdad. His eye wandered along the empty Avenue of Martyrs, across the slow-moving Tigris River, and out towards a desert being slowly unveiled by the rising sun. The view, and the stillness of the dawn, always inspired Wazir. It also provided an opportunity to consider recent events.

General Baban and his army had paid the ultimate price, but their deaths were not in vain. Yet while the Great Satan's head had been a trophy beyond compare, the Guardian Council and Military High Command had expressed doubt and fear in the wake of the infi- del's death. He'd scolded them for their reticence while he himself had rejoiced in the president's assassination. How many lives had Mitchell and his predecessors taken over the years? How many brothers and sisters had died by Yankee bullets and bombs? Who mourned for those victims? Were they buried in national cemeteries, their graves adorned with flags and eternal flames? No. Their bodies were dragged from beneath the rubble of their homes and buried before the sun could cook their mangled remains.

And so, Wazir had revelled in the infidels' misery and had drawn comfort from the pain of Mitchell's family as they'd gathered at his graveside. Perhaps the children who'd stood there, confused and sad, would grow to become more enlightened than the generation before them, and a future caliph would sit across the negotiating table with those same children and find some common ground. Perhaps.

Until then, the caliphate was still at war. Hostilities with the Atlantic Alliance may have ceased, but the conflict with China continued, and now that the vast bulk of his British forces were back on European soil, they could be redeployed to the Eastern front. Wazir took a deep breath and exhaled. He would have to think long and hard about the future of that conflict. Air Chief Marshal Al-Issa and the rest of the High Command were having reservations, and the Guardian Council was concerned about the loss of so many of the caliphate's sons. Wazir shared those concerns, but he had yet to claim a military victory. Until he did, more blood would have to be shed.

He heard soft footsteps on the stairs below and Chitundu appeared, carrying his breakfast tray. He crossed the vast marble floor and set it down on the table by the window. Wazir took a seat, waving the Somali away as he settled down to eat. He poured sweet tea into a glass cup and sipped it, relishing the taste as he watched the sun creep across the Baghdad suburbs. As he chewed a piece of warm flat-bread, he saw a distant airliner climb its way into the dawn sky. These were the moments he enjoyed, the breaking of a new dawn and the promise of opportunities that could —

The bread caught in his throat, and he spat it onto the tray. He took a mouthful of tea and gulped it down to clear his throat. He settled back in his chair, growling and coughing as if a hair was lodged at the back of his throat.

And then he couldn't breathe.

He stood up, snatching at the bell on the tray, ringing it, then dropping it to the marble floor. He knocked his chair over as he staggered towards the centre of the room. Chitundu reappeared, and

Wazir's eyes bulged as he reached out for help, but the Somali stood back watching as Wazir sank to his knees, clutching his throat.

His vision swam, and he fell sideways, collapsing onto the marble floor. Wazir raised a feeble hand, but Chitundu stood motionless, observing with cold eyes...

That's when Wazir knew.

As the icy grip of paralysis seeped through his body, his arm flopped to the floor, no longer under his control.

Time passed as Wazir stared at the ceiling, immobile, choking on his own saliva. He heard the drum of approaching footsteps, saw the anxious faces gathered around him, their hands scrabbling at his clothes, his arms. He wanted to tell them that there was nothing they could do, that someone had accomplished what his nephew Zaki had tried and failed to do, and now his life was over. But he couldn't speak, couldn't move. His mind was trapped inside a suddenly useless body and for the first time since he was a child, Wazir felt frightened.

They placed a pillow under his head and a blanket over his body. They moved him onto his side and Wazir's head lolled, a string of saliva pooling onto the marble floor. He saw the sky outside the window, and the city that he'd imagined as a boy, and as its ruler, had rebuilt. He had achieved much in his life, more than most. Wazir's name would go down in history, and that was all that mattered. He'd performed his duty to God, and to his people, and he'd built a caliphate that was the envy of all the caliphs who'd passed before him.

Outside, the sun climbed higher, heralding another glorious day.

Mohammed Wazir knew it would be his last.

'How is he?'

Air Chief Marshal Al-Issa waited for one of the six white-coated doctors hovering around the Caliph's bed to answer him. Monitors beeped and chirped, and the Caliph himself sat upright on his bed, surrounded by pillows, his skin yellow, his eyes closed and his jaw slack and leaking spit. There was no dignity in death, Al-Issa thought. Perhaps on the battlefield, but even there, men still screamed for their mothers as they bled out, shot, stabbed or eviscerated by shrapnel.

'Well?' he asked again. The Chief of Staff of the Military High Command knew they were terrified of giving an answer, but night had already fallen, and nervous whispers echoed through the palace corridors. Action needed to be taken to protect the continuity of government. The Caliph's personal physician, a man named Tawfiq, cleared his throat.

'The Caliph, much peace be upon him, has suffered a debilitating stroke. Brain function is non-existent, and his vital signs have shown no improvement over the last 12 hours. The Caliph is deteriorating, Marshal Al-Issa. It is in God's hands now.'

One doctor blubbed and blew his nose. Al-Issa glared at the sycophant, then refocused on Tawfiq. 'And if God was a betting man, what are the Caliph's chances of a full recovery?'

Tawfiq frowned at the suggestion. 'None, I'm afraid.'

Standing behind Al-Issa, four senior members of the Guardian Council gasped. He didn't turn around. 'Then we should allow God some room to work, if that is his wish. Make the Caliph comfortable and give him some peace. Notify the family and summon the Imam of Baghdad. His Holiness should have someone to pray over him.'

Al-Issa left the room and consulted with the Guardian Council representatives for several minutes. To the Marshal's relief, they decided that, given the caliphate was in a state of war, Al-Issa himself should assume temporary leadership of the caliphate until a new caliph could be appointed. He thanked them and accepted the role, although he was going to take it anyway. What the caliphate needed was a firm hand and clear political direction, and there was no one better placed than himself to steer the kingdom through its current turbulence.

Hands were shaken and meetings arranged. Al-Issa expected a long night ahead, but with the transfer of power already taken place, much of the rest would be a formality. With the suite now empty, Al-Issa stood at the glass wall and looked out over the lights of the city. The Caliph's manservant, Chitundu, joined him at the window.

'I serve at the Marshal's pleasure,' he said, bowing.

Al-Issa put a hand on his bony shoulder. 'Thank you, Chitundu. This has been a difficult time.'

'The Caliph, peace be upon his soul, was very kind to me.'

'A benevolent man, and an inspiration to all of us.'

Chitundu took a step closer. 'Will there be an autopsy?'

Al-Issa shook his head. 'The body will be cremated privately. Arrangements have been made.'

'I understand.'

'Your bag is packed?' The Somali nodded. 'Good. Meet me at the lift.'

Al-Issa waited in the lobby of the Caliph's private suite, and Chitundu appeared a few moments later, a white shawl wrapped around his shoulders and a leather travel bag in his hand. As they took the lift down to the private entrance below ground, Al-Issa explained the next steps.

'You've performed a great service to the caliphate, Chitundu. Now you must take some time for yourself. Relax. Reconnect with your family.'

'It has been many years since I have seen them.'

'My personal jet will fly you directly to Mogadishu. When the dust has settled, we will speak. I will find you a new position, worthy of your loyalties.'

The Somali beamed a mouthful of white perfect teeth. 'Thank you, Marshal Al-Issa.'

The lift doors opened, and they stepped outside into the concrete cavern where a car waited. The driver threw up a salute and opened the boot.

Al-Issa shook the manservant's hand. 'God speed, my friend.'

'Insha'Allah.'

Chitundu put his bag in the boot and the driver shot him in the back of the head, the pop of the small calibre pistol echoing off the concrete walls of the cavern. The driver caught the body, and Al-Issa helped him tip Chitundu into the boot. The Marshal slipped into the back seat and the driver got behind the wheel. They drove through the long tunnel and out onto the Avenue of Martyrs, where flame torches blazed along its length.

'Take me to the Black Gate, then get rid of the body. They're waiting for you at the drilling rig in Nahrawan. Drop him down the shaft.'

The driver nodded. 'Yes, sir.'

Al-Issa leaned back in his seat as they glided through the wide avenues of Baghdad. As coups went, this had been a benign one, bloodless and well ordered. It required planning, of course, and the cooperation of the black bag of bones in the boot, but the transfer of power had been relatively simple.

The conversations had been going on for some time, and many people, including Al-Issa, were concerned about the direction the caliphate had taken. Too many lives had been lost, too much blood and treasure spent on foolish expeditions like the invasion and subjugation of Britain. And then there was the Chinese conundrum, a war triggered by a nuclear blast that both sides had denied any involvement in. Casualties were too high, but there was good news. The Chinese Premier was not a well man, and with luck, he too would soon find himself the focus of a state funeral. When that happened, Al-Issa would apply the brakes to the war on the eastern front. Faces would be saved on both sides, and everyone could withdraw from the battlefield, their honour intact. That was the hope, at least for Al-Issa.

The car dropped him outside the medieval towers of the Black Gate, a purpose-built dining, entertainment, and accommodation complex for the caliphate's most senior military officials. Behind its thick walls, the High Command had gathered, and tonight, they would thrash out their plans for the immediate future.

Walking through the lush courtyard of palms and flaming braziers, Al-Issa was reminded of his youth, when firebrands had convinced him and many others that the world could be conquered, and its citizens made subjects or enslaved. How easily they'd been duped. Time, experience, and a lifetime spent bending to the whims and dark motivations of those impostors had taught him otherwise.

Above him, the night sky glittered with stars. Tomorrow, a new dawn would signal the beginning of a new era.

[43]
REMEMBER, REMEMBER

'AND WHEN THE FINAL CHAPTER OF THIS WAR IS WRITTEN, historians will look back and say, not only was this the greatest fighting force in the history of the world, but all of its soldiers represented the values of the United States of America in the best possible way, and I could not be prouder to be your commander-in-chief. Thank you, God bless you, and God bless the United States of America.'

The walls of the aircraft hangar shook with the thunderous roar and applause of the thousands of US troops gathered inside it, as President Riley stepped down from the makeshift stage and shook hands with the officers representing the multitude of formations and divisions that had taken part in the campaign to free Britain and Ireland. Harry and his own officers followed on behind Riley's entourage, shaking those same hands as he inched his way across the hangar towards the exit. By the time he got here, his hand ached.

Outside, a cold and drizzly November wind barrelled across the grey expanse of RAF Brize Norton, bringing with it the muted roar of the C-17 Globemaster aircraft queuing along the taxiway as they waited to take off. A short distance away, Harry's convoy of Range

418

Rovers waited in the gathering gloom for the British contingent. As he zipped up the collar of his green parka and walked towards his vehicle, he couldn't help but feel a keen sense of separation, like a child encouraged to travel alone to school for the first time. A foolish thought, he knew, and yet it persisted.

Defence Secretary Simon Chisholm walked by his side, followed by Lee Wilde and young Tom Fuller. The soldiers trailed behind in their own group, led by Chief-of-Defence General Sir David Roland-Jones, his deputy Nick Wheeler, and the other general staff officers. Despite their confident smiles and voices, Harry wondered if they too felt that same sense of relinquishment. The King's Continental Army division was now officially disbanded and the British troops who'd sworn an oath to defend the US Constitution were now free from that obligation. From this moment on, the allegiance of the British army was to the crown and the defence of that realm on behalf of the British government.

They wouldn't be able to do that alone, of course. Only the land forces were under British control, until such time that aviation and naval elements, still operating under the US flag, could be reorganised and redeployed. There would of course be a continued American military presence in the UK, and much of that force would provide air and sea defences, from advanced Patriot missile shields over the British Isles and Ireland to US Navy ships and aircraft securing Britain's and Ireland's territorial waters. However, a significant percentage of US combat troops would head home, and today's ceremony was about thanking those troops for their sacrifice and courage. President Riley had flown in specially to do just that. Now he was gone, and though he didn't care to admit it, the separation troubled Harry.

One of his close protection team opened the door to his Range Rover and Harry was about to step inside its warm cocoon when he heard a shout.

'Prime Minister Beecham!'

He turned around and saw a female US soldier jogging towards him. She paused and threw up a salute. 'Prime Minister, the president would like you to join him for a moment.'

Harry nodded. He'd barely spoken to Riley all day, and now he had an opportunity to share his concerns. He turned to Chisholm. 'I'll see you back in Winchester. Lee, Tom, stay behind, would you?'

Wilde and Fuller nodded, hands in pockets as the damp wind blew. Daylight was fading fast, but the airport remained unlit. The war was over, but the memory of it was still fresh in everyone's minds.

Harry shook hands with his officers and followed the young soldier to a waiting JLTV. It drove around the airfield, past the long line of C-17s, and Harry watched hundreds of troops being swallowed by one such monster. They drove on to another cluster of hangars on the far side of the airfield, all of them cloaked in darkness. The JLTV passed through an open hangar door, and it closed behind them. The vehicle squealed to a halt and Harry's door was opened by another soldier, this one in a black uniform and helmet.

Harry stepped out and stared up at Air Force One, surrounded by its praetorian guard of black-clad troops. The aircraft's livery was set to matte black, and Harry was escorted up the steps at the rear of the aircraft and into the passenger cabin. Flanked by two more guards, Harry followed a crew-member to the presidential suite near the front of the aircraft and was shown into Riley's office, much like the one on the 747, smaller in scale but no less well-appointed. The president was sitting at a small conference table and waved Harry into the opposite chair. He wore a navy fleece with the presidential seal on his left breast, and he spoke only after the door had closed.

'Thanks for coming, Harry. Can I get someone to take your coat?'

'It depends how long I'm going to be here,' Harry said, offering Riley an affable smile. The president was a different man than the one he'd spoken to on the eve of London's destruction. That man was a vengeful one, determined to shed blood at any cost. The man in front of him now had mourned his loss and had time to reflect on his actions. Riley would never admit that he'd overreacted, and Harry couldn't blame him for that — world leaders didn't admit their mistakes to foreigners — but they shared secrets, like the beheadings and the fake nuclear bomb story, which made them co-conspirators. It wasn't the most solid foundation for a friendship, but it was a start.

'Not long,' Riley answered him. 'I need to get back home. There's a lot of work to be done between now and January.'

'Yes, your mysterious power units. I was hoping to speak to you about that.'

'The rollout will be a long process, Harry. America first. You understand, right?'

Harry nodded. 'Of course. However, I thought we might come to an arrangement, given the scale of Britain's regeneration program.'

Riley folded his arms on the table. 'I've seen the reports. Your nuclear power stations were unscathed by the conflict. You can still generate sufficient power and given the reduction in demand due to population shrinkage and industrial contraction, the projected load requirements are well within your production limits.'

Harry sat back in his chair. 'You've certainly done your homework.'

'It's important my administration understands your needs.' He cracked his big knuckles and continued. 'I've spoken to President Orlov. He's prepared to cut you a deal on gas, to backstop your current output. It's a good deal, Harry. You should take it.'

Harry frowned. 'How's that possible? The caliphate still controls all the European transmission infrastructure.'

'The situation has changed. Wazir hasn't been seen for six weeks. There are rumours he's had a stroke, but we think he's dead.'

Harry's eyes widened. 'What?'

'Air Chief Marshal Al-Issa is their frontman now, backed by the Military High Command and the Guardian Council. Let's just say the marshal's tone is a little more congenial than Wazir's, which means Baghdad is prepared to open up the taps to your offshore sites.'

Harry couldn't disguise his frustration. 'Why am I only hearing this now? We're supposed to be allies, for God's sake.' He unzipped his thick green parka, his face feeling flushed. 'You've made it clear that our so-called special relationship means little, but I can't drag this country out of its post-war slump without significant help from the United States.'

'So, take the deal.'

'But we can't pay for the bloody stuff! We have no gold or cash reserves, no industry to speak of, and every trade deal we've ever had will need to be renegotiated. It'll take years to get Britain back on its feet.'

'The United States is not a charity.'

Harry stared at the table as he took a deep, calming breath. He exhaled and looked up. 'Perhaps, but you're about to cash in the biggest lottery ticket ever. Soon, you will own the global energy market. That's a licence to print money.' He waved a finger around the soundproofed cabin. 'And this aircraft, this marvel of technology, it represents a quantum leap in air travel and you own the technology. I cannot imagine the exciting opportunities that these innovations will offer mankind in the coming years.' Harry leaned forward. 'You stand on the brink of history, Curtis, yet you can't bring yourself to throw Britain a bone. Why?'

Riley stood up and stared out of the floor-to-ceiling window that curved around the aircraft's superstructure. After a moment, he spoke.

'You know what *really* bothers me, Harry? Everything that's happened these last few years — the invasion, the subsequent war, the countless lives lost — was avoidable. And yet, the governments of Britain and Europe continued on a path of self-destruction despite the countless warnings of serious trouble ahead.' He glanced over his shoulder. 'That's not to say that Uncle Sam hasn't made similar mistakes, but my administration intends to deal with those past missteps robustly.' He turned back to the window. 'You knew, Harry. Bob told me, after we'd fed and sheltered three million of your citizens. You knew there was a storm headed your way, and you failed to stop it. You didn't even try.'

'It's not as simple as that, Curtis. To become PM, one must be all things to all people. Compromise on issues and policies that go against your fundamental beliefs.'

'You sold your soul.'

'You're lucky you didn't have to.' Harry frowned. 'I'm sorry, that was crass.'

Riley turned away from the window and retook his seat. 'The truth is, I don't trust you. I don't trust your government, and the United States is not prepared to license our technology to Great Britain at this time.'

Riley stared across the table, stony-faced, intractable. Harry fumed, but kept his mouth shut. He changed the subject. 'Can we talk about the British diaspora still living stateside?'

Riley softened, smiled. 'I'm glad you brought that up. Next week I'll be signing a bill into law. The Mitchell Act will guarantee the right of any British citizen currently residing in the United States to become naturalised citizens. That includes all current UK military personnel who served in the King's Continental Army.'

'Excuse me?'

'The Act also applies to UK citizens wishing to migrate permanently to the United States through a buy-in program. The details will be published once I've signed the Act into law.'

'That's very generous,' Harry muttered, still struggling with the ramifications.

Riley glanced at his watch and got to his feet. He held out his hand and Harry shook it. 'Tell Orlov you'll accept his deal, Harry. And don't be too disheartened. There's a long road ahead and things might change.'

Harry stood and zipped up his parker. 'I won't hold my breath.' Riley held all the cards, and he should be grateful for whatever crumbs the US threw Britain's way. Yet it was hard to disguise his frustration. The door opened and two secret service agents waited outside.

Riley smiled for the audience. 'Thank you, Prime Minister.'

Harry forced his too. 'Have a safe trip, Mr President.'

Fifteen minutes later, Harry climbed out of the JLTV and transferred to his Range Rover, the CP officer closing the door behind him. The driver was outside too, banished on Wilde's orders. Tom was keeping the wind-swept man company.

'Well? What did he say?'

Harry sighed. 'Apparently, we're getting a gas deal from the Russians. And Wazir's probably dead. A stroke.'

Wilde was incredulous. 'Wazir's dead?'

'Maybe for the last six weeks. Al-Issa is acting as spokesman and will underpin the Russian deal. So, if there's a loop here, Britain isn't in it.'

'Did you push back?'

Harry shook his head. 'With what leverage? It feels like we've become the 51st state of America.'

'Jesus.'

Harry glanced at his chief of staff. 'It gets worse. Next week, the shiny new Mitchell Act will provide a pathway to all British citizens currently residing in the US to become US nationals. That extends to our armed forces too.'

'But that means...' Wilde didn't finish his sentence. 'Jesus,' he said again.

Harry rapped a knuckle on the window and the others climbed aboard.

'What do we do now?' Wilde asked.

'I need to think, and I can't do that in Winchester, not with the Cabinet clucking around me. I need time to think.'

Wilde tapped a number on his phone. 'I'll ask housekeeping to prepare the flat in Admiralty House.'

'London,' Harry said. 'Good idea. Tom, call ops, get me a helicopter.'

Fuller pulled out his phone. 'Yes, Prime Minister.'

The Range Rover purred into life and headed towards the flight line at Air Operations.

. . .

Later that evening, Harry slipped out of the basement entrance of Admiralty House as Wilde bolted the door behind him. With his protection officer walking close by, Harry crossed the flat wasteland of Horse Guards Parade and skirted the frail shell of Downing Street, now protected by a large perimeter of hoardings and monitored by cameras and security guards. The protection and restoration of his former home was the one item on Harry's agenda the Cabinet didn't bicker over. They all knew his wife had died there, and the famous street also held huge historical and cultural significance. No British government would ever meet there again, not officially, but Harry accepted that. In a hundred years, who would even care?

He followed the crowds wandering along Whitehall, corralled by wide, taped-off walkways and watched by soldiers. Gone were the helmets and war paint, but the guns remained. Life had settled down, though. Since the end of hostilities, the country had suffered no terrorist attacks, no suicide bombings or stabbing sprees. The touchstone of potential rebellion, Wazir, was MIA, and most of Britain's Islamic population had left for the caliphate. Those that didn't make it, the many thousands who'd descended on ports and airports and found themselves trapped, had fled. Many had disappeared into the Channel Tunnel, a temporary escape route that was eventually sealed, but not before countless people had disappeared into its dark tubes.

Harry had flown over Dover shortly after the end of the conflict and was shocked by what he'd witnessed there. As the helicopter hugged the coastline, he'd seen tens of thousands of abandoned cars, a burned-out ship and dozens of scorched buildings. Thousands of pieces of luggage lay scattered everywhere, and amongst them, bodies. They bobbed in the water too, men, women and children, rising and falling with the swell. It was horrible, but Harry found himself almost immune to the horror of it all. Almost.

So, those people who wished to relocate to Europe would be given the opportunity to do so, with the proviso that they would never be allowed to return to Britain or Ireland. Unless they were guilty of crimes, of course. So far, the only criminals they'd found were dead ones, strung up in parks and playgrounds, or stabbed and beaten to death in their homes. Emotions were still very raw, but Harry would not condone death squads and vigilantes and had said so publicly. The killings had abated, not entirely, but there had been progress. What the British people needed was a public trial, so that justice could be served, and the human rights of the criminals be damned.

An ancient form of justice lay ahead, the huge bonfire that burned on the wasteland where the Houses of Parliament had stood. Which was fitting, Harry thought. The crowd was huge, several thousand perhaps. His CP officer moved closer, but Harry was sure no one would recognise him. He wore thick glasses beneath a herringbone flat cap and a scarf over his chin. His overcoat was well worn, as were the scuffed shoes on his feet. Tonight, he wanted to be invisible, to mingle with the crowds and sip the vodka masquerading as a takeaway coffee in his gloved hand.

The fire crackled and roared, the embers drifting high into the night sky, and when the effigy of Wazir went up in flames, the crowd cheered. Harry cheered too, buoyed by the vodka, by the smiling faces around him, the children on their fathers' shoulders, the mothers shepherding their broods, the singing, the dancing, the open alcohol consumption, the pizza and hotdog vendors servicing the long queues. There were no fireworks this time, prohibited as a security risk and the potential to cause trauma, but kids with sparklers ran everywhere, waving them in furious, glowing circles. Harry watched them and prayed they would grow up healthy and happy, that their memories of war and death would fade.

He finished his vodka and wandered away from the crowds, strolling past the newly constructed Westminster Bridge. It was a tactical military bridge, and one of three now connecting the city's north and south banks. As such, it was heavily guarded and accessed only by those with a National ID card, which the British population was now obliged to carry with them. No one complained about freedoms or rights, not even the Cabinet. The world had changed irrevocably.

He passed the soldiers at the bridge, wondering how many would take up Riley's offer of citizenship. He'd discussed it with Lee, and they'd concluded that many would do so. As for the civilians, the take up would be significant. After three long years, many displaced Brits had put down roots in America. Their children were settled in schools, and many had mortgages and jobs. With an economic boom about to be unveiled by Riley, who in their right mind would return to a broken Britain?

The sound of the crowd faded as Harry headed past the Corinthia Hotel towards Admiralty House. He would visit the West End and the City of London tomorrow and see how the clean-up was progressing. Well, he hoped. Because he needed some good news, something to cheer him. Yes, they'd won the war, but in the wake of that conflict, it was time for everyone to roll up their sleeves and get to work. And the Prime Minister would be expected to set that example.

But Harry had no energy, no enthusiasm to knuckle down. He was bone-tired, and now that it was here, fearful of the future. Maybe he really was like Churchill, energised by war and the will to win, only to be left deflated and directionless by its passing.

He crossed Whitehall and glanced to his right, towards the starkly lit Trafalgar Square where giant yellow construction machinery stood lifeless. Nelson was gone, of course, as were all the other statues in London, torn down by the invaders and their disciples. New statues would be commissioned, and Harry wondered if his own might adorn a plinth someday, looking boldly across a prosperous London. One he could barely imagine right now.

He shook his head. What a ridiculous, conceited thought. As the President of the United States had alluded to only a few hours ago, Harry Beecham really was irrelevant.

[44]
TAKE A KNEE

'Come on, Bertie. Pick up the pace. You're like an old man.'

'Cheeky cow.' Bertie smiled and squeezed Cheryl's arm as they strolled up the steep incline of Holly Hill and into the warren of exclusive backstreets of Hampstead Heath. 'I'm out of shape, that's all.'

He knew Cheryl was joking, but her words rang true. He *was* out of shape, no question. The hypothermia had knocked him for six, and his recovery had taken longer than expected. Then, just when he was feeling stronger, a seasonal flu bug had knocked him sideways and set his recovery back by weeks. Dr Ruskin blamed himself, because he was seeing a lot of patients who had the virus. In Bertie's weakened state, he found himself back in bed for the last ten days of November. As December dawned, Bertie was up and moving again, but he still felt weak. That wasn't good because they needed to get out of Kent. People were sniffing around. And not your average nosy parker, either. Whoever was watching, Bertie knew they were wrong 'uns.

So, he'd re-positioned one of the Doc's CCTV cameras and on four occasions, he'd captured the same car parked across the lane with the same four shadowy figures inside it. Despite Bertie's reluctance, the Doc had called the National Police Force – the newly formed civilian law enforcement body – and they'd sent round a patrol which had scared the watchers off, but they'd returned a couple of days later. Bertie knew that someone, somewhere, was onto them. Perhaps the guy who'd serviced the boiler had mentioned two unfamiliar faces living at Doc Ruskin's place. Maybe a neighbour had seen them, or maybe Pauline from the B&B had seen through Doc Ruskin's story and made a call. Bottom line, someone had rumbled them, and it was time he and Cheryl left Kent and struck out on their own.

The Doc was sorry to see them go, and Bertie knew he had a soft spot for Cheryl. They say the way to a man's heart is through his stomach, and Cheryl had certainly pulled out all the stops on the culinary front, as well as making sure the house was spick-and-span for when the Doc came home. Bertie joked that the man was a little bit in love with her; Cheryl had laughed, but Bertie reckoned it was true. The look on his face when they told him they were leaving was … well, the man was devastated.

The going-away present he gave them was priceless, however. Two brand-new ID cards, complete with alternative names. The National ID & Passport Office official had come to the house, a very pleasant man in his late forties who'd recorded Bertie and Cheryl's details on his computer and scanned their eyes and fingerprints. He'd wished them luck before leaving the house, and Doc Ruskin explained the man was a patient; the Doc had saved his little girl's life after a seizure had stopped her heart. The man had owed Doc Ruskin big time. And he'd delivered.

A week later, Cheryl had walked into the bedroom and tipped the contents of a padded envelope out onto the bed. Bertie picked up his ID card – in the name of *Albert Painter* and Cheryl had become *Cheryl Parkes*. They'd agreed it was best to stay as close as possible to their real names, just in case. It made remembering them that much easier.

They'd gathered around the big kitchen table and enjoyed a farewell meal with the Doc, and Cheryl outdid herself with a three-course meal worthy of any London restaurant. They drank wine and champagne, and Bertie toasted the man who'd saved their lives. The next day, Ruskin drove them to Canterbury train station and bid them an emotional farewell. Despite his better judgement, Bertie had left $500 in an envelope on the kitchen table and hoped the man wouldn't be offended.

They'd ridden the packed train into St Pancras International in London. It wasn't where Bertie wanted to go, but they had to start somewhere, and London was a city of opportunities right now, especially for employment. With their new IDs and different wardrobes (Cheryl had cut her dyed blonde hair short and Bertie loved it), he doubted anyone would recognise them.

Bertie's legs and feet ached terribly by the time the train pulled into London, but he forgot all about his discomfort when they saw the enormous Christmas tree on the concourse. No one had seen one for three years, not in public anyway, and people just stood and stared at the spectacle of coloured lights. And the kids? Well, just hearing their voices and seeing their excited faces had lifted Bertie and Cheryl's spirits.

They checked in to the Renaissance Hotel right above the station, intending to stay for only a week as funds were limited, but it was a good enough spot to start their search for work. After a restful night, they sat in a coffee shop down on the station concourse and watched the world go by. It was a big change from the quiet Kent countryside and both Bertie and Cheryl felt energised by the atmosphere, by the crowds of travellers, the train whistles, and the general pace of life. But there were police and army personnel everywhere. War had scarred the city.

'If you took away that tree, I wonder if we'd see as many smiles,' Cheryl said, stirring her latte.

Bertie shrugged. 'Probably not. It's going to be a tough Christmas for a lot of people. Us as well if we don't find work.'

'Do you think about them? Lady Edith and Judge Hardy?'

Bertie grimaced. 'She got what she deserved. Maybe the judge did too, but he saved my life. I wish I could've saved his.'

'I want to go to Hampstead, Bertie. See the house.'

He stared at her. 'Are you crazy? Someone might see us, put two and two together.'

'No, they won't. Look at us. We're different people. Come on, I want to go. We can just stroll past, like we're out walking.'

Bertie felt a faint flutter of fear. The house held a lot of memories for him, mostly bad in those last few months. But then something occurred to him, and suddenly it felt right. The best idea he'd had for a very long time. 'Okay, but I need to go to the room first. I left my ID up there.'

'I'll wait here,' Cheryl said.

And so, they'd taken the Northern Line to Hampstead Station, where a waning sun still shone in the cold December sky.

'I don't remember it being this steep,' Bertie puffed as they trudged higher into the narrow lanes of Hampstead's exclusive neighbourhood.

'Almost there,' Cheryl said, her arm linked through his, but it amused him to hear that she was puffing a little too.

Passers-by smiled and nodded, which was a first for Hampstead. People used to keep themselves to themselves, but maybe things had changed, which wasn't exactly good news. They didn't want some busybody making chit-chat and asking questions.

They turned into the familiar crescent with the enormous houses and the high walls. Bertie forced himself to walk at a normal pace.

'I wonder who's living there now?' Cheryl said.

'Someone with plenty of dough,' Bertie said. 'Remember, no stopping. And no staring.'

'We're just a couple of locals out for a stroll,' Cheryl said, squeezing his arm.

The house came into view, and their pace faltered. Behind huge hoardings, Edith Spencer's Hampstead mansion lay abandoned, its roof partially collapsed, its top-floor windows blackened by fire and exposed to the elements. The house next to it, the one belonging to the textile millionaire Clemens, was still intact, and lights shone inside.

'Vigilantes, I reckon,' Bertie said, his eyes roaming the gutted top floor. 'Thank God we weren't here when they turned up.'

Cheryl held her hand over her mouth. 'What a terrible shame. It was such a beautiful building. Do you think there's anyone inside?'

'Looks derelict to me.' They walked closer, and Bertie peered through a gap between the padlocked gates plastered with signs that read *DANGER – KEEP OUT*. 'Looks like most of the damage is on the top floor. Can't see any lights.'

'I think we should take a look.'

Bertie shook his head. 'That's not a good idea, love. Besides, it's all locked up.'

'I bet the key to the back gate is still there. Why don't we wait until the sun sets? Then we can take a last look around.'

'No.'

She squeezed his arm. 'Please? For me.'

Bertie could see Cheryl was determined. And these days, what Cheryl wanted, Cheryl got. 'Okay, we'll go to the Duke on the High Street and come back in an hour.'

It was the second pub that Bertie had frequented since they'd returned to London, and like the one in Kings Cross, the *Duke of Hamilton* had very little beer and not much atmosphere. The pubs had been closed for three years, and breweries and supply chains had yet to get up and running. Bertie had expected London to party like it was VE Day, but it just hadn't happened. Back then, the country had united against a common foe. In 21st century Britain, your own neighbour could be an enemy. Bertie was tired of it, tired of all the hatred and division. And he doubted things would get better. He put the depressing thought from his mind and focussed on his mission as they drank gin and tonics in a quiet corner.

Bertie had large ones to calm his nerves. When Cheryl went to spend a penny, he took the small box from his pocket and checked to make sure the ring was nestled safely inside its red velvet folds. It was a cheap ring, bought from the hotel gift shop for a couple of hundred bucks, but it would do for now. He breathed on the cheap stones and polished them with the cuff of his sweater. Then he tucked it back in the pocket of his overcoat. Feeling nervous, Bertie escorted Cheryl from the pub, and they looped around Hampstead Grove before approaching their former home from the rear. They strolled in the shadows of the garden wall until they reached the gate. Shielded by the tree-lined pavement, Bertie ran his hand along the brickwork arch above it. The gap in the pointing was small, but Bertie felt the string beneath his fingertips and pulled out the big, rusted key.

'Thank God,' Cheryl whispered, looking up and down the pavement. The sun had set, and the sky had darkened. There was no one around, and Bertie unlocked the gate. Inside the grounds, they kept to the perimeter wall until they reached the rear of the main house. It didn't look as damaged as the front, with only a corner of the top floor burned and exposed to the sky where the roof had collapsed. Bertie poked his head into the garage, expecting to see the bodies of Al-Huda and the black woman rotting in their BMW. But the garage was empty, and everything was gone: garden tools, the mower, the spare furniture, all of it.

They slipped into the house via the unlocked French doors. There was enough light to walk around, but not much to see. Every room was devoid of furnishings and furniture. Even the light switches and fittings were gone, and the house felt bare and cold. It saddened Bertie, but it was also a little spooky, and he wondered if The Witch haunted its rooms and corridors. He imagined her floating down the main stairs towards him, screeching his name, and it gave him chills.

'Let's go to the basement,' Cheryl said.

'Good idea.' They took the stairs down into the corridor, and the memories came rushing back. Bertie heard Chef swearing and the clatter of pots and pans. He heard the buzzer of the security gate and the jangling bells that summoned him upstairs. His old room was empty, as was Cheryl's, and Bertie felt a little sad. This had been his home, and mostly, he'd been content. Life under occupation had been bearable, ensconced in The Witch's cavern, but most important of all, it was where he'd met Cheryl Parker, and where he'd fallen in love – true love – for the first time in his life.

The ring was burning a hole in his pocket as he strolled around the kitchen. Every cupboard was empty, every work surface bare and thick with dust. Bertie ran a finger along the marble worktop of the huge centre island and remembered where he was standing when he'd laid eyes on Cheryl for the first time.

'So many memories,' Cheryl said, echoing his own thoughts. 'Not all good, but not bad either. We were lucky, Bertie.'

Bertie's lips were dry. He'd rehearsed this moment in his head a thousand times and had his speech down pat. The original plan was to do it up on the Heath as the sun set. But coming here was a better idea, the place where they'd met, in a house that had changed both their lives. But now the moment was here, words failed him. And in the absence of words, only action remained.

He took Cheryl's hand and led her towards the door, stopping short. She smiled.

'Bertie, what are you doing?'

He moved her then dropped his arms. 'You were —' He croaked, then cleared his throat. 'This is where you were standing, the day I first saw you. Right here.' His hands were trembling, and he reached into his pocket and covered the box with his fist.

'What's going on?' Cheryl was smiling, her eyes bright, and Bertie knew she'd probably guessed. Cheryl Parker was a smart girl, the smartest he'd ever met. He struggled down to his knee and opened his hand to reveal the box. He eased back the lid.

'Oh, Bertie.' And then those bright eyes filled with tears.

'Will you do me the honour of being my wife?' Bertie said, his voice cracking. His hand shook as he held out the box, like a tribesman with an offering for a stone God. And Bertie did worship her.

'Yes! Of course, yes! Now stand up and kiss me.'

He duly obliged, then he slipped the ring onto her waiting finger. 'This is just a temporary piece. I'll get you something nicer when we're settled and we've got some more money coming in.'

Cheryl held her hand at arm's length and stared at the ring. 'This will do just fine.' She hugged him, holding him tight, and they stayed like that for several moments. It was Cheryl who broke the spell. 'I'm going to the bathroom,' she said, dabbing her eye with a tissue. 'Then we should probably leave.'

Bertie nodded. 'Yes, love. We should.'

She stepped out of the room and Bertie leaned on the island, exhaling a long sigh of relief. He thought she'd say yes, but every man who'd ever taken the plunge knew the woman of his dreams might say no. Cheryl's hand in marriage was never a done deal, so Bertie felt honoured that she wanted to marry him. And happier than he'd ever been. Whatever hard times lay ahead, they had each other, and that would be enough.

He heard a distant toilet flush and then her footsteps in the corridor. He took a last look around the room, absorbing the sights and smells, knowing he would never come back. Cheryl stood opposite him. She pushed a plastic storage box across the island.

Bertie frowned. 'What's this?'

'A wedding present.' Cheryl smiled.

Bertie pulled the box towards him and snapped off the lid. Inside was a worn rucksack. He looked at Cheryl. 'It's what I've always wanted.' He winked and lifted it out. 'It's heavy.' He pulled down the side zip and several plastic-wrapped packets of money spilt across the marble. Bertie picked one up. The denominations were $100. 'Jesus Christ,' he said. 'Where did you get this?'

'The day you brought all that luggage home, remember? You said make an inventory.'

She took the rucksack, unzipped it, and upended it. More money tumbled across the counter. And several small boxes.

Bertie saw a familiar one and plucked it out of the pile. He opened it and took a sharp breath. 'Oh my God.'

'That's the Patek Philippe you told me about. The one that sold at auction for $3,000,000.'

'Jesus,' Bertie said, marvelling at the beauty of the timepiece.

'I thought we needed an insurance policy, just in case. I stashed it behind the vent in the bathroom airing cupboard. Then I prayed it would still be here.'

Bertie looked up at her. In awe of her. 'How much?'

'$400,000, plus the watch. And a necklace. And some earrings.' She winced. 'I couldn't help myself. They were so beautiful, Bertie. Oh, and a ring, just in case someone asked for my hand in marriage.'

Bertie stumbled around the island and snatched Cheryl up in his arms. 'You're amazing!'

'I know, but we should go,' she said, laughing, and he let her go.

Cheryl packed everything back into the rucksack and zipped it up. She smiled and handed it to him. 'Merry Christmas, Bertie.'

'Merry Christmas, love.' He kissed her and slipped the rucksack over his shoulders. A few minutes later, they were back on the pavements of Hampstead and heading for the high street. When they got there, Bertie would hail a taxi, and tonight they would celebrate at the hotel. There would be no champagne corks popping, nothing like that. Just dinner and a few drinks in the bar afterwards. And they would make plans, proper plans, for their future.

As they walked back down the steep incline of Holly Hill, Bertie felt he could fly. A burden had lifted from his shoulders. He had a bag full of money and the smartest, most beautiful woman in the world on his arm.

Maybe Bertie Payne's luck had finally changed.

[45]

CHURCH PARADE

SOMEHOW, ST PAUL'S CATHEDRAL HAD ESCAPED OBLITERATION during the bombing of London. Some argued that the Americans used only laser-guided munitions that day, but others pointed to the damage caused by thousands of cluster bombs dropped across the city, and the fall of stricken aircraft, one of them crashing to the ground less than 200 yards from the cathedral's eastern wall. The iconic building had suffered some damage, but as had happened during the Second World War, the building had avoided catastrophe, reinforcing the fable that God was watching over his most splendid of houses.

Now its aisles, transepts and pews were filled with uniforms from all three services of the British armed forces. Stood amongst them, and wearing his combat uniform and green ISR beret, Eddie stared up at the flakes of snow floating in the scented air of the cathedral, courtesy of the damaged roof and a section of dislodged sheeting, allowing flurries to drift inside. He thought there was something magical about the sight, to see such a thing inside a cathedral lit by thousands of candles and resonating with the voices of the soldiers, sailors and airmen gathered within its ancient walls.

They'd cancelled the remembrance service in November, so the Christmas church parade was an opportunity to celebrate the first festive season after three long years. It was also a chance to remember friends and comrades who'd fallen on the field of battle. There were too many names to be read out, but there were rumours of a monument to be built in London somewhere. Although they served a vital purpose, Eddie didn't need memorials to remember his friends. As voices lifted in prayer around him, Eddie thought about Mac, Steve, and Digger. He would never forget Spike and Griff either, and Eddie had already written both men up so the government might recognise their service and courage. The hope was that his recommendations would be rubber-stamped, and their families would have something official. Time would tell, but it might be a long wait.

Eddie glanced over his shoulder. Behind him, across the aisle, he saw Colonel Butler, the commanding officer of the 2nd Mass – now the 10th Rifles – and his distinctive eyepatch. He recognised a few of the senior officers too, but most of the other faces behind them were unrecognisable. Replacements, probably, to fill the gaps left by Mac and hundreds of others killed and wounded.

As the last hymn note drifted towards the ceiling and everyone took their seats, Eddie thought about the future and the work that lay ahead. It would take years before they cleared every mine in the North Sea, before they discovered and dismantled every booby-trap in every police station and army barracks across England and Wales, before they repaired every road and runway, every track and tunnel. It was a mountain to climb, and the damage to the fabric of society might take a lot longer to mend.

Eddie had read the intelligence reports and attended the briefings. Traitors had been found everywhere, and the ISR team dealing with that particular cancer was working overtime to find out if there were still active cells in their midst. For Eddie, his taskings had been a little more routine. Since the end of hostilities, he'd worked surveillance jobs, spending his time watching residential and commercial addresses for suspicious activity. The few raids he'd been on had turned up little more than weapons stolen from the battlefield by opportunists. The country was awash with guns, and somewhere down the line, Eddie knew there would have to be an amnesty to get them off the streets. Unexploded munitions had killed many people too. It was usually kids messing around with hand grenades, or shooting themselves with recovered weapons, and in too many cases, tripping claymore and anti-personnel mines. Dog walking and country rambles would never be the same, not for many years.

Up in his pulpit, the Bishop of London finished his reading and invited Prime Minister Harry Beecham to take the stand. Eddie remembered the last time he'd seen the man, in that draughty, damp gymnasium in Otterburn, just before they went into the tunnels. He craned his neck and saw Beecham rise out of the front pew and head towards the pulpit. He stumbled on the stairs, and laughter rippled through the pews of uniforms. It died away, and then the Prime Minister was tapping the microphone and clearing his throat...

'BEFORE YOU ASK, NO, I HAVEN'T BEEN DRINKING.'

Laughter greeted his comment, and Harry smiled, gazing at the sea of faces stretching away towards the distant western entrance, and to his left and right, where more service personnel packed the north and south transepts. And yes, he *was* drunk, but just a little. His dress shoes were new, and 300 years of traffic had made the stone steps treacherous for an unsuspecting speaker. Anyone could have slipped.

The booze was a crutch, he knew that. After lunch, he'd felt the first fluttering of a panic attack and nipped a little vodka to ward it off. Harry was suffering from his own brand of PTSD, a suspicion confirmed after talking to the wounded and their medical teams during his many hospital visits. The disorder affected different people in different ways, and though Harry wasn't a soldier, he'd seen his fair share of death and misery, and it had disturbed him. But he wouldn't reveal his condition to a medical professional. Not yet anyway, not until things had settled.

Discussing one's mental health was all very well in some circles, but prime ministers were expected to function, period. A ridiculous concept, of course. No one was immune from the emotional peaks and troughs of life's rollercoaster, especially when those troughs included a loved one being blown to pieces or seeing another thrown from a moving helicopter. And let's not forget putting a bullet through the head of an unarmed man.

A cough echoed through the cathedral, and Harry realised his mind had drifted. He put his hand inside his overcoat, his fingers brushing the silk lining of his pocket. He felt the folded speech beneath his fingers, but when he extracted his hand, it came up empty, and he rested it on the edge of the pulpit. A movement caught his eye, and he saw snowflakes drifting on the cold air of the cathedral. The historic setting stirred something inside Harry, surrounded as he was by flags and uniforms, and where the glow of candles had thrown the walls into shadow, invoking images of clans gathering beneath the straw roof of an ancient chieftain's hut. Expectant faces stared back at him, and he spoke into the microphone.

'I had a speech, a very nice one. I was going to read it, but I've had second thoughts. You've all been here a long time, you see. You've sung hymns and listened to the words of the Bishop and the Chief of Defence, and frankly, there's little I could say that those august gentlemen haven't already said. But as I'm here, stood before you as your prime minister, I feel I should say something. So here goes ...'

He glanced over to the front pew, and saw the fervent whisperings of Faye Junger and other Cabinet members. To hell with the lot of them, he decided.

'We all remember where we were when the war began. I was in my Downing Street apartment when the first bomb detonated. My wife died in the blast, as did many friends and colleagues, not to mention the police officers on duty and the civilians outside Downing Street, either taking pictures or protesting against me.'

No laugh this time, just a pin-drop silence. At least he had their attention.

'At that moment, the world changed, and all of us changed with it. As prime minister, I'd spent little time with the men and women of our armed services. Yes, I'd shaken hands and attended Remembrance Day parades, but one can never understand an organisation until one is on the inside. On that terrible day, the first to arrive was the Special Air Service...' Harry scanned the pews. 'Are there any of those illustrious gentlemen here this evening? Come on, don't be shy, raise your hands.'

Harry laughed at his own joke and was pleased to hear that laugh echoed amongst the thousands of uniforms sat around him. His smile faded.

'They saved my life that night. And two of them died later that same year. They went willingly into battle, like the thousands I spoke to before the fight on the Scottish border. I remember being surrounded by camouflaged faces, barely visible in the dark, and wondering how many would survive. Quite a few, thank God, but not as many as I'd prayed for.'

He turned to his left and nodded at the contingent of US and Irish troops packing the south transept.

'And then America opened her doors to us and gave us the opportunity to retake the lands of our forefathers. And for that, we will be forever grateful ...'

Harry paused as the emotion of the moment got to him. Before he knew it, he was reaching into his coat, not for the speech, but for the leather-bound hip flask tucked inside the other pocket.

'I probably shouldn't be doing this, but to hell with it.' He flipped off the lid and raised it up. 'To all of you here — and to those who are not — I thank you, on behalf of the people of Britain and Ireland. And I drink to your health and to the memory of your fallen comrades. God bless the bloody lot of you.'

Harry tipped the vodka down his throat and swallowed, wincing as the alcohol burned his throat. He snapped the lip back on and looked up. There was complete silence in the cathedral. Harry tucked the flask back inside his coat and leaned into the microphone. 'Now, go and get pissed. That's an order.'

The first clap echoed from the middle of the infantry pews, and then it spread as fast as a rumour of free beer. Within seconds, the whole cathedral was clapping, and by the time Harry made it down the steps and was crossing the floor to his pew, the clapping had grown into a thunderous, cheering roar that threatened to lift the roof off the building. Even the civilians were pumping their hands together, but some of his Cabinet had refrained. Harry couldn't care less. This service wasn't about them. Anyone who didn't like that could take a long jump off a short pier. He squeezed back into his seat.

'Bloody marvellous,' Lee Wilde said, grinning from ear to ear.

The thunder continued, now accompanied by the stamp of boots and cheering voices, the clamour rising into the eaves of the great cathedral and out through the fractured roof into the snowy night air of London.

[46]

RAT TRAP

THE PUB WAS CALLED THE RED LION AND THE NAME OF THE
man drinking at the bar was Clive Harris. At his feet was a supermarket carrier bag with a gift inside, a remote-controlled tank for his
sister's boy. Paying for it had annoyed Harris because the purchase
had eaten into his stash. There was still plenty left, at least a couple
of grand. He used to have a lot of jewellery too, but as several pawn-
brokers had told him, all that glittered wasn't always kosher. He only
had a couple of genuine pieces left, a chunky gold ring and a necklace
with a sparkly little stone that he'd ripped from the neck of a kid after
he'd raped her. That piece was definitely worth something because
the first shylock who'd looked at it had offered him 50 bucks after a
longer than usual examination with his little glass eye. So, at least he
had that in the bank. But he needed money.

'How's the job situation looking, Clive?'

'I've got some irons in the fire,' Harris said, lying to the floppy-
haired, 30-something barman who hovered nearby, polishing glasses.
The pub was quiet today, but Harris didn't mind. It gave him time to
think because he couldn't do it back at his sister's house, not with her
fucking brat running around all day.

'I've got something for you,' he said to the barman, reaching into his pocket and unwrapping a gold ring from a silk cloth as if it were the Hope diamond. He left it on the bar and watched every one of its nine carats and cut-glass glinting beneath the bar lights.

'How about that? Lovely, right? Used to belong to my aunt. We just lost her to cancer.' Harris frowned, the lie rolling off his tongue. 'This was her engagement ring, a proper antique. It would make a lovely Christmas gift for someone. You've got a woman, right?'

The barman shook his head. 'No.'

Harris' eyes narrowed. 'You're not a poof, are ya?'

'Course not,' the younger man replied.

'In that case, you can have it for 250, cash.'

The barman laughed. 'I can't afford that.'

Harris bit his lip. 'As it's you, 200, but I'm giving it away at that price. My nan will be rolling in her grave, God bless her.'

'I thought she was your aunt.'

'That's what I said.'

The barman shrugged. 'I've no use for it, Clive. Sorry.'

Harris scowled and snatched the ring off the bar. He tapped the rim of his glass. 'Give me another. Make it a large one.'

He knew he'd get rid of the thing eventually, but it would mean travelling to another town, then schlepping around its pubs and coffee shops in search of some mug punter who would take it off his hands. And that might be hard work.

Harris dug into his pocket and slapped a note on the bar. The truth was he needed work, but finding legitimate employment was going to be tricky. Cash in hand was all very well, but what he needed was something permanent, with a regular wage, and that meant applying for a National ID card, which, in Clive Harris' case, wasn't a good idea. He needed one that would pass muster and open all the right doors to a normal life. His sister had a real one, and it was tricky looking thing with chips and holograms and all sorts of high-tech nonsense. It wasn't like getting a bent passport back in the day. Still, something would turn up, and if it cost him half of his stash to re-join society, then so be it. The important thing was leaving the past behind him. He'd had a good war, but now it was time to move on and enjoy the peace.

The barman returned with his drink, a large dark rum and coke. Another two or three and he could cope with going home. At first, he was grateful to his sister for taking him in. Her old man had run off with another woman on the estate, so she was grateful for the extra cash. No one had stepped into his slippers either, which was no surprise because the Harris family tree had never borne any attractive fruit. That meant no strange geezers sniffing around the house, which was fine by Harris. But she liked her booze, and when she was pissed, she gobbed off. She'd threatened him with exposure once, after a huge barney. It hadn't happened again, but Harris didn't trust her anymore. If she became a threat, she'd have to go. And the kid. Harris hoped it wouldn't come to that, though. He had enough grief on his plate.

The pub door creaked open, and four men entered. They wore scruffy jeans and yellow hi-vis vests, and they stood at the bar and ordered drinks, joshing amongst themselves. Harris watched them and smiled. He missed a bit of banter, missed all the horsing around and piss-taking with the lads. He stared at one of them, a big fella with blonde hair, and he thought the man looked familiar. Harris had seen a lot of faces these last few years, had met a lot of people, but most of them were dead. This one was alive, which meant he might be like Harris. The big fella paid for the drinks — shots, not pints, which meant they would move on soon enough. That would annoy the barman, Harris knew. The Red Lion wasn't exactly heaving these days. Still, it was a decent pub, with interesting booze and cheap grub. There were a lot worse places to kill time, namely that shithole of an estate he now called home.

'Can I get you a drink, friend?'

Harris turned and saw the big fella was smiling at him. He put a hand over his glass. 'I'm good, thanks, pal.'

He turned away and fingered his change on the bar. The man

spoke again, and it wasn't the voice of a manual labourer. He pronounced his tees and aitches, like the officers he used to salute back in the day.

'Come on, we're celebrating. My firm just won a new contract, demolishing the shopping centre in town. You know, the one that burned down.'

Harris had seen it. A lot of shopping centres had been destroyed during the withdrawal. 'I know the one.'

'I don't suppose you're looking for work, are you? It's cash in hand.'

He passed a business card along the bar, and Harris picked it up. *Regency Construction.* 'What sort of money are you paying?'

'Two hundred a day. And overtime if you want it.'

That was decent coin, but the idea of working eight hours a day put Harris off. He tapped the card on the bar and slipped it in his pocket. 'I might know some people. Good lads, hard workers.'

The big fella held out his hand. 'Appreciate that. What's your name?'

'John.'

The big fella nodded. 'I'm Theo.'

Theo leaned on the bar beside him, sipping his drink and staring. 'It's odd, but I've a feeling we've met before.'

Harris stared back. 'I was thinking the same thing.'

Theo looked over his shoulder, then lowered his voice. 'I used to work around Aldershot, Camberley, that area. In the recent past.'

'Me too. What did you do?'

'Nothing heavy, just driving mainly. You?'

Harris opened his mouth to speak, then changed his mind. *Loose lips sink ships.* The lure of money had clouded his usual caution. A stupid mistake. He looked at his watch. 'Shit, I didn't realise the time.' He slipped off his stool, finished his drink, and tugged on a black puffer jacket. 'It was nice talking to you, pal. I'll call you, okay?'

'Thanks, John.'

Harris picked up the carrier bag and walked towards the door. Theo's words boomed around the bar.

'Wait! I remember now.'

Harris stopped and turned, even though a voice inside him was telling him to get the fuck out. 'What?'

Theo snapped his fingers and pointed. 'It's Clive, isn't it?'

Harris swallowed and shook his head. 'You must have me confused with someone else.'

He saw the barman frown. Harris turned to leave. Two of Theo's lumpy associates had blocked the door. One of them had a police baton in his hand and Harris' heart sank. Behind him, Theo was still talking.

'Clive Harris, erstwhile member of the Aldershot Militia, Penal Support Group.' Harris turned back. Theo was holding up a small black notebook. 'I remember taking your name at Bisley.'

Harris knew the odds were against him, but it wasn't over yet. The lock knife in his back pocket might buy him a bit of time if he could get to it fast enough. He swapped the carrier bag into his left hand and reached for it —

The baton smashed against his elbow. Harris screamed, and then the yellow vests grabbed him and ran him against the bar, knocking the wind from his lungs. Theo leaned over him, waving a badge in front of Harris' face.

'Theo Banks, National Police Force, War Crimes Division. Clive Harris, I'm arresting you for murder. You do not have to say anything, but it may harm your defence if —'

'You've got the wrong man,' Harris yelled, his voice screeching in pain. He felt cold steel ratcheting around his wrists as they locked his hands behind him. Searing pain shot up his right arm. 'That fucking hurts!'

Theo stared at him. 'You really don't remember me, do you?'

'I've never been to Aldershot in my life.' Harris grimaced as the pain ebbed and flowed around his clicking elbow. He growled over his shoulder. 'You broke my fucking arm, you cunt!'

Theo spun him around and slammed him back against the bar, squashing his shattered elbow. Harris screamed. Theo knocked it out of his mouth with a vicious slap. 'Take a good look!'

Harris stared at him through pain-filled eyes. There was something about him, the blonde hair, the height, the voice. He had a fleeting memory of someone similar asking for his name after —

His eyes widened.

'Bingo,' Theo said, but he wasn't smiling. 'I was with Chief Justice Hardy the day we came to witness one of your appalling executions. The churchgoers. The ones you tied to posts and chopped to pieces with a claymore mine. Including that little girl. You remember, don't you?' He pulled back his hand and slapped him again.

Pain ripped through Harris' neck. 'I had no fucking choice!'

'You were just following orders, right?' Theo nodded to the yellow vests. 'Get him outside.'

The vests ran him towards the doors and used his face to open them. Harris felt his nose break and blood poured down the front of his puffer jacket. Then they were outside, his legs stumbling as they hurried across the car park towards a waiting van. They bundled him inside and climbed aboard. Another vest got behind the wheel, and Theo sat in the passenger seat.

'Where are we going?' Harris gasped, blood and snot dripping between his legs.

'You're going to court,' Theo said.

Harris frowned. 'I'm entitled to a doctor. And a solicitor.'

Theo and the others laughed. 'You're entitled to jack shit.'

A yellow vest covered his head with a black hood and Harris kept his mouth shut for the rest of the journey. He hadn't admitted to anything so far, and he intended to keep it that way. And they'd broken his nose and arm, which meant hospital, and the chance of escape.

Harris wasn't sure how much time passed. His nose and elbow were killing him, and the grinding bones were making him nauseous.

Eventually, the van slowed, and he heard shouting and big gates rattling open. The van pulled forward and brakes squealed. They dragged the hood off his head. Outside, dirty grey walls towered around him. A prison courtyard.

'You're remanding me? Already?'

'Move!'

His elbow crunched as Theo led the way into a harshly lit corridor. They turned a corner, then Harris heard voices ahead. Uniforms lined the walls, men and women, some wearing black fleeces and bright orange armbands with NPF in black letters. There were other cops too, in plainclothes like Theo and his crew, who now wore those same armbands. They all saw the blood and the busted nose, but none of them took any notice. Above his head, a sign hung from the ceiling: *JUSTICE MINISTRY – SERVING THE PEOPLE.* Harris knew he was in a world of shit.

There was a queue ahead of him, three men, all cuffed and crowded by cops. The big wooden door in front of them opened and a voice boomed down the corridor.

'Next case!'

They dragged the men into the room, and the door closed again. Before it did, Harris caught a flash of red robes. He spoke over his shoulder.

'This ain't a court, is it?'

'No talking.'

'I want to speak to a solicitor.'

Theo punched Harris in the back of the head. The faces along the wall stared at him with cold eyes. This wasn't like the old days, with snowflake cops and courtrooms that fell for every sob story going. This was something else.

The minutes passed. His elbow screamed and his head pounded, but he'd get no sympathy from his captors. He had to wait a little longer until they banged him up. Then he'd get to see the doctor. The big door opened in front of him.

'Next case!' a court official barked.

Harris grunted as they marched him into the room. He stumbled down a flight of steps and into the well of the court. Three judges in red robes and wigs sat above him beneath a huge crest and the words JUSTICE MINISTRY beneath it. He looked around but he saw no jury, no public gallery, only a bunch of other wigs and a stenographer. A man stood behind a tripod, his video camera pointed right at him. He saw his face in closeup on an enormous TV screen on the wall to his right. Then it disappeared, replaced by his militia ID card. *Fuck!*

'That's not me.'

'Silence!' a judge barked, cracking his gavel down.

Harris bit his tongue. The judge in the middle, a nasty-looking Jew-boy with a hooked nose and cold blue eyes, spoke.

'You have been identified as Clive Harris, a former member of the Aldershot Militia, Penal Support Group. Is this correct?'

Harris shook his head. 'No, sir. There's been a mistake.'

The judge pointed to the TV screen. 'Are you saying that is not your ID card?'

'I don't know nothing about no militia.'

The judge stared at him as if he were an insect. 'This courtroom will not tolerate lies. You have one opportunity to tell the truth – just one – which will be taken into consideration when your sentence is pronounced. Do you understand?' Harris nodded, cowed. 'So, I ask you again, were you a member of the Aldershot Militia, Penal Support Group?'

Harris lowered his head. 'Yes, your honour.'

'Were you a willing participant in the execution of over 1200 people, carried out at Bisley Ranges under the direct supervision of Sergeant Bilal Aziz?'

Harris swallowed. The game was up. 'They forced me into it. I had no choice.'

The judge looked away. 'Officer Banks, can you confirm that this is the man you witnessed playing an active role in a mass execution at Bisley?'

Theo's voice boomed around the court. 'Yes, your honour. He offered me a claymore trigger to give to Chief Justice Hardy as a souvenir.'

'Is this the item?' A green object wrapped in a plastic evidence bag appeared on the TV screen.

Theo nodded. 'It is.'

The judge held a hand over his microphone and conferred with his wigged colleagues. Their murmurings were indecipherable, but Harris knew he was bang to rights. His only option was to beg for mercy. A few tears could be the difference between ten years or life imprisonment. And if there was grovelling to be done, Harris could slurp with the best of them.

He heard the thump of the judge's microphone, and then the man's crisp voice filled the courtroom.

'Clive Harris, this court finds you guilty of war crimes. You will be escorted to this facility's execution room and hanged by the neck until you are dead. May God have mercy upon your soul.'

Harris looked around the court, at the faces watching him, the officials in their black robes, the stenographer, her fingers poised above her keys. Nothing made sense. He turned back to the judge. 'What?'

The gavel cracked. 'Take him down.'

The yellow vests bundled him out of the room and into an empty corridor of grey walls. Theo marched ahead.

'Wait!' he shouted after him. 'What's going on? What did he mean, *hanged*?'

His broken bones crunched, but Harris felt no pain. Fear consumed him as his reluctant feet squeaked and scraped on the tiled floor. Ahead, two guards threw open a set of double doors and they marched Harris into the prison gymnasium.

Only it wasn't.

He saw a stage at the far end of the room, constructed of scaffolding and timber boards standing at least 15 feet high. In the middle of it, gallows, and a dangling noose.

'No! This ain't right! You can't do this!'

They dragged him across the squeaky gym floor past the onlookers. Harris saw medics standing by a wheeled stretcher, more guards, and a group of people, grim-faced men and women standing beneath the stage. One of them stared at him and smiled as he ran a finger across his neck.

A photographer snapped away as they bundled him up the stairs. The boards creaked beneath his trainers, and a priest stood next to the hangman, a purple stole draped around his shoulders as he muttered something that Harris couldn't understand.

'Please! As God is my witness! You've got the wrong man!'

The floor beneath him gave a little, and Harris looked down. A trap door. *This is really happening!* The hangman stepped forward, a big bloke in his sixties, maybe older, his grey hair shaved close. He wore a white shirt and black tie, and he looped the noose over Harris' head, the rough rope scratching Harris' face and neck.

'Please,' Harris whispered, but the man was oblivious. Harris choked as the knot was tightened. The vests let go of his arms and Harris stood alone on the scaffold, the faces below staring up at him. *So, this is it,* he realised. Standing close enough to touch, Theo stared at him, and Harris felt hot piss soaking his jeans as it steamed in the cold air.

'Go fuck yourself,' he said to his silent audience.

The floor fell away. Harris grunted, and then his life ended.

[47]

ET TU BRUTE?

Harry pushed his chair back and got to his feet, placing a hand on the white tablecloth to steady himself. Someone tapped a crystal glass and the conversation inside the ancient walls of Winchester's Great Hall faded away. Harry looked along the length of the room as all eyes turned towards him. Tonight's gathering was a special celebration, a New Year's Eve party thrown by Harry himself as a thank you to everyone who'd worked hard to get his government up on its feet. It was a black-tie event, and the 200 guests sat at long tables lit by large clusters of candles. Earlier, an excellent dinner had been served and now party poppers, buckets of champagne and wine filled the tables. The 12th century building was a magical setting, and even though Harry had enjoyed several drinks already, he recharged his flute in anticipation of the bells. He'd see in the New Year properly, then give up the booze. A recent medical and a dressing down from his doctor left him no choice. From tomorrow, he would embrace a new regime of diet and exercise. Or he'd try at least. He was sure he wasn't the only one in the room making similar vows.

Behind him, mounted on the stone wall, was King Arthur's round table, and he couldn't help feeling a sense of history as the first day of a new year approached. A year when Britain would be free again.

'Can you hear me at the back?' Distant partygoers greeted the comment with raised glasses and cheery responses. 'Good. And don't worry, I'll keep this short.' He cleared his throat. 'It's appropriate that we're gathered here tonight in the Great Hall, where former English rulers and their councils have mustered over the last 800 years. Looking around this stunning building, it's difficult not to feel that sense of history. We, too, are living through historic times, and now a new task awaits us all: the transformation of this country, as we Build Back Britain.'

He saw a few eye-rolls and amused whispers amongst his Cabinet scattered around the top tables. Harry was past caring what they thought of him, and after the weekend, he would announce a reshuffle. Certain people were about to get a rude awakening.

'But tonight, we celebrate and look forward to the coming year with hope in our hearts and a determination to put this country back on its feet. So please, raise your glasses ...' He raised his. 'And to all of you, I wish you a safe, happy, and prosperous New Year.'

Glasses raised up around the room.

'Ten seconds!' a voice shouted, and the room started counting down. Chairs scraped and tables shuddered as everyone got to their feet, the smiling faces already exchanging hugs and kisses ...

'Three, two, one ... Happy New Year!'

Balloons drifted down from the ceiling and the band at the back of the hall struck up a jazzy rendition of Auld Lang Syne. Harry spent the next few minutes shaking lots of hands and kissing cheeks. Lee Wilde chinked his glass against Harry's.

'Happy New Year, Prime Minister.'

'Let's hope so,' Harry said, smiling. He flinched as a popper exploded nearby, and he saw Nina being thrown from the helicopter, her screams snatched away by the roar of the engines —

'Harry?'

'Sorry, Lee. You were saying?'

'I said, it's going to get better.'

He smiled. 'No doubt.'

Harry retook his seat and watched the cheerful faces, saw the balloons batted over the heads of the movers and shakers dancing in front of the band. It was a joyful night, and Harry had every right to feel some of that joy, but it was proving difficult, and he felt very alone. Another drink and he'd call it a night, slip away as quietly as protocol would allow. Tomorrow was a new day. His hangover would be a shocker, but it would be his last for some time.

'Happy New Year, Harry.'

He turned to see Faye Junger standing at his shoulder, looking elegant in a white evening dress. Her copper-red hair had been cut short and expensively styled, and her makeup was flawless. He got to his feet and pecked her cheeks. 'And the same to you, Faye.'

'Could I have a word? In private.'

Harry raised an eyebrow. 'Is everything okay?'

She smiled. 'It won't take a moment.'

He finished his drink and followed her out into the dimly-lit cloisters. He waved away his tuxedoed security officer, and she walked ahead of him, like a ghost moving through the shadows. Without a word, she stepped through a large arched door studded with big iron nails. He'd had his differences with Faye, and she was top of his list for a demotion, so he hoped this wouldn't be an inappropriate encounter. He didn't think she was drunk – Faye was too canny for that – but the mystery of the moment intrigued him.

A small group of people waited inside the shadowy room, most of them from his Cabinet. Foreign Secretary Shelley Walker, the Welsh and Scottish secretaries Maddox and Nicol, the Health and Transport ministers, and several other ministers-without-portfolio. In fact, everyone on his reshuffle list, and Harry wondered where the leak had come from. He saw no drinks in anyone's hand, no smiles on their faces. So, they knew. He feigned ignorance anyway.

'What's wrong? Has something happened?'

Junger was the first to speak. 'We needed to speak to you in private, Harry. Before the New Year gets underway.'

The door creaked open behind him, and Wilde walked in. He stood next to his boss.

'What's going on, Harry?'

'Faye's about to tell us.'

Harry's deputy folded her arms across her narrow chest. 'We'd like you to stand down. Resign your position, before we begin the New Year session.'

Harry wasn't expecting that. He opened his mouth to respond, but Wilde was quicker on the draw.

'You're out of order, Faye.'

'Let's hear her out, Lee.' His temper boiled. They'd ambushed him, and it had clearly been planned for some time. Lee was right. He should've fired Junger a long time ago. His eyes bored into hers. 'Well?'

'We don't think you're the right person to lead the country,' she said. 'Not anymore.'

'Really?' He looked at the others. 'Are you all in agreement?'

Maddox cocked his chin. 'We are,' he said, his broad Welsh brogue emphatic. 'Everyone of us. And there are others too.'

'You should be ashamed of yourselves,' Wilde said. 'You're a disgrace.'

Junger took a step forward. 'It's been tough for you, Harry. You've lost people, but you've taken things too personally. I think that's clouded your judgement.'

'We've all lost loved ones,' Harry replied. 'And yes, I consider the invasion of my country to be a personal violation. It troubles me you don't.' He glanced at the others. 'Any of you.'

Nicol was next to plunge the dagger. 'Your drinking is a problem. Your speech at St Paul's was an embarrassment.'

'Not for the men and women in uniform,' Wilde said, glaring at the scowling Scot. 'Harry has the respect of the armed forces. He's the only person here who can command such loyalty.'

Junger shrugged. 'The war's over. Now we must move forward. Diplomacy will be key, and you've put some important noses out of joint, Harry.'

'You mean Riley?'

'I do. Your resignation might improve relations with the White House.'

Harry smirked. 'He's not interested, Faye. And it's not about me. Riley's not a fan of the UK. He's expressed that view to me directly, and on more than one occasion.'

'US troops caused a hell of a lot of damage in Wales,' Maddox said. 'Civilians were killed. Where was the outrage? The pushback? You didn't say a word.'

Wilde sneered. 'It's complicated, Ceri. I doubt you'd understand.'

'Fuck off, Lee. You're a lapdog, that's all. So, heel, boy.'

'Enough!' Harry yelled, his anger resonating off the stone walls. Tongues were bitten. He took a breath and focused on Junger.

'The Americans are still defending our seas and skies, and the gas deal they brokered is a good one. We should be grateful for that. Trust me, Faye, you won't get any more out of him than I did.'

Junger shook her head. 'There are other players out there. The world doesn't revolve around the United States.'

Harry snorted. 'If it wasn't for them, we wouldn't be standing here having this conversation. You need to park your personal prejudices, Faye, and start focusing on the bigger picture.'

'Others have reached out to us already. The European Congress for starters. They might be a fledgling organisation, but they have a powerful vision for the future, and they've been instrumental in the rebuilding of some of Europe's capital cities after the recent troubles.'

Harry laughed, but there was no humour in his voice. 'Troubles, you say. I believe you're referring to the invasion of Europe. You know, the one that cost the lives of millions of people.'

'We have to look forward, Harry. There are new voices in Baghdad.'

Harry couldn't believe his ears. 'You want to talk to Al-Issa?' He shook his head. 'There are hundreds of thousands of British citizens still missing and you want to cosy up to the caliphate?' His eyes narrowed. 'I've misjudged you, Faye. I thought you were better than this. Now I see you're naïve and opportunistic. You disappoint me.'

'We're all agreed,' Foreign Secretary Walker said. 'We can't rely on the Americans to keep throwing us crumbs. And what's an appropriate length of time to wait before we talk to Baghdad? The Americans have been dealing with them for months, which is why the boats are bringing our people back.'

'The Americans aren't talking,' Harry explained. 'They're dictating. You're the Foreign Secretary, so you should be able to recognise the difference.' He saw her face flush, and it pleased him. 'In five years, the caliphate's economic model will collapse. Other carbon-based economies will die off around the world, so you're backing the wrong horse.'

Junger frowned. 'Do you know something we don't, Harry?'

'I'll put it to you like this. Make an enemy of the United States, and you'll regret it for decades. Whatever we think privately, our public face must be one of solidarity and fraternity with our American cousins. For the sake of the British people and the economic prosperity of this country.'

Strangely, they didn't seem cowed by his warning.

'The Cabinet reconvenes next week,' Junger said to him. 'When it does, I'll table a motion of no confidence. I have the numbers, Harry. This is a battle you can't win.'

'I'm not going anywhere. You're unsuited for the job, Faye.' He looked at the others. 'And I'll be asking for resignations from all of you.'

'Tell him,' Maddox said, staring at Harry.

'Tell me what?'

Junger took a step closer. 'Major Goran Vidich was married with two children. At the time of his death, he was a prisoner of war, with rights under the Geneva Convention. You murdered him in cold blood.'

'So what?' Wilde shouted at her. 'He threw Nina out of a fucking helicopter.'

'Thanks for corroborating,' Maddox said. 'Not that it was necessary. Roland-Jones has a file on the incident. There are witness statements.'

Wilde boiled. 'No soldier will ever take the stand against Harry.'

'If it's a choice between prison and testifying, they will.'

'We'd rather it didn't go public,' Junger told Harry. 'But if it did, you'll face trial for war crimes. You'll go to prison, and your legacy will be shredded. Is that what you want?'

Wilde glared at her. 'You bitch.'

'That's enough, Lee.' Harry could feel everything slipping away. He turned to Junger. 'And if I step aside, this war crime nonsense will magically disappear, yes?'

Junger nodded. 'I'm giving you the chance to get help.'

Harry's temper flared. 'I don't need help.'

'I've been made aware of your medical condition, Harry. As a matter of national security. Sleeping pills, antidepressants, alcohol abuse —'

Harry flushed. 'Why don't you go next door and tell the whole fucking party. That's private information.'

'Not when you're the prime minister.'

'You've no right,' he said, but the rebellious edge to his voice was no longer there. The will to fight was ebbing fast. Junger read his face.

'Give us the room,' she said, and the others filed outside. Junger stared at Wilde and raised an eyebrow.

'He stays,' Harry said.

'Fine.' Junger turned to Harry and softened her tone. 'The vote will go my way, Harry. It's a done deal. But politics aside, you've been through the mill, lost your wife, your friends, Nina...' She offered him a sympathetic smile. 'The stress has been unimaginable these last few years, so you should look at this as an opportunity. You can leave office with your head held high and your reputation intact, and we'll never speak of these things again. Not as long as we are agreeable.'

Wilde growled. 'Blackmail, Faye? Really?'

Harry shook his head. 'It's okay, Lee.'

He stared at Junger for several moments. She was right. This was an opportunity to walk away, to slip the chains of office and unburden himself from all the responsibilities that were keeping him awake at night. He imagined himself rising after the sun for once, to a silent house, to a long, lazy day ahead, to an empty inbox and a calendar that contained only lunches, dinners and social events. No more crises to manage, no more speeches, no guns and helicopters, no more shaking hands, and emotional commiserations. He was exhausted, running on empty. Another nervous breakdown was on the cards, and this time Mike Reynolds wouldn't be there to keep his secret. This time Junger would ensure a very public episode, and Harry didn't want to leave under those circumstances. Already he could feel the first of those shackles slipping from his shoulders.

He smiled. 'You win, Faye. I'll resign —'

Wilde spun towards him. 'Harry, don't do this.'

'But I have conditions,' Harry continued, ignoring his chief of staff. 'I'll draft my own statement, then go public the day after tomorrow. We can do the handover after that, at your convenience. That way you can start the New Year session without me.'

Junger bobbed her head. 'Agreed.'

'And I want the Vidich file destroyed,' Harry said. 'As Lee rightly pointed out, it's blackmail, and I won't be a party to that. Something in writing from the Attorney General's office will suffice. Or I'll take my chance in court.'

'I'll see to it,' Junger said.

And she would, Harry knew, because she craved the power of office more than anything. Harry turned his back on her. 'Come on, Lee, let's get a drink.'

They headed back to the Great Hall, and Harry retook his seat. He topped up his glass with champagne and knocked it back in a couple of gulps. Then he refilled it, and Wilde's glass too. His chief of staff still simmered.

'Don't be disheartened, Lee. We had a good run, and we did our very best. That's all we can ask of ourselves.' Harry nudged his elbow. 'And we won a war, don't forget.'

Wilde necked his drink, then shook his head. 'It's the way they did it, Harry. A bloody ambush. Tonight, of all nights.'

'There's never a good time,' Harry said. 'In fact, I think Faye's done me a favour.'

'Really?' Wilde loosened the bow tie from around his neck. 'How so? She stabbed you in the back.'

'She's set me free.' He smiled and took another sip of champagne. 'I'm going to lie in tomorrow. No alarms, nothing. Faye can deal with anything that comes up.'

Wilde nodded. 'I'll let everyone know.'

Harry sat back, enjoying the atmosphere, a mild sense of euphoria taking hold of him. It was over. He was done with it all, and it made him happy. His chief of staff was wrong about the timing. It was perfect, and he thanked his conspirators for that.

Wilde broke the silence. 'What will you do? Afterwards.'

'Whatever I like,' Harry said, smiling. 'I think I'll get lost for a while, do some reading. And write. Get the whole story down, from the moment I woke up on the day of the invasion.'

'It'll be a best-seller,' Wilde said.

Harry shook his head. 'It's just for me, Lee. So I can purge it all from my system. It'll be good for me, I think.'

'If I can be of any help, Harry, you'll let me know, yes?'

'Of course.' Harry raised an eyebrow. 'What about you? What will you do?'

Wilde jerked a thumb over his shoulder. 'I won't work for that nest of snakes, that's for sure.' He swallowed the rest of his champagne. 'I'm not sure. There'll be other opportunities out there. The private sector, probably.'

Harry held out his hand. 'You've been a good friend, Lee.'

Wilde took his hand and shook it. 'It's been a privilege and an honour to serve, Prime Minister.'

Harry raised his glass. 'Happy New Year.'

'And the same to you, Harry.'

[48]

HOME AGAIN

THE BUS JERKED TO A STOP AND DROPPED HIM BY THE ROAD where the snow lay piled up in high banks. With a hiss of air brakes, the bus pulled away, and Eddie watched its red lights disappear around a distant corner, its grumbling diesel engine fading to nothing.

The wind blew, the Union flag on the pole above him rippling and snapping. Snow flurries rushed to welcome him, wrapping him in their icy embrace. After the warmth of the bus, the freezing temperatures were a shock to Eddie's system, and he stamped his feet as he took his bearings. He was travelling light, just a few personals folded into his daysack, plus some reading material that Hawkins had suggested he bone up on for his next job. It was all public domain stuff, journals, and travel diaries, but it would give him a good insight into the area, the climate, the weather patterns, the nomadic tribes that crisscrossed the region. What wasn't common knowledge was the slave labour, on a biblical scale, Hawkins had told him. It sounded like an interesting tasking, but as far as mission objectives were concerned, Eddie was clueless. Maybe he would find out in due course. If he stayed on.

He crossed the square, passing the snow-crusted memorial where faded poppy wreaths lay partly buried at its base. As he walked, head down into the wind, Eddie cast his mind back to Old London, to the time before Christmas and the service at St Paul's. He smiled when he remembered Beecham's speech, and there was speculation that the man was pissed when he gave it, but nobody in uniform had cared less. Beecham had been there from day one, from the moment the vehicle IED had tried to take him out, killing a bunch of others and his wife instead. The lads from Hereford had got him out, and Beecham was there up on the border, visiting the troops before the attack that claimed Kyle's life. Three years later, the PM had returned with the troops, and thank God he had. Hawkins told Eddie that it was Beecham himself who'd pressured the Americans to pluck them from that Birmingham rooftop.

The prime minister's resignation had disappointed Eddie, and strangely, no one had seen the man since. His successor, Junger, was a bit of a cold fish, and Eddie hadn't taken to her. She liked to use a lot of buzzwords, and he doubted she would beg anyone to get a few squaddies out of trouble. Eddie just didn't get that vibe from her. Still, if she did her job and helped Britain back on its feet, then he'd cut her some slack. Time would tell.

After the service at St Paul's, Eddie had teamed up with his old Charlie Company mates and they'd all got seriously pissed. It was an emotional time, and the lads had questioned him about their disappearance from the battlefield and the deaths of Mac, Steve, and Digger. Eddie couldn't talk about it, but he told all who listened that they'd gone down fighting, and glasses were raised in their honour. Eddie didn't remember much after that.

The next day, at the ISR London headquarters on Jermyn Street, Eddie had used the database to track down Spike and discovered he was working at a prison in Kent. He cadged a ride on a helicopter from London City Airport and met Spike at HMP Barling, a sprawling city of huts and security fences built on four square miles of MOD land close to the Thames Estuary. It was an emotional reunion for them both, and Spike explained his role as interpreter for the Justice Ministry, which he admitted was more interesting than being an estate agent in Birmingham. Both were still amazed by the timing and method of their escape.

After their catch-up, they had a long conversation about Eddie's time in London, primarily about Griff's recruitment and subsequent death. Spike told him what Eddie already knew — that Griff had taken a chance, the same way that Spike had risked his own life. It was cold, but it was the truth. It didn't make Eddie feel any better, and he would never forget Griff's chalk-white face bobbing in that foaming black water as he pleaded for help. Griff had died in pain, frightened, and no doubt regretting the day he'd met Eddie Novak. As Spike said before they'd parted, it was something Eddie would have to live with.

Days later, back in London, Eddie sat down with Hawkins and discussed next steps. He decided HUMINT taskings weren't for him, and Hawkins explained he was an asset, whether or not Eddie liked it. He also ordered him to take some leave and think about it. So, Eddie did.

And there was much to think about. The way Eddie saw it, he had two paths he could take. One led straight back to Charlie Company, and that would mean a predictable cycle of training and deployments, all of them around the UK. But the thought of going back to barrack life didn't exactly motivate Eddie. After everything he'd been through, he felt he'd grown out of it. That he was destined for something else.

The other path would be to stay with 4th ISR, working missions and deployments yet to be defined. A different type of soldiering. There was a third path, outside the armed forces, a job in civvy street, but Eddie's only qualification was a high school diploma from the Massachusetts Board of Education, and that wouldn't get him too far.

So, it was a tossup between the Rifles or stepping into the

unknown with Hawkins' mob, and he wished Kyle was here to advise him. His brother would've shrugged and said, *Do what you want, Eddie. It's your life.* Mac, on the other hand, would've bawled him out: *Is there something wrong with your napper, son? Take the ISR job, ya numpty!*

He'd take his time deciding, enjoy his break, the first since he'd stepped ashore in Ireland a lifetime ago. There would be no distractions, no duties, nothing to do but think. And he might not do too much of that either.

He trudged along the hard-packed snow, past the streets of single-story habitation pods where warm lights glowed behind shuttered windows. He relished the silence as he walked, watching the fresh flakes of snow spiralling down from the black sky above, blowing through the pale wash of streetlamps. Cars passed him by, crunching along icy roads, exhaust pipes smoking in the bitter air. He saw people too, wrapped up against the cold, hurrying for home, and kids playing in the snow. This was normal life, and war was something the people here only saw on TV. They could flip the channel anytime they liked. But to live through it was something else.

War was brutal chaos, where the days were filled with danger and death waited to snatch the careless, the cowards, the innocent, the brave, and often the unlucky. It was depressing, disturbing and sometimes, inexplicably exhilarating. And someplace deep inside him, a tiny part of Eddie missed it.

He turned a corner and saw the familiar half-circle roof piled with snow, the Stars & Stripes flag jutting at an angle on the front porch pole, the single-star banners behind the triple glazed windows, a blue one for Eddie, and a gold one for Kyle. The windows in New London were filled with gold stars.

He kicked the snow off his boots as he stamped up the steps. He took a deep breath and pressed the bell, snatching the beanie off his head and smoothing his hair down. By the front door he saw two pairs of snow boots standing side by side, and he took a deep breath. He heard footsteps inside, then the click of the door latch. It opened.

Eddie tried to smile, tried to say something, but no words would come. The man on the doorstep took off his glasses and stared at Eddie. Then his face crumbled, and he reached out, wrapping Eddie in his arms.

Eddie held him tight. Finally, he found his voice.

'Hello, Dad.'

[49]

SHIP OF DREAMS

BERTIE AND CHERYL STOOD AT THE STERN RAIL OF THE 90,000-ton *Duke of Edinburgh* transatlantic liner and watched the surf pounding the outlying rocks of the Isles of Scilly. The rugged shores of Cornwall had already slipped behind the grey horizon, but this last, remote tract of English soil was still visible. A flock of gulls screeched overhead, as if pleading with them not to leave. They were wasting their breath.

Huddled together beneath the snapping flags, Bertie and Cheryl wore matching navy-blue Canada Goose parkas, winter hats and soft leather gloves on their hands. The sky was a solid slab of slate grey that stretched from horizon to horizon, but the forecast for the five-day crossing to New York City was smooth one. That pleased Bertie because the menu in the first-class dining room looked superb. Cheryl wasn't that bothered. She was still finding her sea legs.

The offshore breezes gusted. Bertie held Cheryl close and reflected on the recent past. After leaving Hampstead with that ruck-sack full of riches, his euphoria had soon worn off. Had someone seen them, reported them? Looting was a serious offence. Back at the hotel, they couldn't fit much into the room safe, which meant one of them had to stay in the room. It wasn't an ideal situation, and Bertie had fretted about their next move.

It was Cheryl who'd seen the news report on TV. A famous British actress was giving up her citizenship to move to the United States. In her cut-glass accent, she had publicly thanked President Riley for introducing the Mitchell Act and for giving people a chance to start new lives. The seeds were sown.

They decamped to the Ritz in Piccadilly, where they took a suite with a large safe. The next day they joined a long queue outside Claridge's. When they finally made it inside, Bertie's nerves were tested when an embassy official swiped their ID cards, but as Doc Ruskin had promised, they were the real deal. Credentials confirmed, Bertie and Cheryl moved into the French Salon, an elegant art deco drawing room, where another official formally invited them to join the citizenship buy-in programme. The price was $25,000 each, plus a deposit in a US bank of $250,000. Bertie felt like a crook handing over a bag of money, but the official didn't bat an eyelid. After a tense hour, she returned with JP Morgan bank cards, temporary US passports and unique Social Security numbers. With a smile and a handshake, she gave them a date in January to return and collect their full passports.

The pressure finally lifted, Bertie and Cheryl unwound a little. They spent most of their days walking around London, and when they ventured south towards the river, the scale of the war damage shocked them both. They mourned the loss of so many historic sites and buildings, now replaced by empty, fenced-off tracts of muddy land. They vowed not to venture south of Pall Mall again.

They returned to Claridge's in mid-January and collected their passports. At the travel desk, they booked a suite on the *Duke of Edinburgh*, which was sailing in three days' time. The sinking of the ferry had terrified them both, but the Atlantic was owned by the US Navy, and they couldn't hope for a safer travel corridor. And for reasons he couldn't explain, Bertie didn't want to fly. He wanted to remember the moment he left the UK behind him.

When the ship pushed back from the dock in Plymouth, a few people were waving from the quay, but their departure beneath sluggish grey skies was an uninspiring one. They spent some time in the cabin, then had lunch in one of the ship's many eateries. Later, the captain announced their imminent passage past the Isles of Scilly and Bertie and Cheryl wrapped up and joined the crowds at the stern rail.

All of them had left now, and only Bertie and Cheryl continued to brave the bitter winds. Bertie didn't mind, however. He held Cheryl close as they stood in silence, watching the waves breaking themselves into white foam against the distant rocks. It still surprised Bertie how his life had turned out. A few years ago, he was driving around London, busting his hump to make a living, trying to compete with Uber drivers who were not much more than tourists themselves. Then he'd become a handyman, and Edith Spencer's manservant, a woman who'd turned on her own people without skipping a beat. And she hadn't been the only one. Given enough incentive, people would do anything to survive. Even him.

The murders of Gates and Al-Kaabi still haunted him. He'd come close to death himself and had to kill to survive. He wasn't proud of what he'd done, but then again, he hadn't asked for war and occupation either.

Bertie had never been an ambitious man. He'd wanted nothing more than to earn a wage, live somewhere decent, meet a good woman, watch his beloved Tottenham, go to the pub, and all the other things that people like him did.

The invasion changed all that.

Now his future lay elsewhere, and he realised there wasn't much he would miss. Pubs had become soulless places, where people were still reluctant to tread, and most of them were now glorified coffee shops and restaurants. As for watching football, a lot of grounds around the country had been used as prisons, and sometimes, as execution sites. Nobody needed reminding of that, least of all Bertie.

So, he'd have to get used to calling it soccer from now on. He'd find some moody Yank team to support and watch the players high-five each other every time they passed the ball. Still, he could live with that. But more important than anything else, he had Cheryl, and she was all he needed. He gave her a squeeze, and she nestled in close. She wore a bobble hat, and beneath it, her cheeks were flushed pink by the sharp air.

'Any more thoughts about where we might live, Bertie?'

He shook his head. 'I've no idea, love. Somewhere warm, but not too hot. A nice house, all the mod cons, a bit of land. And a pickup truck. I've always wanted one of those.'

'What will you do with yourself?'

'I might become an Uber driver.' He laughed, then he turned away from the rail and held her close. 'And what about you? Any thoughts? I know you like to keep busy.'

'Oh, I'll be busy all right. Being a mum is hard work, you know.'

Bertie froze, unable to speak. She reached up and put a gloved hand on his grey stubble. 'It's early days, but the doctor says we're both fine and healthy.' She smiled. 'You're going to be a dad, Bertie. And I get to be a mum again.'

The tears came then, Cheryl first, and then, as he held her tight, Bertie cried too. After a while, they turned to the rail and watched the white wake foaming behind the ship. He squeezed her hand.

'We could ask the ship's captain to marry us. They can do that, right?'

Cheryl beamed. 'I think so.'

'I know it's early, but I've thought about names.'

'Already?'

Bertie nodded. 'If it's a boy, Victor. Or Maggie if it's a girl.'

'Perfect,' she said, kissing his cheek.

They stood in silence for a while, watching the horizon until the distant rocks faded to nothing. Then they turned away and headed back inside, leaving the Old World behind them.

[50]

EPILOGUE

'We are now approaching Kings Cross Station, London. Please ensure you take your luggage with you and thank you for travelling with Amtrak International.'

Harry remained in his seat as passengers around him gathered their things and shuffled along the aisle towards the exits. He waited until the last of them had stepped off the train before collecting his travel bag from the luggage rack and wheeling it off the train. It was the first time he'd travelled on a maglev since the war, and the ride was quite something. After hostilities ended, *Tom* and *Jerry* had continued their work, one drilling north to Edinburgh and Glasgow, the other south, to Manchester, Birmingham, and Oxford. Harry's journey from Glasgow Central had taken less than two hours, and while it was a fast and convenient way to travel, a 450-mile journey below ground wasn't the most picturesque route to take. Still, it was something to tick off his bucket list, and he would make the return journey by air from London City Airport. Harry had read somewhere that improved tunnelling machines were now burrowing their

472

way beneath the Atlantic Ocean. London to New York in four hours, they said. Remarkable.

He queued for a taxi outside the station, then ducked inside the waiting Toyota, tapping his destination on the screen, Dukes Hotel in St James' Place. Although they were part of everyday life, Harry remained a little unnerved as the driverless vehicle navigated the streets of London.

After checking in to his suite, he took a long, leisurely bath, comforted by the fact that no one recognised him. His alternate ID was a factor, the gift of anonymity bestowed on him by the security services, affording him the privacy he craved. And as he stared at his reflection in the bathroom mirror, it wasn't hard to see why no one had spotted him in the busy hotel foyer. Twenty-five years had passed since Harry was prime minister, and his thick grey hair was nothing more than a fond memory. Where his head was now bald and smooth, his face and neck sprouted a trimmed white beard, and he wore prescription glasses with tinted lenses and thick black rims. He used a retractable walking cane out in public, and although his knees gave him some discomfort, he didn't really need it. It was more of a prop, something to divert attention. Because Harry didn't want to be recognised. He wanted to live his life as he had done since his resignation, in blissful anonymity.

He turned on the TV news as he enjoyed a late lunch of chicken soup and a warm baguette, yet there was no mention of the day's significance. He saw Faye Junger speaking to the European Congress, her copper-red hair now a subtle shade of light grey. She'd been a moderately successful PM, but her eye had always been on Europe. Now she was the Congress president, while Harry lived alone in a remote village nestled in the foothills of the Scottish Highlands. He wouldn't have it any other way.

He left the hotel and walked the short distance into Green Park. He strolled the leafy paths down to The Mall and wandered past Buckingham Palace, since restored to its former glory. Above the roof, the Royal Standard rippled in the summer breeze. The King was in residence, and Harry smiled at the thought of making an unannounced house call. Best not, he decided. Like Harry, the King was rarely seen these days. There were rumours of illness, dementia, but no one knew for sure.

The afternoon was warm, and he patted his neck with a handkerchief as he hailed a taxi on his phone. A minute later he was settling into the back seat of glass-roofed, air-conditioned Tesla as the vehicle headed east along The Mall. Alighting at Trafalgar Square, Harry was unimpressed by the bland piazza, now devoid of admirals, columns, and lions. Behind it, the National Gallery was open for business, and though there were many interesting pieces inside, the great works of history that once adorned its walls were still lost to the world.

Rumours circulated after the war, and fingers were pointed at Edith Spencer and her cronies, but she was never brought to justice. Baghdad denied all knowledge of her whereabouts, but they returned many other offenders to Britain, people with serious blood on their hands. But the brutal tyrants who ran their own fiefdoms, the judges and senior civil servants who switched their loyalties as easily as changing electricity providers, were never seen again. Harry could understand why some people wanted to put the whole business behind them, but it was important to remember how the country got here. And it was the reason for his trip to London.

His cane tapped a rhythmic tattoo on the pavement as he headed for Horse Guards Parade. Nobody looked twice at the bearded man in the cream linen trousers, blue linen shirt and a straw Havana. Some glanced at the blood-red felt poppy looped through the buttonhole of his shirt pocket, and he smiled at them from behind his wraparound sunglasses, but no one looked twice.

A huge remembrance garden had been built in place of the famous parade square, and he bought some flowers from two cheery brothers who ran the stall outside. Harry spent an hour wandering around the colonnades with their impressive pillars and Portland stone walls engraved with the names of every soldier, sailor and

airman killed during the invasion. He saw several he knew personally, and he paused at each one, reflecting on their entwined pasts.
Their lives had led here, to these sacred walls. Harry's journey
continued, but the end was closer now.

He left via the Whitehall gate and stood by the pavement,
looking up and down the famous avenue. So much had changed since
that day. The Ministry of Defence building was never rebuilt,
replaced instead by another garden of remembrance dedicated to the
civilians killed during the conflict. The Houses of Parliament had
been reconstructed, and while the architects had made allowances for
practical improvements, the stone and glass structure occupied the
same footprint as its gothic predecessor. The 250-foot-tall glass clock
tower stood where its ancestor once had, but it was certainly no Big
Ben. Harry saw tourists on its high deck, enjoying the views over
London. Inside the Parliament building itself, politicians still argued
across the floor of the House, but the MPs only numbered 100 now,
and the House of Lords had been abolished. Harry couldn't have
cared less. Politics was a game, a charade for the public designed to
fool them into thinking they lived in a democracy. He never truly
understood that until he became prime minister. But that was all in
the past now.

The reason for his trip to London lay further along Whitehall.
The missing Cenotaph saddened him, as the government chose not to
replace it. Its former location had become a focal point for veterans
and others, and every year after the war they had assembled there,
unofficially, until the crowds grew so large it became a public order
issue. So, the remembrance gardens were commissioned, and though
it was a compromise that most accepted, Harry noticed fresh flowers
in the centre traffic island where the Cenotaph once stood, and that
made him smile.

His heart beat a little faster as he approached Downing Street.
The black gates still barred entry, but now they were waist high and
staffed by smiling, uniformed tour guides. Gone were the platoons of
armed police, the anti-vehicle traps, the crush barriers, and check-

points. Downing Street was no longer a seat of British power. It was a tourist attraction, and after a guide had scanned his prepaid code, Harry stepped to one side and set down his flowers at the base of a stone gate pillar. This was where the bomb had detonated, where Ellen had died, and it comforted Harry to see three other floral tributes set against the stone pillar. He wasn't the only one who remembered.

He continued along the street towards Number Ten. He knew the other houses were mere shells, likewise the Foreign and Commonwealth Office building opposite, and although they looked convincing enough, behind their doors and windows there was nothing. Number Ten was a different story.

Harry slipped off his sunglasses and stepped over the famous threshold, yet he wasn't assaulted by a tsunami of memories. Everything felt different, and there were no familiar smells of furniture polish and fresh flowers. As he shuffled behind a family ahead of him, Harry saw the former grandeur of the interior was an illusion, digitally projected onto blank walls by banks of tiny cameras, although he had to admit the effect was stunning. As he filed through the various rooms, a parade of historical figures appeared, so lifelike that Harry couldn't help but smile. He saw Pitt and Disraeli, Churchill and Thatcher, Lloyd George, and Wilson, writing, poring over documents, and passing through rooms before disappearing like the ghosts they were. Then he saw his own apparition heading towards him, a younger, sharp-suited Harry Beecham, complete his signature red silk tie and talking into a mobile phone. Harry watched the digital spectre trot up the famous staircase, fading before he reached the top, then disappearing. One of the tour guides saw his reaction and she smiled at him. Harry returned it.

'Good-looking chap, wasn't he?'

'Yes, sir,' the young lady said, but her accent was heavy, foreign, and Harry wasn't sure she understood the vernacular.

He followed the others, taking the stairs down into the basement. His heartbeat picked up as he remembered the dust and smoke, the sound of the fires cracking and spitting as they took hold of the floors above, the glowing embers swirling through shattered corridors, the distant wail of sirens, the gunfire that rattled across Whitehall ...

He gripped the steel rail as the people ahead slowed, their feet drumming on metal treads as they headed below ground. Harry didn't remember it being this deep. At the bottom of the stairs was a short, wide corridor and, after passing through it, he stepped out into a cavern of light.

Harry took a sharp and involuntary breath. He struggled with his emotions as his eyes roamed the vast cave, the platforms below, the open carriages, and the tunnels, their blue lights stretching into the darkness beyond. Brigadier Forsyth had led him down here, accompanied by his SAS escorts, Mike Reynolds and Chivers, and two more soldiers whose names Harry couldn't recall. He remembered waiting in the control room below, hoping for good news, then realising London was lost. Now, people around him were smiling and taking pictures.

A guide interrupted his thoughts. 'Visitors who have purchased tickets for the Kensington Palace tour, please continue down to the platforms.'

Harry watched as most of the tourists continued down the stairs and boarded the waiting carriages, the children among them jabbering with excitement. Harry wasn't interested in re-entering that tunnel. He simply wanted to see it, partly out of morbid curiosity, but also as a homage to those who'd died down here protecting him.

He headed back out into the sunlight, slipping his shades back on as he left Downing Street — and all those ghosts — behind him. He walked towards Whitehall, his cane tapping, his emotions a mixed bag. What he needed was a drink.

Across the street, on the corner of Westminster Bridge Road, a multi-storey glass building loomed over Parliament Square. A tourist sign told him there were bars and restaurants inside, so he made his way towards it. He checked his watch and saw that it was 5:02. At

6:00, he would stand out in Whitehall and honour the dead by observing two minutes of silence. This was Harry's Remembrance Day, not the saccharine, carefully choreographed event that took place every November at the remembrance gardens, followed by a gaudy peace parade along The Mall. Time and political expediency had watered down the gravitas of the event, to a point where it was no longer televised live. As for today, it was one the politicians wanted to forget, a day the media barely mentioned, and that made Harry angry and ashamed.

As he approached the corner of Parliament Square, a man standing on the pavement saw him and approached. He was much younger than Harry, in his forties perhaps, but like Harry, he wore a poppy pinned to his crisp white shirt. The man handed him a leaflet.

'I couldn't help but notice your poppy.'

'Likewise,' Harry said.

'We're trying to get today recognised as a national holiday. There's a web link on the leaflet that'll take you to an online petition. If you could sign it, that would really help.'

Harry slipped in his pocket. 'Of course. It's the least we can all do.'

The man pointed across Parliament Square. 'There's a pub over there, the Westminster Arms. Anyone who served gets a free drink today. There'll be others there, veterans mostly. You'll find yourself in good company.'

'Thank you, I will.'

It seemed like a good idea. Harry knew the pub from his political days, and the street it was on had survived the war. He crossed Parliament Square, another piazza served by chain restaurants and coffee shops, and crowds sat beneath coloured awnings, eating and drinking while they watched the world go by.

As he approached the Westminster Arms, Harry wondered how it had survived the post-invasion purges. Maybe the owner had boarded up the pub and painted over the sign, like many landlords across the country. Whatever the circumstances, Harry was glad to see its façade restored to its past glory and a Union flag hanging above the door. There were signs posted in the window — *Private Function* — and a large, barrel-chested man wearing a white shirt and a regimental tie blocked the door. Harry tipped his Havana in greeting.

'I was told there was a gathering here. Veterans.'

'Are you a veteran, sir?'

'Not as such. But I am here to pay my respects.'

The man pushed the door open with a very large hand. 'In that case, welcome.'

Harry stepped inside the pub, a den of dark wood walls and floors and a brightly lit bar where it was standing room only. The room was packed with smart-looking men in regimental blazers, many of them wearing berets, the colours representing different corps and regiments that no longer existed. These men — and a few women — belonged to another era, before the invasion. They were jammed between walls decorated with military photographs and plaques, and Harry guessed the drinks had been flowing for a while. There was a lot of laughter and smiles, and Harry felt as if he'd stepped into the warm embrace of times past. Blazers parted as he made his way to the bar. He took off his hat and dabbed his bald head with a handkerchief.

'Rather warm out there,' Harry said.

The landlord was in his sixties, tall and wide, with red, thinning hair, rolled-up sleeves, tattooed forearms, and a moustache any old-school Regimental Sergeant Major would be proud of. Harry recognised the globe and anchor of the Royal Marine Commandos on his tie.

'What's your pleasure, sir?' The man spoke in a deep, resonant voice.

'Iced water, please. And a whiskey. Rosebank, single malt, if you have it.'

The landlord nodded. 'We do indeed.' He poured the drinks and put them in front of Harry, who offered his phone for payment. The landlord shook his head. 'Not today, sir.'

'I never served in uniform,' Harry said, flushed by a sudden bout of imposter syndrome.

The landlord winked. 'My commiserations,' he said, turning to serve another veteran.

Harry thanked him and squeezed his way through the bar, finding a small unoccupied table and a single chair. He sipped his drinks as he watched the surrounding crowd. There were more women and children than he first realised, the ladies wearing ribbons and poppies pinned to their blouses and jackets. Harry guessed that some were widows, and some veterans Young children played around them. Harry sat back, catching snippets of conversation about friends and comrades, postings, and operations. There was lots of grey hair, prescription glasses and middle-aged paunches, and Harry deduced that almost everyone in the pub had walked the same ground as he had back then. He wondered how many he'd met, and if any of the faces around him were the same ones that stared back at him during his many speeches along the Scottish border, or at the airport in Massachusetts, or in darkened halls and gymnasiums before the troops went through the tunnels.

His table wobbled as a man squeezed by, and Harry lifted his drinks to stop them from being spilt. The man turned around. He wore a red beret with a Royal Military Police cap badge, and he held up his hands in apology.

'Sorry about that. I'm not as slim as I thought I was.' He pointed to Harry's almost empty glass. 'Can I get you something? It's almost time.'

Harry shook his head. 'That's really very kind, but I'm fine, thank you.'

The veteran smiled, and then his smile faded. He stared at Harry and frowned. When he spoke again, his voice was a whisper. 'Jesus Christ, you're Harry Beecham.'

Harry swallowed, suddenly embarrassed. He kept his own voice low. 'Please, I've no wish to cause a fuss. I'm only here to pay my respects.'

Two other blazers standing by the table heard his name and stared at him. Eyes widened and jaws dropped. The contagion spread through the pub, a rumble of voices and craning heads, his name muttered and repeated all the way out to the pub door.

'Make a hole!'

The crowd parted and then the landlord was towering over him, his big hands on his hips.

'Well, I'll be damned. It's really you, isn't it?'

Harry winced. 'Guilty as charged,' he said.

The former Marine offered his hand. 'It's a bloody pleasure, Prime Minister.' He turned and bellowed over his shoulder. 'Lofty, bring me a large Rosebank.'

Harry put his hand over his glass. 'I really shouldn't.'

'It's not for you, sir.'

The bar erupted in laughter, and now everyone was pressing closer. Harry felt claustrophobic, and the landlord herded everyone back. A half-circle formed in front of Harry, a configuration he knew well. The landlord pointed to an old-fashioned clock on the wall.

'It's almost six, sir. Would you say a few words? Someone normally does, and we'd be honoured if it was you.'

Harry didn't hesitate and got to his feet. It felt right to address these men and women in such an intimate setting. There was so much he could say, but he decided he would keep it short and to the point.

It turned out Lofty was a short man who carried a handful of drinks and an upturned beer crate which Harry stood up on. Harry gathered his thoughts, and the only sound he could hear was the ticking clock on the wall. It was almost 6 pm.

'The Duke of Wellington once said, "I don't know what effect these men will have upon the enemy, but, by God, they terrify me." I've always felt the same, every time I've faced men and women like you, knowing you've endured harsh battles and seen terrible things that no man or woman should ever see. And yet here you are, survivors, custodians of the memories of friends and comrades.'

Harry reached down and lifted his glass high.

'This one is from me to you, to pay tribute to your loyalty and bravery, and your determination to free this country from tyranny.' Harry sipped his drink in silence, then glanced at the ticking clock. Ten seconds to go. 'The hour is upon us. Time to remember the fallen. May their memory live on.' He raised his glass and the whole pub answered him.

'The fallen.'

Harry downed his whiskey. The clock struck six, and the chimes sang through the pub. Harry lowered his chin and closed his eyes, and the memories flooded back. His last phone call with Ellen, who was only seconds away from home. The terrible blast, as if God himself had ripped the earth asunder, then sirens and gunfire. He remembered David Fuller, covered in blood, his life ending before Harry's eyes as he lay in the garden. The years fell away, and he could smell the burning timber, taste the dust and blood in his mouth ...

The bell rang behind the bar, and heads snapped upright. All eyes were still on Harry.

'Thank you for the privilege, and God bless you all.'

He stepped down, and the landlord began clapping. Those around him joined in, and seconds later, the whole pub was applauding. They surrounded him, those berets and blazers, those regimental ties and medals and ribbons, and he could feel the grip of their hands as they shook his. Harry tried and failed to stop the tears. He smiled through them, greeting as many people as possible, even shaking the tiny hands of the children herded towards him by beaming parents and grandparents. He posed for photographs, and later into the evening, sat and listened to personal accounts of pain and loss. They talked of crossed paths, and he answered questions as best he could, about decisions made, about Birmingham, President Mitchell's death, his own abduction, and a hundred other queries. There was no judgement, no harsh words, or recriminations. The world had moved on, but for this one night, the invasion was relived inside the walls of the

Westminster Arms and the lives of those who died liberating the country, celebrated.

The glass clock tower was striking midnight when Harry left the pub. The landlord and several others escorted him outside, while the voices inside were in full, drunken song. They helped Harry into a waiting taxi and before the door closed, his escort lined the pavement and threw up the sharpest of salutes. With perfect timing, their arms snapped down by their sides. The door closed and the autonomous taxi pulled away.

Harry blotted his eyes with his handkerchief as the car swept around Parliament Square and along the embankment. Around the bend in the river, brightly lit bridges arched across the Thames, and skyscrapers thrust into the night sky, an architectural Phoenix risen from the ashes. Everything destroyed had been rebuilt, transforming the ancient city once more. Life was about moving forward, but sometimes it was important to take a moment and reflect. As he had today.

Tomorrow he would travel to London City Airport and board the shuttle to Glasgow. Then he would head home, away from the city and into the countryside, to the village nestled in the mountains, where the villagers made it their business to protect Harry's privacy. He didn't know how long he had left, given his recent prognosis, but he'd fulfilled the promise he'd made to himself many years ago. That he would return to London, not in any official capacity but as a citizen, as someone who was there all those years ago, when the storm of war blotted out that beautiful June sky. And to pay tribute to those who'd died.

The taxi dropped him outside the hotel. Later, he lay in the dark of his suite, listening to the sounds of the city. He glanced at his watch and realised that at that moment, a quarter of a century ago, he was hiding in a tunnel deep below ground, unaware that the world above him had changed irrevocably. He felt a twinge of guilt, as he had done back then, and every day since.

Despite all his speeches of bravery and sacrifice, there was one aspect of the war that Harry had never discussed, and that was culpability. Why did it happen? And who was to blame?

In hindsight, the subjugation of Britain and Europe was inevitable. The writing had been on the wall for years, but the establishment had ignored those warnings. Like everyone else, Harry had turned a blind eye to the endless waves of fighting-age males arriving on England's shores, to the lone-wolf terror attacks that he scrambled to excuse on mental health grounds. He'd championed diversity quotas and looked the other way when those with dubious loyalties subverted government institutions. He'd ignored and excused Wazir's sabre-rattling even as his armies had gathered on Europe's borders. Harry Beecham was guilty of opportunism and moral cowardice as much as the rest of them. It wasn't until his own life was in danger, after family and friends had been killed, that his eyes were finally opened.

He'd buried that guilt ever since, and again he pondered how different things might've been if someone had drawn a line in the sand and said *Enough*. To his lasting shame and regret, that person wasn't Harry Beecham.

His eyes grew heavy, and he drifted off to sleep...

IN THE DEAD OF NIGHT, THE DARKNESS LIFTED, AND HARRY found himself back in his private flat in Number Ten, pouring a coffee as the clock on the mantelpiece struck six.

A loud bang startled him, and he realised it was just the wind catching the door as Ellen breezed in after her busy day in Greenwich.

He heard no screams, no sirens, no rattle of gunfire, only Big Ben striking the hour across London as the city basked beneath the summer sun.

HAVE YOUR SAY

Did you enjoy *INVASION: DELIVERANCE*?

I hope you did.

If you have a moment, would you mind rating it, or leaving a review?

It would be hugely helpful.

Rate this book!

And many thanks for your time.

NEVER MISS A NEW RELEASE

To learn more about my writing and filmmaking life, and to receive all the latest book news and updates, please visit my official website and sign up for my occasional newsletter.

Sign up!

ALSO BY DC ALDEN

Invasion: Downfall
Invasion: Uprising
Invasion: Frontline
Invasion: Deliverance
Invasion: Chronicles
Invasion: The Lost Chapters
Invasion: Redux
The Horse at the Gates
The Angola Deception
Fortress
End Zone
The Rogue State Trilogy
UFO Down

Join the conversation on social media:

Printed in Great Britain
by Amazon

80491891R10284